Dear Reader,

Okay, I'll admit it—authors have favorite books. I know, I know, books are like children and we don't always want to admit to liking one better than another, but it's true. The Goddess Summoning books are my favorite children.

As with my bestselling young adult series, the House of Night, my Goddess Summoning books celebrate the independence, intelligence, and unique beauty of modern women. My heroes all have one thing in common: they appreciate powerful women and are wise enough to value brains as well as beauty. Isn't respect and appreciation an excellent aphrodisiac?

Delving into mythology and reworking ancient myths is fun! In Goddess of the Sea I retell the story of the mermaid Undine—who switches places with a female U.S. Air Force sergeant who needs to do some escaping of her own. In Goddess of Spring, I turn my attention to the Persephone/Hades myth, and send a modern woman to Hell! Who knew Hell and its brooding god could be hot in so many wonderful, seductive ways?

From there we take a lovely vacation in Las Vegas with the divine twins, Apollo and Artemis, in Goddess of Light. Finally we come to what is my favorite of all fairy tales, "Beauty and the Beast." In Goddess of the Rose I created my own version of this beloved tale, building a magical realm from whence dreams originate—good and bad—and bringing to life a beast who absolutely took my breath away.

I hope you enjoy my worlds, and my wish for you is that you discover a spark of goddess magic of your own!

P. C. Cast

"Outstanding . . . Magic, myth, and romance with a decidedly modern twist. Her imagination and storytelling abilities are true gifts to the genre."
—*Romantic Times*

Praise for *Goddess of the Sea*

"Suspense, fantasy, time travel, all topped off with a very healthy dollop of romance . . . The good news is that this is just the beginning."
—*Romance Reviews Today*

"Captivating—poignant, funny, erotic! Lovely characters, wonderful romance, constant action, and a truly whimsical fantasy . . . Delightful. A great read."
—*The Best Reviews*

"A fun combination of myth, girl power, and sweet romance [with] a bit of suspense. A must-read . . . A romance that celebrates the magic of being a woman."
—*Affaire de Coeur*

"[An] adult fairy tale . . . the audience will cherish."
—*Midwest Book Review*

"Vivid and colorful . . . Splendid blend of fantasy, history, intrigue, and passion . . . Outstanding. Watch out for this author."
—*Rendezvous*

"Most innovative . . . From beginning to end, the surprises in P. C. Cast's new page-turner never stopped. Its poignancy resonates with both whimsy and fantasy . . . I loved it!" —*New York Times* **bestselling author Sharon Sala**

"Sweet and funny."
—*Huntress Reviews*

Goddess of Spring

"One of the top romantic fantasy mythologists today."
—*Midwest Book Review*

"As always, there's a dash of humor and lots of meltingly hot sex."
—*Affaire de Coeur*

"Enchanting . . . Lovely." —*The Romance Readers Connection*

"A veritable feast for readers who just can't get enough fantasy dished up with their romance. Mythology has never been so fun!"
—*Romance Reviews Today*

Goddess of Light

"A charmer . . . Cast continues her unique brand of delightfully mixing a modern-day romance with a mythological legend . . . Creative."
—*Midwest Book Review*

"Pure enjoyment . . . Anything can [happen] when gods and mortals mix."
—*Rendezvous*

"A fanciful mix of mythology and romance with a dash of humor for good measure . . . Engages and entertains . . . Lovely." —*Romance Reviews Today*

Goddess of Love

"Sexy, charming, and fun, *Goddess of Love* is the fantasy romance of the year! You will fall in love with this book. (I did!)"
—*New York Times* **bestselling author Susan Grant**

"Touching, clever, and an excellent heiress to the Goddess Summoning series. Cast's ability to subvert misogynistic mythology . . . and reaffirm what makes women wonderful, is always worth celebrating . . . I bestow my snarky blessings on this book." —*Smart Bitches Trashy Books*

"Scorchingly sensual, utterly delicious! P. C. Cast is a true master of her craft." —*New York Times* **bestselling author Gena Showalter**

Goddess
OF THE
Rose

P. C. Cast

BERKLEY SENSATION, NEW YORK

THE BERKLEY PUBLISHING GROUP
Published by the Penguin Group
Penguin Group (USA) Inc.
375 Hudson Street, New York, New York 10014, USA
Penguin Group (Canada), 90 Eglinton Avenue East, Suite 700, Toronto, Ontario M4P 2Y3, Canada
(a division of Pearson Penguin Canada Inc.)
Penguin Books Ltd., 80 Strand, London WC2R 0RL, England
Penguin Group Ireland, 25 St. Stephen's Green, Dublin 2, Ireland (a division of Penguin Books Ltd.)
Penguin Group (Australia), 250 Camberwell Road, Camberwell, Victoria 3124, Australia
(a division of Pearson Australia Group Pty. Ltd.)
Penguin Books India Pvt. Ltd., 11 Community Centre, Panchsheel Park, New Delhi—110 017, India
Penguin Group (NZ), 67 Apollo Drive, Rosedale, North Shore 0632, New Zealand
(a division of Pearson New Zealand Ltd.)
Penguin Books (South Africa) (Pty.) Ltd., 24 Sturdee Avenue, Rosebank, Johannesburg 2196,
South Africa

Penguin Books Ltd., Registered Offices: 80 Strand, London WC2R 0RL, England

This is a work of fiction. Names, characters, places, and incidents either are the product of the author's imagination or are used fictitiously, and any resemblance to actual persons, living or dead, business establishments, events, or locales is entirely coincidental. The publisher does not have any control over and does not assume any responsibility for author or third-party websites or their content.

Berkley Sensation trade paperback ISBN: 978-0-425-22710-7

PRINTING HISTORY
Berkley Sensation mass-market edition / February 2006
Berkley Sensation trade paperback edition / January 2009

The Library of Congress has cataloged a prior edition under LCCN: 2006576706.

PRINTED IN THE UNITED STATES OF AMERICA

10 9 8 7 6 5 4 3 2

This book is for everyone
who fell in love with the Beast,
and then was truly disappointed when he
turned into a handsome prince.

ACKNOWLEDGMENTS

I would like to thank Mark Stelljes, the rosarian I consulted as I researched this book. Mark, your information was invaluable! Any rose mistakes are mine and mine alone.

A special thank you to my goddess editor, Christine Zika, for understanding that the beast really did need to be a beast. (And thanks for that lovely horn scene, too!)

An adoring thank you to my amazing agent and friend, Meredith Bernstein.

A wink and a thanks to the fabulous "Lunatics" who helped brainstorm the personification of Dream Stealers.

And thank you to my high school students whose brains I picked for the dream-weaving scenes. See? Teenagers really do have brains!

PRELUDE

O NCE *upon a time, when men still believed gods and goddesses walked the earth, Hecate, Great Goddess of Night, was granted dominion over the crossroads of man. The dark goddess took her charge seriously, for not only did she stand watch over mortal roads and byways, Hecate guarded the cross-roads between dreams and reality . . . between the corporeal and the ethereal. Her dominion was the place from which all dreams, and the magick they cre-ate, originated. Thus, the Goddess of Night became Goddess of Magick as well as Goddess of Beasts and the Ebony Moon.*

Ever vigilant, Hecate called to her service a monstrous beast of olde. Willingly the beast swore to be the goddess's Guardian of the Crossroads and to do her bidding. This creature was the perfect melding of man and beast; son of the Titan Cronos, he was a being like no other. As reward for his fidelity in answering the goddess's summons, Hecate gifted her Guardian with the heart and soul of a man, so although his appearance was monstrous, Hecate felt se-cure, entrusting him with the protection of the boundaries of the magickal crossroads, which the goddess christened the Realm of the Rose, as well as the Priestesses of the Blood, who served Hecate there. For centuries, the Guard-ian stood faithful, following the dictates of his sacred trust, for he was as honorable as he was powerful and as wise as he was mighty . . .

. . . Until one Beltane. The Guardian knew his duty. But alas, even a great Guardian can grow weary. Our beast did not err because of cruelty or

greed; his only mistake was in loving unwisely. He broke trust with his goddess, and in a flash of rage, Hecate cast a spell over her Guardian and the Realm of the Rose. The realm would have no High Priestess, and the Guardian would sleep eternally unless the beast was awakened by a woman who carried the magickal blood of Hecate's priestess and was wise enough to see the truth and compassionate enough to act upon it.

And so the Realm of the Rose despaired and the Guardian slept while their goddess waited . . .

Part One

Part One

CHAPTER ONE

"I'VE been having those dreams again."

Nelly straightened in her chair and gave her what Mikki liked to think of as her Clinically Interested Look.

"Would you like to tell me about them?" she asked.

Mikki shifted her eyes from her friend. Would she like to tell her? She uncrossed and then crossed her long legs, ran her hand nervously through her hair and tried to settle into the wingback chair.

"Before I answer that question, I want you to answer one of mine first."

"Fair enough," Nelly said.

"If I tell you about my dreams, how will you be listening? As my friend or as my shrink?"

The psychiatrist laughed. "Please, Mikki! We're at a coffee shop, not my office. You're definitely not paying me a hundred and twenty dollars an hour to sit here with you. And let's not forget"—she leaned forward and exaggerated a whisper—"you've been my friend for years, but you've never been my patient."

"True, but that hasn't been because of my lack of issues."

"Oh, definitely," Nelly said with purposeful sarcasm. "So you gonna tell me, or do I have to use my secret shrink tricks on you to get you to divulge?"

"Anything but that!" Mikki raised her hands as if to fend off an attack. Then she shrugged her shoulders. "Well, they're the same as the others." Noting Nelly's knowing look coupled with her raised eyebrows, Mikki sighed and rolled her eyes. "Okay, maybe they have changed some lately."

"Could you see his face this time?" Nelly asked gently.

"Almost." Mikki squinted and stared at a spot above the cozy brick fireplace in the corner of the coffee shop. "Actually, I think I could have seen his face this time, but . . ."

"But?" she prompted.

"But I . . ." Mikki hesitated.

Nelly made an encouraging sound.

"But I was so preoccupied I couldn't make myself concentrate on his face," she finished in a rush.

"Preoccupied with . . . ?"

Mikki stopped staring at the hearth and met her friend's eyes. "I was preoccupied with having the most incredibly erotic dream of my life. I really didn't give a damn what his face looked like."

"Well, well, *well* . . ." She drew out the word. "I don't remember you describing sex in the other dreams. Now I really am interested in the rest of the story."

"That's because they weren't . . . or maybe I didn't . . . oh, I don't know. For some reason they're changing." She struggled to describe what was happening to her. "I'm telling you, Nelly, the dreams are getting more and more real."

The joking sparkle went out of Nelly's dark eyes, instantly replaced by concern.

"Talk to me, honey. What's going on?" she asked.

"It's like the more realistic the dreams get, the less real my life is."

"Tell me about your latest dream, Mikki."

Instead of answering her, Mikki twirled an errant strand of thick, copper-colored hair and bought time by sipping her cappuccino. She and Nelly had been friends for years. They'd met at the hospital where they both worked and had been instant girlfriends. On the outside they had little in common. Nelly was tall and slender—dark with an exotic beauty—a gift from her mother's Haitian blood. She towered over Mikki's five-foot-seven-inch frame. Where Nelly was dark, Mikki was fair, just as where her friend was slender and graceful, Mikki was voluptuous and earthy. But instead of being jealous of or put off by the differences in their exteriors, the two women had, from the moment they'd met, appreciated each other for their uniqueness.

It was a solid friendship, founded in trust and mutual respect. And Mikki had no idea why she was so hesitant to tell Nelly about the dreams, especially the last one . . .

"Mikki?"

"I'm thinking of where to start," she prevaricated.

Nelly gave her a little half-smile and sipped her own cappuccino before taking a delicate bite from her chocolate biscotti. "Take your time. All good shrinks have one thing in common."

"I know, I know . . . you're all annoyingly patient."

"Exactly."

Mikki fiddled with her coffee cup. She really did need to get this dream stuff straightened out. It was becoming too weird, in a hypnotic, seductive way.

But she was stalling, and not just because she was hesitant about revealing such intimate details aloud, but also because part of her was afraid her friend—who really was an excellent psychiatrist—would have some kind of magic words that would cure her.

She wasn't sure she wanted to be cured.

"Hey, it's just me," Nelly said softly.

Mikki gave her a tight, appreciative smile, drew a deep breath and began. "Okay, this one started the same as the others." She picked nervously at her fingernail polish.

"You mean in the canopy bed?"

"*Huge* canopy bed in the *enormous* bedroom." She corrected and then nodded. "Yeah. It was the same place, only it wasn't as dark as it usually is. This time a little light was coming into the room through a whole wall of windows. I think they're called"—Mikki searched for the word—"mull-something-or-other . . . panes of vertical stripes of glass. Know what I mean?"

Nelly nodded. "Mullioned windows."

"Right, I think. Well, whatever they're called, I noticed them this time because they were letting in some light." Mikki's gaze was trapped by the cheerily burning fire as she relived her dream. "It was a soft, pink-tinted light that must have been dawn," she said dreamily and then caught herself and continued, "Anyway, it woke me." She hesitated and a small, half-laugh escaped her throat. "It even seemed odd in the dream—having my dream self wake up to experience another dream." Mikki shrugged her shoulders. "But I woke up. I was lying on my stomach, and I could feel someone brushing my hair. It was wonderful. The 'whoever' was using one of those big brushes with soft, wide bristles." Mikki grinned at her friend. "You know there are few things better than having your hair brushed."

"I'm with you on that one, but hair brushing is not sex."

"Okay, it's been a long time, but I'm fully aware that hair brushing is not sex. I'm not at the sex part yet, I'm just at the why-I-was-so-relaxed-and-happy part," Mikki said, giving Nelly an impatient look.

"Sorry for interrupting. Just pretend like I'm not here."

"Is that shrink-talk stuff?"

"Nope. It's I-want-to-hear-about-the-sex-part stuff."

Mikki grinned at her. "In that case, I will gladly continue. Let's see . . . I was so relaxed that I could feel myself drifting. It was bizarre—like my soul had become so light that it lifted from my body. It was then that everything got freaky."

"Explain freaky."

"Well, there was a rush of wind. It was like the breeze had all of a sudden picked me up and carried me someplace. But not really *me*. Just my spirit me. Then there was a settling feeling. It startled me, and I opened my eyes. I was back in my body, only now I was standing in the middle of the most incredible rose garden I have ever seen, ever even imagined." Mikki's voice lost any hint of hesitation as she fell into the description of the scene. "It was breathtaking. I wanted to drink the air like wine. Roses were all around me. All my favorites: Double Delight, Chrysler Imperial, Cary Grant, Sterling Silver . . ." She sighed happily.

"Any Mikado Roses?"

Nelly's question brought her back to reality.

"No, I didn't see any of my namesake roses." She sat up, giving her friend an irritated look. "And I really don't think this is happening to me because my mother thought it was clever to name me after her favorite rose."

Nelly made a conciliatory gesture with her hand. "Hey, you have to admit, Mikki," she said, pronouncing the nickname clearly, as if to erase the word *Mikado* from the air around them, "that it's weird that roses, in some form, appear in every one of your dreams."

"Why should it be odd? I'm a volunteer at the Tulsa Municipal Rose Gardens. I raise my own roses. Why should something that has been such a big part of my life not figure into my dreams?"

"You're right. Roses are an important part of your life, as they were your mother's—"

"And her mother's before her, and hers before her," Mikki interrupted.

Nelly smiled and nodded. "You know I think it's a lovely hobby, and I'm completely jealous of your ability to grow such beautiful roses."

"I'm sorry. I shouldn't be so touchy. I guess I'm running short on sleep."

Worry shadowed Nelly's expression. "You didn't tell me that you're not sleeping."

"Oh, no, it's nothing," Mikki said briskly. "I've just been taking too many papers home from the office and staying up too late."

Please don't ask me any more questions about that, she thought, glancing at Nelly as she hastily stirred and then sipped her cappuccino. She didn't want her to know that her exhaustion had nothing to do with lack of sleep or too much work. All she wanted to do was to escape to her dream world and sleep, and even though she never felt fully rested after she'd been to that fantasy world of dreams, she felt compelled to return night after night.

"Mikki?"

"Where was I?" she floundered.

"In the beautiful rose garden."

"That's right."

"And things were getting freaky."

"Yeah." Mikki let her eyes fall back to the fireplace. "For a while I just walked among the roses, touching each of them and appreciating their beauty. My guess was right, it was early morning and the air was fresh and cool; the roses were still sprinkled with dew. Everything looked like it had just been washed. The garden was circular, and the roses and their terraces formed a kind of labyrinth or maybe a maze. I wandered around and around, just enjoying myself."

Mikki's smile wavered, and she paused before beginning the next part of her dream. She could feel her cheeks coloring. Her eyes shifted abruptly to meet her friend's curious gaze.

"Do not tell me you're embarrassed!"

Mikki gave her a sheepish grin. "Kinda."

"Please recall that you and I have gotten Brazilian waxes. Together. In the same room. Get over it and give me the details. Plus, if all else fails, remember"—she took another big bite of biscotti and continued through a full mouth—"I'm a professional."

"Don't remind me," Mikki mumbled. She took a deep breath. "Okay, so I'm in the rose garden and then I suddenly felt him. I couldn't see him, but I knew he was behind me." She licked her lips. Unconsciously, Mikki's hand moved to her throat. Her fingertips slowly stroked the sensitive skin at the base of her neck as she spoke. "I started walking faster, because at first I felt like I should get away from him, but soon that changed. I could hear him behind me; he was gaining on me. He wasn't being quiet or trying to hide. His noises were feral . . . dangerous. . . . it was as if I was being hunted by a fierce, masculine animal."

Mikki tried to force her breathing back to normal. Her body tingled with a flush of heat. She could feel the drop of sweat that made a hot, wet path between her breasts.

"You were afraid?" Nellie asked.

"No," Mikki said in a whisper that her friend had to lean forward and strain to hear. "That's just it. I wasn't afraid at all. It thrilled me. It excited me. I wanted him to catch me. When I ran, it was only because I could tell it provoked him—and I wanted very much for him to be provoked."

"Wow," Nelly said on a rush of breath. "Sexy . . ."

"I told you so, and it gets better."

"Good." Nelly bit into another biscotti.

"I ran naked and laughing. It felt like the wind was my lover as it rushed over my body. I reveled in every grunt, every huff, every growl made by the man-thing who pursued me. And I wanted to be caught, but not until he was very, very eager to catch me."

"Well, for God's sake don't stop there. Did he catch you?"

Mikki's gaze became introspective, and her eyes moved back to the fireplace.

"Yes and no. As I said, I was running and he was chasing me. I came to a sharp corner in the labyrinth and I turned, then stumbled, and fell into a pit. When I hit the bottom it should have hurt, but it didn't because my fall was cushioned." Mikki's lips twitched and then curved into a seductive smile. "It was cushioned by petals. I had fallen into a pit that had been filled with a bed of rose petals. There must have been thousands of them. Their scent filled the air and caressed my body. Every inch of my naked skin felt alive against their softness. And then his hands replaced the roses. They weren't soft. Instead, they were rough and strong and demanding. The difference between the two sensations was incredibly exciting. He stroked my naked body, moving from my breasts down my stomach and my thighs. He caressed me exactly as I would have touched myself. It was like he had the ability to tap into my dreams and he knew all my secret desires."

Mikki paused to brush a strand of hair from her face. Her hand was shaking, but not wanting Nelly to notice, she hurried on with her story.

"It was darker in the pit than it had been in the gardens, and my vision was hazy, almost like the scent of the crushed petals had created a fog of perfume that obscured my vision. I couldn't see him, but wherever he touched me I was on fire. Before then in all of the dreams I had felt his presence, like he was an insubstantial being, a ghost or a shadow. I had known he was there, but he had never pursued me, never touched me. And I had certainly never touched him. But in the pit of roses, everything changed. I could feel his hands on me, and when I reached for him, I could actually touch him, too. I pulled him to me. And he . . . he felt . . ."

Mikki gulped and closed her eyes tightly in remembrance. "He felt thick and strong and incredibly big. I ran my hands up and down the width of his shoulders and his arms. His muscles were like living stone. And I felt something else . . . he was . . . he had . . ." Mikki swallowed around the sudden dryness in her throat. Could she really tell Nelly? Could she tell anyone? Remembering, it was almost as if she was there again, in that pit of sensation and fragrance. Her hands had moved up to bury themselves in the thick mass of his hair. She had intended to turn his face to hers—to open her eyes and to finally, finally see him. Then she had touched them. Horns. The man creature who was stroking her body into an excitement she had never before experienced had horns.

No! She couldn't tell Nelly; it was just too crazy. And her friend definitely knew crazy. Instead, she said in a rush, "He had some kind of costume on. It was leather—hard leather, all across his chest. Like . . . like"—she searched for the word—"like an old-fashioned breastplate. It was unbelievably erotic—those hard muscles being barely covered by that hard leather. I let my hands feel him—caress him. His face was buried in my hair, right here."

Closing her eyes, Mikki's right hand moved slowly up, pulled forward a mass of her reddish curls and sank her hand into them near her right ear.

"This is where his face was, so it was easy for me to hear every sound he made. When I stroked him, he moaned into my ear, except it wasn't really a moan—at least not a moan a human would have made. It was a low, deep growl that went on and on. I know it should have scared me. I should have screamed and fought, or at the very least been petrified, frozen with fear. But I didn't want to be away from him. That horrible, wonderful, beastlike sound excited me even more. I felt like I would die if I couldn't have him—all of him. Arching up to meet him, I could easily feel his erection. He was grinding it against me."

Mikki swallowed again. "And then he spoke. His voice was like nothing I've ever heard—a man's, yet not. An animal's, but not really. The power in it rumbled through me and it was as if I could hear him within my mind, too."

When she paused, Nelly prompted breathlessly, "What did he say?"

"He growled into my ear, 'We must not . . . I cannot . . . It cannot be allowed to happen!' but his words didn't stop me. I could feel his desire in them as surely as I could feel his hardness between my legs. I begged him not to stop as I clutched at his clothes. I wanted them off him; I wanted him naked against me. But it was too late. I was already climaxing, and all I could do was wrap my legs around him as my body exploded. The orgasm is what woke me."

CHAPTER TWO

Nelly cleared her throat before she attempted to speak. "Oh, my dear sweet Lord, I agree with you. That was definitely more realistic than the other dreams—and sexier." She fanned herself with a napkin.

"I could have seen his face, Nelly. It was there, right beside my own face the whole time, and I knew that even though the pit was foggy, there was enough light for me to be able to see him. I could even feel him staring at me, but I refused to open my eyes. I didn't want to see what he was." Silently, she acknowledged that she had lost her nerve. After she'd felt the horns, she'd been afraid to see him. She hadn't wanted the fantasy to be shattered by the reality of what he might be.

"Was that because even though you were excited, there was a part of you that was afraid, too?"

Mikki took her time answering Nelly, wondering if she was talking to her friend or the psychiatrist. "Maybe. But I don't know whether my fear was because of what I might have seen, or because if I saw him the spell might be broken and I would never dream about him again," she admitted.

"The spell?"

Mikki shrugged her shoulders and smiled sheepishly. "What would you call it? What's happening feels more like magic than psychosis. Or at least it does to me."

Nelly returned her smile. "You know my attitude about that kind of stuff. I think there are many magical things about the human brain, but they all have causes rooted in science."

"Now you do sound like a shrink."

"Stop, you flatterer." Nelly's eyes shifted to her watch. "Oh, crap! I have to get going soon."

"Scary freak coming in to unload his problems on you?"

"Of course. It's my favorite part of my job." Nelly dunked her biscotti in the remaining cappuccino. "Wait, didn't you say something earlier about the dreams becoming more realistic and the world around you seeming less real? Did something weird happen?"

"I thought you had to get going."

"Soon, but not this instant. I still have biscotti to devour. So give up the rest of it."

Mikki sighed. "You never forget anything, do you?"

"It's all part of my very expensive training." She waved the soggy biscotti at Mikki. "Continue, please."

"Okay, okay. It happened yesterday. I was crossing Twenty-first Street, going from Woodward Park to my apartment. Thursdays are the evenings I volunteer at the Rose Gardens, remember?"

"Yep."

"Well, it was a little after dusk. I got finished later than usual— there's just so much to do to get the roses ready for winter, and with the pain-in-the-ass construction in the third tier, well, we're way behind. Anyway, I was crossing the street, and I heard something weird behind me."

Mikki paused and squinted her eyes in reflection.

"Something weird?"

"I know it sounds crazy." Mikki gave a nervous laugh. "But who better to tell crazy stuff to than my shrink girlfriend?" Nelly narrowed her eyes at her. With a little unconscious gesture of defiance, Mikki tossed back her hair before she continued. "Okay, I heard this . . . this . . . *noise* coming from behind me. At first I thought it had something to do with the play they're rehearsing in the park."

"Oh, yeah. Performance in the Park runs the first week of November. I'd almost forgotten. What is it they're putting on this year?"

"*Medea*," Mikki said, slanting a grin at her.

"So a weird sound coming from that play wouldn't have seemed too surprising."

"Exactly, except I heard a roar, and even though I haven't read the play since high school, I don't think there are any wild animals in *Medea*."

"You heard a lion?"

"I don't know . . . It sounded a little like a lion . . . only different."

Mikki paused again. She knew very well how the roar had differed from any normal zoo beast. It had sounded lonely—heart-wrenchingly, totally, horribly, lonely. And somehow human, too. But there was no way she was going to admit that to her friend. She wasn't *that* crazy—at least not yet. Instead, she hurried on with the rest of her explanation.

"Yes, I realize the zoo is way over on the other side of town, and even if the lions or whatever animals were roaring their heads off, there's no way I could hear them at Woodward Park. But I swear to you I heard a roar. As you can imagine, it surprised me, so as soon as I reached the sidewalk I turned around. The park was hard to see because the air was filled with waves or thermals or . . . I don't know what the hell to call them. You know, like currents of air rising from a hot black-top road in the middle of summer. I thought something was wrong with my eyes, so I blinked and rubbed at them. And when I opened them again, the park was gone."

Nelly's eyebrows drew together. "What do you mean, it was gone?"

"Just that." She shrugged one shoulder. "Gone. Disappeared. Absent. No longer there. Instead, there was a huge forest of trees."

"Well . . . Woodward Park has trees," Nelly said, as if that was explanation enough.

Mikki made a scoffing sound through her nose. "Oh, please. I don't mean some attractive, well-manicured trees conveniently spaced around man-made waterfalls and azalea hedges. This was a *real* forest. The oaks were huge, and it was dense and dark." She shivered. "If I had walked into it, I would have been swallowed."

"Did you hear the roar again?"

Mikki shook her head. "No, everything was very silent. Weirdly silent now that I think about it."

"Did you experience any other sensory impressions during the hallucination?"

"You sound like a shrink when you talk like that."

"Just answer the damn question."

"I smelled roses." Mikki's lips curled in a smile.

"At least you're consistent." She grinned at her friend. Then her look sobered. "What caused it to end?"

Mikki grimaced. "Some bubba in a pickup drove by, gunned his motor, and honked while he yelled something incredibly articulate like *'Whoo-hoo! You are one hot mamma, Red.'* That effectively killed the fantasy."

"As it would any fantasy that took place anywhere except a trailer park," Nelly said.

"Ugh." Mikki nodded in agreement. "So am I bananas?"

"I don't think 'bananas' would be the medical term I would use."

"Nuts?"

Nelly shrugged. "Clearly, you're some kind of fruit." Then her expression turned serious. "All kidding aside, Mikki, I need to know how this is making you feel. Are you afraid?"

Mikki answered slowly, maintaining eye contact with her friend. "I'll admit it makes me nervous. I wonder what's going on inside my head, but I'm not afraid. It's never made me feel afraid." She drew a deep breath before she finished her answer. "Honestly, I don't want to sound like a freak or some kind of a pervert, but the dreams have become incredibly sexy. Hell, even the weird vision made my heart pound and gave me that fluttery feeling like I'd just been kissed by someone who really knows what he's doing. I hate to admit it, but I'm more horny than horrified." She bit her bottom lip. "Is that awful?"

"Nope," Nelly assured her quickly. "I'm glad you don't feel anxiety or fear. Actually . . ." She gathered up her purse and checked her lipstick. "My professional opinion—although you didn't technically ask for it—is that your imagination is working overtime because it has been forever since you've been laid."

"That's what you'd tell one of your patients?"

"You are not one of my patients. And my friend, you are not crazy."

"I'm just creative and horny?"

"That's my guess. Or I could write you a referral to a good neurologist."

"A neurologist!" Mikki's panic caused her voice to go shrill. "Do you think I have a brain tumor or something?"

"Please do not freak. There are a variety of neurological problems that can cause symptoms like you have been experiencing." She stood, grabbing her briefcase from beside the chair. "If it gets worse and is really bothering you, you might want to have some bloodwork run or whatnot."

"Is 'whatnot' another medical term?"

"Just like 'bananas' and 'nuts.'" Nelly leaned down and gave her a quick, hard hug. "Don't worry about it. Just go on with your life as you normally would, because you *are* normal. Oh, and don't forget that I'm fixing you up with that professor who is in town to lecture at TU."

Mikki groaned. "Now I really do wish you thought I was nuts."

"Stop it. This date will be good for you. Just don't act like you hate all men. It really doesn't make for a good first impression."

"I don't hate all men. I even like men. In theory. It's just that the past thirty-five years have trained me to believe that they will eventually disappoint me."

"Uh, that's not such a positive attitude either."

"Fine. I'll try to be good."

"I didn't mean for you to be good—just don't be cynical, and don't worry. You're totally okay." Nelly hugged her again and then hurried out the door.

Mikki frowned and checked her watch. She'd have to get going soon, too. Drinking the rest of her coffee, she muttered to herself. "Don't worry? Oh, sure. I saw *Phenomenon.* John Travolta thought aliens had visited him—until he died from *his* brain tumor. Aliens . . . a sexy beastlike dream lover . . . what's the difference? I think we're both screwed in more ways than one."

CHAPTER THREE

"NURSING Services, how may I help you?" Mikki answered the ringing phone as she glanced at the clock. It was just a little past noon. Would the day never end?

"May I speak with Mikki Empousai?" the man asked.

"This is she." Mikki tried to keep the impatience out of her voice. It was probably another drug rep trying to schmooze her so he could get to her boss. As executive assistant for the director of Nursing Services at St. John's Hospital, it fell to her to screen salesmen and other time-wasters from her director. But it certainly was an annoying part of her job. Didn't those guys ever give up?

"Mikki, this is Arnold Asher. I'm calling to confirm our date tonight."

"Oh! Uh . . . oh," Mikki stuttered.

"You sound surprised. Did I record the date wrong in my Blackberry?"

Through the phone Mikki could hear him tapping the little electronic screen.

"No, I haven't forgotten. I've just had a really busy morning," she lied. The only thing on her mind after her breakfast with Nelly had been her brain tumor and getting through the rest of the day at work without some kind of tragic, foaming-at-the-mouth psychotic episode. Briefly, she tried to recall if her bra and panties matched. God, it'd be embarrassing to be admitted to the psych ward wearing tacky lingerie . . .

Arnold's voice intruded into her musings. She'd almost forgotten she was on the phone with him. Almost.

"Our mutual friend, Nelly Peterson, told me your favorite restaurant is The Wild Fork, so I made a reservation for seven o'clock. Will that work for you?"

Mikki stifled her urge to break the date. She really was being unfair to the guy. He had a nice voice, and Nelly wouldn't fix her up with a guy who was anything less than attractive and interesting. She ignored the thought that attractive and interesting always seemed to hide arrogant and irritating under their onionlike layers of nice clothes and good manners. She could practically hear Nelly yelling at her, *Give the guy a chance!*

"Yes, dinner at The Wild Fork sounds wonderful, and it is one of my favorite restaurants," Mikki said, forcing her voice to be enthusiastic.

"Great! How about I pick you up at about six thirty?"

"No!" she said a little too quickly, and then to cover her abruptness, she laughed gaily like she'd lost every one of her brain cells. "There's really no need. I live just down the street from the restaurant. I'll meet you there."

"I understand completely. Whatever would make you more comfortable."

Was his tone patronizing?

"That's what I prefer," Mikki said firmly.

"Then it's a date. I'll see you at seven o'clock at The Wild Fork. How will I recognize you?"

Mikki rubbed her forehead, already feeling the beginning of a tension headache. Or was her brain tumor acting up? She seriously hated blind dates.

"I'll be the redhead with the rose in my hair."

Warm laughter filled the phone, surprising Mikki with its allure.

"Well, I definitely won't mistake you for another woman," he said, still chuckling softly.

Hoping he could hear the answering smile in her voice, Mikki said, "That's the idea. And I hope you're as charming as your laugh. I'll see you at seven."

"I'm looking forward to it," he said.

"I am, too."

She hung up and smiled at the phone, realizing that she really was looking forward to meeting the man behind the voice. She was still smiling when her boss, Jill Carter, rushed out of her office.

"Mikki! Call all the other directors' assistants. There's been a major accident on the BA Expressway. A bus filled with senior citizens on their way to Vegas rolled. They're bringing old people in here in droves. We'll need all the hands we can get to process them."

"I'm on it," Mikki said. She was punching phone numbers before Jill finished speaking.

THREE hours later the ER still resembled a geriatric battlefield, but at least Mikki thought it was finally beginning to seem like the hospital staff was on the winning side.

"I think the only ones who haven't been processed yet are those two little old ladies over there." Patricia, executive assistant to the director of security, nodded her head at the far corner of the ER waiting room.

Mikki sighed. "I'll take the lady in the red skirt if you take the one in the orange polyester pantsuit."

"Let's do it," Patricia said, already heading to her charge.

Mikki nodded. Man, she was tired. She felt as old as the ancient grandma she was approaching. Reminding herself firmly that even though she was tired and stressed, she hadn't just been through a bus accident, Mikki plastered a friendly smile on her face. The old woman's eyes were closed and her head was tilted back against the sterile tile of the ER wall. Her wealth of silver-white hair was caught up in an elegant French twist, and up close Mikki realized that the long, full skirt was made of rich-looking cashmere, as was the matching sweater. A thick, iridescent strand of pearls hung almost to her waist, and elegant pearl drops decorated her ears. A white silk scarf was wrapped around her left hand. The middle of the scarf was stained brown with dried blood.

"Ma'am?" she asked softly, not wanting to startle her.

The woman didn't respond.

"Excuse me, ma'am," Mikki said a little louder.

Still no response.

A horrible sinking feeling nested in Mikki's stomach. What if the old lady was dead?

"Ma'am!" Mikki tried unsuccessfully to keep the panic from her voice.

"I am not dead, young lady. I am simply old." The woman's voice was husky and attractive, rich with a soft, rolling accent. She enunciated the syllables of each word carefully.

But she didn't open her eyes.

"I'm sorry, ma'am. I—I, uh, I didn't think you were dead, I just thought you were asleep. It's your turn. I can take your insurance information now."

She opened her eyes, and Mikki blinked in surprise. The old woman's eyes were startlingly clear and a vibrant, deep blue. If hope had a color, it would be the blue of the old woman's eyes, and Mikki was struck speechless by their beauty.

The deep, soft lines at the edges of the woman's eyes crinkled as she smiled.

"You should try to always tell the truth, my dear. You are a dismal liar. But do not fret. I am most certainly alive—for the moment."

She held out the well-manicured hand that was not wrapped in a scarf, and Mikki automatically took it, helping the woman to her feet.

"Yes, ma'am," Mikki said stupidly.

"I have always thought that the title of 'ma'am' should be reserved for young women who desire to appear older, or old women who have given up on life. I am neither. I prefer *signora*, the title Italians give their women. It sounds so much more interesting, does it not? But you may call me Sevillana."

Mikki's smile slipped off her face. "Did you say Sevillana?"

"Yes, that is my given name. Is there something wrong, my dear?"

Mikki helped Sevillana into the chair in front of the registration desk before she answered. "No, nothing's wrong. It's just that I know the name."

"Do you?" The old woman raised one delicate silver eyebrow. "And what is it you know?"

"I know it's the name of a rose, a Meidiland Rose that originated in France. It's a brilliant scarlet in color and very hardy. It makes a great hedge, and it blooms for almost four straight months."

Sevillana smiled with surprised appreciation. "I knew there was something special about you."

Mikki tried to return her smile, but she was still disconcerted by the odd coincidence of their names. Plenty of roses had been named after people—the JFK rose, the Dolly Parton, the Princess Di—but she'd never met anyone else who had been named after a rose. Retreating into the familiar, she tapped her computer and pulled up the new patient profile screen.

"What is your last name, ma'am, I mean, signora?" Mikki asked.

"Kalyca. Spelled k-a-l-y-c-a." She took an insurance card from her purse and handed it to Mikki. "And what is your name, my dear?"

Mikki glanced up from the computer screen. Automatically, she opened her mouth to tell Sevillana her nickname, but something in the old woman's knowing gaze made her hesitate.

"Mikado," she admitted.

The smile that lit Sevillana's face seemed to wash decades from her age. "Oh, my! Another lady of the roses. What a lovely surprise."

"It's certainly unusual," Mikki agreed, with a hint of sarcasm.

Sevillana studied Mikado carefully. "As you age, you will learn to appreciate the unusual, no matter in what form you discover it. Or it discovers you."

Mikki closed her lips on the ready quip that came to her mind. There was something so wise in the old woman's eyes that she felt her normal defenses slip.

"Do you really believe that?" Mikki asked suddenly.

"Of course, my dear." Sevillana's incredible eyes were sharp. "The unusual is as close as we can get in this world to experiencing real magick, and magick is the breath of life."

Mikki would have liked to have questioned the old woman further, but just then a nurse stepped officiously up to them.

"I believe you're my last patient." The RN helped Sevillana to her feet. "Let's take a look at that hand."

"It is nothing but a scratch," the old woman said as she let the nurse lead her from the desk. Then, glancing over her shoulder, she met Mikki's eyes and spoke clearly and distinctly. "I have received far worse wounds from pruning my roses without gloves."

Her words caused a shock of surprise to explode across Mikki's skin.

How did the old woman know?

Mikki was still staring thoughtfully at the doorway through which Sevillana had disappeared when her boss squeezed her shoulder, making her jump.

"Didn't mean to scare you, Mikki. I just wanted to thank you. I appreciate your help today. It was above and beyond the normal call of duty."

"Oh, no problem, Jill. It was a nice change from regular office work."

Jill looked at her assistant closely. She noticed the dark circles under her expressive eyes and the unusual paleness of her skin. Mikki had been her assistant for five years, and the director had come to depend on the no-nonsense way she kept the Nursing Services office running smoothly, but lately her assistant had begun to worry her. She had become increasingly absent-minded, and just two days earlier Jill was almost positive Mikki had been sleeping at her desk. Perhaps it was time her assistant took a vacation. And maybe she needed a raise, too. Jill would hate to lose her to one of their competitor hospitals, and that new heart hospital had just opened on 91st Street. They were probably recruiting heavily for experienced employees. She made a mental note to look into the raise and bring Mikki one of those cruise line catalogs first thing Monday morning.

"Why don't you knock off early today? It's been a long week."

Mikki smiled in surprise. "Thanks! I do have a big date to get ready for."

Jill grinned at her assistant. "I'll keep my fingers crossed." Then she looked around to be sure no one could overhear her before quipping, "You know, a hard man is good to find."

Mikki giggled. "This one's a professor."

"Well, here's hoping that his"—Jill paused, omitting the word and waggling her eyebrows suggestively—"is as big as his brain. See you Monday." Then she departed, swinging her hips jauntily in time with her characteristically saucy stride.

Mikki was still smiling as she turned off the computer. It was as she clicked the mouse that she noticed the laminated insurance card.

"Ah, damnit! I didn't give Sevillana back her card."

Mikki grabbed the card and rushed through the door to the inner area of the emergency room. The nurses' station was located in the middle of the large center arena. Mikki recognized the unit secretary who sat behind the tall counter. As usual, the petite brunette was busy typing orders into the computer.

"Hey, Brandi, what room is Sevillana Kalyca in?"

"Seven." The harried secretary didn't even glance up at her. "That's a name that is hard to forget."

"Thanks." Mikki headed to the door marked 7. "Hope it quiets down for you tonight."

"Fat chance," Brandi muttered.

Mikki knocked on the closed door.

"You may enter." The old woman's distinctive voice called.

Mikki opened the door and peeked hesitantly into the room. Sevillana beckoned her in with her good hand. Her left hand was propped up on an aluminum arm that pulled out of the side of the examination bed. Someone had draped the shiny surface with a blue cloth. Mikki could see the laceration that slashed across the meaty part of her palm. It was slowly seeping blood.

"Come on in, my dear. The nurse has gone to collect some instruments with which to fix this." She nodded at her hand. "Apparently, I need stitches."

"I'm sorry," Mikki said automatically. "I hope it doesn't hurt too much."

"It is a small thing, Mikado." Sevillana gestured to the chair beside the bed. "Please, sit. It was kind of you to look in on me."

"I brought you this." Mikki handed her the insurance card, feeling chagrined that she hadn't really come to check on her.

"Thank you. I would never have remembered where I left it." Sevillana took the card and smiled warmly at Mikki.

Mikki sat. She tried to keep from staring at the old woman's wound, but like a horrible accident passed on a highway, her gaze kept being drawn back to it. And there was something else about Sevillana's palm. Mikki squinted, trying to get a better look at it.

"Blood is fascinating. Do you not think it so?" Sevillana's voice was hypnotic.

"The color always reminds me of roses," Mikki said softly. She forced her eyes from Sevillana's injured hand to her face. "I don't mean to sound like I'm a blood-crazed ghoul. It's just that freshly blooming roses and new blood share such a unique color. I don't understand why that should have a negative connotation," she finished defensively.

Sevillana's amazing blue eyes pierced her. "You are wise for one who is so young. For me, it took many years to understand that there is no negative connotation in what you say. Roses and blood do share many of the same traits, which is, truly, a wondrous thing."

Mikki took a deep breath.

"How do you know about roses and blood?" she blurted.

The old woman's answering smile was wise.

"Here we are!" The nurse hurried into the room carrying a tray filled with sterile instruments. She was followed by a female doctor Mikki recognized as being one of the new residents. "Doctor Mason is going to get you fixed right up."

The doctor glanced at Mikki. "Are you a relative?"

"No, I'm Jill Carter's assistant."

"You'll have to leave."

Mikki nodded and looked apologetically at Sevillana. "I have to go. It was really nice to meet you, signora."

"Wait a moment, my dear." Sevillana reached for her purse, which was lying next to her on the examination bed.

"Ma'am, if she's not a relative, she really must leave," Dr. Mason said.

"I understand that, young woman. I am not asking that she stay. I simply have something I must give her," Sevillana said in a tone a mother would use to admonish an errant child.

Without waiting for a response from the doctor, the old woman's uninjured hand disappeared into the bowels of her huge, baglike purse, and when it emerged, it was holding a small glass bottle. The bottle was no longer than Mikki's little finger, and it was shaped like a slender tube. There were knobby protrusions up and down the length of it. Mikki thought the design looked vaguely familiar.

"Here, my dear. I want you to have this."

Sevillana placed the vial in her hand, and when she touched it, Mikki realized why it looked familiar. It was a perfect glass replica of the stem of a rose, complete with tiny thorns.

"It is a perfume I had made for me when I last visited the island of Crete off the coast of the always lovely Greece. In the past, it has brought me good luck and more than a little magick. My wish is that it may do the same for you."

Mikki's hand closed over the bottle. "Thank you, Sevillana," she called as the nurse ushered her toward the door.

"Remember . . ." The old woman whispered after Mikado.

The door closed with a soft click.

CHAPTER FOUR

MIKKI'S apartment was a sanctuary. She'd signed the long-term lease five years before and hadn't been sorry once. She lived on the top floor of the small complex. It was a spacious, quiet place, but she hadn't decided on it because of its interior. She'd chosen it because of its location. The view from her wrought iron balcony, which wrapped from her living room past her bedroom, looked directly out on Woodward Park. Woodward Park adjoined her favorite place in the world—the Tulsa Municipal Rose Gardens.

Mikki checked her watch as she stepped onto the balcony. Almost six thirty. She had just enough time. She drank in the wonderful view of Woodward Park and noted that nothing wavered or shifted in the air. The park was simply the park. Briefly, Mikki strained to catch even an echo of a lonely roar, but except for the occasional car that whizzed past on 21st Street and the workers who were putting finishing touches on the stage for the play scheduled to open in a couple nights, everything was silent and ordinary. The October evening was pleasantly cool. The sun had just set, but the sky seemed reluctant to relinquish the remnants of its light. Slate blended with mauve and coral in the fading day. Mikki knew the colors would wane quickly, though. Tonight there would be a new moon, which meant the only light afforded by the night sky would be from its stars.

She mentally shook herself. She'd better stop daydreaming and hurry if she was going to get to the restaurant before her date.

The breeze stirred and Mikki breathed deeply, savoring the sweet scent of roses—her roses. The balcony held five large clay pots in which lived five exquisite examples of expertly tended rosebushes. All five were the same type of rose. Mikki had long ago given up mixing her roses at home; she knew what worked best for her—consistency and meticulous care. Her success surrounded her. All five bushes were in full bloom, and the blooms were more than just the typical last-minute blossoming show before winter called them to dormancy. Her Mikado Roses were miraculous.

The outer petals of the fat blooms were red, but not just any red. The scarlet of Mikki's roses had been compared to rubies, fire, and blood. As the blooms unfurled, the brilliant red merged with gold until the base of the rose appeared to have been dipped in a glass of expensive sherry.

Mikki had been winning the amateur category of the annual All-American Rose Selections Garden Show for the past five years. Her co-volunteers at the Tulsa Rose Gardens liked to joke that no one could beat her because she had some kind of magic potion she poured on her roses. Each year they would make a big production of begging her to share her secret.

Mikki smiled and accepted their praise—but she never joked about having a secret rose potion.

Mikki put down the watering bucket and the little toolbox that held her various pruning sheers and other rose gardening implements. She approached the first bush. Frowning, she pinched off a small leaf that to the untrained eye looked healthy, but to Mikki's experienced gaze spelled a potential problem.

"Powdery mildew," she said with disgust. "I knew the last couple nights had been unseasonably cool, but I thought the temperatures during the day would offset any negative effects." She caressed one of the blooms lightly, speaking to the bush as if it were a child. "It's too early in the season. You won't want me to bring you inside yet. I guess I'll have to start covering you at night."

Moving from plant to plant, Mikki inspected her charges. She found no more offending leaves, but she made a mental note to check the forecast before she went to bed. If the temperature was going to drop to anywhere around forty degrees, she would cover the roses.

Returning to the toolbox, she selected a medium-size pair of shears. Quickly making her choice, she moved to the rosebush that sat closest to the sliding glass doors leading to her bedroom. With sure, experienced motions, she held the stem of a delicate, just opening bloom, and in one quick motion made a vertical cut in the straight, green stem. She lifted the bloom to her nose and drank in its intoxicating fragrance.

"I will love wearing you in my hair tonight," she told it.

Once more she returned to her toolbox. Gently, she placed the cut rose on the balcony beside it. Then she put away the pair of shears and searched through the box for the final tool she would need that evening.

She found the pocketknife quickly. It was small, but her toolbox was familiar and well ordered. Nothing could hide within it for long. Mikki opened the knife. The little blade was honed to a razorlike edge, which glinted dangerously in the fading light. Methodically, Mikki opened the bottom drawer of the box. Extracting a small packet, she tore open the alcohol wipe. First she swabbed the palm of her left hand, and then she cleaned the already-sterile-looking blade.

She could hear her mother's familiar voice speak from her memory, *You can never be too careful, Mikado. There's no need to get an infection.*

Satisfied that both surfaces were clean, Mikki discarded the alcohol pad. She glanced around her. Even though her balcony faced a busy street, the apartment's height and the thick foliage of her rosebushes coupled to prevent any passersby from catching much more than a glimpse of her. But on the evening of the new moon, Mikki wanted to avoid even the possibility of being glimpsed.

Nothing was stirring around her except the breeze.

Mikki held her left hand in front of her. The skin of her palm was mottled with slender white scars. She glanced at the palm of her right hand. Yes, she had remembered correctly. Amidst the little bone-colored lines on that palm was a more recent mark, still pink and newly healed, which assured her that this month it was her left palm she must use.

Without further hesitation, Mikki pressed the sharp blade against her left palm, and with a practiced, precise movement, cut herself.

Blood welled instantly, and Mikki was suddenly reminded of Sevillana's injury. It had been in exactly the same place, only deeper and wider. And then with a jolt, she realized what else she had seen on the old woman's palm. Bone-colored scars, slender, well healed, and familiar. Mikki felt a wave of dizziness and closed her eyes quickly on the spinning balcony.

How could the old woman have the same cutting scars as she? It was only the women in Mikki's family who practiced this ritual, and they had done so in strict secrecy for generations. And since her mother had died the year before, Mikki had thought she was the last of her kind, the only person left in the world who knew the secret of blood roses. Mikki had to find out more about her. First thing Monday morning she would pull Sevillana's patient record and get her address. She must see the old woman again.

The vertigo-like feeling faded, and Mikki opened her eyes. Blood was pooling in her palm. Before it could drip onto the balcony, Mikki plunged her hand into the watering bucket. At first the cut stung, but the coolness of the water quickly turned soothing. Mikki swished her hand around, watching the water blush with her blood.

After a few minutes she pulled her hand from the water, shook it and wrapped it tightly in a strip of gauze she pulled from the open bottom drawer of the toolbox. She knew the bleeding would stop soon, leaving a narrow, unobtrusive scab she would cover for the next couple days with a flesh-colored Band-Aid. If the other volunteers at the Rose Gardens noticed it, Mikki would simply smile her way through their admonishments about being more careful when she pruned and making sure she always wore her thick leather gloves.

But few people ever noticed such a small, insignificant cut.

Carrying the bucket with her uninjured hand, she carefully divided the water among the five plants. She poured the blood-tinged liquid slowly over each plant's roots, whispering endearments to them and praising them for their beauty. As always, Mikki thought she could actually see the roses responding to the ritual. The cool breeze filtered through their thick leaves, causing the heavy blooms to nod their heads as if they were saying, *Yes, we are part of you . . . blood of your blood . . .*

And to Mikki, they were more than just plants. They were her legacy and the last vestige of her mother and her family. Without them, she would be alone in the world.

When the water was gone she smiled happily at her charges.

"I'd like nothing more than to pull my rocking chair out here, pour myself a glass of that new red I bought yesterday and spend the evening reading a good book." But she had a date, she reminded herself, with a man who had a nice voice and a charming laugh. Mikki checked the time; it was 6:45. It would take her at least ten minutes to walk to the restaurant.

"Damn!"

Mikki grabbed the empty bucket and the toolbox and tossed them inside the balcony door. She'd clean up the mess when she got home. Rushing to her bathroom, she gave her makeup and hair one last check. She looked good—the black leather skirt was one of her favorites, and the rust color of the cashmere sweater was a lovely compliment to her red-gold hair. Quickly, she chose a long, slender strand of antique black glass beads to hang around her neck and dug through her earring drawer until she found a pair of matching chandeliers.

She rushed from the bathroom, grabbed a sweater for her shoulders and was struggling to zip up her sassy new boots when she remembered the rose for her hair. She'd left it on the balcony. Grumbling to herself about being absentminded, she retrieved the cut flower, trimmed the leaves and the stem, and used the little decorative mirror in the living room to check herself as she positioned it snuggly within the curls over her left ear. Breathing deeply, Mikki smiled at her reflection. What better perfume could she choose?

Perfume . . .

Mikki narrowed her eyes thoughtfully and glanced at her purse.

Deciding quickly, she unzipped the little side pocket that usually held only her lipstick, a compact and her keys. The glass stem was there, nestled among the more familiar items.

"Well, why not?" Mikki asked herself. "Sevillana said it brought her luck. Maybe if I wear it tonight I'll be lucky enough to have a decent date for a change."

Mikki pulled open the tiny cork and raised the vial to her nose. She inhaled and blinked in delighted surprise. The perfume was an earthy mixture of roses and spices. Mikki inhaled again. She'd never smelled any perfume like it. Along with the familiar scent of traditional roses, she thought she recognized cinnamon, ginger and clove, all blended together in a rich, sweet oil. She dabbed the perfume on the pulse points of her neck, throat and wrists before placing the vial back in her purse.

Humming softly to herself, she locked the door behind her and hurried to the sidewalk, loving how the evening breeze mingled the sweetness of her namesake rose and the earthiness of her new perfume. She certainly smelled good.

And suddenly she realized that she really was feeling very lucky.

CHAPTER FIVE

THE Wild Fork was located in the heart of Tulsa's Utica Square—a beautiful area filled with lovely landscaping, mature trees, trendy shops and fine restaurants. As usual, it was a busy Friday night and all the outside tables were already filled with hungry patrons. Mikki glanced surreptitiously around her. No, she didn't see any solitary men. He was probably seated inside. She checked her watch again. It was 7:10. She hated being late. Sighing, she entered the restaurant.

The harried maître d' was taking the names of a party of six. He assured them the wait would not be too long and then with an effeminate flutter of his long, slender fingers, he waved the group into the waiting area. When his gaze shifted to Mikki his businesslike expression was immediately replaced with a welcoming grin.

"Mikki! Get yourself on in here. It's been ages since I've seen you."

Mikki returned his smile, and they shared a soft, girlfriend hug.

"Blair, you handsome thing, when are you going to kick Anthony out of your bed and invite me in?" Mikki teased.

Blair giggled and pretended to blush.

"Hush, bad thing. Tony's working tonight. He'll hear you and turn positively green with jealousy. And you know green is his worst color."

"As a striking redhead, I think it's tragic that some blondes can't wear green," Mikki simpered, batting her eyes coquettishly at her friend.

Blair stepped back and studied her. "And dahling, you *are* looking yummy tonight. That hot little skirt is just to die for! What's the occasion?"

Mikki's grin faltered. She had almost forgotten. Almost.

"I'm meeting a blind date here."

Blair sucked air and clutched his pearls. "Tragic," he said. "Let me guess. Nelly had something to do with this?"

Mikki nodded.

"Not another transient doctor?"

"Well, kind of. This one isn't a medical doctor. He's some kind of professor—an engineer or something. He's guest speaking at TU next week."

Blair's eyes widened. "Get out of town! Sounds dreadfully dull."

"Be nice. I'm trying to be."

Blair's shocked expression froze, and he lowered his voice. "Wait . . . he must be Mr. Dark and Dangerous who's been here for about twenty minutes. Girl, he's not bad at all!"

Mikki felt a little skip of anticipation and tried to remember the description Nelly had given her of Arnold Asher.

"Is he medium height, kind of stocky build, shaved bald head with a small diamond stud in one ear?" she asked.

"That's him. Totally. And he has a yummy mustache. Tony and I were just whispering that he reminded us of a cross between a mob boss and that fabulously sexy Telly Savalas—may he rest in peace." Blair hastily crossed himself.

"Stop it. You're not Catholic."

"Girl, you know I believe in covering all bases."

Mikki rolled her eyes at him. "So what you're saying is that he's cute."

"Cute?" Blair squeaked. "He's simply delicious."

She squared her shoulders. "Well, good. I mean, I didn't expect anything else. You know Nelly wouldn't fix me up with anyone who was hideous." Which was true. But there was a whole hell of a lot more to a man than appearance. "Lead on. I'm ready to meet Mr. Delicious."

Blair took a menu and turned. Over his shoulder in his most professionally snobby maître d' voice, he said, "Follow me please, mademoiselle." He started walking toward the section of the restaurant relegated to its far side.

"Hey." Mikki tugged on his sleeve. "This is the I'm-on-a-sexy-date seating area."

"That's where he asked to be seated," Blair said, eyes sparkling. "Somewhere private."

"Huh," Mikki said.

"You may have gotten more than you bargained for with this one, little missy," Blair said in his truly abominable John Wayne accent.

"Please. No John Wayne tonight. My stomach is already churning from nerves."

"Oh, relax. I have a good feeling about this one."

Mikki followed Blair through the restaurant to the dimly lit side room that held intimate little tables and couples who were close talking. Blair stepped to the side so she could be seen by all the tables. A solitary man wearing a tastefully expensive black jacket and pants with a silk knit sweater underneath that was a lovely shade of cool green looked up from the book he was reading. His head was shaved, and the light caught a small diamond earring in his left ear. Nelly had been honest in her assessment. She had described Arnold Asher as 'attractive, but not in a traditional way.' Mikki had to agree. The man was definitely interesting looking—a little dark and bad boy-ish, and decidedly masculine. She felt a stab of unexpected pleasure. She wasn't attracted to traditionally handsome men—there was something about them that she found too much. After spending time with a "handsome" man, she often felt like she'd eaten too many rich desserts. And all too often she'd discovered that their inside was as empty as their outside was full and attractive. But an unusual or interesting-looking man . . . Mikki watched as he recognized the rose in her hair and waved a hand at her.

"Bingo!" Blair said.

Mikki smiled and strode purposefully forward to meet her date. He stood as she approached his table.

"You must be Mikki Empousai," he said as his eyes slid appreciatively down her body.

"Yes I am, Arnold. It's nice to meet you."

They shook hands. His grip was strong and warm, and as welcoming as his smile.

Blair held her chair out for her, and she sat.

"Wow . . . I . . ." Arnold stumbled over his words, sounding shocked and a little nervous. "I'm sorry, I just suddenly had the overwhelming impression that we've met before, even though I know that's not possible."

"Really?" Mikki laughed a little, enjoying the appreciation that was clear in his eyes. "Do you usually dabble in the psychic? I don't remember Nelly saying anything about that."

His smile stayed warm. "I like to call it being intuitive and willing to be open to new possibilities."

Feeling her face flush with the obvious interest he was showing in her, Mikki's eyes dropped to the book he had been reading. The title was *My Losing Season* . . .

Mikki gasped, reaching for the hardback. "Pat Conroy! You like Pat Conroy?"

"He's one of my top ten favorite writers," Arnold said.

"Mine, too. I love him! *The Prince of Tides; The Great Santini, The Water Is Wide* . . ."

"*Beach Music, The Lords of Discipline,*" he continued for her.

"I adored *Beach Music.*"

"So did I. Almost as much as *The Prince of Tides*. I hated that it got some bad reviews," he said quickly.

"I couldn't agree more! Pat Conroy's prose is magic. I cannot understand how anyone could give him a bad review."

They sat and smiled in happy surprise at each other, and Mikki felt a rush of something she hadn't felt for a long time on a date—hope.

Blair's romantic and totally exaggerated sigh changed into a contrived cough when Mikki glared at him.

"Oh-mi-god, excuse me," Blair said. "Something tickled my throat."

"Blair, honey, you can bring me a glass of my usual chianti." She glanced back at the still-smiling Arnold. "Are you hungry? I skipped lunch and would love an hors d'oeuvre."

"Sounds good to me."

"Fantastic. How about the olive bread? It always makes me think of Italy."

Arnold nodded and Blair hurried away.

"So you're a Conroy fan," he said. "Which is your favorite?"

"Probably *The Prince of Tides*, but I love them all." Mikki stroked the cover of the book before passing it back across the table. "I haven't read that one yet."

"You have to! He gives amazing insight into his life."

"I'll be sure to get it." They shared a look of complete understanding, and Mikki felt another lovely flutter of hope. "You said he was one of your top ten favorite authors. Who are some of the others?"

Arnold leaned forward, obviously warming to the subject as only a true booklover could. Mikki studied him as he talked. No, he was not traditionally handsome, and she did tend to prefer her men taller—and younger. But there was definitely something about him, something intelligent and experienced and sexy.

"It's hard to narrow them down to ten. I suppose with Conroy I'd have to add Herman Wouk."

"*The Winds of War*. What a fabulous book!" Mikki said.

"And don't forget *War and Remembrance*."

"Couldn't do that."

"Then I'd have to go from there to James Clavell," he said.

"*King Rat, Tai-Pan* and the best, *Shogun*," she said, barely nodding at Blair as he brought her wine and their olive bread.

"I didn't like the miniseries, though."

"Richard Chamberlain as Blackthorne? Please. No, no, no. I really hate it when a great book is turned into a cheesy miniseries."

"Unlike one of my other top ten picks—Larry McMurtry's *Lonesome Dove*."

Mikki paused mid-bite of her olive bread. "I loved the book *and* adored the miniseries."

And from there they launched into a lively discussion of the settings depicted by their most beloved authors, from McMurtry's West to Wilbur Smith's Africa and Egypt. Somewhere in the middle of their conversation they managed to order and eat dinner. Mikki felt like she wanted to pinch herself. She couldn't remember the last time she'd had such great dinner conversation with a man. With girlfriends it was the norm to have easy, interesting discussions. With men it seemed—at least to Mikki—almost impossible. Yet before she knew it, she'd killed three glasses of chianti, eaten an excellent meal and was just ordering an Irish coffee for dessert instead of the Death by Chocolate Cake that had been tempting her. She was nicely buzzed and having a great time—and was completely surprised when she glanced at her watch and saw that almost two hours had passed.

She sipped her coffee and felt his eyes studying her. The question on his face was so clear she smiled and said, "What?"

"It's just so amazing."

"Actually, I was thinking the same thing," she said a little shyly.

"I can't believe I found a woman who has actually read, and can appreciate, more than a trashy romance novel."

Mikki felt the beginning of cold water being dashed on her warm, happy buzz. Had he actually said "trashy romance novel"? As in the wonderful Nora Roberts, and the ever-delightful MaryJanice Davidson, Susan Grant, Gena Showalter, Sharon Sala, Merline Lovelace, and a host of other fabulous women authors who had kept her company on long nights and made her laugh and cry and sigh happily?

"What do you mean by that?"

Oblivious to her change in tone, he went on enthusiastically. "I mean that it's unusual that an attractive, available woman has read and comprehended some interesting books."

"I've made it a point to read a wide range of authors and genres. I think it gives an important added perspective to what might be an otherwise narrow view of life," she said carefully, trying to keep her tone neutral. "I was wondering, Arnold, have you ever read any of Anne Tyler's work?"

"Tyler? No, I don't think so," he said.

"She won a Pulitzer for *Breathing Lessons*, you know."

"Did she?" He flashed his smile again. "Good for her."

Mikki cringed internally at his patronizing tone. "How about *The Historian* by Elizabeth Kostova?"

"No."

"I thought you liked historicals," she said.

"I do."

"Hmm. Then how about *The Mists of Avalon* by Marion Zimmer Bradley?"

"The Arthurian myth told from a woman's point of view?" His laugh was sarcastic and condescending. "I wouldn't consider that historical."

"Did you read it?"

"No, of course not. I choose to stick with Tennyson or T. H. White." His hand rubbed his forehead as if she was causing his head to hurt. "I like things that are tried and true."

"Okay, then what about any of Nora Roberts's books? I read a statistic once that said that every sixty seconds someone buys a Nora Roberts novel. Sounds as if she is definitely tried and true. And statistically, at least, you might have read her—maybe even on accident."

"Nora Roberts? Doesn't she write those bodice rippers?"

Blair fluttered up to the table. "I'll just leave the check here." He put it next to Arnold's arm. "But there's no rush for you two, take . . ." Blair's words trailed off as he recognized the look of narrow-eyed annoyance Mikki had trained on her date. He cleared his throat. "What I meant to say is that I'll be happy to take this for you whenever you're ready." With a worried glance at Mikki, he retreated to watch from the waiter's station.

Blair's abrupt departure made Mikki realize that she needed to fix the expression on her face, but when she glanced at Arnold she saw she needn't have worried. He wasn't looking at her. He was frowning over the bill.

"Is there a problem?" she asked.

He looked up at her and then slid the bill over so she could see it. "No. No problem at all. I was just figuring up my part of the bill."

"Excuse me?"

"Well, you were the one who ordered the appetizer. You had one more glass of wine than I did, and that Irish coffee certainly wasn't cheap."

Disbelieving, Mikki blinked and tried to find her voice.

He reached into his wallet and got out a twenty and two tens. "That should take care of my part, plus a tip." Then he looked expectantly at her. "Are you paying with cash or a credit card?"

Mikki burst into laughter. "You want me to pay for my half of dinner?"

"Of course," he said with a perfectly straight face. "Times have changed. Today's women want to be treated equally and with respect. I'm just showing you the respect you want."

"Perfect," Mikki said, still laughing. She could feel the lovely redheaded fit brewing just under her breastbone. This was going to be truly delicious.

"This is just perfect. Okay, here's the deal Dr. Asher—that is how one formally addresses you, isn't it?"

He nodded, looking vaguely confused.

"Good. I want to be sure I get this right. Here's the deal, Dr. Asher. It's not showing me respect to use rhetoric about what today's women want as an excuse to be cheap. It's actually showing me the opposite. I don't care what year it is. If this is a date—and I was under the impression that it was—then it should be a point of pride and good manners for a gentleman to pay for a lady's dinner. That's being respectful. But you wouldn't understand that because you clearly do not respect women. Your attitude about what you believe women read is as patronizing as your obvious disdain for female authors." Mikki reached into her purse, pulled out three twenty-dollar bills and plopped them on top of the check. "And here's a newsflash for you—those so-called trashy romance novels outsell all other genres of writing. Many of the authors are insightful and well educated. They create worlds filled with strong, passionate women and honorable, heroic men. You should try reading some of them. Those female romance authors you disdain could definitely teach you a thing or two about being a man." She stood up and put her purse over her shoulder. "Good night, Dr. Asher." He started to stand, clearly struggling to say something. "No, please. Don't get up. I want to remember you just like this—confused and speechless. It's a good look for you; it certainly beats patronizing and chauvinistic."

Grinning wickedly, she turned and sauntered lazily out of the dimly lit room.

She was still grinning as she strolled down the sidewalk. God, she was glad she'd told him off and walked out! She had never been a wimpy, doormat kind of a woman; she had an extraordinarily low bullshit meter. God, didn't it just figure! He had seemed interesting and sexy at first. But like most men, he had turned out to be a disappointment.

Whispering through her subconscious was the thought that no man had been able to get close to her because she had never been able to allow herself to share the secret that pulsed through her blood . . . but the thought was fleeting, and she quickly stifled the stark honesty of it with a tipsy laugh and a little impromptu twirl in the halo of light under a streetlamp.

She'd never actually walked out on a date before.

It was exhilarating!

Her steps slowed. Lately, she'd been thinking more and more that maybe she wasn't meant to have a permanent relationship. Maybe tonight had been the final sign she needed. Something like a modern omen. She *was* different, and it was becoming more and more clear to her that there was no "right" man for her. He didn't exist. Oddly enough, the thought didn't make her feel sad or lonely. Instead, it made her feel wise, like she had come to a realization that her friends weren't mature enough yet to understand. It gave her a sense of release that was almost overwhelming.

Mikki walked past McGill's, a popular local pub, and considered ducking in for a quick drink. But the door opened and a current of noise rolled out, changing her mind. She didn't feel like dealing with shouting above a din of music just to order a drink. Plus, she'd probably had enough—not that that was a bad thing. She wasn't driving—she was flying! Mikki laughed and walked on, breathing in the cool October air.

As she left the business district and got closer to Woodward Park and her apartment, the buildings changed from posh shops and restaurants to the stately old oil mansions that surrounded the park. Mikki loved this part of Tulsa. It made her wish she had lived during the 1920s. She would have been a flapper. She would have cut her hair short, worn loose beaded dresses that shimmied when she moved, had too much to drink and danced all night. Between parties she would have crusaded for equal rights for women.

Kind of like she'd done tonight, she thought happily. Well, minus the dress, the haircut and the dancing. She did a happy little skip step under the next light and laughed at herself. Maybe not minus the dancing. She'd have to go back to the restaurant tomorrow night for dinner and get all the gory after-she-left details from Blair and the gang.

The sidewalk was interrupted by the road forking in front of her. Mikki was at the juncture of where the mansions gave way to Woodward Park. Here was where she usually crossed the street to her apartment. Hesitating, Mikki looked into the park. She didn't detect any strange shifts in perception that might signal one of her episodes. Actually, until that moment she'd forgotten about the weirdness that had crept into her life with her recent dreams.

"Just goes to prove dumping a man is good for what ails me," she said pleasantly to herself.

And everything did look utterly normal. The free-standing antique streetlights scattered throughout Woodward Park speckled it with pools of creamy light. The wind whispered through the well-tended oaks, calling softly the change of seasons and causing a cascade of leaves to scatter like mini-tornados that had been taught to heel. And smack in the middle of it she could see the soft illumination of the stage lights for the Performance in the Park rehearsal. Faintly she could hear the actress speaking her lines . . .

> *"A little love is a joy in the house,*
> *A little fire is a jewel against frost and darkness . . ."*

She started to cross the street toward home but hesitated, looking longingly at the park, awash in light and sound. It was so lovely. It looked like a magical oasis in the middle of the night—a special little sub-city of her very own. A teasing breeze whisked from the park and twirled around her body, enticing her forward with the cinnamon scent of autumn leaves.

Why not?

Mikki checked the time. It was only nine. The park and the rose gardens didn't close till eleven. Nelly had specifically told her to go on with her normal life. It was definitely normal for her to walk through the park and visit her roses. She'd make her way around the rehearsing actors and then take a quick stroll through the gardens. She really should check on the roses that surrounded the construction site. She'd been concerned that all the tromping of the workmen's booted feet with their clumsy comings and goings was overstressing the roses.

Mikki glanced up at the darkening sky, reminding herself that it was the night of the new moon. If the roses needed help, what better time could she choose to give it to them?

She'd make one pass through the central tier and be sure the workers had cleaned up their mess and not manhandled the roses. Then she'd go home, pour herself a glass of bedtime wine and curl up with a good book . . . by a female author!

Or, her errant thoughts whispered enticingly, she could just go to sleep. Wouldn't she rather revisit her dream lover than do anything else?

With a supreme effort of will, she steered her mind away from that line of thinking. She couldn't start living life around her fantasies. Then she really would be crazy.

CHAPTER SIX

MIKKI stepped into the crossroads between the park and the street and then onto the sidewalk that twisted past the lovely waterfall-fed ponds that framed the north edge of Woodward Park. At the next fork in the walkway she headed up and away from the northern street side, walking toward the central area of the park, which was currently abuzz with activity around the raised stage that had only just been erected the night before. Bits and pieces of poetic lines drifted around her, teasing her with snippets of the play.

"The holy fountains flow up from the earth,
the smoke of sacrifice flows up from the earth,
the eagle and the wild swan fly up from the earth, righteousness also
has flown up from the earth to the feet of the goddess . . ."

Intrigued, she searched her memory for details of *Medea*'s story. She vaguely remembered that the play was an ancient Greek tragedy and that the plot centered around Medea, who had been jilted by her husband, Jason, for . . . Mikki scrunched up her face as she tried to sift through the dregs of long-forgotten high school English.

. . . But women will never hate their own children.

Floating to her on the soft wind, the line jogged her cobwebby memory. Medea had been pissed at Jason because he had dumped her for a younger woman, the daughter of the king of wherever it was they had fled to after she'd betrayed her homeland to save Jason.

"Figures," she muttered to herself. "Just like a man . . ." She slowed as she approached the busy group of people who were rearranging lights and hauling pieces of freshly painted plywood setting here and there. Several actresses were onstage, but they had fallen silent. Three grouped nervously together on stage left. Another woman was standing by herself opposite them stage right. They were wearing drapey toga-like outfits, and their hair flowed long and loose down their backs. All of them were looking around as if they expected someone to materialize from the shadows at the edge of the stage. Mikki stopped to watch, wondering why they seemed so uncomfortable.

"Where in the hell is Medea?"

The voice boomed from a little open-ended tent not far from her, causing Mikki to jump.

"She . . . she said she had to take a break," the lone woman said sheepishly.

"That was half an hour ago!" the shadowed voice yelled, clearly annoyed. "How are we supposed to finish the sound check without Medea?"

Mikki's eyes slid to where the voice was coming from. All she could make out from the interior of the tent was an illuminated soundboard that had lights and switches blinking away on it, in front of which the dark figure of a man stood.

"I could wear two mikes and read her lines as well as mine," one of the three women said, shielding her eyes from the spotlights trained on the stage as she peered toward the man who Mikki decided must be the director.

"That won't work. We can't get an accurate check that way. God-damnit! I'm tired of Catie's theatrics. The little twit thinks she *is* Medea." The man paused, and Mikki could hear him pacing irritably back and forth over the leafy ground. Then, as if her gaze had drawn it, his head turned in her direction. "Hey you! Would you mind giving us a hand?"

Mikki looked around. No one was near her. The guy was actually talking to her.

"Me?" She laughed nervously.

"Yeah, it'll just take a few minutes. Could you go up onstage, let them key a mike to you and say a few lines?"

"I don't know the lines," Mikki said inanely.

"Doesn't matter." The man gestured at a worker who was standing near the stage. "Get the lady a script, and tell Cio to mike her." Then he turned back to Mikki. "How 'bout I give you a couple tickets to opening night for helping us out?"

"O-okay," Mikki stammered. What the heck? Nelly loved this kind of stuff—she'd take her.

Feeling only a little foolish, she let two men lead her to the stage. One thrust an open script into her hand, and the other guy, the one the director had called Cio, pushed back her hair, fitting a neat little mini-mike into her hairline.

"Hey," Cio yelled back at the director. "Her hair's as thick as that wig Catie wears."

"Good, it'll give us an accurate test."

"There's your mark," Cio told her, pointing to a line duct taped on the floor of the stage. "All you have to do is stand there and after the Corinthian women say their lines, I'll point to you and you read Medea's invocation of Hecate." He paused, took a pen from his shirt pocket and circled a paragraph in the script. "That stanza right there. Face the audience and try to speak as slowly and clearly as possible. Got it?"

Mikki nodded.

"Great." He patted her shoulder absently before exiting the stage.

"You'll be fine," one of the three ladies said, smiling at her. "This is easy-peasy."

"I don't know," Mikki whispered back at her. "I've never invoked a goddess before."

"Hey, don't worry about it. You won't invoke one tonight unless you really are Medea," the friendly looking woman said, still grinning.

"Or unless you're one of Hecate's blood priestesses," another lady chimed in.

"Or have delusions of grandeur and diva yourself into believing you're both." All of the actresses rolled their eyes at the first woman's comment. Clearly the absent lead actress had let the part go to her head.

"Ready, ladies?" the director called.

The four women sent her looks of encouragement as Mikki moved center stage to her mark.

"All right, let's get this done so we can go home. First Corinthian Woman, start us out please."

The First Corinthian Woman's voice was strong and clear as she repeated the lines Mikki had overheard earlier.

"The holy fountains flow up from the earth
the smoke of sacrifice flows up from the earth,
the eagle and the wild swan fly up from the earth . . ."

A little thrill tingled through Mikki's stomach, and her nervousness was suddenly replaced by excitement. The actress's words seemed to fill the space around her, chasing away her trepidation.

The Second Corinthian Woman spoke her lines earnestly to Mikki.

"Women hate war, but men will wage it again.
Women may hate their husbands, and sons their fathers,
but women will never hate their own children."

Mikki's eyes followed the lines on the script as the First Woman's voice trembled with emotion.

"But as for me, I will do good to my husband,
I will love my sons and daughters, and adore the gods."

From the edge of the stage Cio pointed to her, and like a horse goaded by spurs, Mikki plunged into Medea's lines.

"You will be quiet, you women.
You came to see how the barbarian woman endures betrayal;
watch and you will know."

On the script were written the words *(Medea kneels and prays)*. Mikki glanced questioningly at Cio. He nodded and gestured to the stage floor. Drawing a deep breath, Mikki knelt and began reading the invocation.

"Not for nothing I have worshipped the wild gray
goddess who walks in the dark, the wise one,
whose dominions are the crossroads of man, wild
beasts, and ancient secret magicks,
Hecate, sweet flower of the ebony moon."

As Mikki spoke, her voice gained power and the small electric thrill that had lodged in her stomach when the First Corinthian Woman began to speak swelled throughout her body. Excitement rushed, adrenaline-like, into her throat, so that when she continued the invocation, her voice strengthened and magnified. Had she been looking at the director, she would have seen him frantically adjusting switches and turning dials. Had she glanced at the actresses onstage with her, she would have seen their mildly amused expressions change to confusion and shock. But Mikki looked nowhere except the script before her and the words that suddenly appeared, glowing, on the page as if her voice had called them alive.

"Queen of Night, hear your errant priestess's prayer.
Forgive me that I have forgotten your ways."

Mikki faltered. The small, Band-Aid-covered cut on her palm throbbed painfully. There was a great rushing sound in her ears that reminded her of the ocean. She felt the night wind, which had only moments before been gentle and cool, whip in a sudden heat around her, lifting her hair as if it, too, along with her body, had been electrified. Caressed by the wind, the unusual scent of the perfume she'd dabbed on her pulse points lifted with the breeze to fill her senses. She breathed deeply, inhaling rose and spice and heat. Overwhelmed by the exquisite beauty of the rich oil, the glowing words on the script blurred until Mikki could no longer see them. But it didn't matter. Unbelievably, she heard the lines within her mind, and with a sob, she opened her mouth and cried the words that were echoing through her head.

*"I call upon you now Hecate, by the blood that runs thick in my veins
and ask that you help me to return to your service and your realm
so that I might once again remember the use of the blood magick and
the ancient beauty that is the Realm of the Rose."*

A great roar split the night, ringing in Mikki's ears with an intensity that washed her in dizziness. She blinked tears from her eyes, looking around her as if she had just awakened from a dream.

Ah, hell! I'm having one of those damn episodes! Mikki frantically tried to make sense of the bright lights and the women who were staring open-mouthed at her. *The play! Crap! Crap!* Mikki looked down at the script she still clutched in her sweating hands. The words printed there in ordinary black and white made no sense. They weren't the lines she had just said. What the hell had happened to her?

Three single claps came from the rear of the stage.

"Lovely job of ad-libbing. Truly moving." The voice was filled with sarcasm.

Mikki managed to get awkwardly to her feet as an attractive petite woman wearing a gold toga and a long, dark wig stepped up to her.

"But the star has returned. So I'll take my mike and my stage position, and you can run along."

Mikki felt frozen with humiliation as the actress reached up to yank the neatly hidden microphone from her hair.

"Ouch! Fuck!" the diva shrieked, pulling back her hand and sucking on her bleeding finger. "The damn thing stabbed me."

Woodenly, Mikki raised her hand to touch the rose that still sat behind her ear.

"Sorry," she muttered, quickly pulling the mike from her hair. "Mikado Roses don't usually have prominent thorns."

"Catie, darling, it's all right. She was just helping us out with the sound check." Cio rushed onstage.

Catie snatched the mike from Mikki and turned her back dismissively as the sound manager hastily began working the tiny microphone into the hairline of the star's wig.

"Someone get me a Band-Aid before I bleed to death! And my God! What is that smell? Who has on too fucking much perfume? It's like I'm standing in the middle of a bordello, not a stage. For Christ's sake! I leave for half a second and everything goes to shit!"

Two more people hurried onstage, and Mikki sidled off, ignoring the director when he called insincere thanks and reminded her that she could pick up her tickets opening night at the Garden Center.

CHAPTER SEVEN

I T took several minutes for Mikki's cheeks to cool down. She could easily imagine the blazing red of her blush. Jeesh, what a humiliating experience! She left the sidewalk and retreated up the side of the gently sloping hill that would lead her to the uppermost entrance to the rose gardens. Shuffling her feet through the dry leaves that browned the soft grass of the park, Mikki tried to make sense of what had just happened. Everything had seemed fine—even fun—when she'd gone up onstage. Then she'd started reading her lines and . . . she looked down at the script that she had forgotten to leave behind. The light was too dim, and she couldn't make out the words, but she didn't have to read them to know that what had come out of her mouth had definitely not been what had been written on the script. She remembered all too well seeing the lines glow and then hearing them ring in her mind. She ran a shaky hand through her hair.

What was happening to her? She should go home. Maybe she should call Nelly. If having a totally embarrassing hallucination in front of multiple people didn't constitute an emergency of enormous girlfriend proportions, she didn't know what did.

Just then Mikki topped the little rise and came to a halt. The Tulsa Municipal Rose Gardens stretched before her like a familiar dream, comforting her frayed nerves. Just what exactly was so terrible about what she'd just done? What had really happened had probably more to do with three glasses of wine and being freaked out by suddenly being thrust onstage than with psychosis. She shoved the script into her purse. When she got home she'd reread Medea's words. What she had said was probably close to the original text. She needed to quit being so hard on herself. It was ridiculous to focus on every little mistake she made and every little daydream she allowed herself. She grinned suddenly. She'd even pick up the free tickets and consider heckling diva Catie on opening night.

Mikki felt the pull of her beloved gardens dissipate the last of her nervous stress as she gazed out across the expanse of roses. The gardens had been built in the shape of a gigantic tiered rectangle that always reminded Mikki of a huge, Italian wedding cake. There were five sections of terraced gardens, which climbed almost 900 feet from street level. Each tier was filled with row after row of meticulously tended roses. The gardens were styled after the gardens made popular during the Italian Renaissance, and amidst the more than 9,000 roses and imported statuary were Italian junipers, sheared by hand into formal, conical shapes, southern Magnolias, as well as deciduous holly and mugo pines.

Each level also held its own distinctive water element. The gardens boasted everything from peaceful, deep reflective pools and ancient-looking spouting wall fixtures to the graceful, cascading fountain situated as the garden's water showpiece in the magnificent center of the third and largest level.

It was fully dark, and, unlike Woodward Park, the rose gardens didn't have freestanding lights. Instead, each water feature was lit from underneath. The effect was spectacular. The gardens seemed to glow, suspended in the flickering illumination of rose-scented water. A whimsical breeze lifted Mikki's thick hair, pulling her forward. Eagerly, she crossed the boundary between the two parks and drew in a deep breath. Roses filled her senses.

"Heaven couldn't smell any better," she whispered.

As if her feet made the choice for her, Mikki started down her favorite walkway, working her way slowly toward the center most garden area. Some nights the grounds remained filled with people almost until closing. They brought chairs and picnic baskets, books and sketch pads. That night Mikki was relieved to see that the only other human activity was a couple of lovers who were making out on a blanket at the edge of the top tier. She ignored them, and they ignored her. Mikki preferred it that way. She loved to have the roses to herself. She walked lazily through the gardens, pausing often to visit beds of her personal favorites. The night was quiet, and except for the wind playing through the trees, the hypnotic tinkling of water and the muffled tap-tap of her boot heels against the pebbled cement of the pathways, there was little outside noise. It was like the roses created a sound barrier between their gardens and the rest of the world.

The disappointing date in the past and the *Medea* fiasco forgotten, Mikki was thoroughly enjoying herself once again as she chose the wide stairway that ran down the right side of the third tier. Hurrying, she almost skipped down the steps that led to the heart of the gardens. The bottom of the rocky stairs was framed by a large archway made of heavy rock. She stepped through that amazing arch of stone and, as always, she felt like she was entering another world. Mikki smiled and glanced to her left.

"And you know you're a big part of the reason why." She spoke to the enormous statue that perched imposingly between the archway she had just walked beneath and the second stone archway, which framed the set of steps to its left—a mirror image of the stairs she had just descended.

She walked to the statue and looked up at it, breathing in the scent of the profusely blooming Double Delights that surrounded it.

"Hello, old friend," she said softly.

The flickering light from the large, circular fountain situated a few yards from them threw a strange, aquatic glow over the statue, illuminating it with an eerie, ever-changing light. For a moment Mikki felt a tremor of unease; the thing looked almost alive in the blue-tinged light. Its marbleized skin seemed to borrow a glow from the water that pulsed, giving it the facade of living flesh. The ancient statue appeared to breathe. Then she mentally shook herself.

"Don't be ridiculous," she said firmly. "It's the same statue that's always been here. And it's supposed to be scary-looking, that's why it's called the Guardian of the Roses."

As Mikki spoke, the statue settled into the familiar marble lines she had known since she was a child. Local legend said that the statue had been a gift from an eccentric Greek heiress in 1934, the year the gardens were christened. No reason had ever been given for her largess—the local assumption was that she had visited and had fallen in love with the design of the gardens.

Mikki drifted forward and let her fingers play over the raised words of the plaque that proclaimed it: *Beast of the Greek Goddess of Night—This statue is a restored copy of one found in the Parthenon and is thought to have been the inspiration for the Cretan myth of the Minotaur.*

Mikki's lips twisted in a crooked smile. The beast had never looked like the Minotaur to her. Yes, he had always evoked exotic images of fantasy and myth, reminding her of late, sleepless nights and the shadowy fairy tales her mother used to read to her throughout her childhood, but she just didn't see that much similarity between the statue and the mythological creature who was supposed to have had a man's body and a bull's head.

"It's more like you're from another world than ancient mythology," she told the marble creation. Actually, Mikki admitted to herself as she studied him for the zillionth time, the statue was a wonderful, frightening mixture of raw male power and beast.

He was huge, at least seven feet tall, and more human than Minos's Minotaur, but the fact that he was manlike didn't make his appearance any less imposing. He crouched on the top of a wide, ornately carved marble pedestal. His rear legs were thick, much like a world-class sprinter's, except that they were covered with a coat of fur and ended in cloven hooves. His hands were massive, and they curled clawlike around the top of the pedestal. The thick muscles in his arms, shoulders and haunches strained forward. His face had been carved with indistinct lines, almost as if it had been half finished. It gave the appearance of a man, though he was decidedly fierce and bestial. His eyes were wide, empty marble under a thick, bestial brow. Mikki cocked her own head as she studied him. A beast, yes, but in a man's skin. Not really a bull, yet vaguely Taurean. On his head were thick, pointed horns, and an impressive mane of hair cascaded around his enormous shoulders. The sculptor had carved the creature's mane so it was swept back, making it appear as though he was straining against a raging wind.

Mikki felt a jolt of recognition. That's right, the statue had horns! Like the creature in her dream last night. She narrowed her eyes. Maybe this was where her fantasy had originated. She wanted to smack herself on the forehead. Talk about too much imagination! Was the answer to her supposed obsession as simple as that? She had always loved the rose gardens, especially this particular tier. And as her mother would have reminded her if she had still been alive, she did have a tendency to be overimaginative. How many times had her mother admonished her to quit daydreaming and get her room cleaned up . . . or her homework done . . . or the dishes washed?

Nelly had been right. Again. Her recent dreams were probably nothing more than a reflection of her obsession with roses and all that surrounded them. And the rest of her hallucinations were nothing more than daydreams from a sleepy, daydreaming (and clearly horny) mind.

A mind that had no one else to fantasize about, she reminded herself. She'd faced the truth tonight—her real life was decidedly void of men about whom she wanted to fantasize.

So the dreams had just been an elaborate fantasy she had created to amuse herself.

Mikki felt a wave of disappointment, which she quickly squelched.

"Would you rather have had a basketball-size brain tumor?" she chided herself as she absently kicked at a loose pebble. "And if it wasn't a brain tumor, what did you think? That you were actually having some kind of magical experience? That a fantasy lover was going to step from your dreams into your life? How pathetic. Get a grip, girl. And try to remember why you're here."

Mikki turned her back on the statue and marched toward the roped-off construction area, shaking her head in self-disgust. Already annoyed, she approached the construction site with determined steps. That particular part of the terrace wall had begun to crumble, so masons had been hired to repair it, with explicit instructions *not* to mess up the roses that had lived happily in the beds around the wall for decades.

Mikki let out her breath in a huff of disgust. Just as she'd suspected, litter had been left all over. She bent under the yellow construction tape and entered the rose bed, picking up the garbage that dotted the otherwise neat rows of bushes and shoving it into an empty plastic bag she'd untangled from the thorny trap of two rosebushes. When she found the small plastic cooler lying on its side in the middle of the bed, she felt her temper snap.

"This is just bullshit!" she exploded.

Tomorrow was Saturday, so the master gardener wouldn't be on the premises, but first thing Monday morning Mikki would call her and make a full report about the workmen's negligence. And tomorrow she would be sure she was there all day to supervise those Neanderthals and keep them from creating any further havoc.

She finished picking up the trash and then focused her attention on the roses themselves.

"Oh, no!" She felt her stomach clench as she examined the stressed-out bushes. She had thought they had looked wilted yesterday, but she had hoped it was just her overprotective nature rearing its maternal head. Today she knew she had been right to worry. The normally thick, shiny foliage looked markedly dull, even in the subdued light from the fountain. And the blooms were in bad shape. The blossoms were limp, and prematurely loose rose petals sprinkled the ground like sad feathers from dying birds.

Mikki shook her head slowly. "What incredibly bad timing," she told the damaged bushes. "After all this, you won't be strong enough to fend off much cold weather. If the winter is too harsh, we could lose this entire bed." Mikki clucked and fussed with the bushes like an irate kindergarten teacher.

The possible loss of the bushes tugged at her heart. Mikki knew most people wouldn't understand her love of roses—her girlfriends had certainly told her enough times that they were only plants, not people or even pets. But whenever Mikki touched a rose or breathed in the heady fragrance of the gardens, she was reminded of her mother and her grandmother; through the roses, if only for a moment, she could feel their love again. Mikki was tired of losing those she loved.

She had to do something. She stopped and looked around her. The tier was empty. Nothing stirred except the water and the wind. Absently, Mikki picked at her already chipped fingernail polish.

Just do it! she told herself. *No one will know.*

The empty cooler beckoned. Mikki made her decision.

"Okay!" she said to the nearest wilting bush. "Just don't tell anyone."

She grabbed the cooler, ducked back under the construction tape, and walked quickly to the fountain. She dipped the empty cooler in the water, and with a grunt, pulled it out. Filled with water it was heavy, and she had to strain to lift it. Water sloshed around her feet when she set it awkwardly on the ground beside her.

It only took a second for her to work the Band-Aid free from her left palm. The cut was already scabbing over, but her flesh was still pink and tender from the knife wound. Mikki rested her right thumbnail against the little slash line. Holding her breath, she closed her eyes and pressed her nail into the wound, forcing it open again.

Mikki sucked her breath in at the sudden pain. But when she opened her eyes, she was relieved to see the darkness of fresh blood flowing into her palm. With a grimace, she dunked her hand into the pool of water held by the cooler.

She certainly had a lot of disinfecting to do when she got home.

Trying not to think about how much her palm ached, she began dragging the full cooler across the stony path back to the bed of sick roses. Once inside the construction area, she straightened, unsure of her next move.

"There are so many of you," she told the bushes. It was obvious that she couldn't pour the usual amount of blood-tinged water on each bush. She felt her lips twitch in a sarcastic smile. She'd have to open a damn vein for that—and that was probably not a very good idea.

Assuming a businesslike stance, Mikki put her hands on her hips and addressed the roses. "How about I just sprinkle you guys with some of this water?" The bushes didn't answer, so Mikki counted that as a yes. Bending, she used both hands and began scattering the blush-colored water over the roses that surrounded her. Snapping her wrists and flicking the liquid off her fingers soon became a game. The cool evening breeze mixed with the darkness and the sweet scent of roses and earth. Mikki laughed and sprinkled the blood-kissed water all over, pretending she was a garden fairy raining magic on sleeping children.

Mikki was breathless and smiling by the time she had finished. She studied the damp bushes. It might just be her overactive imagination, but she was sure they were responding already. In the dim, watery light, she swore she could see the limp leaves straightening and the wilting blooms healing. There was more water in the cooler than she had anticipated, and she bent to pour it out onto the nearest bush when a flicker of light caught the corner of her eye as it danced over the guardian statue.

Why not? Mikki thought. Glancing around to make sure she was still alone, she carried the almost-empty cooler quickly to the marble statue.

"Your roses deserve a little extra boost, too," she told the silent beast. "After all, you've been watching over them a lot longer than I have."

Grinning, she dunked her still bleeding hand into what was left of the pink water. With practiced motions she rained drops over the roses that surrounded the statue. When she was finished she stashed the cooler near the wall next to where she had left the full bag of garbage.

Noticing that she had inadvertently sprayed some of the water on the statue, she patted one of the creature's big hands.

"Oops, I didn't mean to get you wet," she said fondly. "But I'm pretty sure you understand. I mean, please. We, more or less, have the same job. You watch 'em—I watch 'em."

Digging into her purse, she retrieved a Kleenex, which she wrapped around her left palm, wincing at the tenderness of the reopened cut. She didn't really care about the pain. It had been worth it. She was certain now the roses would survive the winter to thrive and bloom again next spring.

With feet that felt light, she retraced her path out of the third tier, passing under the stone arch and climbing up the stairs. With languid, lazy steps, she walked through the second tier, staying close to the side of the path so she could occasionally reach out and brush her uninjured hand gently over a delicate bloom.

The gardens were absolutely deserted, and Mikki imagined that they were hers—that she was a great lady who lived in a huge mansion and whose only job was to tend to and enjoy her roses.

The night seemed to agree with her. There was no noise at all, not even any echoes of the actresses from Woodward Park, which relieved her because it meant they must have finished and gone home. Thankfully, she wouldn't have to face them again.

It was so silent that Mikki imagined a soundless bubble had been formed around her made of roses and cool October air.

The silence lent itself to listening, so Mikki noticed the noise immediately. It began as a strange, shattering sound, and it came from somewhere behind her—somewhere on the third tier. The sound made her jump in surprise. It reminded her of the crack of faraway thunder. She even glanced up at the sky, half expecting to see clouds announcing the coming of a storm.

No, the night was clear. Thousands of stars spattered the thick ink of the sky; there was not even a hint of clouds above her. Mikki stopped and listened carefully. When she heard nothing more she decided the sound must have been caused by a rabbit or maybe a wandering cat.

"Probably knocking over some of the construction workers' garbage," she told the rosebush nearest to her.

Mikki walked on, ignoring the fact that her feet were carrying her forward more quickly and the hair on the back of her neck felt prickly and on edge.

The other noise started as soon as she reached the middle of the second tier. At first she thought it was the echo of her boots bouncing back from the rock wall that framed one tier from the next. Two more steps forward were enough to assure her that she wasn't hearing an echo. She was hearing independent footsteps. They crunched on the pathway with a decidedly heavier tread than her neat little boot taps.

But it wasn't the footsteps themselves that were odd. Lots of people liked to walk the rose garden paths, even after nine o'clock on a cool fall night. It was the distinctive noise that went along with the steps that caught Mikki's attention. She heard it once and discounted it.

She heard it a second time and halted, pretending to stop and smell a particularly lovely Princesse de Monaco. Actually, she was listening with every fiber of her being.

The third time she heard it she was sure. It was an achingly familiar grunt . . . a deep, rumbling exhalation that was somewhere between a growl and a snarl. It passed through her body in an intimate wave that caused her to shiver. Mikki's eyes widened in shock. There could be no other noise like that, and no other being could make such a sound except the creature from her dreams. And it was coming closer to her with every heavy step.

No fucking way! her rational mind screamed. *That's utterly impossible.*

It's just a delusion, she reminded herself firmly. *Nothing more than a symptom of my overactive imagination.*

But no matter what common sense told her, Mikki knew that what she was hearing was real—at least to her. At this moment what was happening had become her reality.

Her heart was beating erratically. *Get out of the gardens and into the park where I'll be surrounded by lights and people!* Her mind nagged at her, belying the rush of sexual excitement that stirred low in the pit of her stomach.

She wasn't dreaming. She was not safely asleep in her apartment or retelling an erotic fantasy to her girlfriend, or even mixing up lines on a script because of nervousness and too much chianti. Something out there was stalking her. She had to get to safety. As soon as she left the rose gardens, she would be away from the shadowed darkness of their paths and the night-shrouded privacy they afforded. Then she could scream for help. Even if the actors and stagehands had all packed up for the night, someone was always within hearing range in Woodward Park. Plus, she would be well illuminated within the park's free-standing light fixtures. Easy for rescuers to see her.

And easy for *him* to see, too, that "other" part of her whispered seductively.

Mikki quickened her pace.

A muffled grunt—a mighty burst of breath that sounded as if it came from a blacksmith's bellows rather than a living being—came from the path that ran parallel to the one on which she was walking. Separating them was only a neat bed of profusely blooming Tiffany roses. Mikki sent a furtive look across the pink-faced flowers.

She wasn't close enough to the park for the city lights to help her see him very well. She only caught the flash of glowing eyes before he spun away from her. Size—she gasped—the creature was immense. Against her will, her body flushed with a wild rush of excitement.

A sudden, violent snarl made the hair on the back of her neck stand on end. He was flanking her. He meant to cut her off from the lights of the park.

Faster! her rational mind warned. *Get out of the gardens and into the light of the park and then scream for help!* Fear overshadowed excitement, and in a frightening parody of her dream, Mikki ran.

WHEN he felt her presence, he thought he was dreaming. Again. He didn't understand them, but he welcomed the dreams as rare gifts. They relieved the unending darkness of his entombment. They almost gave him hope . . . almost.

But the fabric of this dream was different. At first that didn't surprise or alarm him. He'd been there generations and had only infrequently been allowed the wisp of a thought . . . the enticing aroma of the living world . . . any living world. Each time it had been a little different. Over the years he'd strained to hear the sound of a voice, the touch of a soft hand, the scent of roses and spice. Sometimes he'd be rewarded; most of the time he had not.

Until recently. The dreams had come to him. That was when she had entered his prison and he had begun to live again.

He had reveled in the dreams, inhaled her until he felt drunk on her essence. Dreams . . . who better than he knew what magic they held?

Perhaps he would dream of touching her skin again. Perhaps . . .

Then her blood had spattered against the cold stone that entombed him, and the pain that jolted him shattered the past two centuries like ice cast against marble.

He hadn't believed he had been freed. He'd thought it was just a cruel delusion. It might have taken a decade for him to attempt even a small movement of one of his massive muscles if her scent hadn't begun to wane.

She was leaving him. Escaping from him.

No! Not again!

Embracing the pain, he flexed his great muscles and broke the barrier of shrouding darkness.

He scented the air. Yes, there, layered within night smells of roses and blood, was the anointing oil. He commanded his stiff body to move, and he followed the fragrance he knew too well through the dark, unfamiliar garden. With an enormous effort of will, he did not crash through the few rosebushes that separated them and seize her. He forced himself to wait until he was able to more carefully control the beast within him. The creature had been penned too long . . . his needs were too raw . . . too brutal. It would not do to rend her flesh with his claws. That would solve nothing. He must capture her gently, as he would a delicate bird, and then return her to the destiny she had thought to escape.

Controlling the ferocity within him, he stalked her. He could not see her well, but he did not need to. The anointing oil drew him; she drew him. And she was aware of him. He could feel her panic. But there was something else—something unfamiliar that radiated from her. He frowned. Something was wrong. He picked up his pace as she left the rose gardens and burst into a small pool of light. He stopped abruptly.

This was not the priestess he sought. Disappointed and confused, he stood frozen, watching as she struggled with the opening of the leather satchel she carried, clearly looking for something. A weapon? Her eyes frantically searched the dense shadows behind her—the shadows in which he stood.

"COME on! Where is that damn cell phone?"

He heard her unfamiliar voice and saw that she was trembling as she searched through the satchel—trembling so badly that the slick leather of the bag slipped out of her hands and fell to the stone path with a sickening crunch.

"Shit! Shit! Shit!" the stranger said.

She dropped to her knees and slid her hand into the purse, and he heard her breath rush from her lips, as if in response to a sudden sharp pain. She jerked her hand back. He could see that her fingers were sticky with blood.

The scent hit him hard in his gut—blood mixed with the anointing oil of a High Priestess. She was not the betrayer, but she had clearly been marked by the goddess. And he must obey the goddess's will. He began moving toward her again, this time using his newly freed powers to call the darkness to thicken about him so his body would remain cloaked with night. Still, her head jerked up and she stared wide-eyed in his direction.

"Do not fear," he murmured, attempting to gentle his powerful voice.

She gasped. "Who are you? What do you want?"

He could feel her terror, and for a moment he regretted what he must do. But only for a moment. He knew his duty. This time he would fulfill it. Before she could dart away from him, he used his inhuman speed to reach her where she still crouched on the leafy ground. She stared up at him, unable to see through his mantle of darkness.

She was so small . . . so very human . . .

With a gruff command, he ordered the darkness to cover both of them, and for a single breath he wrapped his great arms around her, engulfing her in a tide of vertigo. The cool breeze that earlier had been friendly and inviting suddenly beat against them in a frenzy of scent and sound. They were caught in a vortex of confusion. The ground seemed to open to swallow them. It trembled . . . shifted . . . rocked. The world around them faded and then disappeared altogether, and the shimmering air was rent by a tremendous roar.

Like a snake slithering into its hole, darkness and the beast retreated, carrying Mikado Empousai with it.

Part Two

CHAPTER EIGHT

SOFTNESS . . . she was surrounded by softness. Curled on her side, her face rested against a pillow. Mikki rubbed her cheek against its sleek surface. Silk. It had to be silk. She snuggled more deeply into the thick comforter, breathing in the rich scent of expensive, down-filled bedding.

While she lay there, someone combed through her hair with a wide, soft-bristled brush. Mikki sighed happily and rolled over on her stomach so the someone could have better access to more of her hair. Dreaming . . . she had to be dreaming.

And, she told her sleeping self, her dreams had certainly been wonderful lately. She should just relax and enjoy.

The person hummed a wordless tune while she brushed Mikki's hair. Her voice was a gentle waterfall of notes that blended with the soft strokes of the brush lulling Mikki into an almost hypnotically relaxed state.

Mikki sighed with perfect contentedness.

Somewhere in the lullaby-like humming, the whispered words *Welcome, Priestess* echoed in her sleep-heavy mind.

Mikki breathed another dreamy sigh; she was definitely going to have to do more sleeping.

Another pair of hands touched her. These new hands focused on rubbing her feet. With the confidence of a master masseuse, the hands drew firm, soothing circles across her insteps.

Mikki felt like she was liquefying. Well, she certainly deserved an excellent dream, especially after the night she'd had. Her mind traveled languidly back. The crappy blind date . . . humiliating herself by screwing up the lines of that play . . . then being stalked by some terrible imaginary beast through the rose gardens . . . cutting her fingers on the broken perfume bottle . . . the deafening roar and the horrible sense of suffocation . . .

Memory tried to break through the dam of contentment her dream had built. She had to be dreaming, but how had she gotten home? Just what exactly happened before the weird dizzy spell that had overwhelmed her in Woodward Park? A sliver of unease skittered spiderlike through her body. She needed to wake up.

Mikki opened her eyes.

A flutter of activity sounded behind her. Mikki spun around. Two women stood next to her bed.

No—it wasn't *her* bed.

Mikki snapped her eyes shut.

No. No. No. This wasn't right. It was the bed from her dreams. The *huge* canopy bed in the *enormous* bedroom, to be precise. Mikki pressed the palms of her hands against her closed eyes. Then she rubbed her face vigorously. She could feel her body, too damn well. The feeling was distinct, not like the sweet, erotic fog that filled her dreams. With her eyes still closed, she slapped her own cheek. Hard.

"Ow, shit." Mikki flinched. It definitely hurt. She was certain she was awake now.

She opened her eyes.

Sticky tendrils of fear laced their way through her stomach. Nothing had changed. The bed was still there, as was the bedroom and the two women. They were wearing long shimmering robes that wrapped toga-like around their bodies and brushed the lushly carpeted floor. They were young and beautiful, especially silhouetted against the wall of mullioned windows behind them.

"Shit on a shingle!" Mikki automatically used her favorite curse as her breath left her body and her heart slammed against her chest. "Who the hell are you?" she squeaked. Fear clenched her. Had she been attacked in the park and killed? "Am I dead? Are you ghosts?" she blurted.

The women's eyes widened, and the brunette held out a delicate hand in a gesture that was probably meant to have been reassuring, but the fact that she was there at all, and that she could respond to Mikki's question, was definitely not comforting. Mikki immediately shot backward, crablike, over the bed until she was pressed firmly against the headboard.

"My Lady! We are of the living. You have nothing to fear." Her voice was soft and melodic, and Mikki recognized it instantly as the one that had recently been humming the lullaby to her. "We are here to welcome and to serve you, Priestess."

The other woman, the one with the lion's mane of wheat-colored hair, nodded in agreement. "Yes, Priestess. We are all very much alive."

Clutching the comforter to her chest, Mikki tried to control the shaking in her voice. "Wh-where am I?"

"You are home, Priestess!" The brunette smiled magnanimously.

"And just exactly where is 'home'?" Mikki asked, feeling numb around her mouth, like she'd eaten a Popsicle too fast and was having a hard time making her lips work.

"You are in the Realm of the Rose," the blonde assured her.

"I have finally done it," Mikki moaned. "I have finally gone stark raving, totally fucking crazy." She buried her face in her hands.

Instantly, the two women rushed to her, patting her shoulders and stroking her hair. Mikki jerked back from them.

"Don't touch me!" she yelled. "You're only making it worse. I can damn sure feel you when you touch me, even though I should be sleeping and this should all be a dream, and . . ." She broke off her babble. Breathing hard, she just shook her head at the women. "No. Stay back. You're just giving me more proof of how kooky I am!"

The women took nervous little half-steps away from her.

Obviously the leader, the brunette spoke quickly. "Let me assure you, Priestess, you are of your right mind. We are not imaginings, nor are we deranged fantasies." Her smile was hesitant but sweet. "I know this must seem very odd to you"—she glanced at her partner, who mirrored her smile—"but you truly are in the Realm of the Rose, and we are your handmaidens."

The blonde nodded her head, the waves of her hair bouncing in perky agreement.

Mikki felt her right eye begin to twitch.

"Maybe I'm drunk," she muttered, trying to remember how much she'd had to drink before she'd dumped her date. Three, or had it been four glasses of that fabulous chianti? Oh, Lord . . .

"We would be happy to bring you wine, Priestess," the blonde chirped.

"Oh, be quiet and let me think," Mikki snapped. "And stop calling me priestess. It's not my name, nor is it my job title." Then she rolled her eyes at herself. What a totally moronic thing to say. Not her job title? Being a kook was bad enough. Being a stupid kook would be completely humiliating.

But the handmaidens seemed oblivious to her idiocy. They were busy exchanging startled glances.

"But," the brunette began hesitantly, "you must be our priestess. You awoke the Guardian."

Mikki made an exasperated sound in her throat. "The only thing I *must be* right now is crazy."

The women went on talking to each other as if she had not spoken.

"She is beautiful," the blonde said. Studying her carefully, she sniffed in Mikki's direction. "And she has been properly anointed."

The brunette squinted at Mikki. "But she is not as young as the other priestesses who were Chosen."

Her partner nodded silently, her brow wrinkling in concern. "Perhaps that is for the best." Her voice dropped to a whisper, and Mikki had to strain to catch her words. "You know how badly the last one turned out."

"Silence!" the brunette snapped.

The blonde paled and clamped her lips together.

"You are a maiden, are you not?" the brunette asked Mikki matter-of-factly.

"That's it!" Mikki swung her legs over the side of the bed and stood up so abruptly that the two women each took a startled step back. "It's bad enough that I'm having some kind of psychotic break with reality, but I really have to draw the line when my delusions begin talking about my age and questioning my sexual history." Mikki made little shooing motions at them. "Go on. I prefer to sink into psychosis by myself."

"We did not mean to offend, Priestess," the brunette said, instantly contrite.

The blonde nodded again—vigorously.

"You didn't offend me. My mind, or more accurately, my lack of it, offended me." The women blinked at her like Kewpie dolls. "Oh, just leave me alone for a while. I have a lot of thinking to do."

"You have only to call for us if there is anything you desire," said the brunette. "Of course, Priestess, we will return when the sun has set to prepare you for the goddess's evening ritual. We all hope that once again—"

Mikki's raised hand cut off her gushing words. "No! Nothing else right now. To quote an idiot accountant I once had the misfortune to date, 'My bucket is too damn full right now to deal with anything else.' Just leave." At their hurt looks she added, "Please." They were fabrications of her mind, but (as she was sure her mother would have reminded her) there was really no reason to hurt their feelings and be impolite. They couldn't help her kookiness.

Reluctantly, they walked gracefully across the room. Mikki expected them to pass through the wall like proper figments of imaginations, but the blonde opened the large, ornately carved door, which clicked closed softly behind them. Even her hallucinations didn't behave properly.

"Insane," Mikki said firmly. "You are completely insane."

Her legs felt weak, and abruptly Mikki sat back down on the bed. The thick down comforters billowed around her like clouds of handspun gold. Unable to help herself, she ran her hand over the rich, silk surface of the duvet.

"Unbelievable," she muttered. The bedding was sumptuous and incredibly beautiful, richer than even the linens from The Blue Dolphin, the expensive boutique she liked to browse through at Utica Square. And *browse* was the key word—she could never have afforded to buy her bedding there. Now she was surrounded by material that made The Blue Dolphin look like K-Mart.

At least she was having an expensive delusion.

Actually, *expensive* didn't begin to describe the room. It was more like obscenely *RICH*. Definitely spelled with capital letters.

The stuff of fairy tales, her mind prodded.

Mikki ignored her mind, which had already proven totally untrustworthy, and looked around. She knew the room. Her fantastic dreams always began in this very room, but the images her sleeping mind had retained had been fleeting. Typically, when Mikki awoke she could only remember that she had been in "the room" again and that the room had given her a sense of comfort, setting a pleasurable stage for the rest of her dream experiences.

What was it the brunette had said? *You are home, Priestess!*

Impossible. Home was a nice little apartment in a great location, not a room fit for a princess. Mikki's admiring gaze took in her surroundings. Princess, hell, the room had been made for a goddess. The light from the wall of windows was dim, but three huge crystal chandeliers hung suspended from the ceiling on golden chains. Their many candles mixed with the freestanding candelabrum that perfectly accented the corners of the room, as well as the enormous fireplace in which a fire crackled and popped cheerily—the entire effect was to cast the chamber in the warm glow of living flame. The gold and scarlet color scheme of the bed linens was reflected in the rest of the room. The carpet was plush, incredibly soft, and the color of untouched snow. The marbled walls were the color of clouds streaked through with delicate veins of gold and hung with ornate tapestries. Their intricate designs were all—Mikki grinned in pleased surprise—roses! Each tapestry was a woven marvel. Not able to stop herself, Mikki drifted over to the closest of the works of art and sucked in a sudden breath.

The tapestry rose was the Mikado.

Her eyes went from wall to wall. Each hanging was filled with artistic renditions of roses so real Mikki almost expected to be able to smell their delicate bouquet. And each and every one of them was of the Mikado Rose.

"Consistency should count for something, even if it's delusional," she said firmly.

Intrigued by what her mind was concocting, Mikki explored the room. Beautifully carved wardrobes rested elegantly between wall hangings, and a huge mirrored vanity was placed not far from the canopied bed. It seemed to be waiting for a fairy princess or goddess to sit before it and primp. The tinkling light of the closest chandelier caught Mikki's eye, and she looked up. The walls stretched to an incredible height. Mikki had to tilt her head back to see the domed ceiling far above, which was painted with delicate frescos of blood-and-gold–colored Mikado Roses.

Incredulous, Mikki muttered, "Where the hell am I?" How could her mind have fabricated such an amazing "reality"? *Maybe I didn't fabricate this . . . maybe this is real and my old, boring, uneventful life was the dream.* The thought, more elusive than smoke, drifted through her bedazzled mind.

Trying not to feel like an interloper, she stood, wiggling her bare toes into the lush carpet.

Bare toes?

She looked down at herself. She was wearing a long, white robe that V-ed deeply to expose a generous amount of cleavage. The sleeves were trimmed in lace that circled her wrists. The entire garment was embroidered with tiny scarlet roses. Mikki rubbed a finger against the material; she had never felt anything like it. It wasn't exactly silk, but it was too soft and slick to be cotton. Expensive linen? Whatever it was, it was certainly flattering. It flowed in a diaphanous wave down her body, showing just enough flesh to be seductive without being sluttish. Mikki swung one long leg out in front of her, loving the richness of the fabric against her naked skin.

"Naked?" She froze. Then, holding the top of the dress away from her chest, she peered down at her body. "Very naked," she whispered, feeling her cheeks warm.

How had she gotten that way? Or more to the point, *who* had gotten her that way? Probably the little handmaidens, she told herself (*please, oh please*, her mind shying away from the memory of the beast that had so doggedly pursued her). Even though they were strangers, they were definitely female. Having talked herself into feeling relieved, she let one hand absently caress her sleeve. The tangible touch of the fabric soothed her frayed nerves. She lifted her hand to look more closely at the filigreed lace, and she noticed the pad of her hand was scabbed over but still sore when she pressed on it.

She clearly remembered cutting them when the perfume bottle had broken last night. Mikki pressed the healing scabs again and winced. The cuts were real. She breathed deeply and, sure enough, the scent of the exotic perfume she'd dabbed on her pulse points, as well as smeared all over her hand, wafted distinctly to her nose. Surely a hallucination couldn't include so many of her senses. Could it?

Mikki sighed and walked to the wall of windows. As she got closer to them, she realized that the middle panes had marble handles and opened outward to an enormous balcony. She pressed her face close to the glass, trying to see through the fading light. All she could make out was the distant outline of the balustraded balcony. Beyond that, she could only see vague, dark shapes. And then the glass fogged over with her breath.

"Don't be such a sissy," she told her reflection. Ignoring the fluttering of her heart, she turned the handle and stepped out into the cool evening.

The balcony seemed to stretch on forever. It was a smooth pane of pearl-colored marble that curved gracefully in an elliptical shape. On either side of her it wrapped out of sight around that section of the . . .

. . . Castle!

Mikki gulped and turned to face the imposing structure behind her.

"Ohmydearlord!" Stunned, she stared wide-eyed. The building was made of the same opaque marble as the balcony, and, on closer inspection, looked more like a huge palace than a traditional castle. It rose above her like a man-made mountain and stretched to either side of her as far as she could see. It appeared to be elevated, as if it had been built on a cliff. Mikki gawked, totally amazed. From where she stood, she could tell that there were several rounded wings that climbed above what appeared to be the basic palace structure. Through huge picture windows she glimpsed flickers of light. She gazed at the palace and a key turned within her.

"I couldn't have made this up," she said, letting the sound of her own voice reinforce her words. "If I was going to dream up a palace or a castle or whatever, I would have made up something like Cinderella's fairy-tale castle, and I mean straight out of Disney." She shook her head. "Not this—I could not have fabricated this." Her hands lifted and then fell helplessly. "I don't know where I am, or what has happened, but this can't be taking place only in my mind."

Behind her a sputtering, popping noise drew her attention, and she turned. Past the edge of the balcony, lights flickered. Swallowing hard, she started forward. It took her more than thirty steps to reach the carved balustrades that supported the balcony's edge. The flat marble top reached just above the level of her waist, and with a catch in her breath, she leaned against it as she gazed down upon the grounds.

"Roses!" Mikki cried in delight. The palace was surrounded by an enormous circle of mazelike rose beds intermingled with ornate trees, hedges, fountains and statuary. In the heart of the gardens she thought she saw the dark outline of another structure, but fading day had not left enough light for her to distinguish anything clearly, even though sprinkled throughout the grounds were winking sconces of open flame that were either suspended from branches of trees or held by thick torches that sprang from the ground. The muffled sputtering noise sounded again, and Mikki watched as the wispy outline of a silk-draped girl lit one of the torches. Soon, Mikki noticed many such girls moving soundlessly along the garden paths and, cometlike, leaving flickering tails of flame in their wake. Staring out at the unbelievable sight, she felt a rush of nausea.

"See!" Mikki waved her hand in a frustrated gesture, fighting back the dizzying sickness. "There's another thing I don't think I could have made up—little nymphlike servants lighting tiki torches."

"You are not fabricating what you are seeing, nor are you going mad, Mikado Empousai."

Mikki sucked in a breath and jumped as a woman's strong, throaty voice surprised her. Shock chased away the weird vertigo feeling that had gripped her. She turned quickly to a woman who had suddenly materialized and who no doubt reigned supreme over them all. Overwhelmed, Mikki couldn't find her voice. She could only stare at the woman like an awestruck child.

She was tall and wide shouldered with a statuesque, appealing body and a strong, intelligent face. Her lips were full and crimson, and her wide, watchful eyes were a startling, piercing gray. She wore a gown that was layer upon layer of shining black silk, draped to flowing perfection around her body; the curve of her waist was girdled with a chain of silver roses linked together by stems of rubies. Through a slit in the shimmery gown Mikki could see part of her long, slender leg—so perfect it appeared to be carved from living marble. Her feet were covered with golden sandals, and beside them reclined two of the most enormous dogs Mikki had ever seen. The black creatures unblinkingly met her gaze with eyes that glowed an unearthly red, and Mikki hastily looked away, her startled gaze skipping from the flaming torch the woman held in one hand, to the gleaming headdress that was wrapped around her head. Nestling in her dark, intricately braided hair was a waterfall of shining pinpoints of light. They twinkled like miniature stars in the night of her hair.

Then the woman spoke again, and the power that filled her voice sent a thrill of fear through Mikki.

"I am the Goddess Hecate, and I welcome you to the Realm of the Rose."

CHAPTER NINE

"HECATE?" Mikki's mouth felt numb again. There was something unnamable about the woman that caused her knees to go to liquid as she automatically moved back until she was pressed against the marble railing. "Medea's Hecate?" she rasped, her voice barely above a whisper.

"Indeed, I am Medea's goddess." Hecate spoke in hard, sharp words. "If you faint like a typically weak woman, I will be very displeased, Mikado."

"I've never fainted before." Mikki blurted the first thing that came to her amazed mind.

"Do not start now," the goddess said.

Mikki could only nod with a jerky motion of her head.

Hecate studied Mikki silently. Her strong face was inscrutable, and Mikki had a childish, nerve-filled desire to wring her hands and fidget, but she forced her arms to her side and stood still, even though the goddess's gaze was so sharp she imagined she could feel its touch.

"I am not simply Medea's goddess." Hecate broke the silence suddenly. "I am Goddess of Beasts, Magick and the Ebony Moon. I have dominion over the dark of night, dreams and the crossroads between the known and unknown." The goddess's words rang with authority, and Mikki felt the power of them slide over her skin like hungry, searching snakes. Then Hecate's voice lowered dangerously, and Mikki had to work hard not to cringe away from her in fear. "I knew your mother, Mikado, and her mother before her, and hers before that . . . for generations I have watched the women of your family. I continued to watch and stay faithful to them, even after the women all but forgot me."

Complete surprise had Mikki crying, "My mother! My grandmother! How? I don't understand any of this."

Almost imperceptibly, the goddess's expression softened. "Have you never wondered at the origin of the gifts you've been given, Mikado?"

"Gifts?"

"Yes! Think!" the goddess snapped. The dogs at her feet growled restlessly. "Do not stand there stupidly as if you are a man and can think with naught but the flesh that hangs between your legs! Acknowledge your gifts, Empousa!"

Mikki responded automatically to the goddess's command with a voice that shook only a little. "My blood makes roses grow. I mix my blood with water and during the new moon . . ." She paused, eyes widening as she realized what the title, Goddess of the Ebony Moon, implied. "During the new moon I feed my roses with my blood."

"And your roses always grow," the goddess finished for her.

"Always," Mikki whispered.

"That is one gift. The other is also something the women in your family have carried with them from generation to generation," Hecate said.

Thinking, Mikki frowned. Then her face cleared. "My last name! All the women in my family always keep their last name, Empousai. We never change it—no matter what. It's tradition, an unwritten rule that we've followed for generation after generation. Even when it was unheard of for a woman to insist that she keep her own name and not automatically take her husband's, the Empousai women stuck to their tradition. Trust funds have been set up and whole wills have been written under the strict provision that the Empousai women always retain their name. My mother told me stories about Empousai brides who broke off engagements when men refused to follow the tradition." Mikki clamped her mouth shut suddenly, certain that she was babbling like a hysterical fool.

Hecate dipped her head in brief acknowledgment. "That is because within the veins of the women of your family runs the rich blood of the Empousa—my most cherished priestesses. It has been a long wait, but it gladdens my heart that finally you have rekindled the goddess flame within you, anointed yourself, mixed blood and water, and called upon my name." For an instant the goddess's formidable face almost looked kind. "You can see that I rewarded your faith. You awakened my Guardian, and you have returned to the Realm of the Rose."

"But it was an accident! I didn't do any of it on purpose." Mikki felt like sobbing.

"Explain yourself. How could you possibly have anointed yourself and invoked me *accidentally*?" The goddess spat the word like it had a foul taste.

The marble of the balcony railing felt like cold iron as it pressed through the back of Mikki's sheer nightdress. The huge dogs at the goddess's feet pricked their ears at her, as if they, too, were curious about her answer. Mikki wondered semi-hysterically if Hecate would command them to eat her when she found out that this whole thing had been nothing but an insane mix-up.

Mikki drew a deep breath and met the goddess's icy gray eyes. "You say I anointed myself—by that I assume you mean the perfume I'm wearing."

Hecate raised both brows. "Perfume? Indeed. And how did you manage to acquire a perfume that is the exact fragrance of my High Priestess's ceremonial oil?"

"It was given to me by an old woman I met earlier today . . ." She paused. Had it been earlier today, or had several days, or for that matter years, gone by? She couldn't think about that now; it really didn't matter. The only thing that mattered was that Hecate understand that she didn't belong here. Or none of this mattered at all because she was wrong about this place being her new reality, and she had really gone stark raving mad and was curled up in a fetal position in the middle of the Tulsa Rose Gardens drooling on herself.

"I told you before that you are not suffering from hallucinations or delusions, Mikado. Nor are you mad," Hecate said firmly.

"Can you read my mind?"

"I always know the deepest fears and the most passionate desires of my Empousa. Now, Priestess, continue to explain this *accident* to your goddess."

Your goddess . . . an unimaginable thrill shocked through Mikki's body when Hecate spoke those two simple words. It was as if a memory, long forgotten, had begun to stir, restless with the possibility of new life.

Your heart remembers, Empousa, as does your blood. The goddess did not speak, but the echo of Hecate's voice whispered through Mikki's mind.

A voice in her mind? Mikki shook her head, suddenly afraid again. She spoke quickly, hoping the sound of her voice recounting events she knew had happened in "the real world" would anchor her shifting sense of reality.

"An old woman gave me the perfume. She and I hit it off because she had been named after a rose, too."

"And what was this crone's name?"

"Sevillana Kalyca," Mikki said, noting how Hecate's eyes immediately narrowed. But the goddess didn't interrupt her again, and Mikki continued. "I had a date that night, so I thought I'd wear the perfume," she grimaced, remembering the arrogant Professor Asher. "But the guy turned out to be awful. I left and walked home."

Hecate nodded thoughtfully. "Few men are worthy of an Empousa."

Mikki looked into the goddess's eyes and was surprised to see understanding there. She smiled tentatively at Hecate. "I've definitely not been lucky in love."

Hecate snorted. "Men are inconsequential."

Mikki felt some of the tension in her shoulders relax. They had certainly been inconsequential in her life. "Well, I decided not to go straight home, so I cut through the park because I wanted to walk in the rose gardens."

"You live near rose gardens?" the goddess asked.

Mikki nodded. "Right across the street from the city's rose gardens. I volunteer there year round."

Hecate looked pleased. "It is proper. As Empousa, your most important duty, after honoring me, is to care for your roses."

"I have always cared for roses. So did my mother and my grandmother—"

Hecate's impatient gesture cut off her words. "The women of your family are tied by blood to the roses. I know that. What I do not know is how you invoked my name."

"It really was an honest mistake. I was walking through the park to get to the rose gardens, and they were rehearsing the play *Medea*. They needed someone to step in for the actress who was supposed to play Medea at the same time I happened by. The director asked if I would read a few lines, and I did . . ." Mikki's words trailed off as she remembered how the lines on the script had blurred, glowed and then seemed to be spoken of their own accord. "It was like once I said the goddess's name, everything changed."

She hadn't realized she'd spoken the thought aloud until Hecate's stern voice answered her.

"Your soul and the very blood that pounds through your heart know my name, and they called for their goddess, even though your mind has forgotten me."

"It seems so impossible . . ." Mikki shook her head and wiped a shaky hand over her face.

"But there was no blood sacrifice made. The wind would have stirred at your words, the earth would have trembled, and the waters wept as flame blazed, but you could not have awakened the Guardian and been carried to my realm without the letting of your blood."

"I fed the roses," Mikki said faintly, remembering the cacophony of sound that had swelled around her as she had read the goddess invocation. Wind . . . earth . . . water . . . fire . . . had they really all responded to her? The thought thrilled and overwhelmed her. Then the goddess's impatient frown brought her quickly back on track. "Some workers in the gardens had trampled the roses. It was the night of the new moon, and I'd already fed my roses—the ones on my balcony at home. It was a simple thing for me to reopen the cut in my hand and help them, too. I guess I went a little overboard, because I was sprinkling water everywhere. I even got some on the Guardian statue—" Mikki sucked air and stared at Hecate. "The statue. That creature. It . . . It . . ."

"He," Hecate corrected her. "The Guardian is male. And, yes, your call to me—coupled with the sacrifice of your blood—awakened him. He brought you here. It was his duty to return my priestess to her proper place."

Mikki's eyes darted from the goddess to the shadows that were lengthening with the thickening of night.

"He is not near. He has been absent from his charge for too long. There is much that he must correct; many things are amiss to which he must attend. You are not to concern yourself with him. And you have nothing to fear from him. The Guardian's only purpose is to protect the Realm of the Rose, to make sure the threads of reality are woven into dreams and magick."

Mikki shook her head. "Threads of reality? How does he—"

The goddess cut her off. "It is not important that you understand his purpose. Just know that he is not a danger to you. He guards all who reside within my realm."

"If he's your Guardian, then what was he doing being a statue in the Tulsa Rose Gardens?" *And,* Mikki's mind shrieked, *what was he doing seducing me in my dreams?*

Hecate's gaze shifted from Mikki, and the dark goddess stared out over the flame-lit gardens that stretched in a seemingly limitless expanse of beauty before them. When she spoke, it was more to the shadows than to the woman who stood beside her.

"I am a goddess, but I am also fallible. It was through an error of my own judgment that my Guardian was banished. It is my desire to correct that error."

Mikki didn't know what to say. If she had thought about the ancient gods and goddesses before today, her basic assumption would have been that they were powerful, omnipotent beings who were immune to simple mistakes in judgment. And now she was standing before a being who proclaimed herself Hecate, who radiated power and authority, and this same goddess was admitting to having made a mistake? It made no sense. But then, none of what was happening to her made any sense.

Again Hecate spoke without looking at Mikki. "Yes, a goddess can err. I have a heart and a soul. I have passions and dreams. I love and I hate. How can I be a wise goddess, worthy of worship, if I do not intimately understand the mistakes of humanity? To understand those mistakes, I must experience some of them," she concluded in a somber voice.

"I'm sorry," Mikki said softly.

Hecate's gray eyes returned to rest on her. "I have missed the presence of my Empousa in the Realm of the Rose. Even though your return appears *accidental*," this time she added a touch of humor to her voice when she said the word, "I am pleased you are here. I have grown weary of waiting."

"But I still don't know why I am here." Could she really be priestess to this amazing goddess?

"You are here for the roses!" Hecate spread her arms in a magnanimous gesture to include all the gardens before them. "You will reinstate my rituals and bring health and life renewed to my realm."

"Hecate, I don't know how," Mikki said.

"Of course you do!" she said fiercely. "The knowledge has been written in your blood. All you need do is turn your eye inward and learn to read what my hand printed there generations past."

The patter of slippered feet running on marble interrupted Mikki's reply. She and the goddess peered down on the gardens as four women hurried up the nearest path to the staircase that led to Mikki's balcony.

"Your handmaidens approach." Hecate glanced at the darkening sky. "I see that at least they haven't forgotten the proper order of things, though the Realm of the Rose has suffered with the absence of its Guardian and my Empousa."

Like a wave lapping eagerly on a thirsty beach, the four women rushed as one onto the balcony and instantly fell into deep, graceful curtseys, heads bowed, with their long, unbound hair falling forward to shade their bright faces. The handmaiden who wore buttercup yellow silks, a perfect compliment to her golden hair, spoke first. She lifted her face to the goddess and cried in a voice filled with gladness, "Hail Hecate! Great Goddess of the Ebony Moon!"

Next spoke the girl dressed in brilliant red whose fall of glossy scarlet hair blazed like fire. "Hail Hecate! Wise Goddess of Beasts!"

Mikki realized that she recognized the two remaining girls when the handmaiden dressed in sapphire blue with the waves of sea foam–colored hair lifted her head.

"Hail Hecate! Beautiful Goddess of Magick!"

Before the sound of her sweet voice had faded the brunette, who was tonight dressed in moss green silks the color of her large, dark-lashed eyes, lifted her head, face glowing with obvious joy.

"Hail Hecate! Goddess of the Crossroads between reality and dreams and mighty proctress of the Realm of the Rose."

"Rise, daughters. Come! Kiss my hand. I have missed you."

The handmaidens rushed to Hecate. Mikki realized that they were much younger than she had at first thought—really, they looked little older than teenagers, especially as each of them pressed her lips to the goddess's hand, giggling and cooing like happy children. Hecate touched their heads and greeted them, clearly pleased to see the youths. The enormous dogs at her feet wriggled, totally (and shockingly) puppylike, sniffing enthusiastically at the girls, accepting kisses and caresses from each as was their due. Then Hecate raised her torch high, and the handmaidens fell instantly silent.

"Handmaidens of Hecate, I bid you welcome the return of my Empousa!" At her proclamation, the torch blazed, sending a cascade of sparks falling in a whirlwind around the goddess.

The handmaidens gasped, whispering excitedly to one another as they curtseyed to Mikki. She was sure she heard the brunette hiss a clear "I told you she had returned!" to the others.

Hecate raised her hand for silence.

"Go within. There you will prepare the Empousa for the self-initiation ritual, which will be performed in the heart of my realm."

Once again Hecate lifted her torch, only this time she faced outward, looking over the vast gardens.

"Let the Temple of Hecate be lit once more!"

At the goddess's command, lights suddenly blazed from deep in the gardens. The handmaidens reacted with exclamations of excitement and joy. Wide-eyed, Mikki watched the silhouette of a columned temple suddenly illuminate.

"Go now," Hecate told the handmaidens gently. "The priestess will join you shortly."

The girls curtseyed deeply to the goddess and then scampered across the wide balcony and into the bedroom in which Mikki had awakened.

"You must do two things tonight, Mikado," Hecate told her sternly. "First, cast a sacred circle. The handmaidens will aid you in this until you learn to listen to the knowledge that sleeps within your blood. Second, you will perform a self-initiation ritual. In that ritual, you will dedicate yourself to a new life as my Empousa, a Priestess of the Blood of Hecate."

"But I don't know how to perform an initiation ritual! I don't know how to perform any ritual," Mikki said, exasperated at how inept she felt.

"Mikado!" Hecate's gray eyes pierced her. "You invoked my presence. You awakened my Guardian. There lives within your blood the knowledge of generations of my priestesses. If you do not have the courage to partake of that knowledge, cast the sacred circle and then choose to step from within it. I give you my oath that the moment you leave the circle, you will return to the life you left in that mundane world at the far side of my crossroads." The goddess's lip curled in disgust, and the flesh on Mikki's arms prickled in response as Hecate's divine anger sizzled around her. "Perhaps you shall marry . . . perhaps you shall not. Doubtless, you will produce a daughter, another Empousai, as you have come to call yourselves. You will live and die an ordinary life. And I will look to other generations for the return of my priestess. But if you do not break the sacred circle and instead choose to complete the ritual, know that as surely as your heart beats and your lifeblood flows you will forever after be my High Priestess, Empousa in the Realm of the Rose." Hecate lifted her blazing torch once again. "Decide tonight, Mikado Empousai, and know you will never receive another chance at changing your destiny!" Sparks showered from the torch, and with a great roar of wind, Hecate disappeared.

CHAPTER TEN

T HOROUGHLY confused, Mikki stood alone, blinking away the bright spots of the goddess's light from her eyes. She was supposed to cast a circle? Wasn't that witch stuff? And if she managed to bumble her way through that, without being struck by lightning or swallowed up by Satan or who/whatever, she was supposed to listen to her blood to know how to perform a self-initiation ritual because she was an Empousa, a Priestess of Hecate. How?! What the heck was she going to do?

Girlish laughter drifted from the open doors of her room. Mikki sighed. She was also supposed to be getting dressed. And deciding on her destiny.

"Damn, my head hurts." She rubbed at her throbbing forehead. The newly illuminated temple tugged at her gaze, and she found herself staring across the dimly lit gardens at the domed building. A little rush of excitement fluttered through her stomach. If this was real . . . if all this was actually happening, then she was being offered the opportunity to be High Priestess of a powerful goddess—a goddess who had watched over the women in her family for generations. Mikki couldn't deny that the possibility fascinated her.

And if none of this was real? If she had fabricated all this and the world and the goddess were nothing more than figments of her delusion?

If that were true, then it didn't matter whether she chose to stay or return. Either way she was screwed—figuratively speaking.

So why not ride it out? Why not choose to become High Priestess of Hecate over being a psych patient?

She thought about the goddess. Hecate was powerful and intimidating. What would it be like to be her priestess? The thought was like a bright flame, and it drew her with its exotic warmth. Hecate had said that her first duty as Empousa would be to care for her roses. Mikki stared out across the dark expanse of gardens. The soft night breeze swirled around her, carrying with it the compelling and familiar scent of roses. She closed her eyes and drew a deep breath.

It smelled like home.

The thought startled her. Could it be possible that she belonged here? Was she brave enough to consider believing this was her reality . . . her future . . . her destiny? She was many things—stubborn, opinionated, too cynical—but she was not a coward. Resolutely, she crossed the wide balcony and entered the beautiful, rose-themed room.

Like a small school of exotic, silk-finned fish, the young women turned to her and bobbed down and up in quick curtseys.

"Empousa! Your ceremonial dress awaits," said the brunette. She gestured to a fabulous length of glittering purple silk that cascaded over the edge of Mikki's bed.

"Thank you," Mikki said automatically and then her mind caught up with her words. "But before we go on, I think introductions need to be made. My name is"—she paused for only an instant—"Mikado. As you probably already know, I've been brought here by rather unusual circumstances, and all of this is new and more than a little overwhelming to me."

The brunette frowned. "Are you not Empousa in your own land?"

"No," Mikki said.

The four young faces registered mirrored expressions of shock.

"If you were not Empousa, then what did you do?" the brunette asked.

"I was . . ." Mikki hesitated, carefully choosing her words. "I was an assistant to a very important woman. She made sure sick people were cared for."

The brunette's frown deepened. "This woman could not have been as important as Hecate."

"No!" chorused the others.

They had her there. "Maybe working for a less important, uh, goddess"—Mikki's lips twitched at what her boss would think of being called a goddess—"was preparing me for this job."

"Job?" the flame-haired girl tittered. "Empousa is not a job; it is a destiny."

"A divine privilege!" added the handmaiden dressed in buttercup silk.

"Yes, I'm beginning to understand that." Mikki felt like she was futilely trying to hold the reins on a runaway horse. "But where I'm from, things are a lot different. It's going to take some time for me to get used to my destiny."

The brunette suddenly gasped, green eyes bright with understanding. "You are from the mundane world!"

"Yes, yes I am," Mikki said.

Clearly horrified, the handmaidens stared silently at her. The golden blonde pressed her hand against her mouth as if to hold back a sob.

"It's really not that bad there," Mikki said, feeling the need to stand up for, at the very least, Tulsa. "It's filled with interesting people and things. Like the Internet and"—she grasped at straws—"and some really excellent restaurants. Especially around Utica Square." Far from convinced, they continued to stare at her. "So," she said, purposefully changing the subject, "how about you tell me your names and then I'll get dressed and you can give me some pointers about how to handle the rest of the night."

"How incredibly rude of us, Empousa!" the brunette said quickly, giving the other three girls a hard look. "I am Gii."

"I am known as Floga," said the striking redhead.

"You may call me Nera," said the blonde who had been there to welcome her with Gii.

"And I am Aeras," said the final girl.

"It's nice to meet the four of you," Mikki said, smiling warmly at them and mentally crossing her fingers that they would become her allies as she took in the unusual names.

"Shall we dress you, Empousa?" Gii asked.

Mikki wanted to say "Thank you very much but *no*." Then she looked at the long length of silk and realized she had not one clue about how to put it on. Did it wrap like a toga? What held it together? (And where were her panties?)

"Fine. Let's get me dressed."

"I cannot go out in public in this. Really. There has to be another piece to it." Mikki stared at herself in the full-length mirror. The royal purple silk was caught in a braided silver tie over her right shoulder. From there it swept down her torso in a graceful drape, leaving her left boob and her right leg, from waist to ankle, completely, utterly, totally bare.

Gii's frown was back. "But Mikado, this is the traditional dress for the Empousa's ebony moon ritual."

"Why would you want to add anything to it? You look quite lovely," Nera said, confusion wrinkling her smooth brow.

Mikki pointed at the reflection of her bare breast. "I'm half naked!"

Like those little bobbing-headed figures that sat on the dashboard of tacky cars, the four handmaidens nodded at her.

Mikki sighed and tried again. "How can I walk around with one of my breasts exposed?" Not to mention her entire right leg and part of her pantiless butt. "It just can't be right."

"Of course it is right," the redheaded Floga said, clearly disconcerted by Mikki's negative reaction. "It is how Hecate's Empousa has always dressed for this ritual."

With a sudden flash of understanding Gii said, "Is it not normal in the mundane world for a priestess to perform rituals with her breast bared?"

"Actually, in the mundane world it's very abnormal to be seen in public with a bare breast—at least in my part of the world."

Gii shook her head sadly. "Women must be horribly restricted in your old world."

Mikki opened her mouth to set Gii straight—to tell her that women in modern, albeit mundane, America had equal rights with men and . . . But the image of the last rape victim she'd read about in the *Tulsa World* surfaced in her memory. The girl had been young, only twenty-one or twenty-two, and she had been attacked while she had been clubbing downtown. The newspaper report had made several slanted references to the seductive way she had been dressed, vaguely implying that she had caused her own rape. Hot on that memory came the voice of the newscaster she'd listened to as she'd dressed for work that morning. Seems a serial molester had attacked yet another Tulsa woman. As in the other instances, he'd come in through the woman's open bedroom window. Police and the media advised the public—the female public—to be more careful about locking their doors and windows. Mikki felt the stir of anger low in her gut. Women had been lectured, judged, and warned. Neither of the men had been condemned as the animals they clearly were. She met Gii's gaze.

"I think you might be right, even though on the surface it doesn't appear that way."

"Like hidden thoughts, it is the world beneath the easily seen one that most often controls us," Gii said.

Mikki nodded slowly. Then she turned back to her reflection in the mirror, straightened her shoulders and lifted her chin. The woman who stared back at her looked exotic and incredibly feminine draped in liquid purple with her hair hanging free around her shoulders and her bare skin flushed a delicate blushing peach in the flickering candlelight. On an impulse, she swung out her bare leg, pointing her naked toes. The soft material of the ceremonial dress fluttered attractively in response. Sexy . . . she was definitely sexy—and that ten pounds or so she always seemed to battle with only added to her sensuous look. She was curvy and full-bodied and more beautiful than she had ever thought possible.

"I'm ready," she said firmly, more to herself than the four women who were watching her so intently.

Gii's smile was instantaneous. She grabbed Mikki's hand and tugged gently toward the open doors to the balcony. "Come! Hecate's Temple glows with light once more. Let us hurry and fill it with life, too!"

On a tide of silk and laughter, Mikki let herself be led across the balcony and down the pearl-colored stairs that emptied into the gardens. Another odd wave of dizzy sickness engulfed her as she followed the handmaidens. She gritted her teeth and did her best to ignore it, thinking that it was logical that changing worlds would be hard on one's system. Wide-eyed, she tried to take in everything as the girls hurried her along one of many curving marble paths that wound between row after row of roses. She could make out bubbling water features and benches, but everything was gently cloaked in night and shadow and the warm light of the fragrant oil lanterns that hung from the limbs of ornamental trees.

Then everything left her mind as the temple rose like a dream before them and Mikki stumbled to a halt. Torches blazed inside and out, illuminating tall, slim columns supporting the dome of a raised, open-air temple. In front of the temple sat a huge, multi-basin-shaped fountain. Crystal water cascaded from it, spilling all around its edges and into four marble troughs that appeared to carry the musical water out into the gardens.

The temple itself was elegant in its minimalist design. There was nothing inside the building except a single flame that burned brightly from the center of a broad, circular expanse of slick marble floor.

"Hecate's torch has been lit," Floga said in a voice choked with emotion. The beautiful scarlet-clad handmaiden was the first to ascend the stairs and enter the temple. "I felt it in my soul, but to see it once again makes my heart leap with gladness!" And then to Mikki's astonishment, Floga walked straight to the fire and caressed the flame as if it was a beloved child. Instead of burning her, the fire appeared to rejuvenate her. Her hands glowed where it touched her, and her red hair crackled around her as if it was alive.

"She's touching the fire!" Mikki gasped. "But it doesn't burn her."

"Of course it doesn't burn her," Gii said. "She is Flame."

With an effort, Mikki pulled her gaze from the scarlet handmaiden, turning her attention fully to Gii. "What do you mean 'she is Flame'?"

Gii studied her carefully. "Empousa, do you not recognize your own handmaidens? I know you did not act as if you understood who we were when Nera and I welcomed you, but surely you know who we are now that you have seen the four of us together."

"Gii, I've never had handmaidens before. How could I recognize you?"

"You truly don't know us?" Nera said sadly.

Mikki had the sudden urge to shout that she didn't even know herself anymore—how the hell could she know four women who were total strangers! But the hurt in their eyes made her check her words.

"In my old world I didn't worship any goddess." Mikki carefully met each young woman's eyes. In the silence that followed her words, she heard Floga approach. Without speaking, the handmaiden rejoined her friends. Mikki continued, slowly and distinctly. "I have never cast a circle. I have never performed any ritual. I had no idea I was a Priestess of Hecate until the goddess told me so herself. So it's not just that I don't recognize the four of you, it's that I don't recognize anything in this world."

The women stared at her, wide-eyed and shocked.

"There are no goddesses in the mundane world?" Gii finally said in a hushed voice.

Mikki considered her words carefully before answering. She remembered that Hecate had told her she had been watching over the women of her family for generations. And there was no doubt that the Empousai women had a magical something in their blood. *Goddess touched* ... the thought flitted through her mind. The women in her family were goddess touched, which means that, acknowledged or not, goddesses must exist, even in Tulsa, Oklahoma.

"I think goddesses exist in my old world," Mikki said, thinking of the women in her family and letting instinct guide her words. "But most people—most women—have learned to live without them."

"How terrible," Aeras whispered.

"So if you don't want to call me Empousa, I won't blame you," Mikki said. "I don't really deserve the title."

"Hecate named you her Empousa. It is the goddess's right to do so, and only she can remove the title," Gii said. "If the goddess acknowledges you as such, then so shall we."

The other three women nodded, but Mikki thought they did so less than enthusiastically.

"And do not forget," Gii added, looking sternly at the other handmaidens, "Mikado awakened the Guardian. That is something only Hecate's Empousa has the power in her blood to do."

At the mention of the Guardian, Mikki felt a chill move across her skin. She'd almost forgotten about it—*him*—she corrected herself. The statue. Only he wasn't a statue anymore. He was out there somewhere, alive again because her blood had touched him. What part did he play in all of this? Why had he visited her dreams? And suddenly she was truly sick of unanswered questions.

"Gii, you said Floga didn't get burned by the fire because she is Flame. Please tell me what you meant by that."

But Floga didn't give Gii a chance to answer her. Instead the fire-haired handmaiden stepped forward so she stood beside Mikki. She raised her hand, palm up, and then, smiling, Floga blew a small breath, much like she was blowing a kiss, onto the palm of her hand. Mikki felt the unusual heat of her breath even before the rust-colored flame spouted from her palm.

"Gii meant what she said literally, Empousa. Your personal hand-maidens are carefully chosen by Hecate from all other women in the Realm of the Rose. Each of us was selected because we carry within us a special affinity for one of the four elements. My element is Flame. I can conjure it; it will never burn me; when the thread of my life has been followed to its end, I will return to it."

"Unbelievable . . ." Mikki breathed. Hesitantly, she reached a finger to the fire that burned steadily in Floga's hand. It was like touching the flame of a candle. She could bear it for an instant, but she knew it would burn her if her finger stayed too close for too long. Then Mikki's gaze slid to the other three women.

"I am—" Gii began but Mikki shook her head sharply, interrupting her. "No, don't tell me. If I am really Hecate's priestess, I should be able to figure out some things for myself." She squinted her eyes, thinking . . . *The four elements . . . Floga already said she is Flame. So what's left?*

As she considered, her eyes remained on Gii, at first unconsciously, and then more purposefully. She took in her moss-colored robes that matched the rich green of her eyes, accenting the thick length of her mahogany hair. And she knew.

"Earth!" Mikki said. "You have to be Earth."

Gii's smile was a brilliant reward. "Yes, Empousa. Floga is Fire. I am Earth . . ." She paused and nodded encouragement.

Mikki turned her attention to the two remaining handmaidens, Nera and Aeras. Nera was wearing blue and had hair so light it could be reminiscent of clouds, but Wind just didn't seem to fit her. Nera was too voluptuous. Her body was lush; the blue silk lapped around her like translucent waves. Petite Aeras wore butter-yellow robes that seemed to move gracefully around her in time to a secret breeze of their own. Her long, straight hair was the golden color of summer sunlight.

"Nera is Water, and Aeras is Wind."

The handmaidens clapped their hands happily, making Mikki feel inordinately proud of herself.

"You see, Empousa," Gii said. "You did recognize your handmaid-ens."

"With your help I did. Now with your help maybe I can figure out how to cast a circle, too."

"You have everything here you need to cast the sacred circle, Empousa," Gii said. "You have the spirits of the four elements, and you have your own affinity."

"My own affinity? But there are only four elements. What could I represent?"

"You represent the heart of the circle—its spirit," Gii said. "That is why you wear sacred purple. It is the color of Spirit. And that is why your position will be in the center of the circle."

"We will show you, Empousa," Aeras said, skipping up the stairs into the temple. "We each have our positions."

Mikki squared her shoulders and moved with the handmaidens into the temple. Aeras walked purposefully to a place a few feet away from the ever-burning flame which was in the center of the temple. She turned to face Mikki. "Wind is always positioned in the east."

Floga moved around an invisible circle to Aeras's left. "Flame is allied with the south."

"Water prefers the west," Nera said, taking the position directly across from Aeras.

"Earth's place is always in the north," Gii said, completing the circle. "And your place—Spirit's position—is in the center of the circle near the heart of the goddess's flame."

Not giving herself time to hesitate, Mikki moved into the center of the circle made by the elements personified and stood beside Hecate's flame. Then, feeling a little lost and a lot foolish, she moved her shoulders restlessly. "I don't know what to do next." She whispered the words, but her voice carried eerily in the stillness of the temple.

"It is a simple thing, really," Gii said gently.

"A natural thing," Nera added.

"A wondrous thing," Floga said, with barely suppressed excitement.

"You always begin with me," Aeras said, smiling brightly. "Greet me and call Wind to you, welcoming my element. Then move deosil around the circle and call the other elements to you."

"Deosil?"

"This way," Floga said, moving her hand in a clockwise motion.

Mikki nodded. "Okay, I've got that."

"As you call each element, think of the energy you beckon forth to protect and support you, Empousa," Gii said.

"Will a circle really appear?" Mikki asked tentatively.

"That depends on you, Empousa," Gii said.

Mikki's stomach fluttered with nervousness. *Just do it!* she told herself. Mikado Empousai lifted her chin and approached Aeras.

CHAPTER ELEVEN

"Hello, Aeras."

"Empousa."

The handmaiden sank to the marble floor in a graceful curtsey, and Mikki's mind frantically searched for something, anything, to say. She was supposed to focus on the elemental power as she called it. She drew another breath to calm herself. She drew a breath . . . air . . . which was really wind . . .

"I call to the circle the element Wind," she said, mentally crossing her fingers that she wasn't totally messing up. "It is what we breathe in when we are born. Without it we would all die." As Mikki had begun speaking, Aeras had risen from her deep curtsey. The handmaiden lifted her slender arms, closed her eyes, and tilted her head back. Mikki swallowed around the nervous dryness in her throat and continued. "When I think of Wind I think of movement and invisible power. It is a contradiction—a paradox. It cannot be contained, but it can be harnessed. It can gently fill a newborn's lungs, and it can destroy cities." Suddenly, the ethereal yellow silk that clothed Aeras began to lift and stir, and then, in a rush of white sound, wind whipped around the handmaiden like she stood in the vortex of a magick tornado. Wind moved against Mikki's skin, too, but not as violently. It felt caressing, causing her bare nipple to harden in response. Surprisingly, Mikki didn't feel embarrassed or exposed. Instead, the nakedness of her body seemed natural, and the fact that the element had come at her call and touched her body so lovingly, bolstered her confidence. She smiled and met Aeras's shining eyes. "Welcome, Wind!"

Then she turned to the right. Her steps were much surer as she approached the scarlet-clad handmaiden.

"Hello, Floga."

"Empousa," she said. And she, too, sank to the floor in a respectful curtsey.

"I call to the circle the element Flame." As Aeras had, Floga stood, lifting her arms and closing her eyes. Mikki thought the handmaiden's face look rapturously expectant, as if she was prepared to greet a lover. Inspired by the element's personification, Mikki continued, "Fire is passion and heat. It consumes, but it also feeds and warms. Without fire our nights would be dark and cold." Floga's glossy scarlet hair began to lift, and in a whirl of heat the girl's body became outlined by a luminous glow. Mikki could feel the heat radiate from Floga. It licked against her skin, too, causing a fine sheen of dewy sweat to glisten over her body. "Welcome Flame!"

When she turned to her right again she thought she caught a glimpse of a delicate silver thread of light stretching between Aeras and Floga.

"Hello, Nera."

"Empousa." Nera dropped to the floor. Her thick, blond-white hair covered her face like a wave.

"I call the element of Water to the circle. It surrounds us before we are born, and it nourishes us during our life. It cleans and purifies, feeds and soothes." Nera stood slowly, and Mikki watched as the voluptuous outline of her body appeared to liquefy. And then her hair really was sea foam and waves, and the blue of her silk robes rippled like the changing tide. Mikki was engulfed in a misty coolness that smelled of spring rains and warm, tropical beaches. "Welcome, Water!"

Mikki's feet felt incredibly light as she hurried to where Gii waited.

And this time she clearly saw the sparkling silver ribbon that connected Aeras to Floga and now also Nera.

"Hello, Gii."

"Empousa." She curtseyed as had the other handmaidens.

"I call to the circle the element Earth." Mikki smiled fondly at Gii as the handmaiden stood, lifting her arms and awaiting the approach of the spirit of her element. "Earth is really our mother. It's as fertile and nurturing as farmland, as moist as soil and as dry as sand. It's home for all the other elements." Gii's mossy robes shifted and changed until they were more ivy than silk. Her dark hair seemed to lengthen, blanketing her shoulders and falling down her back with the richness of a newly ploughed field. Mikki's senses were filled with images of Earth. She smelled the sweetness of cut hay. She tasted ripe fruit and berries. She felt cradled in warmth and security, as if her mother's arms were once again around her. With a catch in her voice, Mikki said, "Welcome, Earth!"

"And now, Empousa, you must greet your own element," Gii said, pointing to the place at the center of the circle beside the sacred flame.

Mikki moved to the center of the circle. She closed her eyes and raised her arms, mimicking the other women.

"I call to the circle the element Spirit."

Then the handmaidens' voices flooded her thoughts and senses until Mikki couldn't tell if they were actually speaking or if they were only voices within her soul.

"Spirit is present everywhere," Aeras said in her sweet, clear voice.

"It is the great alchemist." Floga's voice was filled with passion.

"Spirit is the element that unites all others." Nera spoke with the sound of a cascading stream.

"It has the power to shape the very nature of all things," said Gii, in a loving mother's voice.

"Welcome, Spirit!" Mikki cried. There was a crackling snap, and the air within the temple sizzled with energy. Mikki opened her eyes to see that she stood in the middle of a circle ringed by four women who were bound together by dazzling gossamer threads of silver woven to create a boundary that pulsed with light and power. The flame burning beside her had taken on a lovely violet tint.

"Wow! It worked!"

The handmaidens laughed, filling the temple with sounds of feminine happiness. Their laughter was like music, and Mikki wanted to twirl and dance.

Dance, Empousa . . .

The silent words settled into Mikki's mind like a remembered dream. She didn't stop to question her next impulse or hesitate until she could second guess herself. Mikki danced. Within the circle she twirled and swayed. The handmaidens took up the tempo of her movements and began humming a seductive melody. She felt beautiful and powerful and utterly joyous. And she knew what her decision for the rest of her life would be. She would choose this world—this magickal life—and not because she was afraid of snapping out of it and finding out she was crazy. She chose this life because it had awakened a joy deep within her that she had never before experienced. Reality be damned! This was real enough for her.

Speak the words that will bind you to me, Empousa, commanded the voice within her head.

Automatically, Mikki answered the goddess. As she spoke, her own voice grew stronger and more confident.

"Hecate, Goddess of Crossroads, Beasts, and the Ebony Moon, I have cast your sacred circle and been given a chance at a new life—a new destiny. I stand on the threshold between my old life and my new . . ." Mikki hesitated, but only long enough for her to turn to face the violet-tinged flame. "My decision is that I am willing to become your Empousa."

"What two perfect words do you offer your goddess to bind you to me?" Hecate's somber voice hung heavy in the midst of the sacred circle.

Mikki stared into the spirit flame. She had no idea what words to speak. What could bind her to Hecate? What did her instincts tell her?

She wasn't sure, but she knew what her heart was telling her. There were only two words that should ever bind one person to another . . .

"Love and trust," Mikki said.

"Then it shall be, Empousa. You are bound to me through blood and by love and trust!"

The violet flame leaped, shooting almost to the ceiling of the temple's dome.

"Blessed be your feet that have brought you on this path," Aeras said. The Wind spirit held her hands out to her Empousa. Mikki grasped them, feeling a surge of energy swirl into her.

"Blessed be your sex, source of love and power," Floga cried. Mikki retraced her path inside the circle to the spirit of Flame. When she took Floga's hands, power filled her with a rush of heat.

Nera's voice called her farther around the circle. "Blessed be your breasts, and the heart that beats within." The Water spirit's hands were a wash of cool energy that reminded Mikki of a deep, clear well.

Gii's blessing had her moving to the head of the circle. "Blessed be your lips that will speak the rituals of the goddess." Mikki clasped hands with the Earth spirit and felt the strength of ancient trees and ripe meadows enter her body.

Then, without needing to be prompted by anything except an innate feeling of rightness, Mikki returned to her place beside the spirit flame and whispered, "Blessed be my eyes that will see clearly the new path before me."

"The Empousa is mine, and I am hers—body, mind and spirit." Hecate's powerful voice filled the temple. *"The ritual is complete; so mote it be!"*

Suddenly Mikki was aware of a multitude of voices cheering in celebration. She looked beyond the circle to see what must be hundreds of women, young and old. They crowded the gardens around the temple and were all clapping and waving her way.

The watching crowd began to hum a wordless melody, and soon the seductive beat of drums joined the voices. Then the gathering of women danced, barefoot and exuberant, in the torch-lit garden of the goddess.

Intrigued, Mikki watched them frolic. In the shadowy gardens, they looked like beautiful night flowers waving in the breeze. Briefly, she wondered at why there were no men present, but the thought was fleeting and Gii's voice chased it completely from her mind.

"Close the sacred circle, Empousa, and we will join the people's celebration!" Gii said.

Before she had to ask, Aeras's soft voice lifted above the noise of the crowd like a warm summer breeze. "Walk in reverse order around the circle. Touch each of us in turn, and visualize the web of light fading away."

Smiling her appreciation, Mikki retraced her steps, lightly brushing her hand over each woman's head as she sank into a curtsey at the approach of the Empousa. She watched the woven thread of light unravel, and eventually, as she returned to her place in the center of the circle, it disappeared completely, leaving only the goddess's flame to burn a bright, but ordinary yellow.

Then Gii took one of her hands and Aeras another, and flanked by Earth and Wind, the newly christened Empousa was led to her people and the celebration that awaited its priestess.

THE Guardian watched from beneath an ancient oak. The lighting of Hecate's temple had drawn him. When it blazed again in the heart of the realm, he had been pulled to it unerringly, even though his body was wracked with the pain of newly awakened muscle and sinew. He had wanted to kneel beside the flame—to again beg the goddess's forgiveness and to ask that he be allowed to resume all the duties that had been his before he had broken faith with Hecate. But before he could move, the night breeze shifted and brought her scent to him. His nostrils had flared and his bronze skin quivered.

The priestess approached.

He knew it was she by her scent—spices and roses distilled by the heat of her soft skin. He recognized it because he drank the fragrance of her in his dreams, and, waking, he had touched that skin when he held her in his arms as the power of the goddess transported them to Hecate's realm. He closed his eyes and leaned against the tree. He had frightened her then, though he had not meant to. His awakening had been abrupt, and the beast within him that seemed at constant war with his humanity had been too strong, too eager to capture and possess. Remembering, his body shuddered and his heart ached.

He should go, retreat to his lair and prepare himself for tomorrow. He had long been absent from the Realm of the Rose, and he could already tell that all was not as it should be. He must be diligent—focused—he must resume guardianship of the realm as was his duty; and, if the goddess was merciful, he would also be allowed to use all his magickal gifts again.

But he stayed.

When his keen hearing detected the light tread of her feet, he spoke a command in a language long dead, and the lanterns that hung from the massive tree's limbs instantly extinguished, wrapping him in shadow. Under the thick ridge of his brow, his expressive eyes opened in time to see Floga rush into the temple. He paid little heed to the Fire spirit though, or to any of the other handmaidens. Like a bewitching Siren, *she* commanded his attention.

He watched her.

Her awkwardness was obvious to him, as he was certain it was to the handmaidens, too. They were accustomed to an Empousa who moved with practiced confidence, who knew each ritual of the goddess so well she could perform them as if it was as natural to her as breath and heartbeat.

This woman was different.

The handmaidens had to prompt her on how to cast the sacred circle. He saw her overcome her initial hesitation as she moved from element to element, calling Wind, Flame, Water, Earth, and Spirit alive again within the goddess's temple. Despite her inexperience, her power was evident in the tightly woven thread that bound the circle together.

She danced.

His breath went thick. A low growl rumbled almost inaudibly in his throat. Lust surged, hot and insistent through his body in time with the beat of his heart. His inhumanly keen eyesight became blessing and curse. Because of it he could see the sweat-slickened flush of her naked skin as she moved in a seductive dance around the circle. The nipple of her exposed breast was tightly puckered, elemental and alluring. He turned his massive head away from the tempting sight, pressing his forehead into the rough skin of the oak until the tips of his ebony horns rested against the tree. The betraying breeze flirted around him, once again bringing him the scent of her—woman and roses, oil and spice, now heightened by the heat and sweat of her. He snarled a curse, damning his preternatural senses.

Goddess help him, the longing was still there.

Why? He raised his hands. They became claws as razor-edged talons dug into the thick bark of the tree. Why hadn't his long imprisonment cured him of this terrible, futile desire?

He heard Hecate's voice commanding the new Empousa to bind herself to the goddess with ritualistic words.

"Love and trust . . ."

She spoke the words, and the night took them and carried them to him so he felt the power of her oath fold over his skin.

Why had she chosen those two words? For countless generations, Hecate's Empousa had always chosen words such as *knowledge* . . . *power* . . . *beauty* . . . *strength* . . . *success* . . . to bind herself to the goddess. Yet to complete the self-initiation ritual, this Empousa had chosen *love* and *trust*.

The Guardian bared his teeth. What did a priestess know of love and trust! What did any mortal woman know of such things!

He sensed the crowd approaching the temple and commanded more shadow and night to surround him. The women of the realm could not see him as they passed the great oak, but they sensed his presence and averted their eyes from the darkness that hid him, nervously making a wide path around the tree. When they shouted with joy at the completion of the ritual and began to welcome her with song and dance, the

Guardian felt as if he had become a great island of misery amidst an ocean of rejoicing.

And still he could not stop himself from looking at her again. She was closing the circle. The changing light of the goddess's flame caressed her naked skin. Her body enticed him as she acknowledged each of the elements and bid them depart. Without conscious thought, his claws tightened on the tree, slashing deep grooves into the ancient bark.

In response to the flexing of his muscles, pain shot through his arms and chest. He welcomed it. The pain reminded him of his banishment and the reason for it. He had been bespelled for generations because of his weakness. What perfect irony. He was a beast. He had physical strength that no mortal man could match, yet weakness had caused him to betray his duty, and, ultimately, himself.

Not again. I will not allow it to happen again.

Then his mind cleared as a new thought formed. Perhaps all of this—the dreams of her, the awakening and now the return of the agony of his desire—perhaps it was all part of the goddess's test.

Yes . . . he straightened, sheathing the daggers that were his claws. It did make sense. Hecate was providing him the opportunity to regain her sacred trust. He was being tempted so he could prove to her that it would not happen again.

Never again would he betray his goddess and his realm.

He would perform his goddess-appointed duties as Guardian of the Realm of the Rose. And when it was time for Beltane's Spring Ritual, he would complete his charge, sending this new Empousa to meet her destiny.

With a mighty effort of will, the Guardian repressed the longing within him. He would not give in to his weakness again. For countless generations he had protected Hecate's magickal realm. He had been ever vigilant. He had been tireless in his devotion. And he had been alone, even during the brief moments when he had imagined that his solitude might come to an end.

He remembered the pain of discovering just how wrong he had

been and knew that the misery of that rejection had been greater than all the years of loneliness that had preceded it.

What the last Empousa had said had been true. He was a beast. A woman might become fond of him, might treat him with compassion, as she would a favorite cat or an especially loyal hound, but a woman could never truly love a beast. It mattered little that the goddess had gifted him with the heart and soul of a man. The heart and the soul were within the body of a beast. It was his destiny to be alone, and destiny could not be changed.

With one last look at the new Empousa, he turned away. Duty. That must be his life.

But part of my duty is to ensure the Empousa's safety . . . to make certain she is well cared for . . . The man within him whispered temptation. *Would any of the handmaidens remember that the Empousa must eat and drink after the ritual to ground herself? Of course not. And she . . .* He paused and glanced over the corded muscle of his shoulder at where laughing women surrounded her. *She was so inexperienced she had to be led in the casting of a circle. She would not know that she must ground herself and use food and drink to replenish her strength.* Again, he forced his gaze from the Empousa. Snarling a hasty command, he drew darkness closely about him and made his way unseen from the temple celebration. When he was clear of the crowd, he picked up his pace, clenching his teeth against the pain that radiated from leg muscles that had just the day before been dead stone. *It is only another part of my duty as Guardian to order her meal prepared and to be certain that she partake of it. Yes, only another part of my duty . . .*

His cloven hooves thudded against the soft ground with a shy, secretive voice that seemed to echo the word *liar . . . liar . . . liar . . .*

CHAPTER TWELVE

I T was only when she stopped dancing that Mikki felt the return of her sick dizziness. So many women . . . she put a hand to her sweaty forehead and brushed back a mass of tangled hair. And every one of them had a word of welcome for her, just as they each wanted to dance and twirl and laugh with her. She was breathing hard and her legs felt wobbly. She was definitely all danced out.

"Empousa?" Nera peered into her face. "Are you well?"

"I'm just tired. It's been a long day."

"Come with me." Gii was suddenly beside her, tucking a steadying hand into her elbow. The handmaiden began to lead her in a weaving path between the revelers, heading back in the direction of the palace.

"Do you wish the other handmaidens to accompany you, Empousa?" Gii asked when Nera, Floga, and Aeras noticed they were leaving and paused in their celebration.

"No!" Mikki said hastily, gesturing at the young women to stay. The last thing she wanted right now was to be fussed over. Actually, solitude and something to drink sounded perfect. "And you don't have to leave, either, Gii. I'm sure I can find my way back to my bedroom."

"It is my honor to accompany you," Gii said firmly. Then she smiled and spoke the Empousa's regrets to the women who would have drawn Mikki back into the celebration, smoothly extracting the High

Priestess from the throng. Mikki sighed and resigned herself to Gii's mothering.

The well-lighted palace looked warm and inviting, and Mikki was incredibly glad to see it grow quickly closer. She wrapped her arms around herself. Now that she wasn't dancing, she was all too aware of the chill of the night air as well as her hunger. When was the last time she'd eaten a real meal? Had dinner at The Wild Fork only been last night? How did time work in this magickal realm? Little wonder she was starving and felt so sick and shaky inside . . .

Mikki stumbled up the marble stairs that led to her balcony. Gii halted suddenly, almost causing Mikki to trip and fall over her. The handmaiden was staring at a lovely little table someone had placed near the open doors leading to her room. It sat invitingly in a pool of light on the otherwise dark balcony. A thick blanket was draped over the back of the single wrought iron chair, and a pair of slippers was placed strategically in front of it. The table was, blessedly, laden with food.

"Oh, man! Whoever did this is my new hero." Ignoring Gii's reticence, Mikki hurried across the dark balcony to slide her cold feet into the slippers. Then she groaned aloud with the pleasure of a woman who truly loves her food. There were several platters on the table, each filled with delicacies. Aromatic cheeses, olives, thin slices of meat, and a loaf of bread that was still warm from the oven. Before she fell into the food like a starving fool she remembered Gii, who was still standing near the entrance to the stairs. Oddly enough, it appeared that the handmaiden had forgotten her. Gii's attention was focused on the deepest of shadows that nested at the far side of the balcony. Mikki cleared her throat to get the girl's attention. The handmaiden jerked, as if Mikki had startled her and, though she was too far away for Mikki to be sure, she thought Gii looked almost frightened when their eyes met. She smiled at the handmaiden, wondering what was bothering her. Had she committed some kind of cultural faux pas by rushing to the food without inviting Gii to join her? She certainly hadn't meant to be rude to the person who had shown her the most kindness in this world. So even though she preferred to be left alone to eat and relax, she gestured to the table.

"I know there's only one chair, but we can pull another out here from my room." Her mouth already watering, Mikki looked back at the table. "And there's plenty for two. Why don't you join me?"

Slanting one more nervous glance at the shadows, Gii returned her smile but shook her head. "No, Empousa. You are weary. It is best that you are given the privacy to eat and then sleep." The handmaiden started to depart. Then, changing her mind, she turned back and took a few hurried steps toward Mikki until her delicate face was more clearly visible. "Mikado, please forgive my impertinence, but I cannot remain silent."

"What is it, Gii?"

The young handmaiden closed the distance between them and knelt beside Mikki, taking her hands in her own. Though her voice was hardly louder than a whisper, she spoke with quiet intensity that demanded Mikki's attention. "Your destiny and that of this realm are now woven unalterably together. The choices you make affect more than you know."

Though she was feeling like a fish out of water, Mikki did recognize Gii's concern as real.

"I'll remember, Gii." Not knowing what else to say she added, "I'll be careful. Promise."

Looking relieved, Gii nodded and squeezed her hands before letting them go. "You did well tonight, Empousa. Welcome to your destiny." She curtseyed deeply and then padded softly to the stairs and disappeared as swiftly and silently as if she really had been only a dream.

Finally, she was alone. What had that been all about? Too damn tired to give Gii's weird behavior and cryptic advice much thought, Mikki stretched and then rolled her shoulders. Her neck was killing her, and her body felt stiff and sore. What the heck was wrong with her? She should spend more time in the gym (who shouldn't?). But she didn't think she was in such bad shape that frolicking about for an hour or so should make her feel like an old woman, or like a young one who had just taken a beating.

Her hands shook as she forked cheese and meat onto her plate, but as soon as she'd swallowed a few bites of the delicious fare she began to feel more settled. Mikki shivered and pulled the blanket off the back of the chair and wrapped it around her shoulders. Warmer, she broke off a hunk of bread and sighed happily as she bit into the soft center. She imagined that it somehow fed her soul as well as her body. A beautiful candelabrum sat across from her place setting, like a silent dinner partner who came to the table just to illuminate. Its light danced off a crystal goblet filled with dark red wine. She lifted it, admiring the elaborate rose design etched into its surface and appreciating that someone had already filled her glass as well as left an entire pitcher of wine for her personal use. If any occasion called for wine drinking—lots of wine drinking—tonight was one. Mikki glanced around her, trying to see if there was any movement in the deepening shadows of the balcony. Everything was still; it seemed she really was completely alone.

Raising the goblet to her lips, she paused, brows drawn together in confusion. Floating in the middle of the tiny scarlet sea was a rose blossom, so deeply red that it appeared almost black.

What the heck was a flower doing in the middle of her glass of wine? Not sure of the correct protocol for extracting a rose blossom from wine, Mikki glanced from the table to the crystal goblet. Should she pull it out with her fingers? Or was she supposed to use a fork? Maybe a dessert spoon would be more appropriate?

"I can't even call for a new glass," she muttered, thinking that finding a rosebud in her wine was a perfect punctuation mark to a truly bizarre day. "What would I say? Hey, waiter, or in this case, handmaiden, there's a rose in my soup, uh, glass, uh, wine." She shook her head and laughed aloud. "Doesn't it just figure?"

"The Ancients believed that a glass of wine could not be fully enjoyed unless there was a rose blossom afloat within it." The deep, powerful voice rumbled from the area of the balcony that was shrouded in the darkest shadows, washing around her and causing the hair on her body to prickle. "It is a belief to which I adhere."

Mikki jumped and fumbled with the glass, almost dropping it.

"Forgive me for startling you, Empousa."

"I just wasn't expecting a . . ." Mikki faltered, trying to see through the shadows. She could discern only darkness within darkness, but she didn't need to see him. She knew to whom the voice must belong. Her stomach tightened. She took a deep breath and pulled the blanket more securely around her shoulders, suddenly very aware that she hadn't changed from the ceremonial dress that exposed far too much of her body. "I thought I was alone," she said, amazed that her voice sounded so normal.

"I did not mean to disturb you. I came only to see that you grounded yourself after the ritual."

Mikki stared blankly in the direction of the faceless voice. Ignoring the rose blossom, she took a long drink of wine. *It was him—the statue—the beast from her dreams—the creature who had stalked her through the rose garden.* Unlike her voice, her hands could not hide their emotions so easily and she had to wrap both of them around the goblet so their shaking didn't clatter the crystal against her teeth.

When she didn't respond, he continued speaking in that preternaturally powerful voice that was at such odds with his civilized words.

"Again, Empousa, I ask that you excuse my lack of judgment. I thought only to see that all was acceptable to you so your grounding could be completed. I did not intend to disturb or to discomfort you."

She stared into the dark space from which the voice originated.

"You did all this?"

"I directed the servants, yes. Empousa, you must always remember to eat and drink after you cast the sacred circle and perform any ritual. In that way you will once again be grounded to this world. If you do not, you will feel weak and sick at heart."

Mikki had to swallow down a hysterical bubble of laughter. She was conversing about post–goddess ritual rules with the living statue of a beast who talked like a college professor in a voice that could have belonged to Godzilla.

It was totally fucking Loony Tunes.

Mikki took another long gulp of wine. This time the scent of the rosebud tickled her nose and she noticed the way its elusive sweetness heightened the richness of the wine. She put down the goblet and looked out across the table. Fine linens. Beautiful porcelain china. A crystal goblet and pitcher etched with a rose design. Plates heaped with carefully chosen delicacies. A blanket and warm, comfortable slippers. He had ordered all of this for her?

Mikki glanced at the corner of the balcony and then hastily averted her eyes and poured herself some more wine. His silence was making her even more nervous than his inhumanly powerful voice. Had he left? Was he sneaking up on her? Stalking her?

The erotic chase scene from her last dream teased through her memory, causing her cheeks to flush and nervous words to rush too loudly from her lips.

"I didn't know about the grounding. And everything is delicious. I guess I owe you my thanks." She wanted to bite her lip at her idiocy. She *guessed* she owed him her thanks?

"You owe me no thanks, Empousa. I am Guardian of this realm, and as such it is my duty to see to the welfare of those within the realm, which includes Hecate's High Priestess," he said gruffly.

"Oh, well," she mumbled, feeling awkward and not knowing what to say, but wanting to be polite. "Still, I appreciate—"

"Do not!"

She felt the force of the command against her skin. It battered her and made the flush that had heated her cheeks drain white and cold. Hecate's assurance that the beast wouldn't harm her seemed only weak, faraway words. Mikki pressed her hands into the arms of the chair and bunched her legs under her, preparing to sprint for her room. Maybe he wouldn't come inside the palace. Or maybe she could call for help and . . .

"Forgive me. It seems I have again frightened you. That was not my intention. It is just that your appreciation is not appropriate. What I did for you is out of duty. It is why Hecate called me into her service. Do you understand?"

He was clearly trying to modulate his voice to a softer, less-intimidating timbre. She recognized the attempt, even though he was being only partially successful. Instead of answering right away, Mikki took her death grip from the chair handle and, two-handed, lifted the wineglass to her lips. After she'd had another fortifying drink she stared into the darkness again. This was ridiculous and twice as scary because she was talking to a disembodied voice and letting her imagination fill in all the gory details of his appearance.

"I'm trying to understand, but it's not easy. Especially when I can't see who I'm talking to."

There was a long pause. And then he stepped from the darkness. The crystal goblet slid from between her numb fingers and shattered against the marble floor. He made a movement like he was going to approach her, and with a rush of adrenaline, Mikki surged to her feet, knocking over her chair with jerky, panic-laced haste. Shards of broken crystal crunched under her feet.

Instantly, he halted. "Have care where you step. The glass can cut through the soles of your slippers." The words were meant to be gentle, but the voice that spoke them rumbled with an inhumanly thunderous warning.

Mikki couldn't breathe. She couldn't make her vocal cords work. She could only stare at the creature. Then he sighed, and it was in that lonely, wordless sound that she heard the echo of a familiar roar. That one small thing pushed through her panic, allowing her to draw a gasping breath.

"I did not come to you tonight to harm you. You have my oath that you are in no danger."

Her lips felt cold and numb, but she forced herself to speak. "You're the statue. The one from the rose gardens."

He nodded his massive head. "Yes, you have known me only as I was in your world, entombed in marble amidst the roses. Now that I have awakened, I have resumed my rightful position as Guardian of the Realm of the Rose."

Mikki brushed a shaking hand across her forehead, trying to clear her mind.

The creature took a step closer to her, his hooves thudding inhumanly against the silent balcony.

"No!" she blurted, blood pounding in her ears. "Stay away!"

As if to show that he meant no harm, he raised one huge hand toward her, palm up. Except for its size it appeared normal, but Mikki was sure she caught a flash of the candlelight glinting off something sharp and deadly. She stared at his hand without blinking.

He closed the hand and let it fall to his side, where it was enveloped in shadow. "I was only concerned that you might faint."

"I'm fine," she said automatically, but she did pick her way carefully among the pieces of broken glass, righted her chair and sank into it before her legs gave way. "I don't faint." She forced herself to sound as normal as possible. He said he wouldn't hurt her. Hecate said he wouldn't hurt her. And, anyway, if he was going to attack her, it would do no damn good for her to hyperventilate and freak out. She clasped her hands together to stop them from shaking. "Really, I'm fine," she repeated, more for her own assurance than his.

"You should eat," he said. "It will strengthen you."

She just stared at him. How the hell was she supposed to eat with him standing there?

She was surprised to easily recognize comprehension on a face that was so alien. And at the same time she recognized something else, something that clouded his powerful voice like fog. Sadness . . .

Did he really sound sad, or was she just imagining it?

"I should leave you to your meal. First allow me to . . ." He broke off and spoke a sharp, unintelligible command. He held out one large hand, and instantly a crystal goblet, identical to the one she had broken, appeared in midair. His hand closed around it.

A noise, somewhere between a sob and a scream, squeaked from Mikki's lips.

"Did you not desire another glass?" he asked.

Mikki could only nod. Her swarming thoughts semi-hysterically said that what she really wanted was a valium to go with the wine.

He was watching her closely, and she thought his expression might have softened, but his face was so fierce that it was hard to tell. "May I bring this glass to you?"

She hesitated and then nodded again with a quick, slight movement.

Slowly, he stalked forward with an athletic grace that was as powerful as it was feral. His ebony hooves echoing against marble sounded unnaturally loud in the silence of the balcony. Mikki couldn't look away from him. As he moved closer to her, she couldn't help pushing herself against the back of her chair, where she sat rigid and unmoving. Her heart was pounding hot and loud in her ears, and for a moment, she thought she might make a liar out of herself and actually faint.

Would he catch her if she did? The thought of him touching her shivered through her body.

When he reached the broken glass he made a dismissive gesture with one hand and muttered a word under his breath.

The shards instantly obeyed him, blowing off the balcony in a tiny crystal tornado.

Then he stood beside the table. This close the light from the candelabrum flickered over him, illuminating the hard, inhumanly muscular lines of his body. He kept very still, allowing her time to study him and to become accustomed to his nearness.

The statue in the park had not been clothed, but the living Guardian was. He wore a black leather breastplate over a short tunic. The outfit reminded her of something Russell Crowe would have worn in *Gladiator*, except had the two stood side by side, the Guardian would have made the Aussie actor look like a boy in dress-up clothes.

The creature was huge. He had to stand almost seven feet tall. His hair was the unrelenting black of a new moon night. It fell thickly around his massive shoulders. Two dark horns protruded from his head. They curled forward and tapered to dangerous-looking points. His face . . . Mikki's breath caught in her throat. The face of the statue had been roughly hewn and indistinct, but the living Guardian was no unfinished rock; he was powerfully masculine, with a thick brow; high, distinct cheekbones and a square jaw. Taken by itself, his face reminded her of ancient images she'd seen stamped on foreign coins or carved into statues of warriors long dead, but mix his classic features with the horns and the sharp glint of a carnivore's teeth, and it was obvious that the man did not completely dominate the beast that lay so close to the surface.

His breastplate and tunic left quite a bit of his muscular body bare. The skin that covered his torso was dark and looked like living bronze in the candlelight. She let her eyes travel down his body. She knew what she would see, yet still she sucked in a shocked breath at the reality of it. His thick legs were covered in dark fur. Instead of feet, the flickering light glinted off cloven hooves.

He was the personification of animalistic power, and though he did not move to threaten her, the aura of feral viciousness that surrounded him was almost palpable. Mikki shivered and pulled the blanket more closely around her shoulders.

"The night is getting cold," he said as softly as possible. "I should have had them set your dinner within by the hearth."

"I—I like it out here," she stuttered.

"Do you? Or are you just being polite?"

"No, I often eat dinner on my balcony at home," she said, feeling a tremor of homesickness. There wasn't a lot she'd miss about her old life, but her comfortable apartment and her view of Woodward Park was something that would always be a bittersweet memory.

"Then I am pleased that I chose to set your dinner on your new balcony, Empousa."

Slowly he placed the goblet on the table and, with a gentlemanly gesture that was in direct contradiction to his bestial appearance, he poured her another glass of wine. Each of his movements was unhurried and carried with it a catlike grace.

Like a predator, she thought.

When he was finished pouring he took a step back from the table and nodded at the full glass.

"Drink. It will soothe you."

Mikki did as she was told, barely tasting the excellent red. Her body felt detached and unreal, but the wine warmed her and helped anchor her senses. She drank deeply, for the moment not caring if it made her tipsy or muddled her thoughts.

Her thoughts, after all, were highly suspect. Perhaps they could use some muddling.

"I dreamed of you. Back there, in your old world . . . at your old home. I dreamed of you often."

His words jolted through her, and she put down the goblet before it, too, broke. Mikki raised her eyes to his. They were almond shaped and as dark and bottomless as a quarry.

"I know," she whispered. "I dreamed of you, too."

"It was a shock," he said, pulling his gaze from hers to look out into the darkness. "After all those countless years of nothingness . . ." He shook his head and his mane moved softly around his shoulders. "It seemed impossible that I was aware again. At first I sensed you, but I could not see you. I only knew your presence." His voice was deep with a low, hypnotic sound, but his face remained expressionless, as if part of him had become stone again. He did not meet her eyes. "Then the dreams changed. They became more real. I could see you and feel you. Finally you called to me and I awakened completely. I knew you were Hecate's Empousa; only she could have awakened me. My mastery over magick returned to me, and so I brought you here."

"I thought I was going crazy," Mikki said, wishing he would look at her or give her some hint about what he was feeling. But he only stared, stone-faced, into the night.

"No, Empousa. You are not mad. You are fulfilling your destiny."

CHAPTER THIRTEEN

"YOU know that's not really my name," she blurted. Now why the hell had she said that?

He turned his head and finally looked at her again.

"Of course not. Empousa is a title of respect, not a name."

"Well, it doesn't really seem like it's me yet," she said. "Like just about everything here it seems foreign . . . odd . . ." Mikki stifled a sigh, wondering how it could be that she was talking so easily with this man-creature.

"If not Empousa, then what shall I call you?" he asked.

"Mikki," she said.

His thick brow furrowed, and for a moment she thought she caught the glint of humor in his dark eyes.

"Mikki? That is a name?"

"It's not my given name, but it's what everyone calls me."

"What is your given name?"

"Mikado," she said.

"Ah." He nodded, and the candlelight glinted off a quick flash of too-sharp teeth as he smiled. "The Mikado Rose. It is appropriate."

Mikki took another drink of wine. With its spread of warmth through her body came a sudden, delicious sense of heady courage. She cleared her throat and spoke quickly before she changed her mind. "What is your name?"

"I am Guardian of the Roses."

Mikki frowned. "But what do I call you?"

"I have always been called Guardian."

"Guardian?" Mikki said doubtfully. "That sounds like Empousa—a title, not a name."

"It is what I am. Title or name, there is no difference for me."

His face changed again, and this time Mikki was sure she saw sadness there before his expression settled into an unreadable mask. He was such a mass of contradictions. One second he was scaring the breath from her, and the next he was making her feel pity for him. Her head was a little woozy. She was definitely more relaxed—not exactly grounded, but relaxed enough to allow the next question to spill from her mouth.

"Am I making you up? Is this all happening just in my mind?"

"No. We are real, you and I. As is the Realm of the Rose and the goddess we both serve."

"So I'm not asleep and dreaming this?"

"No, Mikado." He enunciated her name carefully. "Not this time."

His eyes caught hers, dark and expressive with the knowledge of what their dreams had become. "You are very much awake, as am I. Finally."

"Sometimes my dreams of you felt more real than the world around me."

Slowly, not taking his eyes from hers, he moved closer to her and lifted his hand so his fingertips brushed lightly over her cheek. "You broke the spell that entombed me. For that I will eternally owe you a debt of gratitude."

The heat of his brief caress made her shiver, and he quickly dropped his hand and stepped back.

"But why me?" Her voice was rough, as equal parts of fear and fascination struggled within her. "How could I have broken a spell I didn't know anything about?"

"You carry the blood of Hecate's priestess within you. None other could have broken the spell and awakened me."

"I awakened you . . ." Mikki repeated. "And I'm here because you needed a spell lifted from you."

"No, Empousa," the Guardian said firmly. His words were stone, and the power that he had been keeping in check roiled between them once more. "You are not here for me. You are here for the roses."

Inadvertently, she cringed away from the force of his voice, once again fearful of the monstrous creature who stood before her.

The Guardian sighed wearily. When he spoke, he had tamed his voice so it was no longer overpowering.

"I will leave you to finish your meal in peace. If you have need of anything, simply call and your handmaidens will attend you. I bid you good night." He bowed neatly to her, turned and blended back into the shadows from which he had emerged.

When she was sure he was gone, she unclenched her hands and wiped them across her face.

Breathe. Be calm. Breathe. Be calm. She let the words sink from her mind into her body. Instead of reaching for the wineglass, she began to methodically eat meat and cheese. She needed to be able to think clearly. Food made her feel more normal, so she ate and let the simple act of refueling her body rejuvenate her mind. She didn't take another drink or think more about the impossible conversation she had just had until the edge of her hunger was gone and the woozy feeling in her head had cleared.

Mikki slowed her eating and sipped the wine. The food worked exactly as he had told her it would. She was full, and she felt normal again—if she could use the word *normal* to refer to anything she was experiencing in this fantasy world.

The creature . . . how could anything so terrible and powerful walk and speak like a man? As a statue she had always thought of him as more man than beast, but seeing him alive—hearing him speak—had made her understand all too well that he was not, *could not,* be only a man.

You are not here for me. You are here for the roses. The words seemed to echo on the empty balcony, accusing and mocking her. She remembered the sadness that had shadowed his face. Did beasts feel sadness? Would a beast think to have a sumptuous table set for a woman and then float a rosebud in her wine? Could a beast enter a woman's dreams and fantasies? And why would a beast touch her face with such gentleness?

He was not, *could not,* be only a beast, either.

Mikki tried to wrap her mind around the things he had said. He wasn't a dream. He wasn't a hallucination. He was all too real.

You are here for the roses. He had told her that, and so had Hecate. But what did it mean?

"Tomorrow," she said aloud. "Tomorrow I'll find out."

She drank the last of the wine and then with a groan of protest at her stiff muscles, she dragged herself from the balcony and into her bedroom. While she had been busy circle casting and conversing with a living statue, someone had blown out the chandeliers and all but one candelabrum. The fire was banked, but the room was pleasantly warm after the coolness of the night. The thick bed linens were pulled back in preparation for her and a nightgown, a twin of the one she had been wearing earlier, lay across the foot of the bed.

Before she changed into it, Mikki nervously closed the doors to the balcony and drew the thick velvet drapes. Then she hastily peeled off her scanty ritual dress and gratefully slid on the soft nightgown. As she curled up in the middle of the opulent down comforters she thought about how much she'd like a warm soak in a bath. Man, her body was stiff. She sighed. She could tell she'd be sore as hell tomorrow. Her eyelids felt weighted. It was impossible to keep them open.

Her final thought before she slipped into sleep was to wonder if he would visit her dreams that night . . .

THE Guardian paced back and forth across his lair's sleeping chamber. He should be pleased. He should be celebrating his release. At last, after all those silent, frozen years, he lived and breathed again. And she was here. It mattered little that she was inexperienced or that she was from the mundane world where he had been entombed for so many centuries. She had Hecate's blessing. Mikado was the new Empousa. The Realm of the Rose would, once more, be set aright.

He remembered the fear in her eyes when he had stepped from the shadows, but he had watched as that fear had changed, as it had become tempered with fascination, even while his power had intimidated her. He knew what she was feeling. It was fascination for her that had awakened him. He had known it before, when she had invaded his mind as his consciousness had been trapped within the marble body. He had not wanted to admit it, not even silently to himself. But now that he'd seen her . . . talked with her . . . smelled her living fragrance and touched the warmth of her skin . . . he could not delude himself any longer. His desire for her was like air—it filled him, sustained him, and he only felt truly alive when he breathed her in.

"Why?"

He growled while he paced. A test. That was the only answer for it. Hecate had given him this burden to bear, and by all the immortal Titans he would bear it!

Spring came early to the Realm of the Rose. Surely then the goddess would relieve his agony. Then he could return to the loneliness that had been a comfortable enemy. Until that time he would keep busy with his duties, which, he admonished himself, did not include watching the Empousa eat. It had all been a lie his mutinous desire had rationalized into temporary truth. He hadn't needed to stay and watch, nor had he needed to speak with her. The ritual had made her hungry and thirsty. Her body would have shown her naturally what it needed to be grounded, and even the empty-headed Elementals would have eventually gotten around to explaining such a basic concept to the inexperienced priestess.

He must not delude himself. Staying away from her was the wisest choice. And that would be easy. He didn't need to see her to know when she was near; he knew her scent. His hands curled and he quelled the urge to smash them into the smooth walls of the cave. Her scent would warn him if she was near, as would the sun glinting off the rich copper of her hair. He had touched that hair in his dreams. He had run his hands along the length of her smooth skin, reveling in its softness. And she had touched him in return, stroking his body as if they were lovers. He had seen the memory of that touch reflected clearly in her eyes. He had longed to respond to it, just as he had longed to respond to her body as it had shuddered beneath him in the last dream.

"No!" he roared.

He could not allow it to happen again. He had one chance to right his past wrong. He must not love her. He could not. And this time he would not delude himself into believing that there was any chance she could love him in return, though in reality her feelings mattered little. She was Hecate's Empousa; therefore, she must die.

The Guardian sank down on the thick pallet of furs on which he slept and buried his face in his hands. He wanted to weep, but he felt empty of everything except pain and despair. There were no comforting tears within him.

"Are you sorry that I allowed her to awaken you?"

The Guardian's head snapped up and he beheld his goddess in her full regalia—headdress of stars, cloaked in the veil of night, with her torch blazing in one hand and the other resting on the head of one of her massive hounds. He fell to his knees before her, supplicating himself with his head bowed so low that his horns touched the ground at her feet.

"Great Goddess! I rejoice that I am in your presence once again."

"Arise, Guardian," Hecate said.

"I cannot, Goddess. Not until I beg you to forgive my crime."

"You did not commit a crime. You simply succumbed to the humanity I placed within you. I was mistaken when I punished you so harshly for a weakness that I was ultimately responsible for gifting you."

His shoulders shook with the effort it took for him to maintain control of his turbulent emotions. "Then I beg that you forgive my weakness, Great Goddess."

Hecate bent and touched his bowed head. "I demonstrated that forgiveness when I allowed my new Empousa to awaken you. Now arise, Guardian."

Slowly he stood. "Thank you, Goddess. I will not disappoint you again."

"I know that. We will not speak again of a past which is dead. You have finally returned to me. The realm has felt your absence keenly, as have I."

"I am prepared to resume my full duties, Goddess, if you will grant it so."

"I do." Hecate scooped her hand through the air, gathering invisible power until her hand glowed. Then, with a quick throwing motion, she tossed the brilliant pile of light on him and said, "I hereby return to you dominion over the threads of reality."

The Guardian's head bowed again as the magickal power resettled into his body, filling him with its familiar warmth. When he was able, he met his goddess's gray eyes.

"Thank you, Hecate."

"There is no need to thank me. I return to you what is yours. In all the time you were gone, the handmaids never got the knack of it, not even the Elementals were as adept at turning reality into the threads that bind the garment of mortal dreams as you."

"I am eager to begin again, Goddess," he said.

"I expect no less of you. But tonight I command that you rest. Tomorrow is soon enough to begin."

"Yes, Great Goddess," he said. He bowed his head again, expecting that she would disappear as she normally did in a shower of stars. When she didn't, he glanced up, curious as to her hesitation.

"Goddess?"

"As you know, my Empousa has returned."

Silently, he nodded his head.

"She is . . ." Hecate paused, choosing her words carefully. "She is not like the other Empousa. She is, of course, from the mundane world. This realm is strange and new to her."

"And she is older than the other priestesses," he said. Hecate's quick, knowing gaze made him silently curse himself for speaking at all.

"That is true. It is also true that she is inexperienced in the duties of my High Priestess. Keep a watchful eye on her, Guardian. She has much to learn and very little time in which to learn it. Beltane is not far away."

He bowed his head. "I will do your will, Goddess."

When she glanced up at him, her gray eyes were piercing. "This time I have taken steps to insure that you will not be so easily tempted to err. With the return of your power over the threads of reality, I have given you a"—she paused and her lips tilted up in a humorless smile— "let us call it a special thread of reality of your own. I know your body burned for my Empousa and that she used that desire against you as you sought the impossible. So you will never be tempted to betray yourself for lust again, know that I have made it impossible for you to consummate your desire for a woman unless that woman loves and accepts you for the beast you are, as well as the man who lurks within the creature's skin. Henceforth, you will be safe from your own impossible dreams. Do you understand, Guardian?"

Awash in shame, he bowed his head again. "I do, Great Goddess."

Her voice softened. "I do not do this to be cruel. I do this as protection for you, as well as the realm. For what mortal woman could ever truly love a beast?"

Awaiting no response from him, Hecate raised her torch and disappeared in a whirlwind of light, leaving her Guardian as he was before, alone and filled with despair.

Chapter Fourteen

Unlike the first time, there was no confusion or lingering sense of displacement when she woke up. Mikki knew exactly where she was. She opened her eyes to the perky light of full morning shining in a golden wave through the wall of windows. Someone had drawn back the curtains, and she could see that the table she'd eaten dinner at the night before had been reset for breakfast.

Had *he* directed that breakfast be prepared for her? Was he out there again, watching? Mikki's stomach gave a sickening lurch as she wondered what it would be like to see him in the full light of day. Last night he had belonged to the darkness, like the boogey monster or a nightmare creature. *Or . . .* her imagination murmured . . . *a forbidden lover.*

"Get a grip on yourself." Mikki sat up, shaking her head as if the physical movement would clear the ridiculous thoughts from it, and she was struck again by the beauty of the room that was now hers. Pushing the Guardian from her mind, she intended to leap out of bed and glide gracefully to her balcony, as should any woman lucky enough to live in a room this incredible, but the leap turned into a stagger, and the glide became a stiff limp accompanied by a groan when she made her body straighten fully.

Oh baby, she was sore! She hobbled to the door. When the handmaidens had first met her, they had seemed to think she was unusually old for an Empousa. Maybe that was because it took a damn teenager to withstand the hidden torture of casting a circle and dancing around with a gaggle of women. Who knew? Even her hair hurt. She sniffed at herself. And she needed a bath. A long, hot one.

She opened the door and was met by a cool, rose-scented breeze. It pulled her attention from the waiting breakfast, her sore muscles and the mysterious Guardian, and drew her across the wide balcony so she could look out over the vast gardens.

Mikki was awestruck.

The land that stretched before her was filled with bed after bed of roses. They blazed clouds of color in the green sky of their branches. White marble paths circled labyrinthine around the beds, connecting them to trees and shrubs and an occasional water feature. She could see the creamy marble of the domed roof of Hecate's Temple and the dancing reflection of the sun off the great central fountain that stood near it.

It was so beautiful that it weakened the disbelief and cynicism she had learned from a very young age to carry as her shield. She could be happy here . . . she could belong.

"It is your charge, Empousa."

This morning Hecate's presence did not startle her. The goddess materializing beside her felt comforting—a reinforcement of the miracle that lay before her.

"This is where I belong," Mikki said without looking away from the gardens.

"Yes, it is your destiny." The goddess sounded pleased by her acknowledgment.

Mikki turned to face Hecate and flushed with surprise. Last night the goddess had appeared an indeterminate age, anywhere from thirty-something to fiftysomething. This morning Hecate wore the same night-colored robes and star-studded headdress. The gigantic dogs lounged by her feet, as they had the night before. But the goddess had shed decades. She had the fresh face and tight figure of a teenager. Her smooth cheeks were kissed with a blush of youthful peach.

Hecate frowned and raised gracefully arched brows. "You do not recognize your goddess, Empousa?"

Mikki swallowed hard. She might look like a teenager, but Hecate had certainly not lost any of her powerful aura.

"It's not that I don't recognize you; it's just that you're so young!"

"Of my triple forms I simply chose the Maiden today. But do not be fooled by the facade of youth. You should already know that the exterior of a woman does not define her interior."

"It may not define her, but it certainly affects her. I'm old enough to know that," Mikki said automatically. Then, appalled at the brusque tone she had inadvertently used, she added, "I didn't mean any disrespect."

Intelligent gray eyes looked unnaturally mature and out of place in the goddess's smooth young face. "I rarely find it disrespectful when an Empousa speaks honestly to me, Mikado. And you are correct. Too often our exterior is what we are judged by, especially in your old world, one that has largely forgotten the lessons of the goddesses." Hecate shrugged her smooth shoulders. "Even in my realm where a woman's appearance should not be the basis on which she is judged, my daughters too often forget the lessons of the three-faced goddess." Hecate's wise gray eyes sparkled. "For instance, some would say that an Empousa of your advanced years is too old to assume the role of my High Priestess. They would not say it in my presence, but they would say it. And how would you answer their impertinence, Mikado?"

Mikki ignored the stiffness in her back and her sore muscles and met the goddess's steady gaze. "I'd say that I may be older, but that also means I've lived through more experiences, so I suggest they watch their silly young selves. Age and treachery usually triumph over youth and exuberance."

Hecate laughed, and as she did so, her appearance shifted so she was, once again, the beautiful, middle-age woman Mikki had met the night before. "I will tell you a secret, my Empousa. Of the three, this is the form I prefer. Youth is often overrated."

"Especially by the young," Mikki agreed.

The two smiled at one another, and for a moment, they were not goddess and mortal. They were just two women in perfect agreement.

After a short, compatible silence, the goddess said, "I imagine this"—she gestured with one hand to take in the gardens and the palace—"all seems quite unusual to you."

Encouraged by the goddess's approachability, Mikki smiled crookedly. "It is strange and unusual, as well as more than a little overwhelming, but I do feel drawn to everything here." She hurried on, not wanting Hecate to know included in that "everything" was her cloven-hoofed late-night visitor. "When I cast the circle and performed the initiation ritual I felt more beautiful and powerful and *right* than I've ever felt in my life."

Hecate nodded. "The Empousa blood runs thick in your veins, Mikado. You could not have felt true belonging in the mundane world. Part of you longed to take your proper place in my realm. I suspect even your mother and her mothers before her knew the unease of not quite fitting in."

Mikki thought about her mother, remembering how she had always seemed to prefer to be alone—or to spend time working in her garden with her roses—than to socialize. How she hadn't ever seemed to miss her father's presence and when Mikki asked about him she only said that he had been an indulgence of her youth, but that she would always be grateful to him for giving her the most important gift in her life—her daughter.

Her grandmother, too, had not been a woman who had many friends outside her daughter and her granddaughter. She rarely spoke of the man who was her grandfather, except to smile surreptitiously and say that they had had two different viewpoints on marriage—he had enjoyed it; she hadn't. Men had not been important in either her mother's or her grandmother's life. Not that either of them hadn't been wonderful, loving women. They had been, and Mikki missed them both desperately. Her grandmother had died of an unexpected heart attack five years ago, and breast cancer had stolen her mother four years after that. Mikki thought of both women as beautiful and ageless, like they'd stepped out of one of the fairy tales her mother used to read to Mikki when she was a young girl. They had been otherworldly . . .

"They are at peace now, Mikado. Even from the mundane world across the far edges of my crossroads, their souls were able to find the paradise of the Elysian Fields, and, finally, true belonging. You need not weep for them."

Mikki reached up, surprised to feel the tears wetting her cheeks. She looked at Hecate. "They belong here, too. That's why they didn't really fit in back there."

"Part of them belonged here, but the magick in their blood was not as strong as the magick within you. If it had been, they would have awakened the Guardian and returned."

Mikki wiped her cheeks dry. "The Guardian . . . I met him last night."

The goddess cocked her head, studying her priestess. "And what was your reaction to him?"

"He scared me," she said quickly. And then more slowly she added, "And he made me sad."

"Sad?" Hecate's brows lifted into her dark hair.

Mikki moved her shoulders restlessly. "I don't know . . . there's something about him that feels so alone."

"There is no other creature like him in existence, so by his very nature he is alone. Ages ago, when I took dominion over this realm, I knew I needed a guardian to stand watch over it. This is the realm from whence all the dreams and magick originate; it must be protected. So I called upon the great beasts of olde—the immortal offspring of the Titans. Though I am Goddess of the Beasts, I do not hold dominion over them. Even I could not force one of their kind into my service. The creature you met last night bound himself willingly to me. He took up this eternal burden when it was not his own. I have gifted him with some powers that are unique to this realm, but the Guardian has an ancient magick of his own—he ties the threads of reality to that of this realm."

"Has he always been as he is now?"

Hecate's sharp gaze seemed to look within her. "The Guardian has never been a man, nor will he ever be. Do not ever make the mistake of believing otherwise."

With effort, Mikki didn't flinch at the goddess's anger, but she quickly changed the direction of her questioning.

"He's called the Guardian, and you said he is needed to protect the realm. From what does it need protection?"

"Dream Stealers and those who desire to possess the fashioning of magick for themselves. Dreams and magick belong to all of mankind, even those who live in the mundane world. No one has the right to steal such things for himself."

Mikki didn't really understand what the goddess was talking about, but she was damn tired of sounding like a blundering idiot. As she had implied to Hecate, she was old enough to figure things out for herself. So she'd keep her eyes open and learn. And she wouldn't ask too many personal questions about the Guardian—clearly that made the goddess angry, and a pissed-off goddess couldn't possibly be a good thing.

But there was one question she needed to ask, whether it made her look moronic or not.

"Where do the roses fit in to all this?"

Hecate smiled as she gazed out at the expanse of dream-colored flowers.

"Roses are beauty, and beauty is at the heart of all dreams and magick; it is its foundation, its support. Without beauty, the mind cannot reach beyond the corporeal to grasp the ethereal."

Mikki's brow furrowed as she frowned. But hadn't the goddess just talked about the exterior not defining the interior? Now she was saying that beauty was everything.

Hecate laughed softly. "There is more than one kind of beauty, Empousa."

Mikki said the first thing that came into her mind. "Well, you wouldn't know it by the tastes of the majority of the men in my old world."

"Why should you sound so cynical? Your form and face are pleasing, Mikado."

"That's just it. I'm pretty. I have good hair, nice boobs, and decent legs. And that's all men see. They don't bother to look deeper." Her conscience reminded her that she hadn't often given any man the opportunity to look deeper . . . to discover her secrets . . . the truth of which only made her scowl harder.

"I think there is much you can teach this realm, Mikado. And it has much it can teach you in return. It will be an adventure for you, as well as your destiny."

Mikki sighed softly. She'd only been here for a day, and already she was sick of mysteries.

"I'm here for the roses," she said, unconsciously mimicking the Guardian's words.

"You are. They are the foundation on which dreams and magick are built, as well as the boundary between worlds."

"The boundary between worlds? Do you mean that literally?"

"I do, Empousa. Roses fill this realm, and the strength of their beauty gives life to dreams and magick. Their strength also forms the border of my realm." Hecate pointed out across the gardens and made a sweeping motion that encircled them. "The edges of the gardens are bound by a great wall of roses. Past that wall is a vast forest, a kind of netherworld, which is the crossroads between reality and magick. On one side of the forest rests the ancient world where gods and goddesses are still honored; on the other your old world can be found, that of the mundane. The rose wall is what defines the boundaries between those worlds and ours. See to the health of the roses, and, in turn, all else in my realm will prosper. If the roses sicken, so, too, will this realm. You should know that this realm has long been without its Empousa. The roses need your care, and you do have other duties, too. You are High Priestess of Magick, and as such the people of this realm will come to you for advice, spells, and rituals. Be wise, Mikado, for you stand as my Incarnation. When you speak, it is my power that answers."

Mikki felt the blood drain from her face. "Hecate, I don't know anything about spells and magick and rituals!"

The goddess's serene expression remained unchanged. "Your mind doesn't know, but your spirit does. Look within, as you did last night, and you will find what you seek. No matter how things appear on the surface, follow your instincts. They will not fail you. And use your experience, Mikado. I believe I will enjoy having an *aged* Empousa."

"So just trust my gut?"

"Crude, but correct," Hecate said. "Your handmaidens are here to aid you, but remember—you alone are my High Priestess. They personify the Elements over which I lend you dominion. Befriend them if you will; use their powers as you need them. Just as the handmaidens are at your disposal, so, too, is the Guardian. He is a magickal creature whose powers have been pledged to protect the Realm of the Rose. If there is a problem in the realm, do not hesitate to call upon him."

Mikki felt a little jolt of excitement at the mention of the Guardian. Guiltily, she said, "But if I think the realm is in danger, shouldn't I just call you?"

"My duties are vast! I do not have time to answer your summons as if I were a mere handmaid!"

Mikki took an involuntary step back, surprised by Hecate's sudden burst of anger. "That's not what I mean. I—"

Hecate cut her off with a brisk wave of her hand. "I forget that you are inexperienced in the ways of an Empousa. I do reign as supreme goddess over the Realm of the Rose, but you and the Guardian have been given the task of caring for and protecting it. I would like to spend much of my time here, but my duties do not allow me that luxury." Hecate studied Mikki carefully. "You must not fear the Guardian. I have told you that he will not harm you."

"I know." Mikki bit her lip. Avoiding Hecate's eyes, she stared out at the gardens. "It's just that he's like nothing I've ever imagined before."

"Is he?" Hecate's voice was soft. "Didn't you tell me that you spent much of your time tending the roses in the gardens in which he slept, frozen in the form of a statue?"

Mikki nodded her head. "Yes."

"Well then, how could he be like nothing you've ever before imagined?" Hecate said matter-of-factly.

"I suppose when you put it like that . . ." Mikki's words trailed off doubtfully as she turned back to the goddess.

"There is no other way to put it," she said briskly. "He stood silent watch over your roses then. He does the same now, only not so silently. If it is easier for you, simply forget that he is a beast—think of him only as a Guardian." Not giving Mikki time to answer, Hecate continued, "Excellent. I must leave you now. Break your fast and then call the handmaidens to you so you can be dressed and begin the day's duties. The roses have gone too long without the touch of an Empousa. They are in need of your care. Remember, follow your instincts, Mikado. Allow your spirit and the knowledge held in your blood to guide you, and you will do well . . ."

The goddess raised one elegant hand, and she and the dogs disappeared in a shower of star-colored sparks.

Shaking her head, Mikki walked to the table that was laden with fruit and bread and cheese. "It might be easier if I really was kooky," she muttered. Pouring herself fragrant, rose-spiced tea from a steeping pot, she wished desperately for a couple aspirins and some BenGay.

CHAPTER FIFTEEN

THE food really was delicious, especially the cheese. Mikki took one last bite of a creamy white cheese she'd spread on a slice of chewy bread. She'd been carrying on a passionate love affair with cheese for as many years as she could remember—as her curvy butt could certainly attest to—and the selection someone had laid out for her breakfast was even more extraordinary than last night's feast.

Was that because the Guardian knew what she liked best? Could he, like Hecate, read the passions and fears in her mind? Had he plucked her favorite foods from her subconscious? If he had, then that would mean he would also know that she was thinking of him . . . and that she was intrigued as well as intimidated at the thought of seeing him again.

I am here for the roses!

She jumped guiltily. He was a beast. A creature from a strange world who had sworn an oath to guard Hecate's realm. Clearly, something had happened a long time ago and he had screwed up, Big Time, and ended up a statue in Tulsa.

What had he done? Whatever it was, she'd bet he wouldn't do it again. Mikki sighed. There were so damn many mysteries and unanswered questions here it was overwhelming. No! She shook her head and took a last sip of tea. She'd take things one step at a time and figure them out as she went. She just needed to think of this as a new job. It might be daunting to learn all the new . . . well . . . procedures, but not impossible.

And the Guardian? If she thought of him at all she should think of him like she would any security guard. For a moment the image of the Tulsa Rose Gardens' night watchman, Mel, flashed into her mind. He was short and round and very gray. Actually, he reminded her of a balding Santa Claus. Mel couldn't have been more different from the magnificent creature who had turned from stone into living flesh. Her lips curved up at the comparison. The Guardian and Mel? She really was crazy if she started thinking of the two of them as similar.

Mikki bit nervously at her lip. She didn't know how she was supposed to deal with the creature, the roses, the magick . . .

Before she could get overwhelmed—again—she stood and stretched carefully, focusing on working the stiffness out of her muscles. Her body had definitely felt better. Then she made her way slowly back into her bedroom. Busy. She needed to get to work and keep busy. It would help her muscles loosen up and her brain not to obsess on horns and hooves. And she was anxious to check out the roses. Her roses. Hecate had said that she was in charge of caring for them, that it was her destiny. She was no longer just another volunteer who daydreamed about making the gardens her own.

Eagerly, she looked around the room. Hecate had said to call the handmaidens to help her get dressed. Did that mean there was some kind of bell/rope system in her room? Isn't that how they did things in palaces "back in the day"? But this wasn't a scene from some old English movie with castles and such; this was a realm of myth and magick, something her personal life experiences hadn't exactly prepared her for.

"Maybe I should try calling a messenger owl. Talk about Hogwarts," she grumbled to herself. "Okay, you're being ridiculous." Mikki put her hands on her hips. "It can't be that hard. Hecate said to call them. So I'll call them." Actually, she thought she'd just call Gii. She felt the most connection with her, and, quite frankly, all four of the girls at once were a little more than she wanted to deal with so early. She cleared her throat. "Gii?" she said tentatively and then a little louder, "Gii, could you come here, please? I could use your help."

Nothing. Nadda. Zip. The handmaiden didn't suddenly materialize. No pitter-patter of little feet were heard rushing across her balcony.

"Okay, there must be another way to do this." Mikki paced while she thought. She was supposed to call the handmaidens . . . she came to an abrupt stop. The handmaidens were really the personification of their element. She'd called each of their elements into the circle last night. Maybe she could do something like that now. She closed her eyes and thought about Gii . . . the element Earth . . . last night the element's presence was preceded by scents that invoked the fertility of the earth and the harvest . . . the sweetness of newly cut hay . . . the ripeness of fruit and berries. Mikki could almost smell and taste the richness of a green and growing Earth.

"Gii," she said softly. "Come to me."

Almost instantly two quick knocks sounded on the far wall of her room. Mikki opened her eyes in time to see a door open seamlessly into the opulent bedroom, giving Mikki just a glimpse of a wide, moon-colored hallway as Gii hurried in. The handmaiden's arms were filled with several lengths of amber and cream and gold cloth.

"Good morning, Empousa." She curtseyed gracefully.

"I did it!" Mikki grinned. "I called and you came."

Gii's smile was warm. "Gladly, Empousa! It is a true pleasure to once again have Hecate's High Priestess within our realm. We have been idle too long." She paused and looked around her. "Did you not call the other handmaidens as well?"

"Actually, since I'm not used to having any handmaidens, I'd like to start with just you for today. Is that okay with you?"

"Whatever you wish, Empousa. It is an honor to be chosen to serve you."

The young woman's exuberance made Mikki feel a lot less nervous about not knowing what the hell she was doing. She was where she belonged. Everything else would fall into place. She nodded at Gii's laden arms. "I was going to say I needed you to help me find something to wear, but it looks like you already have that taken care of." Mentally Mikki crossed her fingers that today's outfit would cover both of her breasts.

"Naturally, Empousa. I knew you would be eager to oversee your gardens. When you summoned me I made certain that I was prepared."

Gii began helping Mikki out of her nightdress, and with the words *your gardens* echoing delightfully in her imagination, Mikki shrugged her way out of her clothes and held very still as the handmaiden took the long, rectangular length of gold fabric and wrapped it once around her body. With gold pins that appeared from the voluminous folds of her own robe, Gii fastened it at the shoulders. Thankfully, it formed a full bodice, covering both of her breasts. Then she unwound one of the elaborately braided belts from around her own waist and hung it low on Mikki's hips.

"Gii, I don't mean to complain, and I think this"—she hesitated, trying to think of the right word for the rectangle that had become a flowing, toga-like garment—"this dress is flattering and very feminine, but don't you have something else that's better suited to working in the garden?"

Gii straightened and gave Mikki a confused smile. "How could any garment be better suited than a chiton?"

"Well, it's an awful lot of material. Won't this"—she pointed at the length of golden fabric that hung gracefully to her feet—"just get in the way?"

"Not if you tuck it here and here." Gii demonstrated tucking her own lovely mint-colored chiton up into her belt so her long, strong legs were left mostly bare. The Earth Elemental held out her arms. "Our arms are not hindered by cumbersome sleeves, but if you feel chilled, you can easily wrap your palla around your shoulders."

"Palla?"

Gii wrinkled her forehead at her High Priestess. "Empousa, have you never before worn a chiton with a palla?"

With an effort, Mikki didn't shriek her frustration. "Gii, I explained to you last night that my old world is totally different. There I didn't know about priestesses or goddesses, and we don't dress anything like this. If I was going to work in the garden I would wear jeans"—here she mimicked stepping into a pair of pants—"and a short T-shirt that I'd pull over my head, and it would cover the top half of my body."

Gii looked horrified. "I do not mean to speak ill of your old world, Priestess, but it sounds barbaric! Why would a priestess, or any woman, choose to dress in such an unflattering, uncomfortable manner?"

Mikki meant to say that she'd never thought of jeans as unflattering or uncomfortable, but her eyes were caught by her reflection in the full-length mirror and the words stopped before she could form them. She looked like a queen from an ancient world. She walked slowly forward, studying herself carefully. The fabric was soft and unbinding, feminine and alluring. She had nothing on under it to crawl up her butt or to bite into her shoulders and leave red marks at the end of the day. Compared to this outfit, a bra, panties, jeans and a T-shirt were barbaric and uncomfortable.

"Teach me about this, Gii. You called it a chiton?"

"Yes, Empousa. It can swathe the female form in almost endless ways, especially when you add a palla or various other types of mantles." Taking a wide, soft brush from the vanity dresser, Gii fussed with Mikki's hair as she spoke, brushing it back and then tying it in place with a gold thread. "We believe our clothing should idealize a woman's body, rather than attempting to conceal its natural shape. Or bind it unnecessarily."

"There's no doubt that it's beautiful, but can I work in it?"

"Shall we see, Empousa?"

Mikki took the amber-colored palla from where it lay like a spilled treasure across the end of her bed and wrapped it around her shoulders. "Absolutely."

MIKKI knew something was wrong as soon as she approached the rose bed that had been planted so close to the stairs that led from her balcony that the roses brushed against the marble railing. It was the same sick feeling she'd had the night before, only this morning it was far stronger. Her stomach clenched, and she had to fight a bizarre impulse to be sick. The smile that had lit her face when she recognized the Old Garden Rose, Blush Noisette, faded along with the color in her cheeks. The bed was large and the plants well spaced, but the closer she got to them, the more obvious it was that they were not as healthy as they had appeared to be from above. She hurried down the rest of the steps. She ignored the sick feeling that had hit her as soon as she approached the roses and left the marble path, ploughing directly into the bed, muttering under her breath while she touched leaves and lifted canes to get a better look at the heart of the plants.

"Empousa?"

"They look terrible!" Mikki said without pausing in her inspection. "The leaves are yellow and limp. The canes are spindly. The blossoms, which seem fine from a distance, are really undersized and several don't look like they're going to open at all. When's the last time they were fertilized?"

Mikki didn't look up from the roses until she realized that Gii wasn't answering her. The handmaiden was staring uncomfortably at her tightly clasped hands.

"Gii, what's the problem? I just asked when was the last time the roses were fertilized. It's something that should be done regularly enough that . . ." Mikki's words trailed off as she realized that Gii was becoming more and more obviously upset.

"The Empousa cares for the roses," Gii blurted, without looking at Mikki.

"Are you telling me that for the entire time you've been without an Empousa no one's taken care of these roses?"

Gii finally lifted liquid eyes to Mikki. "It is the Empousa's sacred trust to care for the roses. Without their Empousa, Hecate bespelled them. They slept."

Just like the Guardian.

Mikki's mind whirred. Nausea rose in her throat again, and she was hardly able to concentrate on what else Gii was saying.

"There was nothing we could do for them. The roses wouldn't respond to us. They had stopped blooming." She lowered her voice to a whisper. "We believed they were dying."

"And none of you thought to mention this to me while we were frolicking around last night?" she cried, exasperated with herself for being so starry-eyed that she hadn't noticed how sick the seemingly beautiful gardens really were. And where the hell was her intuition last night? Today just getting near the beds made her feel like she was going to throw up her breakfast. Wait . . . maybe her intuition had been firmly intact. Last night she had just attributed it to nerves and lack of food, but she'd definitely been light-headed—her stomach had clenched and she'd felt sick. And then this morning she'd felt like she'd been beat up. It hadn't been because she was having a nervous breakdown or because she danced too much. Her body was reacting to the sickness in the roses.

Why hadn't Hecate warned her about the sorry state of her roses? Mikki frowned. What was it the goddess had said? *You should know that this realm has long been without its Empousa. The roses will need your care . . .*

Need her care? Mikki let her eyes sweep over the beds nearest to her, recognizing more Old Garden varieties, Eglantine and LaVille de Bruxelles. She narrowed her eyes at them. They looked sickly as hell, too! They definitely needed a lot more than a little of her care.

"We thought all would be well now that you are here. We even knew the moment you arrived because the roses suddenly began to bloom again."

"Gii, these roses aren't getting well. They're underdeveloped and anemic! And these pathetic things aren't normal blooms, they're . . . they're . . . they're more like final death throes than healthy blossoming."

Then, as if Hecate was still standing beside her, she heard the goddess's voice replay through her mind. *The edges of the gardens are bound by a great wall of roses . . . The rose wall is what defines the boundaries between that world and ours . . . If the roses sicken, so, too, will this realm.* A chill swept through Mikki, and she felt the warning in it pound with her blood.

She had to call the Guardian.

Chapter Sixteen

"Gii, do the roses in the rest of the realm all look like these?"

The handmaiden nodded and then, sounding childlike, she repeated, "We thought everything would be well now that you are here."

Mikki put on a smile she hoped didn't look too fake. "I think it will be, but it'll take some work. The first thing I want you to do is to gather all those women we were dancing with last night. Have them meet me at Hecate's Temple. And get the other three handmaidens, too."

"Yes, Empousa." Gii curtseyed and then hesitated before she turned away. "You do not come with me?"

"No, go on. I'll be at the temple soon. I have something I need to take care of here first."

Gii flashed a relieved look at her before hurrying away. Mikki waited until the girl disappeared around the corner of the path that curved between two more beds of sick roses. Then she straightened her shoulders and walked purposefully back to the wide marble stairs that led to her balcony. Was she doing the right thing? She thought so. No, she knew so. When she'd realized how sick the roses were—*all* the roses were—she felt the unmistakable chill of danger deep within her.

Mikki climbed up two of the steps, stopped, reconsidered, and climbed up one more. There. That should make her tall enough.

She closed her eyes. Just as she had called Gii to her earlier, she called him. She thought about the strength of his body . . . the power in his voice . . . the care with which he had directed dinner be made ready for her . . . the slippers and the rosebud that floated in the crystal goblet . . .

"Guardian," she said softly, "come to me."

The air seemed to thicken and press with an angry hum against her skin.

"Why have you summoned me?"

For the length of one breath Mikki pressed her eyes more tightly closed. *These are my gardens now. He is a security guard. Think of him as nothing scarier than a difficult employee.* She opened her eyes.

He was standing only a few feet from her. How could any living creature be so massive? She'd been smart to move up that additional step. In the revealing light of morning he looked less manlike than he had the night before. He was dressed the same, in the short, military-looking tunic and leather breastplate, but the clothes seemed to extenuate the bestiality of his cloven-hoofed legs and horned head rather than dress him up as civilized . . . controllable. Mikki's mouth went dry, and she had to swallow twice before she could find her voice.

"I called you because Hecate told me that was what I should do if I thought the realm was in danger." She had to fight to make herself speak, and the result was that her voice was unintentionally loud and angry. When the Guardian's black eyes widened in surprise, she decided that her new (albeit unintentional) firmness might be a good thing.

"What is the danger, Empousa?" he rumbled.

With an effort, she kept herself from biting nervously at her lip. "I don't know exactly. All I know is that the roses are sick, which means the rose wall that surrounds the garden is probably sick, too. My intuition tells me that possible weakness is somehow dangerous." She held her breath, waiting for his snarl. Instead, he surprised her by bowing his head slightly to her.

"You were right to summon me, Empousa. I should not have questioned your authority. If the boundary between the worlds is weakened, I must guard against those who would use it as an opportunity to slip into our realm."

"So as I try to heal the roses, I need to focus on the rose wall first?"

"That would be wise, Empousa."

Mikki nodded and said, more to herself than to him, "That's what my gut was telling me. Good thing I listened."

"Your gut?"

"Yeah," she said hastily. "Hecate said I should follow my gut and I'd do the right thing."

He snorted. "The goddess said *gut*?"

Was it possible his dark eyes were glittering with humor?

"That's not exactly how she put it." Surprising herself, Mikki smiled at him. His eyes locked with hers, and Mikki could feel the sudden weight of his stare as if his look could bridge the space that separated them and touch her with its intensity. And she felt something else, something that she recognized from her dreams. Mikki felt the stir of desire. He was dangerous and frightening, but he was also a powerful, overwhelmingly masculine being. As in her dreams, she was drawn to him by a hot chain of fascination. Holding his dark gaze, she said, "Hecate told me to follow my instincts, and that's exactly what I intend to do."

As if he had become tethered to her gaze, the Guardian moved to her until he stood near enough that he could easily touch her. "And what is it your instincts are telling you right now, Mikado?"

Mikki's breath caught. She could feel the heat from his body. Standing up several steps had brought her almost eye level with him, and she was, once again, struck by the impossible contrasts that made up his face . . . handsome and fascinating . . . bestial and dangerous.

He's not part man, part beast. He's more than that. He's part god . . .

Slowly, he lifted his hand and took a thick strand of her hair that had escaped from its golden tie between his thumb and forefinger. While Mikki stood frozen, he let her hair slip like water through his fingers. His deep voice rumbled intimately between them.

"Can you not speak, Mikado? Where is the brave priestess who commanded me into her presence? Is my nearness enough to frighten her away?"

"I'm frightened, but I'm not going anywhere," she said resolutely and was pleased to see his eyes widen with surprise at her honesty. Purposefully mimicking his gesture, she reached up and touched a shiny length of dark mane that spilled over his shoulders.

As if her touch was an electric charge, the Guardian jerked back from her. His voice was raw and hoarse. "Have a care, Empousa. You might find the beast you awaken is not as tame as the roses that are yours to pet and pamper." Then, with a growl, he whirled around, his hooves biting into the marble pathway. He was leaving, abruptly and without warning . . .

"Wait!" she yelled after him.

The great creature froze, his broad back turned to her. With a jerky motion his head swung so he glared over his shoulder.

She met his eyes again and could almost see herself reflected there—a weak, indecisive woman who, like an inexperienced young girl, had called him back to her without knowing for sure what she wanted to say.

The image angered her.

Hecate had chosen her as High Priestess, Empousa of the Realm of the Rose. *She* had summoned *him*. It had been her instincts that had alerted them to a possible danger. It didn't matter that she didn't totally understand the danger. She was doing what Hecate had chosen her to do. And damnit! He had touched her first! What the hell game did he think he was playing, and by what right did he think he could dismiss her? She was no girl child dressed up in the robes of power. She was a grown woman—independent and intelligent. She didn't tolerate patronizing men, with or without hooves and horns. Mikki slitted her eyes at him and spoke slowly and distinctly.

"There are things I need to know before you run away."

"I do not run—"

"No!" She shouted the word, ignoring the warning in his voice. "I speak with Hecate's authority. This time it's your turn to listen and answer."

His face was alien in its mixture of man and beast, but she was certain she saw approval register in his dark eyes.

"What is it you wish to know, Empousa?" he said. Turning, he walked the few paces back to her.

She felt his approach as if he changed the pattern of the air around them. She swallowed hard, careful to keep her voice businesslike and her mind from wandering.

"I need to know if there is one area of the rose wall that is more easily penetrated than the rest of it. Maybe a place where there is a break in the roses, like around a door or a gate."

He considered, then nodded, his shaggy mane spilling over his broad shoulders with the movement. "Yes, there is a gate in the roses, and it makes sense that that is where the barrier might be most easily breached."

"Do the handmaidens know about this gate?"

He nodded again. "Yes, Empousa."

"Then I'll have them show me where it is after I have them collect fertilizer."

His thick brows shot up. "You expect the handmaidens to tend the roses?"

She looked at him like he was totally nuts. "How do you expect me, all by myself, to tend this many roses? They need to be fertilized, pruned and deadheaded, and that's just for a start. I'd kill myself trying to do all that alone, not to mention that I wouldn't get it all done. That's not smart or productive."

His face had hardened again into an unreadable mask. She blew out a burst of frustrated breath.

"Are you telling me that the other Empousas did all that by themselves?"

"I do not recall an Empousa commanding the women to do anything to the roses except to cut bouquets to decorate her room."

"What about the fertilizing and pest control and the general care roses always need?"

"These roses have never before needed that kind of care. They simply required the presence of the Empousa to thrive."

"They've never been sick before?"

"Never."

"And before the, um, time you spent as a statue, you'd been here a long time?"

"I have been here since Hecate claimed dominion over the realm."

Which, Mikki guessed, had been a damn long time ago. So for literally eons the roses had been healthy, without needing any care except for the presence of Hecate's High Priestess. Until now, when she had suddenly become Empousa. Great. The news just kept getting better and better.

"Well, it looks like times have changed, or I'm a different type of Empousa, because the roses need care now. I can't do it on my own, so the women are going to have to help me."

He looked at her silently for what felt to Mikki like a long time before saying, "I believe you are a different type of High Priestess."

"Is that good or bad?"

"Neither," he said gruffly. "It is simply a fact."

"I think it's good," she said firmly, determined to be undaunted by his cynical attitude. She knew from her personal propensity for cynicism that the attitude usually hid feelings that were too painful to let the world see. Her cynicism had hidden the fact that she never felt like she truly belonged. She wondered what his was covering. Did it have something to do with what he had done to cause Hecate to turn him to stone and banish him? She realized she had been standing there gawking at him, and she hastily continued. "But I suppose changing worlds has made me more likely to think different is good."

"Odd," he said, his deep voice edged with sarcasm. "It did not have the same effect upon me."

"I imagine if I'd been turned to stone I wouldn't be so willing to think 'different' was synonymous with 'good,' either. But at least you know I can't cause you to turn into a statue," she said and wanted to cover her flapping mouth with her hand and stop her stupid words as she watched his face go rigid with tension.

"Is that all you wish to ask me, Empousa? I should go to the rose wall and inspect the boundary."

"Yes, I'll get the women and meet you at the gate." Mikki had to shout the last part of her sentence at his swiftly departing back. "You're welcome," she muttered. God, he was confusing! One second he was all smoky-eyed and erotically dangerous—talk about the classic bad boy! And the next second he was withdrawn and cynical. It was like he was two people.

"What the hell am I thinking?" She shook her head at herself. "He's not two people; he's a person and an animal, and I need to quit having delusions of a young Marlon Brando (with horns) and remember He Is Not Human." Interracial dating was fine. Interspecies dating? "Please, Mikado. Just please. Relocate your common sense and take care of the roses." With a sigh she started down the path Gii had taken to the center of the gardens, heading into what she was sure would be the continuation of a vastly difficult day.

THE gathered women parted like a sea of delicately colored flowers to make a path for Mikki to join the four handmaidens who were standing within Hecate's Temple. Many of the women called greetings to her, but they were decidedly more subdued than they had been the night before. Mikki hoped they were in the mood to work. She climbed the temple steps, smiled a quick hello to the Elementals and then turned to face the crowd. *Please don't let me sound as nervous as I am*, she thought. Immediately, Hecate's stern voice spoke from her memory. *When you speak, it is my power that answers.* The memory boosted her confidence. She ignored the lingering soreness in her body and the vague nausea she seemed unable to get rid of and looked out at the crowd, purposefully meeting the eyes of several of the women as she spoke.

"The roses are sick."

Frightened murmurs ran through the group, and Mikki had to raise her hand to silence them.

"But that's why I'm here. I understand roses. I know what they need, and with your help, we can make them healthy again." Mikki was pleased at the attentive expressions of the listening women. "The first thing we must do is fertilize them. So I need you to gather things that roses need to thrive." She paused, ordering the thoughts in her head. She'd already realized the obvious—that she would have to depend on wholly organic methods of fertilizing and pest and disease control, and that wasn't all bad. Many times the natural ways were the best. Last night she'd eaten meat that tasted like prosciutto. That was pork, wasn't it? Which meant they had to have pigs somewhere. It was a start . . .

"Hog manure," she said, and the bright, attentive expressions dropped into frowns. "You do have pigs, right?"

A few heads nodded hesitantly.

"Good. I want you to fill baskets with pig manure." Hardly taking a breath, she turned to Nera. The Water Elemental was watching her with large, round eyes. "Nera, is there a lake or sea nearby?"

"Yes, Empousa, there is a large lake within the realm."

"Excellent." She turned back to the crowd. "I'll need fish heads, entrails—anything you'd normally throw away instead of cooking. Actually," she continued as if the group of women wasn't staring slack-jawed at her, "I need dead organic matter, both plant and animal. Gii, I'm assuming that the forest outside the rose wall is dark and dense?"

"It is, Empousa."

"Then the forest floor should be rich with loam. Bring buckets or baskets or whatever, along with something to turn over the ground around the roses so we can mix the fertilizer into the soil."

"But bring them where, Empousa?" Gii said.

"Oh, I'm sorry." Mikki spoke so her voice carried out over the crowd. "Bring everything, empty baskets and those filled with the fertilizer I've mentioned, along with gardening tools, to the gate in the rose wall. We'll start there."

No one moved.

"Now would be good," Mikki said firmly. "The roses have been ignored too long."

Still no one moved.

Floga cleared her throat and moved closer to Mikki. "Empousa, this is highly irregular."

"What is? That I've told you we need to fertilize the roses or that you're refusing to do as an Empousa asks?"

Floga paled. "I would not refuse your bidding, Empousa."

Mikki looked at her other three handmaids.

"None of us would refuse you, Priestess," Gii said quickly, and the girls nodded agreement.

Mikki swung her gaze out to the crowd and raised her voice, making sure she sounded well and truly pissed. "Then is it only the women of the realm who refuse to obey Hecate's Empousa?"

The crowd stirred restlessly. One woman, who was probably about Mikki's age, stepped forward and curtseyed quickly.

"My sisters and I will gather the baskets for the forest loam, Empousa."

Another woman moved to the front of the group. "I will bring the fish offal."

"As will I."

"And I."

"We will see to the hogs," a young girl said from the middle of a group of teenagers.

Mikki wanted to weep with relief and thank them all profusely. But her gut told her that was not the reaction the people expected, or deserved. So instead she simply said, "Then I will meet you at the gate. You'll need to hurry. We have a long day ahead of us. The quicker we get started, the better." She turned her back to the dispersing crowd and caught Gii's eyes. "I'll need you to show me where the gate is," she whispered.

Gii smiled her approval before bowing her head and dropping into a deep, respectful curtsey. "As you wish, Empousa."

CHAPTER SEVENTEEN

"THERE! This is the rose wall. The gate is just around that bend in the hedge." Gii pointed a little way ahead of them at an area of the wall that curved back toward the gardens.

"Multiflora roses—that figures." Following the imposing boundary that seemed to materialize out of the air, Mikki shook her head. "Well, they have been called a living wall, but I've never seen them contained in such an orderly way."

She'd seen multiflora roses take over pastures and completely destroy them in less than a couple years, but stretching before her was a huge wall of the wild roses that had apparently been tamed. She and Gii turned with the curving wall. Mikki gazed up. The mass of climbing roses had to be at least twelve feet tall. "Do they ever spread and threaten to take over the forest?" *Or the rest of the realm*, she mused silently.

"The rose wall obeys Hecate's command."

Mikki felt Gii's body jerk in response to the Guardian's deep voice, and she was profoundly grateful that she, too, hadn't jumped out of her skin when he spoke. But then, she'd known he was going to meet her at the wall. Subconsciously, or maybe not so subconsciously, she'd been waiting for him to appear. Her gaze shifted from the roses to the Guardian. He was standing on the other end of the curve they had been following, framed by what looked like an immense gate made entirely of multiflora roses. As per usual, his strong face was somber and his expression unreadable, but his eyes . . . his eyes seared her. *He is not going to intimidate me. He's a security guard—a big, grumpy security guard. I'm Empousa, which would translate at the very least to his supervisor.* Mikki smiled pleasantly.

"I know more than a few ranchers in my old world who would pay just about anything to have Hecate command roses like these to behave themselves."

He frowned. "Hecate is not a merchant who can be—"

"I didn't mean that literally. I was just kidding," Mikki interrupted, working hard not to roll her eyes. She glanced at Gii. The Elemental had her lips pressed tightly together in a thin white line, and her eyes darted nervously back and forth from the Guardian to Mikki. *Huh. I guess no one kids with the Guardian. Or maybe the Empousa has never had a sense of humor before—the others were probably too young to have acquired one.* Yet another thing she was going to have to change.

"Okay, well, obviously this is the gate." Mikki ignored both of them and marched over to stand not far from the Guardian. From the corner of her eye she noticed that Gii followed her but was careful not to get too close to the man-creature. Mikki moved nearer the gate, observing that the roses that made up the wall looked only marginally healthier than the sickly plants in the gardens. The leaves of the multiflora roses were still mostly green, but there was a disturbing amount of yellowed foliage mixed in with healthy growth. There were a few half-hearted light pink buds, but none of the blooms had opened. She touched leaves, turning them over and looking in amidst the mass of plant that made up the body of the hedge, checking automatically for black spots and insects.

"I don't see anything specifically wrong with them—no obvious disease or insect infestation." She sighed and chewed her lip. "Like the rest of the roses in the gardens, they just look sick."

The Guardian moved closer to her. He, too, was studying the rose wall. "Can you make them well?"

"Of course," Mikki said with much more confidence than she felt. "I've never met a rose that didn't like me." Of course she'd also never met a wall of multiflora roses that listened to the commands of an ancient goddess, either, but she thought it'd be counterproductive to mention that. "We'll just start at the beginning and work our way forward from there. Step one—make sure the roses are well fertilized. It doesn't get much more basic than that."

At that moment a little breeze carried to them the sound of chattering women. The Guardian cocked his head and drew a deep breath. Then he looked down at Mikki and raised his eyebrows.

"You must smell our approaching fertilizer. What is it, fish heads or pig manure?" Mikki said.

"Pig waste."

This time it didn't matter that his face was like no other living creature; Mikki easily recognized the glint of humor in his eyes.

"Good!" she said brightly.

"You are, indeed, an unusual Empousa if pig waste causes you happiness."

She grinned. "I am and it does. Now it's time we get to work."

He flashed a smile that showed very white, very sharp teeth. Then he bowed to her. "I am yours to command, Priestess."

Ignoring Gii's sudden surprised intake of breath, Mikki tilted her head in what she liked to think was a goddess's acknowledgment of his goodwill before turning to begin giving directions to the approaching women.

THEY weren't doing a half bad job for women who had never worked with roses. Mikki stood and stretched, carefully circling her shoulders to try and relieve the tension that always found a way to rest between her shoulder blades. She wiped her hands on the outside of one of the tucked-up edges of her chiton and surveyed her surroundings.

The women were spread out along the rose wall for as far as she could see. Those she had stationed at the wall had three jobs—one group dug shallow trenches up and down the area near the roots of the roses. Another group covered the fertilizer with the freshly dug dirt after yet another group of women dumped the baskets of organic matter into the trenches. A steady stream of women carried baskets back and forth from wherever the pig poo and fish guts came from to the hedge.

There was also a chain of women who passed baskets filled with the loam of the forest floor from outside the rose gate back through to the women waiting to mound it snuggly around the base of the living wall.

Mikki glanced toward the open gate. Sure enough, she had only to wait a couple seconds to see the Guardian. All morning he had paced restlessly back and forth on the forest side of the gate. The playful goodwill that had begun to exist between them had dissipated when Mikki had insisted that the women be allowed to go into the forest to pile the rich loam into the baskets. The Guardian had been, quite simply, thoroughly pissed at her.

"It is not wise that the gate be left open," he'd growled when she'd explained how she intended to fill the empty baskets.

"The roses need the nutrients that are found in the organic matter that makes up the forest floor. So the gate has to be open because the women need to go into the forest," she'd told him, in a clear, unafraid voice right in front of all the women.

"The forest is not safe," he'd said stubbornly.

"Isn't that why you're here?"

He growled something unintelligible at her that made her skin prickle, but she'd refused to look away from him, just like she'd refused to back down in her insistence that the women go into the forest. She knew what the roses needed, and some of it could be found out there. Mr. Grumpy would just have to deal with it; he wasn't going to scare her out of what she knew was the right thing to do. And anyway, what could he do to her in front of the women in the realm? Eat her? Bite her? Pick her up and shake her? Please. She was Empousa—he was supposed to make sure she was safe. He couldn't very well be what caused her damage. She figured the worst he could do would be to throw a fit and stomp away. If he did that she'd just have to listen within and figure out how the hell to open a gate made of roses that didn't have a handle or a latch or a . . .

"I insist none of the women leave my sight."

"Whatever you say. Security is your job, not mine."

He'd cocked his head and sent her a black look.

"Well, I mean whatever you say as long as the women go into the forest and collect the loam," she'd amended sweetly.

"I still do not like it."

"And yet I am still insisting." Mikki had felt the weight of the women's staring eyes when she contradicted the Guardian. It was as if they were shocked that she stood up to him, and it made her wonder how the other, younger Empousas had handled disagreements with the intimidating Guardian. *It doesn't matter,* she told herself firmly, *I'm Empousa now, and he needs to learn that I'm not some virginal infant he can bully.*

"Huh," he'd snorted. But he'd gone to the gate, raised his hands and spoken words Mikki could not understand but the power of which rippled like warm water over her skin. The rose gate opened slowly, and only far enough for the bulk of the Guardian to pass through. She'd followed him, and the women, led by Gii, had followed the beast and their Empousa into the edges of the dark forest.

The forest was dark—and it should be. The trees were enormous, ancient oaks, so thick at the trunk that even the Guardian's wide reach couldn't have wrapped around one. The interlocking branches formed a canopy of lush green, through which very little sunlight managed to escape. But it seemed perfectly normal. Birds chirped. Squirrels scolded. Mikki even thought she caught sight of the rear end of a startled deer as it bounded away.

The women who scooped the leafy loam from the forest floor and into the baskets were unusually silent, and none of them wandered very far apart, but no boogeymen or monsters jumped out at them. And all the while the Guardian paced, his sharp eyes focused past the women and into the depths of the forest.

Gii's sweet voice interrupted Mikki's musings. "It is midday, Empousa," the Earth Elemental said after delicately wiping the sweat from her brow. She pointed to a line of women who were approaching from a different direction than the chain of fertilizer had arrived. "I see that women from the palace come bearing food."

"So late already?" Mikki hastily took her gaze from the Guardian's ever-vigilant form and smiled at the handmaiden.

"Yes, Empousa, and several of your rose workers must eat and then be allowed to change places with the Dream Weavers within the palace."

"Dream Weavers?"

"I forget that you are new to this realm and its ways, especially today, after watching you work so easily with"—Gii paused and her gaze slid to the open gate and the grim guard who stood beyond it— "the roses," she finished.

Mikki ignored her reference to the Guardian because she was not sure what to make of it. She was dying to ask questions about him and about the High Priestesses who had come before her—for instance, where were they now? Did the women retire? If so, couldn't one of them be called out of retirement temporarily to . . . well . . . train her properly?

But intuition told her that asking a bunch of personal questions about the Guardian and the previous Empousas would make her look even more inexperienced and insecure than she already was. She'd gained a measure of respect from the women today. She didn't want to lose ground. And there was something else, too. Something in the way the women averted their eyes from him and avoided standing too near him.

"May I, Empousa?" Gii was saying.

"Oh, I'm sorry, Gii. Yes, it is time we took a break. Then I'd like to hear more about these Dream Weavers." Which, she decided, should at least be a safe topic. As Gii sent a couple young women who were working close by to inform the other three Elementals that it was time to break and refresh with the midday meal, Mikki retreated to one of the many marble benches placed in lovely rose alcoves all around the gardens. She sat, realizing how tired her achy muscles were now that she'd stopped moving, and was sincerely grateful that Gii was so capable and able to quickly call the women to order. They broke into little groups, clustering around benches and fountains, and the soft sound of their conversation mixed with the ever-present scent of roses, creating an atmosphere that Mikki found soothing, despite her tired muscles and the general feeling of sickness that clung to her.

She breathed deeply, thinking how wonderful the gardens would be when they were healthy again. Letting her mind wander with her eyes, she imagined the beds and the rose wall in full, magnificent bloom. Her daydreamy interlude was interrupted when her gaze landed on the frowning Guardian as he ushered the last of the women back through the rose gate. He looked so damn serious and gloomy. Why? What was it about the forest that made him so uptight? Hell, maybe he was always uptight. No . . . she remembered the glint of humor in his eyes and the touch of his hand on her hair . . . clearly he wasn't always uptight. Still, she needed to have a frank talk with him. No mysteries, no evasions. If the forest was that dangerous, she needed to know the specifics.

The Guardian spoke a terse command and the wall closed seamlessly. Mikki yawned and stretched and tried not to be obvious about watching him. One of the palace servants approached him and offered him a basket of food. He ignored it, but he did accept a floppy skin, which he raised to his mouth and drank deeply from. He handed it back to the woman, and she hurried away. Then he paced over to a tree that grew near the rose wall and seemed to disappear within the shadow of its trunk.

Gii hurried up with a basket of her own, which was filled with tempting smells, and sat beside Mikki, placing the basket between them.

"Is the food not to your liking, Empousa?" she said when Mikki made no move to begin eating.

Mikki hastily looked away from the shadow under the tree. "No, everything is wonderful." She broke off a piece of bread from the long, thin loaf and added a slice of cheese to it. Nonchalantly, she said, "I was just wondering why he doesn't eat."

Fixing her own sandwich, Gii said, "I have never seen him eat." The Earth Elemental shrugged. "Not that he doesn't. He must. The food that is left at the mouth of his lair disappears and must be replaced."

"Lair?" Mikki sputtered, almost choking on the piece of cheese she'd just swallowed.

"Yes, his lair." Gii paused, looking confused at Mikki's surprise. "The place in which he sleeps—where he goes when he is not out amongst the roses."

"I guess I assumed he lived in the palace, like I do."

"Oh, no, Empousa, he is a beast." Gii sounded appalled. "It would not be proper for him to live in the palace."

Mikki studied Gii, trying to read the handmaiden's face as well as her words. The Earth Elemental was kind and compassionate. So much so that Mikki naturally sought out Gii's company more often than the rest of the handmaidens, and she already felt as if the two of them were becoming friends. Yet here Gii was, sounding cold and unfeeling. The Guardian was an animal. Period. So he didn't deserve the same luxuries or consideration the rest of them did, yet he was the being who protected their realm.

Deep in her gut it felt wrong—terribly, hurtfully wrong.

But she didn't correct Gii or question her further. Mikki didn't know enough about what was going on here. Not yet. Something wasn't right, and it had to do with the Guardian. She'd already learned from getting close to the roses that everything in this realm was not as it first appeared. She'd keep her eyes open and watch the Guardian. Her instinct told her that if she got close enough to him she might discover what was hidden beneath his facade, too. That is, if he let her—or if she dared. Until then she would watch and learn, and follow her gut.

"Tell me about the—what did you call them—Dream Weavers?" She purposefully changed the subject.

Gii brightened. "The Dream Weavers have the ability to take the ordinary—and the not so ordinary—and weave it into dreams and magick, which they then send from this realm out into the other worlds. It is from what is created here that all the dreams and magick of mankind are born."

Mikki struggled to take it all in. "And by 'the other worlds' you mean?"

"Your old world, that of the mundane. And then there is also the ancient world, where the gods and goddesses are still revered. It is the ancient world from where the women of this realm and I were chosen."

That was what Hecate had said when she'd talked about the crossroads between the worlds. It had confused Mikki then, but today her mind felt more able to absorb the seemingly impossible details of her new home. And she realized that at least one of the questions she had been pondering had been answered. The other Empousas had obviously come from the ancient world, and that must be where they retired to. In a slightly crazy way, it did make sense.

"You said the women had to go back to the palace to take their turn as Dream Weavers. So they're doing that—creating dreams and magick—right there in the palace?"

"Yes, Empousa."

"I'd like to see that. Is it possible that I could watch?" Mikki asked eagerly.

"You could do more than watch. As Empousa, you have the ability to weave dreams and make magick, too."

CHAPTER EIGHTEEN

S HE had the ability to weave dreams and make magick . . .
Gii's words remained with her all the rest of the day, circling
around and around in her imagination, which stayed as busy as her
hands. Just the concept that dreams came from somewhere other than a
sleeping subconscious was bizarre enough. But to think that she had
the ability to create them! It was the most extraordinary thing she'd
ever imagined.

"Empousa."

The Guardian's deep voice startled her, but she was careful to cover
her jumpiness with a show of wiping her hands briskly on her muddy
chiton while she straightened from crouching under an unusually large
cluster of a Felicite Parmentier shrub. He was standing so close that his
shadow seemed to engulf both her and the rose on which she'd been
working, making her feel flushed and nervous. Buying time to steady
herself, Mikki said briskly, "Oh, Guardian. Just a moment." Then she
called to Gii, "Gii, the roses in this bed will need to be staked. Would
you remind me that tomorrow we'll need to have wood cut and brought
out here?"

"Yes, Empousa," Gii called back.

Then, composed again, Mikki turned to face the Guardian. "Sorry
about that. Now, what can I do for you?"

"Dusk approaches. The women cannot be in the forest after dark."

Mikki squinted over his shoulder at the sun that was, indeed, beginning to settle into the massive canopy of the forest. "I've really lost track of time today. I keep being surprised at how late it is. You're right; it is time we stop."

"You have accomplished much, Empousa."

Mikki smiled softly. It looked like he'd gotten over being pissed at her. "That sounds like a compliment."

He bowed his head in slight acknowledgment. "Indeed."

Since he seemed to be in an agreeable mood again, Mikki said, "It would really be a help if you would check out the rest of the rose wall and let me know if there are any other parts of it that look weak. The thing is huge; it seems to stretch on forever. I want to make sure it's fertilized, but I also feel like it's important that we begin working on the roses in the gardens."

"It is logical. The garden must have your care, too. I will inspect the wall at first light."

She tried not to stare at the way the setting sun glinted red off the gleaming tips of his dark horns. "Thank you. That would definitely save me time." Then since he showed no sign of leaving, she added, "I was thinking that it would be smart to have Gii or someone draw me up a map of the gardens and then I'd divide the area up into fourths—north, south, east, west—and have each of the Elementals take their direction and a group of women, and that would be the section of the gardens they'd be responsible for fertilizing and anything else I can see they need. I'll still go from section to section supervising, but at least dividing up the area might help organize things."

"The idea has merit." He seemed about to say more and then looked away as if he changed his mind.

"What is it? Hey—I'll take any advice I can get about this. Don't worry about stepping on my toes."

His broad brow wrinkled as he looked from his thick cloven hooves to her slippered feet. Mikki burst into laughter, calling curious looks from several of the women. "No! I didn't mean that literally. It's just a saying—stepping on my toes would be you offending me because you're giving me advice when I didn't ask for it."

"Oh," he snorted. And then, amazingly, the beast laughed. It was a full, rich sound that had the women of the realm staring openly at him.

"You're not laughing because you're actually considering stepping on my toes, are you?"

"Not now that you agreed the women should leave the forest."

A joke? Was he actually kidding around with her? Well, wonders would never cease.

"Gii," she called, not taking her gaze from his. "Would you please tell the women that we are done for the day? Be sure you call the women in from the forest first. The Guardian would like to close the gate as soon as possible."

"Yes, Empousa," Gii said, sending the Guardian a nervous, sideways glance.

"Thank you, Mikado. I can never consider the realm safe while the gate remains open," he said.

Wondering if this was the right time to ask him about the specifics of the dangers in the forest, Mikki bent to reach a pair of shears she had been deadheading roses with and the slim shoulder strap of her chiton slipped down her arm. Before she could shrug it back into place, she felt a prickle of heat run the length of her arm. As if in slow motion, the beast tilted his great head and deftly hooked the tip of one slender, ebony horn beneath the linen strap and then lifted it back to its proper place over her shoulder.

Their eyes met and held.

"I'm . . . I'm not used to wearing a chiton yet," she stuttered.

"It becomes you."

"Th-thank you," she said breathlessly. Though her voice was little more than a whisper, the intensity of his dark, sensuous eyes compelled her to ask, "Is that just more of you being the Guardian and doing your duty?"

His face, which had seemed so readable just a moment before, suddenly closed down. As if remembering himself, he took a quick step away from her. His voice was clipped and he didn't look at her when he spoke. "My duty . . . yes. Caring for you is my duty."

Mikki frowned. What the hell was up with him? His mood swings were wearing her out. So was the uncomfortable silence that had settled between them. She was searching for something . . . anything to say when he finally spoke.

"I could draw the map for you, Empousa."

His voice was deep and as unreadable as his expression, but he looked at her and then quickly away, as if he had become suddenly, inexplicably nervous.

"A map?" she said stupidly and then she remembered. "Oh! A map of the gardens so I could divide the area up among the Elementals. That would be great," she said quickly. "Why don't you give me time to get things wrapped up here and get cleaned up and then you meet me on my balcony? We can discuss the map while we have dinner. You could even bring your drawing supplies and sketch something out for me."

"No!" The word rumbled from him, causing several heads to turn in their direction again. He lowered his powerful voice. "No," he repeated. "It would not be proper."

"I don't know why not," she said easily. "I have to eat; you have to eat. We need to talk about this, and the sooner the better so I can give the new directions to the handmaidens first thing in the morning." She wondered briefly at the certainty with which she felt she must push him. Did it have something to do with the callous way Gii had talked about him earlier? *It's time I stopped questioning myself and followed my gut!* she told herself firmly. "But if you really don't want to come to my balcony—which I don't understand at all because you were just there last night—I could always have dinner brought to wherever you live. We could eat there while we dis—"

"I will come to your balcony!" he said hastily.

"Good." She was careful not to show the rush of exhilaration she felt when he gave in. "But don't forget that I have to finish up here and then take a bath or something because I am definitely a mess and—"

He held up one powerful hand to cut off her words.

"Would you rather I just called for you when I'm ready?" she asked sweetly.

"Call and I will come to you."

Then he turned and stalked back to the gate.

"I think that went well," she told the Felicite Parmentier shrub.

"I would give just about anything for a long, hot soak in a whirlpool bath," Mikki said to no one in particular as the four tired handmaidens walked slowly back to the palace with her.

"Empousa, can you describe what you mean by 'whirlpool bath'?" Nera asked.

"Absolutely—and you'll like this because it definitely has to do with water." She grinned at the Water Elemental, who giggled in response. "A whirlpool bath is a large tub of warm water that bubbles around you and almost magically soothes dirty, tired muscles," Mikki sighed wistfully. "It's possible through technology, which is my old world's version of magick."

"I believe your new world can do better." Gii smiled knowingly at the other handmaidens.

Nera added, "We can certainly provide more for our Empousa than a tub of bubbling water."

"It's true," said Aeras.

"And if you would like it hotter than merely warm, I can arrange that," the Fire Elemental said mischievously.

Gii took one of her hands and Nera the other. With renewed energy, the handmaidens hurried Mikki around the side of the palace that held her chamber and the curving balcony. They walked on a path that led between two rows of ornamental shrubs that had been trimmed into cones. The path turned and almost immediately fell away to reveal a wide staircase that spiraled gently to the right. Before they had reached the bottom, Mikki felt the temperature of the air get warmer and she smelled something that was vaguely familiar . . .

The stairs emptied on a white marble landing. Mikki stepped out onto it and gasped in pleasure. "It's a hot spring!" But it was like no hot spring Mikki had ever seen. It was two levels. The first held the smallest pools—five of them, Mikki quickly counted. Each was roughly double the size of a modern whirlpool bathtub, and it was like each one had been hollowed out of the lumpy white rock by a giant ice-cream scoop. They were filled with lazily bubbling water so blue it was turquoise. From the lip of the tier, steaming water cascaded down to a larger pool. Mikki walked over to the edge and peeked down. The pool was deep and ringed by more of the white rock, and she could easily see through the clear water to the white sand of the pool's bottom.

"The upper baths are hotter than the large pool below," Nera said. "They should be perfect for soaking away your aches."

"Amazing . . ." She breathed the word on a sigh. "The only thing that would make it more perfect would be soap, clean clothes and lots of wine."

The words had no more left her mouth than the patter of feet were heard on the stairs behind them. Wordlessly, Mikki watched several young women hurry onto the landing. Some of them were carrying trays of goblets and pitchers of wine. Others' arms were filled with clean lengths of fine linen, and still others had baskets packed with delicate glass bottles, soft sponges and brushes.

Gii laughed at Mikki's expression. "Empousa, if you wish for a thing, it will appear. These women are palace servants whose sole responsibility is to be certain that Hecate's Empousa is well cared for."

"Like magick," Mikki whispered.

"Not *like* magick. It *is* magick. Your magick," Gii said, gently unpinning the brooches that held her dirty chiton precariously at her shoulders.

"So my wishes are actually commands?" Mikki asked, feeling numb with shock as the servants placed their treasures on the landing, curtseyed and disappeared back up the stairs.

"They are," Gii said.

"Good lord, what if I wish for something inappropriate?"

Gii looked searchingly into her eyes. "I believe you are too wise for that, Empousa."

She certainly hoped so. Good thing she'd be busy with hard physical labor for some time to come. Wishing for triple fudge cake late at night might not be classified as dangerously inappropriate, but without exercise, it would definitely be unwise.

Lost in thought, Mikki let the Earth Elemental unwind her from her chiton and, with a moan of pleasure, she slipped, naked, into one of the bubbling pools. Nera, Aeras and Floga had already poured five goblets to the rim with white wine the color of sunlight and dragged baskets filled with bottles and sponges over to within reach of each of the pools. Gii passed Mikki a goblet before she began to take off her own clothes.

"I'm so glad you chose this cold white instead of a red!" Floga said from the pool on Mikki's left. "I was dreaming of this very wine all afternoon."

"But I didn't . . ." Mikki began and then closed her mouth as she realized that, yes, she had been picturing in her mind a cold, refreshing white wine when she'd spoken. *Unbelievable . . .*

The icy wine was a wonderful contrast to the hot, bubbly water, and Mikki shivered in pleasure. She rested back against the smooth side of the pool and gazed at the beauty that spread before her. The springs were situated on the rear of the cliff on which the palace had been built. The view was spectacular. Mikki looked out across an area of the gardens filled with what appeared to be all the same type of rose. They had been planted in beds that each formed a spiraling circle, and even though Mikki knew that they, too, had to be sick, it seemed that these roses were greener and healthier than those in the rest of the realm. Beyond the beds of roses, she could see the thick multiflora hedge, and past it the forest. The sun had already sunk beneath the leafy horizon, but the sky still held its dying colors. Mikki sipped her wine and let her eyes linger on the circular rose beds, appreciating the symmetry and style of the unique beds. She could just make out the hint of some blossoms, and it even seemed that a few of them had bloomed. They were scarlet, with a touch of gold at the base . . .

Mikki sat straight up, causing water to slosh over the smooth, white rocks around the pool.

"I wondered when you would notice," Gii said softly.

"Have these beds always been filled with the Mikado Rose?"

"No. They change with each new Empousa. This area of the gardens is sacred to Hecate's High Priestesses. If you look carefully, you will see that in the middle of the central bed there is a small temple. It is your private shrine, a place in which you will never be disturbed."

A sudden thought drifted through Mikki's mind like smoke, and almost without meaning to, she asked the question. "Where is the Guardian's lair?"

"The entrance is beneath these springs. Hecate fashioned it there so his protection would never be far from her Empousa."

Mikki could hear the frown in Gii's voice, and she turned to look at the handmaiden. "You don't like him."

"It is illogical to like or dislike him. He is a beast. It is simply his duty to protect the realm—his sole purpose for being." Gii sounded unusually terse.

"She's worried that he will err again and cause the realm to become bespelled once more," Floga said.

Mikki noticed that the Fire Elemental's expression was as cold and disapproving as her voice.

"You sound like you're worried about that, too," Mikki said.

"I am."

"And are the rest of you?" She looked from Nera to Aeras. Both Elementals nodded quick agreement.

"Okay, what exactly did the Guardian do that made Hecate so angry?" Mikki asked, wondering why she felt so damn annoyed at the handmaidens and so damn defensive of the Guardian.

When no one answered, she turned back to Gii. The handmaiden squirmed and wouldn't meet her eyes. Mikki sighed. "Will you please tell me what in the hell is going on? I mean, how terrible can it be? Hecate did finally let him return."

Gii's gaze rose to meet Mikki's. Her eyes were bright and round with unshed tears. "I cannot tell you, Mikado."

"You've got to be kidding! Why in the world can't you tell me?"

"Forgive me—forgive us, but we are not permitted to speak of it. We shouldn't have said as much as we did." Tears spilled down the little Elemental's cheeks.

"Please don't be angry, Empousa," Nera said.

"She tells you only the truth, Empousa," Aeras cried. "We have been forbidden to speak of it."

"Gii is right; I should never have mentioned it. Hecate commanded that it remain in the past. We may not speak of it ever again," Floga said.

"Well, how about the Guardian? Will he talk about it?"

"Oh, Empousa, no!" Gii's face, which had been flushed from the bath, suddenly drained of its color. "You must not speak of the past with him!" The other Elementals echoed her with horrified No's of their own.

"Okay, okay! I won't ask him. It's all right, Gii, please don't cry. Let's just forget I said anything about it." Mikki hastily assured her, hating that she had caused the young women to become so upset. "Here, help me figure out which of these bottles holds what. I don't want to accidentally pour oil instead of shampoo on my hair."

Sniffing and wiping her eyes, Gii pointed out the soaps and oils in Mikki's basket. Mikki only half listened to her. Her thoughts kept circling around unanswered questions. Even after the warnings she still wanted to ask the Guardian what had happened. Not tonight, of course. Not so soon. But what if she got to know him better? Today he had actually smiled and joked with her. And touched her . . . she shivered, remembering how his horn had prickled the skin of her arm and how his eyes had seemed to see into her soul.

Admit it. He totally intrigues you.

It was true, but she squelched the thought, pulling her mind from the beast to the mystery that surrounded the realm he guarded. Hecate couldn't honestly expect her to live here and *not* want to find out what had happened that caused the sequence of events that led to her becoming the goddess's Empousa. Maybe the truth was that Hecate didn't want her to hear about it secondhand, like common gossip, and that was why she had forbidden the handmaidens to talk about it. Gii hadn't specifically said that the Guardian had been forbidden, too; she'd just freaked out and said not to ask him about the past. Well, it was obvious that the handmaidens, as well as the other women in the realm, tip-toed around the Guardian, vacillating between treating him like a rabid dog and a god.

She didn't think of him as either.

Mikki uncapped the cork from the bottle Gii had said was shampoo and poured a generous amount of it into her hair. As the night cooled, steam from the pools lifted in thickening waves, veiling each bather in warm mist. In a world of her own, Mikki inhaled deeply, noting that the soap was the same fragrance as the exotic perfume the old woman had given her. She finished washing and rinsing her hair and uncapped the other bottles, too. All of it—the soap, shampoo and oil—were the same rich fragrance.

"It is the anointing scent of the Empousa. None other may ever wear it."

As each woman sipped wine and bathed herself, the pools had grown still, and Floga's voice startled her. Mikki peered at her through the steam and noted that the Fire Elemental's expression was odd—it was almost as if she looked angry.

"Do you wish you could wear it, Floga?" Mikki asked pointedly, lowering her voice so her words were for Floga alone.

The handmaiden instantly looked chagrined. "No, Empousa! Of course not," she whispered.

But as the handmaiden turned away, avoiding her eyes, Mikki wondered . . .

CHAPTER NINETEEN

"NO, thank you, Gii. I'll be fine. I'm going to eat a quick dinner and go straight to bed. I'm totally exhausted, and tomorrow will be another busy day." Mikki smiled brightly, telling herself she wasn't really lying to Gii. She was just failing to tell her everything.

"But, Empousa, are you quite sure you wouldn't like me to help you into your nightdress?"

"No need." Mikki glanced down at the simple yet elegant butter-colored dress. "I think I'm finally getting the hang of the way these chitons wrap."

Gii smiled, "Did it serve as proper work attire for you today?"

"Actually, it did." And Mikki meant it. After some initial awkwardness at getting used to tucking in the trailing skirts, she found that the outfit was comfortable and easy to work in, even if it had required some help from the Guardian to stay on straight. Actually, maybe it was because it had required his help that she liked it so much . . .

"So you like it better than the . . . jens?"

"Jeans." Mikki laughed, forced her thoughts back to the girl beside her and gave Gii an impulsive hug. "You know, I think I do like chitons better than jeans."

Gii returned the hug with an affectionate squeeze. "Then rest well, Empousa."

"You, too, Gii. Why don't I call you and the other handmaidens as soon as I wake up, and we'll all have breakfast together? I have some new ideas I want to discuss with you."

"As you wish, Empousa." Gii curtseyed, and then skipped lightly to the balcony steps and away into the night.

Alone at last, Mikki had time to be nervous about the next part of the evening. As it had been last night, the little table was placed just outside the glass doors to her bedroom. It was, again, laden with meats and cheeses, bread and wine. Only one place had been set, but tonight there were two chairs instead of one.

Mikki frowned. He wasn't going to get away with this. She'd invited him to dinner, and dinner it would be.

She closed her eyes and thought about the servants who had magickally appeared when she'd wished for wine and soap and clean clothes. "I need another place setting. Please," she said.

In less time than she could count to ten, she heard two sharp knocks on her bedroom door. She stuck her head inside her room and called for them to come in, and one of the women she recognized from the hot spring hurried in, carrying a tray on which was another complete place setting. Mikki met her halfway across the room.

"I appreciate you coming so quickly." Mikki held out her hands for the tray.

"I apologize, Empousa. Had I known you were not dining alone, I would have made certain the table was already set for two."

"Don't worry about it. Actually, these are last-minute plans," Mikki said quickly, hoping the servants could just tell when she wanted something and not when she was lying. "I'll take it from here."

The woman looked confused, but she nodded. "Of course, Empousa. Shall we bring you more food and wine?"

"No. There's plenty. No need to bother."

"It is never a bother to serve you, Empousa."

Mikki reminded herself not to sigh. It might not be a bother for them to serve her, but she could already tell that such diligent service could very easily become bothersome.

Changing tactics, Mikki asked her, "What is your name?"

The servant blinked in surprise. "Daphne."

"Daphne—that's pretty."

The servant blushed.

"Daphne, I'll be fine carrying this to the table myself." She took the tray from the disconcerted Daphne. "But I'll definitely need you in the morning. I'm going to have breakfast with the four Elementals. Could you be sure to bring enough for all of us?"

"Yes, Empousa."

"Wonderful! Now, you and, um, the rest of the women can relax tonight. I won't need anything else." Daphne opened her mouth for what Mikki felt sure would be a protest, so she added firmly, "Good night, Daphne. I'll see you in the morning when I call for breakfast."

Reluctantly, Daphne curtseyed and left the room.

"A pain in the ass . . ." Mikki muttered to herself as she set the table. "All this 'Yes, Empousa, what can I do for you, Empousa?' might sound like a good idea in theory. In practice it is a pain in the ass." *Of course it probably wouldn't be if I wasn't sneaking around like a teenager meeting a thug boyfriend against her parents' rules.* "I'm not a teenager," she told her reflection as she brushed through her drying hair. "And he is not my boyfriend. This is no different from a business dinner." She pressed a hand against her fluttering stomach. "So stop being so damn nervous!"

The table was ready. She was ready—or as ready as she was going to be. Mikki walked to the balcony and sat down. She put her hands in her lap, closed her eyes, and thought about the Guardian . . .

. . . The way he had kept such careful watch over the women today . . . his laugh . . . the heat of his body when he was near her . . . his touch . . . and how alone he'd looked disappearing into the shadow of the tree instead of being included in one of their groups at lunch . . .

"Empousa, you look sad. Is anything amiss?"

She opened her eyes. He was standing, just outside the pool of light cast by the candelabrum that sat on the table.

"I'm not sad. I was just concentrating. I'm not used to calling someone by just thinking about him."

"It is a gift given to each Empousa by Hecate."

"Oh, I appreciate it—it'll just take some getting used to." She motioned to the chair at the other end of the table. "Please, join me. I don't think I realized how hungry I was until just now when I smelled this food."

He stepped from the shadows slowly, as if giving her time to readjust to the sight of him. Mikki realized that she shouldn't stare—that she was being rude. But he was such an incredible being she couldn't just smile and make polite conversation and pretend like each new sight of him didn't send shockwaves through her mind. In the silence, his hooves rang against the marble, pulling her gaze down. He was wearing another short, military-looking outfit, which left much of his muscular legs bare. She noted that except for the fact that they were covered with a coat of slick fur, his legs were fashioned more like a human man than an animal. The leather breastplate molded to his chest and abdomen so it clearly outlined the definition of his muscles, which were completely manlike. *No*, Mikki mentally corrected herself, *no normal man could have a chest like that. He's not stone anymore, but he looks like he could have been carved from marble.*

She realized he'd reached the table and stopped and was just standing there, letting her study him. Mikki felt her face heat with an embarrassed blush.

"What is that called?" she blurted, trying to cover for her rude staring.

"Empousa?" His wide brow wrinkled in confusion.

"That leather top you wear. I'm new to all of this." She lifted an edge of her own clothing. "It was just this morning that Gii taught me that this is called a chiton. So I was curious about what yours is called." She didn't think she sounded too terribly moronic. Maybe.

He looked down at himself and then back at her. "It is a warrior's cuirasse."

"Cuirasse," she repeated the word. "Is it over a chiton?"

"No, this is a short tunic. A warrior would not wear a chiton into battle."

Because his expression seemed to tell her she was amusing him, she pointed to his bare legs. "I'd think you'd need more covering for battle."

His face hardened. "I would, were I a man. For protection, Greek men go into battle with leather enemides strapped on their legs from ankle to knee." He lifted one massive hoof and set it down with a heavy, dangerous sound. "I do not require such protection."

A little tremor that was fear mixed with fascination shivered over her skin. She looked into his dark eyes and was immensely proud that her voice sounded perfectly normal. "Huh. Built-in protection like that must come in handy in your line of work."

"Being Hecate's Guardian is not my work; it is my life."

Mikki forced a little nonchalant laugh and started to lift a slice of cold meat onto her plate. "You have no idea how many men in my old world say that about their jobs."

"I am not a man," he growled.

This time Mikki did sigh. Deliberately, she put down her fork and met his gaze. "I'm well aware of that. Just like I imagine that you—as well as the rest of the inhabitants of this realm—are well aware that I'm not like any other Empousa. But am I all prickly about it? No. Do I feel the need to constantly remind you that I'm probably a good twenty years older than the norm, and that I'm totally confused by almost everything surrounding me? No. For two reasons: one, because it's annoying and, two, because bemoaning the fact won't change a damn thing. I mean, I could complain constantly about wanting to be taller or thinner, but that wouldn't ever change the fact that I'm five-seven and weigh"—she hesitated and reconsidered—"ten pounds more than I wish I did." She pointed to the chair with a sharp, frustrated motion. "Now would you please sit down and have some dinner. I'm hungry, and when I'm hungry I get grumpy. So let's eat."

To her surprise, he didn't snarl at her or whirl away. He sat.

Mikki picked up the fork and resumed loading her plate with a variety of the delicious selection of meat and cheese. Tonight they had added dark, flavorful olives and roasted sweet peppers as well as fresh, plump figs. She glanced up when she realized he was still just sitting there. Mikki raised one brow at him.

"I am unaccustomed to eating in the company of others," he said slowly.

She didn't have to ask him why. Gii had already answered that question for her. The rest of the realm saw him as a beast, little more than a walking, talking animal. Even the goddess herself had reminded her sternly that he had not ever been, nor would he ever be, a man.

Well, Mikki was different. No, he wasn't a man, but he wasn't an animal, either.

"Where I'm from it's mean-spirited to make someone eat alone while everyone else excludes him."

"And you are not mean-spirited, Mikado."

He didn't phrase it as a question, but she answered anyway. "No. Sometimes I'm selfish and stubborn, and even cynical, but I can promise you that I've never been mean-spirited."

As she spoke, something in his face changed. It was like she had somehow peeled away a protective layer that he kept wrapped around himself, leaving him terribly, unexpectedly, vulnerable. She remembered that awful, lonely roar she'd heard echoing from a dead statue all the way through a modern world and into her dreams. Mikki wanted to reach out and touch him, to tell him that everything would be okay, but she was suddenly afraid, and not of the fantastic beast who sat so awkwardly across the table from her. Mikki was afraid of herself.

She looked away from the raw emotion revealed in his eyes and busied herself arranging the food on her plate. Soon she heard the clanks and rattlings of cutlery, which told her that he, too, was filling his plate. Mikki filled her goblet with the cold white wine that was beading its pitcher and was pleased that it was the same excellent wine she'd had earlier at the springs. She glanced up at the Guardian.

"Wine?"

He nodded, and she poured. Then she lifted her own goblet and smiled.

"To the roses," she said.

The Guardian hesitated. He made a small gesture with his hand and spoke a single word under his breath. Then he, too, raised his goblet. His powerful hand engulfed the delicate crystal, and he held it awkwardly, as if he was afraid of crushing it.

"To our new Empousa," he said.

When she lifted the glass to her lips, she saw the perfect white rose blossom floating in the sea of wine. It hadn't been there before; he'd made it appear—for her. Mikki closed her eyes and drank, inhaling the sweet perfume that was the perfect accompaniment to the crispness of the liquid.

Later, she would remember it as the moment she began to fall in love with the beast.

Chapter Twenty

SHE'D wanted dinner to be easy and casual, but in truth, there were several awkward moments. The Guardian was silent and clearly self-conscious and uncomfortable. Which made total sense. He always ate alone. The entire realm considered him an animal, an outsider. How was he supposed to know anything about polite dinner conversation?

She was careful not to stare at him, because whenever she looked his way, he quit eating. Trying to make him more comfortable, she dispensed with the niceties of using knife and fork and picked up the meat and cheese with her fingers, purposefully chewing more noisily than was her norm. Still, he sat stiff and silent, eating little and drinking only when her attention was elsewhere.

Mikki glanced across the table and awkwardly met his eyes, then looked away quickly, for what seemed like the thousandth time. Too bad they didn't have a TV they could sit in front of or, at the very least, other diners they could eavesdrop on. He needed something to get his mind off the fact that he was sitting at dinner with her. And then she had it!

"The map of the gardens," she said. "While we're eating, you could sketch one for me." Her mind was racing. "I'll bet those little servants who bring dinner and such could scare up some paper and a pencil." She'd stand by the door and not let them come in her room. They wouldn't even know he was here.

"I created it while I awaited your call." He held out one massive hand and spoke a word that sounded like a growl mixed with vowels, and a rolled-up parchment burst into being in his hand. He offered it to Mikki, and she took it from him gingerly, half afraid it would disappear at her touch.

"You know, it's amazing the way you can make things appear like that." She cleared her throat and, only half kidding, added, "Could you teach me to do it?" It didn't seem possible, but in this world, who knew?

"I'm afraid you must be born the child of a Titan to have the ability to conjure inanimate objects."

"That's too bad. It'd come in handy to be able to conjure up a hoe or pruning shears whenever I needed them instead of lugging them around."

His lips tilted up in the hint of a smile. "But I do not have the ability to call the Elements to me, or to cast Hecate's sacred circle."

She smiled. "There are definitely good things about being Empousa."

"Agreed." He lifted his wineglass to her again, and this time seemed more at ease holding the crystal goblet.

Mikki pushed some of the dishes to the edge of the table, making room for the wide parchment paper. She unrolled the Guardian's map and placed four of the smaller plates at each of its corners so she could study it. It was all done in what looked like quill and ink. He'd drawn a thick, wide, spherically shaped circle, which clearly represented the rose wall boundary. Within the boundary, created with amazing attention to detail, was the garden's blueprint. The palace was placed in the north. He'd even sketched in the southern-facing balcony on which they sat, as well as the cliff behind the palace where the springs were located and the unique beds of roses it looked out on, which were Mikki's private gardens.

Hecate's Temple was drawn in as a domed shape, with the enormous fountain beside it, which Mikki could see was, indeed, situated in the geographical center of the gardens. Spiraling out, like spokes on a wheel, he'd drawn bed after bed of roses nestling within a labyrinthine series of interwoven pathways.

She had expected the crude map equivalent of a stick-figure drawing, but he'd created something filled with detail and rich with beauty. Completely caught off-guard, she looked from the map to the creature who had drawn it with such obvious care and unexpected talent.

"Guardian, this map is wonderful! Not only does it have everything on it, so I can easily divide it into fourths and show the handmaidens exactly which area of the gardens I want each of them to be responsible for, but it's a great resource for me. Now I don't have to worry about not knowing my way around." She couldn't help looking at his hands, which more closely resembled massive paws than an artist's delicate tools. "How did you do it?"

For a moment he didn't answer and then, slowly, he lifted his left hand. It was man-shaped, but bigger, with thicker, more powerful fingers than even what she imagined would be normal for a pro football linebacker.

"They're really more dexterous than they look," he said. "I have spent centuries learning to wield them."

Spreading his fingers, his hand quivered, and from each fingernail bed a long, pointed, talonlike claw extended.

"Shit on a shingle!" she gasped.

He barked a rough laugh. "Is that a curse?"

She drew her spine up straight. "Yes. A very bad one. I should watch my language, but you . . ." Her words ran out and she could only gaze at the five dangerous knives his fingers had become.

"I frightened you," he finished for her.

"No," she said quickly. "You didn't scare me, you just surprised me." She met his eyes. "May I touch them?"

"Yes . . ." The word rumbled from deep within his chest.

She touched one of the gleaming claws. "You're like Wolverine."

"I'm like a small, mean-tempered animal?"

"No." Fascinated, she stared at the claw. It felt cold and hard against the pad of her finger. "It's the name of a fictional character who was created for something called comic books in my old world. Actually, he probably was named after the animal. He's a man who has special abilities. One of which is that he can make claws come out of his hands, like you can."

The Guardian didn't take his eyes from his hands, where she was still tracing his claw with the soft warmth of her finger.

"And is this Wolverine a demon, shunned and rejected by the rest of the comic book characters?"

"He seems to get himself in more than his share of trouble, but he's really a man with a good heart who tries hard to do the right thing." She finally raised her eyes to his. "After you get to know him you understand that the only demon within him is the one he imagines in his own imperfections." Mikki couldn't look away from him. His dark eyes devoured her sense of reason. Reality bent until it wasn't important what he was, as long as he kept looking at her like that—like she was his world.

With a little tremor, she felt his claws retract and she realized that her hand was resting within his. With a nervous laugh, she pulled her hand quickly to her side. "So you actually use your claws as quills?"

"Yes, Empousa." His expression hardened into unreadable lines again.

Mikki's stomach clenched. She didn't want him to retreat from her, so before she sat back down she reached over and placed her hand gently on his forearm. His eyes shot to hers, but he didn't speak, nor did he pull away from her touch.

"Thank you for this beautiful map. It is exactly what I need to organize the women tomorrow."

"You are most welcome, Empousa."

She smiled and then returned to her chair. "I wish you would call me Mikki. I like being High Priestess, but there are times when I just want to be me."

"If you would not mind," his deep voice rumbled between them, "I would prefer to call you Mikado. It is a lovely rose, and I find that it reminds me of you."

She felt a thrill of pleasure at his compliment. "I don't mind. I like the way my name sounds when you say it—like there's some kind of secret hidden within the word."

"Perhaps there is," he said.

"Perhaps . . ." she said. She was falling into his gaze again, losing herself . . .

"I should go," he said abruptly, breaking their gaze and beginning to stand.

"Not yet!" Leaning forward, she caught his hand and felt the jolt that went through him when their flesh touched. "Stay a little longer and have one more glass of wine with me." When he relaxed back into his chair, she reluctantly released his hand and then busied herself re-filling both of their wine goblets. "I know I should be exhausted, and my body is, but my mind keeps going around and around with all the things I need to do tomorrow and all the things I should have gotten done today."

"You accomplished much today. You should be pleased."

"I am. I'm just impatient to get to work on the rest of the gardens."

He nodded. "It is important that the roses heal and thrive. They are the foundation of our realm and its strength. It is dangerous for them to be unwell."

"Can you tell me what it is in the forest that you're so worried about?" she asked quietly.

"Dream Stealers."

"That's what Hecate called them, too, but I have no idea what that means. All I know is that you and she, and by the way the women who went into the forest stayed quiet and frightened looking, everyone in this realm believes they're dangerous. I get that, but I don't get what they are."

"Dream Stealers take different forms, depending upon their victim. That is one reason they are so dangerous. The face they would show you would be different from the one they would show one of your hand-maidens."

"So they're physical beings?"

"They can take physical forms, yes." He paused and studied her carefully. "In your old world, there must have been Dream Stealers. Perhaps they just chose to personify yet another form there."

She thought about the young gang members who were regulars in the ER until they inevitably ended up in the morgue or the state penitentiary—about the statistics that reported Oklahoma as one of the states with the largest number of teen pregnancies, as well as reports of child abuse—and about the ridiculously high number of Oklahoma women who lived in poverty.

"You're right. There are Dream Stealers in my old world. Young men throw away their lives; girls repeat cycles of abuse until they can see no way out; terrible things happen every day."

"And what causes those things to happen? What is at the heart of those tragedies?"

"Hatred, ignorance, apathy," she said.

"Exactly. And those are just some of the Dream Stealers that lurk in the forest of the crossroads between worlds. If they would enter our realm, they would be able to not simply destroy people's lives, but the dreams on which generations survive."

"You'll keep them out, won't you?"

"I have sworn a life oath to do so."

"You should have told me all this earlier." Mikki shivered, feeling sick at the thought that she'd insisted he open the gate and let the women go into the forest. "No, it's not your fault. You tried to tell me that it was dangerous; I should have listened to you."

"You did what you believed was best for the roses. No harm was done; I was there to guard the gate. I will always be there to guard the gate."

"But if those things are in the forest, why is there a gate at all? Shouldn't we seal it up and be sure it's never opened again?"

"We cannot. Mikado, not everything in the forest is evil. You should know that even dreams must be tempered with reality from time to time. Our reality comes from the forest and the threads of reality that drift there from the worlds beyond."

"First thing tomorrow you'll check all the rest of the hedge to be sure no other area has been weakened by the roses being sick?"

"I will. You may rest easily, Mikado. The realm is safe under my protection."

She knew what he said was the truth—she knew it because she felt it deep within her blood. All her intuition told her that this incredible man-beast would give his life to keep the Realm of the Rose, and its Empousa, safe.

"Thank you."

This time instead of bristling at her appreciation, he simply bowed his head slightly.

For a while they sipped their wine, each lost in their own thoughts.

"May I ask you another question?" Mikki said.

"You may." He was looking at her with an open, interested expression.

"When I asked you if you could teach me to conjure things, you said you couldn't because only someone born of a Titan had that ability. Just exactly who were your parents?"

He didn't respond to her question for a long time, weighing whether he should tell her his story, or whether he should stay silent and remain a mystery to her—a mystery that she would eventually tire of trying to solve.

The thought made him feel crushingly alone.

When he began to speak, his powerful voice was unusually subdued, and he could not look at her. Instead, he stared blankly out into the night.

"My father is the Titan Cronos. One day he visited the ancient island of Crete and was struck by more than the beauty of the land amidst sea. He saw and instantly fell in love with the fair Pasiphea. But she was no mindless maiden. Pasiphea knew that mortals who become lovers of the gods usually come to tragic endings, so she refused the Titan. Cronos was not dissuaded by her rejection—he waited and watched. When Minos, king of Crete, chose Pasiphea as his bride, my father saw his opportunity. On Minos's wedding night, he drugged the king and took his likeness, as well as his bride's virginity. Minos was fooled, as was Pasiphea. But Cronos's wife, Rhea, was not. She suspected her husband's infidelity and confronted Cronos. He denied loving Pasiphea. And in truth, he did not lie. Once he'd sated his desire for the mortal woman, his love faded. Still, Rhea was not satisfied. She watched Pasiphea, discovering that the new bride was pregnant. In a fit of jealous anger, Rhea cursed Pasiphea's child. If, indeed, it was the son of a Titan, the child would be born not man or god, but an abomination, a creature like none other in the ancient world. That is how I came into being."

"You *are* what the myth of the Minotaur was based on!"

Bottomless and empty, his eyes found hers. "That is the name Minos gave me. He loathed me from the moment I was born."

"And your mother?"

"Pasiphea was kinder than her husband. She even used to secretly visit me, and I remember when I was young, she sometimes sang me to sleep." He paused, struggling to control his emotions.

"Your mother loved you."

He flinched and felt as if her words physically hurt him. "I like to believe that she tried to love me. She named me Asterius, refusing to call me by the name Minos had given me, but even in her kindness she could not forget that I was a beast. She knew that because of my monstrous form, Cronos had somehow been successful in entering her bed, the very thought of which was abhorrent to her. The sight of me was a constant reminder that the Titan had tricked her and invaded her body. So she persuaded Minos to build an enormous labyrinth, saying that in the center of it was where he should hide the fortunes of Crete, and that I would guard it for him. The labyrinth on Crete is where I lived, away from my mother's eyes and those who would hunt me for sport. It is where I would still be today if not for Hecate."

"My God! They tell stories about you. Stories that say maidens and boys were sacrificed to you."

The stunned expression on her face made him feel hot and cold at the same time.

"You should know that I have not always been as I am now. Before I answered Hecate's summons, I was as Rhea cursed me to be—an abomination, of both body and soul. When I pledged myself to the goddess, she lifted Rhea's curse and gave me the heart and soul of a man, though there was nothing even the Great Goddess could do to alter my physical form."

His hand was resting on the table near the open map. The Empousa reached out and put hers on top of his. He looked down at her hand.

"I don't see an abomination when I look at you," Mikki told him.

"Perhaps you should look deeper. There is still a beast within me."

"I'd like to believe in the man, if you'll let me, Asterius."

"The man . . ." His words were barely audible. He looked from her hand into her eyes. "The man hears you, Mikado, even if it seems your voice is speaking from his dreams."

"Maybe I am." She smiled softly. "You and I have been in each other's dreams before."

He turned her hand over in his and let his thumb trace the delicate lifeline that bisected her palm, following it until it met the pulse point at her wrist. Then, with a caress softer than the brush of a butterfly's wings, he smoothed his thumb in sensuous circles over her pulse.

"I can feel the beat of your heart," he murmured.

"Can you feel that it's beating faster?"

He lifted his eyes to hers. "I can." Her face was so close to his that he could feel the warmth of her breath on his skin. Her eyes had gone soft and her lips were parted. He wanted to taste her! He wanted to drink her in and lose himself in her sweetness. With a low growl he bent his head, replacing his thumb with his lips. He could feel her life's blood pulsing, and he tasted the salt of her skin. She shivered under his touch, and he let his lips move to the delicate indentation of her elbow. Then he lifted his head. Her breathing had deepened, and she was staring at him with wide, liquid eyes. Before reason and common sense could make him change his mind, he leaned forward and touched his lips to hers. She made a little gasping sound that seemed to call to his soul, and he deepened the kiss.

Pain lanced through his body. His blood had turned to white-hot lava, and it pounded with ferocious intensity within him. For a moment he was so disoriented that his claws automatically shot from his skin and he bared his teeth in a snarl, ready for the stealthy enemy that had attacked him. Then he understood. Hecate's spell!

The Empousa did not love him; therefore, her passion would not be allowed.

He raised tortured eyes to hers. Mikado looked pale and shocked, and she had scooted back in her chair as far away from him as she could get.

Abruptly, he stood, knocking over his chair and causing the little table to rock dangerously. "This was unwise. I should not be here with you."

"What's wrong? What's happened? You look like you're in terrible pain."

She reached one hand hesitantly toward him, but he lurched away from her, not able to bear her gesture of kindness.

"You must not touch me!"

"Okay!" She dropped her hand shakily to her side. "I won't touch you. Just sit down and tell me what's going on."

"No." He took another step back. "I should have obeyed your command to create the map, delivered it to you, and returned to my lair."

"I didn't command you to make the map. I asked you to, just like I asked you to have dinner with me. You didn't do anything wrong—*we* didn't do anything wrong," she said, looking utterly confused by his sudden change.

"That is where you are mistaken. You did nothing wrong, but I did. Today I began to twist the threads of reality into a waking dream, something that, even in this realm of dreams and magick, is as impossible as it is dangerous. This cannot happen again."

The Guardian flung himself from the balcony. With the agility of a beast and the power of a god, he distanced himself from her, and as he did the pain in his body subsided, leaving him exhausted and empty.

So this was what his life had come to. This was what it was to be.

He was a man within a beast, tethered by a goddess. He was to know desire but not surcease. Like Tantalus, he was to live in torment—his relief in sight, but unattainable. Asterius stumbled to a halt, threw back his head and roared his agony to the deaf heavens.

CHAPTER TWENTY-ONE

MIKKI woke up with a headache and puffy, red eyes. Yawning and stretching, she walked to the wall of windows and opened the door. The sun was just starting to peek over the horizon, and the morning was so cool she could see her breath. Someone had already cleared away all the dishes from dinner. It made Mikki sad, as if the night before, the good along with the bad, had been wiped away without a trace. She walked over to the chair in which he had sat, her fingers lingering on the back of it.

Asterius . . .

He'd never be just the Guardian to her again, not after what he'd told her last night, and not after what she'd seen in his eyes—a soul-deep loneliness, and, for just a moment, a longing that struck an answering cord within her.

But it didn't matter that he'd given her a glimpse of his soul. Nothing could come of it. And not just because of the obvious—that he was a beast, or, more accurately, he was a creature, a mixture of mortal and god, a being like no other, as he had explained last night. *Asterius* . . . No. It wasn't because of the obvious; the obvious mattered less and less to her. If she was honest with herself, she'd have to admit that, even back in Tulsa when he'd first begun to seduce her in her dreams, his appearance hadn't been a deterrent. The truth was quite the opposite. His appearance had been a fascination from the beginning.

It was impossible between them because he was making it that way. It was as if there was some kind of unwritten rule that no one was allowed to get close to him. He'd touched her—kissed her—clearly desired her. Yet he'd run from her as if she was the one who was dangerous. His behavior was confusing and just plain annoying.

Mikki rubbed at her eyes again. Okay, maybe it *was* a rule. Maybe no one was allowed to be close to him. The smart thing to do would be to talk to Hecate about him. To ask the goddess about . . . about . . . about what? Did she really want to ask the imposing Hecate if it was okay that her new Empousa had a crush on the man-beast that was her Guardian? Please. Mikki wasn't an idiot. It wasn't okay. Asterius had made that clear. If she asked the goddess outright and Hecate commanded her to stay away from him, then what would she do? She'd have to keep her distance from him. Wouldn't she?

Better not to ask at all.

Was she actually considering pursuing him, even after what had happened between them the night before? Yes. Yes, she was. Mikki had no idea where it would take them, but she couldn't forget the physical jolt that passed through his body when she'd touched him. She rubbed her wrist absently, remember the heat of his lips. And beyond his physical magnetism, she'd seen the vast loneliness that seemed to shadow his every unguarded expression, even as he rejected her touch. *But he's so used to being treated like an abomination that maybe his rejection is more about fear and habit than the desire to push me away.*

She needed to think more about where she was heading. She needed to think more about Asterius. Mikki shivered as the early morning breeze whipped through her sheer nightdress. The hot springs would be all dreamy and steamy on a cool morning like this . . . what better place to think?

Before she started down the balcony stairs to follow the path around the side of the palace, Mikki closed her eyes and sent Daphne a quick thought.

MIKADO was thinking about him as she bathed. He could sense it—feel it. Not because she was calling to him. It was nothing that specific. She was just *thinking* about him. He shouldn't be able to sense it. He shouldn't know. But he did.

This had never before happened. In all the eons he had been Hecate's Guardian, and all the generations of her Empousas who had presided as High Priestess within the realm, he had never felt the thoughts of one of Hecate's chosen.

Just as he had never felt the gentleness of any Empousa's touch. Not even the priestess he had loved . . . and who he thought might possibly have loved him in return. No woman had ever touched him caressingly. He only had a vague recollection of his mother sneaking into the labyrinth a few times. One of those times he thought he remembered her touching his cheek. But it had been so long ago and such a brief caress. Yet this woman, this mortal from the mundane world, had not just touched him willingly. She had accepted his caress in return; she had shivered beneath his lips.

The touch of a woman . . . such a small, ordinary thing, really. Mortals and gods alike thought little of it. They touched on greeting and on parting. They touched as they laughed and talked. They touched when they loved. Yes, such a small, ordinary thing . . . unless it had been a thing denied. How he had longed for the kindness of a woman's touch to soothe the beast within and without.

Mikado's touch had undone him.

His moan of frustration changed to a rumbling growl as he propelled himself from his sleeping pallet. She had called him Asterius and said she believed in the man within the monster. Then she had allowed him to kiss her! Surely she meant nothing more than kindness. She couldn't realize that her touch and her words were seducing the man as well as calling the beast to her. His hooves cut into the marble floor of his lair as he paced. She couldn't know how desperately he had wanted to kneel at her feet and beg her never to stop touching him . . . thinking of him . . . talking to him as if she truly did believe in his humanity.

And then what? In the spring she must be sacrificed. In despair, he looked down at his hands as his claws extended. He could still feel the softness of her skin against their razorlike tips. Would he allow her to escape, as he had the deceiver who had come before her? No. He could not. The roses were sick, and he had little doubt as to why. Their last Empousa had fled without completing her destiny. What would happen to the realm if this one did the same?

He knew what would happen. It wouldn't survive.

If he would be the only one to pay the price, he would gladly do so. He knew it for truth, even though the thought shamed him. It meant he was willing to betray his goddess again. But no matter how desperately he longed for Mikado, he would not allow his own desires to cause the destruction of the Realm of the Rose.

His growl deepened, and he had to fight against the urge to rend and tear. The man within him held the beast at bay, but only just. The ache and yearning for the impossible that caused his emotions to be in turmoil also roused the monster within. She might believe in the man, but he was joined with the beast—they were one in the same. If she stirred the man, the beast roused. He had to remember that no matter how sweetly she may speak his true name, or how sweetly she might touch him and let him touch her, she would be imagining the man. What would happen when she realized that she was seducing the beast, too?

She would reject him. Anything else was only a dream. And he, of all creatures, knew how insubstantial dreams really were. He must forget the dream and deal in reality, which was what he did best.

And none of this mattered. He could not love her—he could barely touch her without feeling the raging pain of Hecate's spell.

Asterius's head suddenly lifted and his eyes widened. That was it! He didn't have to hold the beast at bay. The goddess had tethered the monster for him. He could stay as close to Mikado as she would allow; the goddess's spell would ensure that he never went too far . . . all he need do would be to bear some pain. When it became too much, too unendurable . . . he remembered the feel of her skin against his lips and her small hand within his. Yes, he could endure a taste of the goddess's punishment for the miracle that was the touch of Mikado's skin.

If she allowed him near her again. He resumed his frustrated pacing. After the way he'd left her last night it would be understandable if she avoided his company completely.

But perhaps she would not always avoid him. She was so different, so unlike any of the other women. She had asked him if he would seal the gate! No other Empousa would ever have asked such a thing. Of course, she didn't know her fate. Didn't know that her only escape from it was through the rose gate and back to the world of the mundane that lay beyond the forest. Part of his mind whispered that even if she knew, she might still choose to stay for the roses . . . for him . . .

He went to the mouth of his lair. The sun was calling the sky awake with young tendrils of light. He could feel Mikado's thoughts slide away from him as she left the baths and then he could no longer feel her at all. He imagined that she was preparing to summon the Elementals and begin her day. He, too, must begin his. She had asked him to inspect the rose wall, and her request had been a wise one. He left his lonely lair and began his solitary trek along the boundary between worlds.

Choosing to remain invisible, Hecate watched her Guardian. His powerful stride was weary, and she clearly saw the strain of conflicted emotions in his dark, expressive eyes. The goddess smiled and let her hand absently caress the head of one of her great hounds.

"It goes well . . ." she whispered.

"SEE how I've divided the gardens into fourths?" Mikki had hated to tamper at all with Asterius's map, but it was necessary that everything be clear for the Elementals, so she'd had Daphne bring her a quill and some ink, and she'd drawn her own considerably less-attractive lines to quarter the blueprint. "As I said before, each of you will take the area that corresponds to the direction of your element. Nera, you'll be west; Aeras, east. Gii and Floga will, of course, be north and south. You'll each have your own group of women. Start by fertilizing the beds, like I showed you yesterday. I'll make my way through each area, checking to see if the roses need any other special attention. Do you have any questions about your areas?" Mikki asked the four Elementals. As she'd done the night before, she'd pushed the dishes aside and spread Asterius's map out on the dining table. The handmaidens were gazing at it raptly.

"This is a lovely map, Empousa," Gii said, touching the delicate sketch that represented the realm's central fountain.

"And accurate, too," Aeras said. "I think every one of the paths have been duplicated here."

"Your baths are even drawn in," Nera said, obviously delighted with the squiggly water lines that represented her element.

"Who did this for you, Empousa?" Floga asked.

Mikki lifted her eyes from her own contemplation of the map to meet the Fire Elemental's sharp gaze.

"The Guardian drew it for me," Mikki said, careful to keep her voice casual, her expression placid.

"The Guardian!" Gii exclaimed. "But how could he have—"

"She commanded it," Floga interrupted the Earth Elemental. "He would do whatever she commanded."

Unruffled by her odd tone, Mikki said, "Actually, I didn't *command* him. I just asked." She lifted a shoulder. "That's all. Apparently it wasn't that big of a deal. He has claws that he can extend and use as built-in quills. And he's been here for ages. No wonder he knows all the nooks and crannies of the realm." She gave Floga a tight smile. "But thank you for reminding me. I do need to command him to come here. I asked him to inspect the rest of the rose wall and make sure there are no other weakened parts of it we need to pay special attention to." Mikki didn't need to close her eyes to concentrate on him. After last night, he never seemed to be far from her thoughts. She turned her back to the handmaidens and looked across the gardens. "Come to me, Asterius," she whispered into the wind.

She only had time to wonder if he minded that she called him by the name his mother had given him, before the pressure of the air on the balcony changed. It felt heavier and thick against her skin. Then she heard his hooves pound forcefully on marble as he climbed the balcony stairs. Though his stride was powerful, that unmistakable mixture of animal and man with which he moved, Mikki thought he looked tired and was almost as annoyed as she was disappointed when he bowed and spoke formally to her without meeting her eyes.

"You commanded that I come to you, Empousa?"

"Yes. I was hoping you'd had a chance this morning to inspect the rest of the rose wall."

"I have, Empousa."

"And?"

"I see no area that appears particularly weak except that which surrounds the gate."

"So you agree that we can focus on the roses within the garden?"

Finally, he met her eyes. "Yes, I am in agreement with you."

"Good," she said briskly, ignoring the fluttering he caused deep in her stomach. She turned to the handmaidens. "So each of you collect your group of women and set up your own line of fertilizer baskets. Prepare the beds just like we did the area around the roots of the multiflora roses. I'll visit each area, and we'll go from there."

"Yes, Empousa," the Elementals chorused. They curtseyed and began to leave the balcony, along with the Guardian.

"Floga, Guardian—I need to see the two of you," Mikki said.

Mikki thought that though the Fire Elemental had carefully arranged her face into a blank expression, her eyes gave away her uneasiness at being singled out. *She doesn't trust me.*

"Floga, your area of the garden is the section that is most southerly. This happens to include the rose gate. I know it would be quicker for your women to go to the forest and use the loam for fertilizer as we did yesterday, but I'm concerned about having the gate open again today."

Floga looked surprised, and Mikki couldn't really blame her. Just yesterday she'd insisted, in front of everybody, that Asterius keep the gate open, danger be damned. Mikki looked at him. "What do you advise?"

"I believe you are wise to be concerned about reopening the gate so soon," he said.

"So we are agreed that maybe in a day or two Floga can allow the women to collect more loam, but right now it's not a good idea?"

"Yes, Empousa. We are in agreement."

"Good." She knew the smile she gave him was obvious in its warmth, and she could feel the handmaiden's eyes watching her every expression, but she didn't care. Let them all know she valued the Guardian's judgment. She would not treat him like an animal when he was not one, and neither would they. Not while she was Empousa. There was a new boss in the realm, and they'd better get used to it. Still smiling, she turned to Floga. "Do you understand what I need you to do?"

"Yes, Empousa."

"Good. Then you're free to get started. The Guardian and I will be along shortly."

Floga's eyes widened, but she said nothing as she curtseyed and then hurried from the balcony, leaving the priestess and the beast alone.

"Good morning, Asterius," Mikki said softly.

And that was it. The sound of his true name on her lips undid him. He could not fight his desire for her and his need to be in her presence. Despite the spell Hecate had placed upon him and the pain it would cause him, come spring or come the very gates of the Underworld, for as long as they had together he had to hear the sweet sound of her voice and, if fate granted it, feel the touch of her hand again.

"Forgive me, Mikado."

"For what?"

"For the way the night ended. I have no practice in . . ." He paused, struggling for words he'd never before spoken.

"There's nothing to forgive," she said. "It's hard to know the right thing to say or do, especially when you're faced with a completely new situation. Sometimes it's easier to run away."

"That makes me sound like a coward."

She smiled. "No, it makes you sound human."

He looked shocked, and then, slowly, his lips turned up into a smile that eventually reached his eyes. "You are an extraordinary woman, Mikado."

"Well, let's see if you still think so at the end of the day."

He raised a questioning brow.

"I'm going to put all those muscles of yours to work. Tonight you'll be too tired not to sleep."

His dark eyes caught hers. "You knew I didn't sleep last night?"

"Don't be too impressed by my powers of observation. It doesn't take a goddess to figure it out. You look pretty rough this morning."

"And I am usually so handsome," he said dryly.

She gasped. "Do not tell me that you just made a joke!" Mikki's laughter floated musically on the breeze as the two of them made their way from the balcony. Neither noticed the women who peered wide-eyed from the palace windows, watching them go.

Chapter Twenty-two

MIKADO hadn't been exaggerating when she'd said she was going to put his muscles to work. Asterius had never lifted so many baskets or dug so many holes in all the long centuries of his immortal life.

And he'd never been so happy.

He'd been working beside Mikado all day. She actively supervised, which meant she did not shy from even the dirtiest of jobs. He could tell that the women of the realm were not pleased with the messy, tiring tasks she had given them, but they were visibly pleased that their Empousa was right in the middle of the mess with them. She worked twice as hard as they did; she seemed to be everywhere at once. And perhaps most surprisingly, she was cheerful about the work. The High Priestess appeared to actually enjoy getting her hands in the dirt as she demonstrated exactly how the earth needed to be worked around the roots of the bushes. She didn't shy away from the rank fertilizer; she did the opposite. The Empousa helped scoop it into the dirt and even laughed and made jokes about the irony that such a horrid smell could make sweet roses thrive.

He ignored the looks the women gave him. He was used to it. No matter how often he walked amongst them, the women of the realm were always uncomfortable around him. More so now than ever before.

They all knew what he had done and the rage his actions had evoked from their goddess. They, too, had paid for his error. They hadn't been encased in stone and banished from the realm, as he had. They had only to wait . . . without aging . . . without changing . . . unable to do more than watch time pass around them for all the centuries he slept. He could only imagine how disturbing it must be for them to see him beside their new Empousa, especially when she made it clear that she appreciated his opinion and she treated him like . . .

Mikado treated him as if *he were a man*.

What a true and wondrous miracle she was. And she did stay in his presence—or rather, he stayed in hers. She began the inspection of the roses in the east, and after thoroughly examining all of the beds, with Aeras promising to follow each of her directions, she had moved to the south.

He would never forget how he'd stood there pretending to be busy piling empty baskets easily within the women's reach as Mikado waved a bright farewell to the little Wind Elemental. He thought he would stay there in the east and continue working, that perhaps later in the day he would catch a glimpse of her as she moved amongst the plants, but she'd had other ideas. When she'd realized he wasn't leaving with her, she'd marched right back to him and said, "I need you to stay with me. I would very much appreciate your help today."

"Of course, Empousa," he'd said formally, but the joy that had rushed through him hadn't been formal and he hoped she could see its reflection within his eyes. As they'd hurried away from Aeras and her women, Mikado's palla had fallen from her shoulders and snagged on a nearby rosebush. Deftly he had extricated it and then placed it back around her, letting his palms rest against the roundness of her shoulders until he felt the stinging burn of pain.

But when she smiled up into his eyes, he forgot the pain and remembered only the warmth of her skin against his hands. Little wonder the handmaidens' eyes followed them wherever they went. He couldn't keep his hands from her, and she . . . she *smiled* at him, often taking obvious pleasure in his company.

206 P. C. Cast

It had taken Mikado longer to inspect the southern section of the gardens. The roses were more ill there, though he didn't need to look at the plants to know that. Watching Mikado become grim faced and pale told him more than inspecting the rosebushes ever could.

Midday came quickly. He was readying a bed of wilting, multicolored roses called Masquerade for their baskets of fish entrails fertilizer when he caught the scent of food. He didn't look up when the women from the palace arrived with the midday meal. He kept working. The most uncomfortable part of the day before had been at exactly this moment. The women had separated into their little groups to talk and laugh and eat together—things that were denied him. He could guard them, but he would not be accepted by them, not enough to share a simple meal with them. Last night Mikado had granted him a great gift when she'd shared her table with him, and he silently cursed himself for ruining the evening.

He could hear the women breaking for the meal. They grouped around the fountains in the area, letting the garden's clear water wash their hands free of dirt. Their laughter came easily, and it mixed musically with the sound of the tinkling fountains. He wondered where Mikado was—probably in the middle of the laughter. She laughed readily, and the women of the realm responded well to her. He hoped she was busy, distracted enough that she would not notice him and see how they shunned him. He did not want her pity.

He knew one of the palace servants would soon find him and offer him food and drink—not because she wanted to, but because it was her assigned duty. Without looking around, he slipped from the rose bed in which he'd been working and headed toward the rose gate. A large tree sat near it, under which he could call its shadows to him and attempt to cloak himself from prying eyes. There he would rest and perhaps drink some of the wine the servant would offer him. Of course he was hungry, but he would not eat. He could not stand their stares. It was as if they expected him to fall to his haunches and tear at the food with his teeth. Perhaps he should! That would cause quite a stir amongst them. No . . . he stifled a weary sigh. It would cause nothing more than a reinforcement of their belief that he was, indeed, a mindless, heartless beast.

"There you are!" Mikado hurried up to him, a little out of breath. "Good thing you're so tall or I would never have found you out here."

He stopped and looked down at her. She was carrying a large basket. Her hands and face were wet, as if she had just washed, and as she smiled up at him she used a fold in her dirt-speckled chiton to wipe a trickle of water from her cheek.

"I completed readying the bed of Masquerade. What is it you would have me do next?"

"I'd have you eat!" She grinned, nodding at the well-laden basket. "I made sure this one had enough for both of us."

He wondered if she could hear the blood rushing in his veins, pumping shock and disbelief through his body. He drew a deep breath. When he spoke, he struggled to keep his voice low and for her ears alone.

"You should eat with the women, Mikado."

"No. They've already formed their little cliques. If I butted into one, it would just be awkward, kinda like eating with the boss who crashed a workers-only party. And as many orders as I've given them today, I'm sure they need a break from me. Plus, I'd rather eat with you," she finished simply.

"But it has never—"

"Stop!" she interrupted, causing several of the women's heads to turn their way. In a more sedate, but no less firm voice, Mikado continued. "I'm tired of hearing what hasn't been done before. I'm Empousa now and things are going to be different, and not just with the roses."

"As you wish, Empousa," he said, using comfortable formality to cover his turbulent emotions.

"Good. Let's go eat under that tree you disappeared beneath yesterday. I want to take another look at the gate anyway."

"As you say, Empousa." He began to walk toward the ancient tree that shaded the area near the rose gate, careful to shorten his stride so she didn't have to struggle to keep up with him.

When they got to the tree, he felt a rush of relief when he saw that no group of women had chosen to eat nearby. With a long sigh, Mikado sat and leaned her back against the wide trunk of the oak and gazed at the rose gate.

"It doesn't look any better than it did yesterday," she said.

"It also does not look any worse."

"I suppose that's something. You know, I don't sense anything horrible coming from the forest. If you hadn't told me about the danger there, I wouldn't have thought the forest was anything more than an old, dark woods."

"Dream Stealers choose their time carefully to appear. Remember to be on your guard always when you are near the gate or in the forest itself."

"But you'll be with me, won't you? I mean, I can't open the gate."

He raised a brow at her. "Of course you can, Empousa."

Her eyes widened as she looked from him to the gate and back to him again. "I'll be careful," she said. Then she turned her attention to the basket of food. "Let's worry about the forest later. Now, let's eat."

Hesitating only a moment, he sat and made an almost imperceptible gesture that caused the shadows around them to thicken. He wanted to be able to watch her without schooling his expression, and that was not something he would do if the other women could easily see them.

"You look tired," he said.

"So do you," she countered as she pulled a wineskin from the basket and then took a long drink.

"Your face is pale, Mikado."

"That doesn't surprise me." She tossed him the wineskin and then began taking cheese and bread from the basket. Mikado glanced up at him. "Drink," she ordered.

He drank, thinking that he could taste the essence left by her lips, and that lingering touch was more intoxicating than wine could ever be. Then he realized what she had said and commanded himself to stop daydreaming.

"Why is it that you are not surprised by your pallor?"

"The roses in this part of the garden are sicker than the ones in the east," she said between bites.

"Yes, I thought so, too."

"Somehow I'm connected to them. They make me feel sick, too."

"I guessed as much. You seemed to change when we entered this part of the gardens."

"Do you know if this has happened to any other Empousa?"

"Each Empousa has a special bond with the roses," he said slowly. "It is in the blood of Hecate's High Priestesses."

"I already know that. Even back in Tulsa I had a connection to roses, and so did all the women in my family. We always have. It's—it's a kind of family tradition."

He thought she looked uncomfortable. Perhaps she missed her family? Or her old world? The thought made his chest feel tight. Could there be a man for whom she was pining? Is that why she suddenly sounded so awkward when she mentioned her old life? Before he could consider asking, Mikado continued.

"But what I want to know is have any of the other Empousas felt things because of the roses?"

"They may have, but I would not have known. The other Empousas rarely spoke to me."

She looked surprised. "But you're Guardian of the realm. Didn't they need to talk to you about"—her hand fluttered in the direction of the rose wall—"protection and whatnot?"

"Each Empousa knew I would do my duty. None felt the need to speak with me about it. If an Empousa felt that any danger approached, she would call for me. Other than that, we rarely had the need to speak together." He thought of the Empousa who had come before Mikado and realized, again, shame at the ease with which she had fooled him into believing she might care for him. That for generations the Empousas had shunned him, taken his guardianship for granted, had been precisely the reason her ruse had worked so easily on him. One or two kind words and he had been blind to anything except the chance that she might show him another kindness.

Could that be what was happening with Mikado? Was he still so desperate for a woman's gentleness that he was becoming lost in yet another game?

But what game? Mikado did not know her destiny, so she had no reason to falsely seduce him.

"Asterius?"

The sound of his true name broke into the turbulence of his thoughts. "You must not call me that when any of the women might overhear you." His voice sounded rougher than he had intended, and he hated the hurt that was reflected in her eyes.

"I'm sorry. I should have asked if you minded that I call you by your given name."

"I do not mind." He met her gaze, willing her to read within his eyes all that he was feeling and all that he could not find words to say. "It is just that to the rest of them, I prefer to remain Guardian."

"I understand," she said.

"Do you? Do you know what power there is in a true name?"

"No," she said softly, "tell me its power."

"When you speak my true name, I hear it not with my ears, but with my soul. With that one word, you touch my soul, Mikado."

"The soul of a man, Asterius."

"So the goddess tells me," he said.

"You don't believe her?"

"I would never lack belief in Hecate," he said quickly.

"Then it's yourself you don't believe in," Mikado said.

He looked away from her too-knowing gaze and didn't answer for several moments, during which he unconsciously flexed and contracted his claws over and over. Then, reluctantly, he said, "Perhaps it is the man inside the monster in which I have trouble believing."

Then it was her turn to be silent. He could feel her thoughts. He couldn't actually read them, but he knew that she was thinking of him . . . considering . . . weighing her response.

"Maybe you need someone else to believe in the man, so you can quit seeing nothing but the monster."

The meaning of her words jolted Asterius, and hope surged so sweetly within him that he felt the beast shiver in response. "How can you see anything but the monster?" The depth of his emotions made his voice rumble with the force of a growl, and even though he noticed that this time she didn't flinch away from him, he struggled to regain control. Through gritted teeth he said, "Look at me. Listen to me. I cannot even gentle my voice to speak soft words to you! There is little that is manlike in my appearance."

"Then I suppose I'll just have to look deeper than your appearance."

The smile that tilted her full lips made his heart beat painfully against his chest. He wanted to pull her into his arms and crush her to him. But he could not—not here and now, and perhaps not ever. But he could touch her. Just for an instant . . .

Asterius lifted his hand and let his fingers brush the side of her cheek. "Mikado, you make me believe that I still dream," he murmured as gently as possible.

She met his eyes. "Sometimes I think that would be nice. Gii told me that I have the power to weave dreams. Maybe I'll figure out how to weave one for us."

His fingers began to sting, and reluctantly, he took them away from her face. She sighed, as if she, too, was disappointed that he wasn't still touching her. Then she gave herself a little shake.

"Dreams are for later. Right now let's hurry up and eat. I'm still not done here, and I really do want to check in with Nera and Gii before it gets too dark."

So amazingly, he and Mikado ate the midday meal together within sight of many of the women of the realm, who did often steal looks in their direction, trying hard to peer through the shadows of the ancient oak.

His inhumanly acute hearing caught the sound of the Elemental approaching before Mikado noticed her, and he surreptitiously motioned for the shadows under their tree to lighten. Then he stood and moved aside, purposefully giving the appearance that he might only be there to wait on the Empousa's next command instead of sitting close beside her, sharing an intimate meal.

"Empousa, the women have finished their meal," Floga said after sliding a narrowed glance at the Guardian.

"Good! We're done here, too."

Then, very deliberately, Mikado held out her hand to him. Asterius hesitated only an instant before taking it in his own and helping the priestess to her feet. She smiled and thanked him as if he were a man accustomed to the touch of a woman's hand. Then she turned to the staring Fire Elemental.

"Let's get back to work."

CHAPTER TWENTY-THREE

"I'M glad the palace is situated in the north so Gii and her group of women are in charge of the roses surrounding it," Mikki told Asterius as they watched the Earth Elemental pass the word to her women that they were done for the day.

"It's obvious that you and she are becoming friends," Asterius said.

"Yes, we are," she said, thinking that it was just as obvious that the Elemental was uncomfortable with her Empousa's familiarity with the Guardian.

"It's not surprising that the two of you are compatible. Earth and roses fit naturally together."

"You're right—they do."

Gii would just have to get used to having Asterius around. Mikki didn't think it would be too tough for the Elemental to do that. All she needed to do was to quit thinking of him as a beast, and she'd soon see what Mikki saw—the man within. It hadn't been that hard for her. How difficult could it be for the rest of them?

"I should go now, Mikado. The handmaidens will want time alone with you, and there are duties to which I must attend."

She looked up at him, surprised that she could be sad to part from him after spending the whole day in his company. She usually got sick of being around a man in less than half that time. "Will you come back?"

Mikki watched his eyes darken and he said, "If you call for me, I will come to you."

"Then I'll call," she said.

He bowed formally to her just as the four handmaidens approached them. Mikki noted how each of them looked obviously relieved when Asterius turned and disappeared into the shadows of the darkening garden. She pushed down the annoyance she felt. They had worked hard today; they were all tired. And it really would be unreasonable of her to expect the women to change the way they felt about Asterius in just a couple days. The other Empousas had treated their Guardian like an animal; it was logical, then, that was how the women of the realm would treat him. Mikki would just have to lead by example. They were smart girls—they'd catch on.

"Are you four as ready for a long soak as I am?"

THIS evening was even cooler than the one before, and steam from the baths veiled everything in a warm, damp mist. Mikki leaned back against the smooth side of her private bath and fed herself another grape. She was pleasantly full and a little tipsy from the wine. She hadn't planned on having dinner with the women. She'd planned on taking a quick bath and then retreating to her room and another private dinner with Asterius, but the women had been hungry, and, after all, who could bathe quickly when the "tub" was this spectacular and the company was so enjoyable?

And Mikki was sincerely enjoying the company. The handmaidens were tired after another long day, but they didn't whine or complain. Instead, they talked about the work they'd done in their separate areas and asked Mikki countless questions about rose care. Already plans for tomorrow were discussed. The fertilizing would continue, but some women would begin deadheading old blooms or blossoms that looked like they were too far gone to ever open. Mikki agreed to show the Elementals examples of both in the morning.

"I think we've conquered the hardest part of what we need to do to coax the roses into recovery. Most of the fertilizing will be finished tomorrow. Then we'll focus on the deadheading and cutting off of any useless canes. After that, we just keep an eye on them and wait."

"How long before they begin recovering?" Gii asked.

"It doesn't take long for a good fertilizer to start working, especially if all that's wrong with the roses is that they needed to be fed. We should see a change in them soon."

"And if we don't?" Floga asked.

"Then I try something else. I have more tricks up my sleeve." She raised her wet, naked arm and wiggled it around, causing the young women to giggle.

"Perhaps you should cast a health spell for the roses," Nera said. "You know, as you would if one of the women of the realm asked you to cast a spell to rid her of a persistent ague."

"It is a good idea," Aeras said.

"It certainly couldn't do any harm," the Fire Elemental said as she nibbled at a fig.

"And it might very well do a great deal of good," Gii added.

Feeling totally out of her realm of experience, Mikki wished desperately that her new job/destiny had come with an owner's manual.

"It would be like the self-initiation ritual. The four of us will be there when you cast the sacred circle and then you simply follow your heart." Gii's smile was filled with kindness. "You'll know what to do, Empousa."

"You may as well begin with a spell for something you know as intimately as roses; it will be easier that way. And anyway, it's only a matter of time before the women in the realm begin coming to you for the typical love spells and such," Floga said.

"She's right, Empousa," Gii said.

"Love spells and such?" Mikki sputtered.

Aeras sighed wistfully. "Love spells . . . it has been so long."

"Too long!" Floga said.

"Actually," Nera began hesitantly, "I have been wondering. If perhaps—well, if you might . . ." The little Water Elemental paused. She looked nervously at the other handmaidens, who nodded encouragement. She sank a little lower in the steaming water, as if drawing strength from her element, and then she finished in a rush, "I wondered if you might agree to cast an invitation spell for me and, well, a few others."

Mikki noted the pink flush that colored the Elemental's cheeks, and she didn't think it was from the warm water.

"I'd be happy to cast an invitation spell for you—and your friends. But what are we inviting and where?"

"The what is men," Nera said shyly, her cheeks turning from pink to red.

"And the where is here," Floga purred.

"Huh," Mikki said. "I was going to ask about the absence of men."

"There are no men in the Realm of the Rose," Gii said.

"You mean except for the Guardian," Mikki said.

Gii frowned. "The Guardian is not a man. He is a beast."

Mikki opened her mouth to protest, but Floga was already speaking. "There are no men in the realm because they can only come here if the Empousa sends an invitation spell to the ancient world. There has been no Empousa in the realm; hence no men have been invited."

Mikki stared at the Fire Elemental. "Are you telling me that for as long as the Guardian was banished and the Empousa gone you have been here without any men?"

"Yes," the Four Elementals said together.

"How long has it been?"

For a moment no one answered her. Then Gii whispered, "It has been a very long time, Empousa."

And she thought her love life sucked. She was queen of romance compared to these girls.

"Then I'll definitely do an invitation spell. A big one—right away."

Gii laughed. "Tomorrow will be soon enough, Empousa. Tonight we are too tired to have the invitation be of much use to us."

"Then tomorrow it will be. How about we only work till midday and then I'll cast a circle and try a little spell work?"

"Just don't make my invitation little," Floga gibed. "*Little* men do not interest me, even after all this time."

Nera giggled and flicked her wrist at the Fire Elemental, causing water to spew from her bath all over Floga. Gii called her too hot-blooded, and Aeras joked that if Floga needed a breath of cold northern wind she could certainly provide it for her. Mikki smiled and watched their good-humored play, but her mind was not on the handmaidens. She thought instead of bronze skin, a deep, powerful voice, and how candlelight looked glinting off ebony horns.

WOULD she always be nervous before she called him? Mikki looked around the balcony, for the zillionth time checking that she was alone. The table was ready. It was set with a pitcher of wine and two goblets. She hoped he had not waited to eat with her. She hadn't asked him to. Had she? No—no, she remembered asking only if he would come to her—not come to her and have dinner again. She ran a hand down the soft material of her chiton. This evening it was made of some kind of fabulous material that hugged her body like silk, and it was the exact green of her eyes. She knew it flattered her, just as she knew Daphne had brought it to her at the baths because she had been wishing for something beautiful to wear. She wanted to look beautiful for him. For Asterius . . .

"Come to me," she whispered into the night.

She could feel him approaching. Like an electrical storm, he was a great gathering of energy and force.

"Good evening, Mikado."

"Hello, Asterius." Still nervous, she gestured to the table. "Would you like some wine? I hope you've already eaten. The handmaidens wanted to have dinner with me at the baths, and they'd worked so hard today I didn't feel like I could tell them no."

"That is as it should be. Your Elementals need the presence of their Empousa. Do not be concerned, I ate as I awaited your call."

"But you'll join me in a glass of wine?"

"Of course."

Again, when Mikki lifted the goblet to her lips she found a rosebud swimming in the wine. She savored the delicate fragrance as they drank.

"You'll spoil me," she told him with a smile. "I won't be able to really enjoy a glass of wine unless it has a rose floating in it."

"That is as it should be, too."

She watched him sip his wine. Tonight he seemed more relaxed than the night before, and she was able to look at him openly. He was such a paradox—monstrous strength and a body that melded man and beast, yet he was humane enough to conjure a rose for her wine.

"What do you think when you look at me thus?"

Mikki jumped guiltily at the question.

"You need not answer that," he said quickly, looking away from her.

"I don't mind. I just . . . well . . . I know it's rude of me to stare at you."

"I am accustomed to women's stares."

She felt a rush of anger for the kind of stares he'd had to endure. "Then I will tell you what I was thinking. I was thinking that it's amazing that you're so powerful and at the same time so kind."

"Kind?"

"Oh, don't sound shocked. Of course you're kind. Who ordered my dinner the first night I was here? And you told them to put a blanket and slippers out here for me, not to mention the rose blossoms you never forget to add to my wine."

"That doesn't make me kind. That just shows that I'm fulfilling my duty in caring for the Empousa."

She snorted. "Please. You're not just kind to me. You're like that with all the women. I watched you today. Even though they act weird and skittish around you, you're completely patient with them."

"Mikado, that is my duty. Nothing more."

"Are you telling me that you never get frustrated or annoyed at them?"

"I do," he said.

"Then why don't you show it?"

"That would be dishonorable, and it would . . ." He stopped suddenly, realizing he was saying too much.

"It would what?" she prompted.

"It would be wrong," he said.

"Would it be wrong, or would it be proving that what they say about you is true?"

His dark eyes found hers, and she read her answer there.

"What they say about you is not true," Mikki said softly.

"You don't know that."

"Yes I do. I know it here." She pressed a hand to her heart. "And I know it here." She reached across the small table and placed her hand gently on the leather breastplate that molded to his chest. Through the pliable leather she felt the strong beating of his heart and the way his breathing deepened at her touch. They stared at each other. Mikki wished he would return her touch, cover her hand with his own, do something that told her it was okay for her to touch him. But his only movement was the pounding of his heart and the drawing of his breath. Reluctantly, she took her hand from his chest.

"It went well today, Mikado." His voice sounded unnaturally loud in the stillness that had settled between them.

"I think so, too. Tomorrow we're just going to work until midday. Then I'm going to try some spell work.

His lips tilted up. "That should prove interesting."

"Especially because I have no idea what I'm doing."

"You will. Just listen within. And remember, the Elementals are there to assist you. When you cast a spell, you can call anything within their power to aid you with the spell."

Mikki perked up. "For instance?"

He sipped his wine and considered. "For instance, let us say a maiden comes to you because she has been cursed with terrible pains in her head. She asks for a spell to cure this pain. Lavender has long been associated with health, peace and relaxation. So you command Gii to provide you fresh lavender and Aeras to fill the breeze surrounding the maiden with the scent of the herb."

"That does make sense," Mikki said enthusiastically. "So all I need to do is to think about what each Elemental can provide to support whatever spell it is I want to cast."

"Then you complete it with your words and Hecate's power."

"Wow," she breathed. "Incredible."

"And, you'll find, very effective. Hecate's High Priestess wields great power. Your spells will be strong and binding."

"In other words, I better think before I speak."

"I have no doubt that you will be wise, Mikado."

"I wish I was as sure," she muttered. Then she sighed. "There's just so much I don't know."

"You will learn," he said.

"Will you help me?"

"If I am able," he said carefully.

"Good! There's something you can help me with tonight." She ignored the way he instantly retreated behind his all-too-familiar expressionless mask. "It's a little like drawing the map for me last night." That seemed to reassure him, and when he nodded slightly, she said, "You know the gardens so well, I assume you know the palace equally as well."

He looked surprised but said, "I do."

"Well, I don't." She jerked her thumb at the glass doors leading to her bedroom. "The only way I've left my room is through there. I've not stepped so much as a foot into the hall outside my bedroom. I know there's some kind of fantastic dream making and magick brewing going on out there in the rest of the palace, though." Unspoken between them was what she had said earlier—that she wanted to weave a dream for the two of them.

"There is, indeed."

"I'd love to see it, but I also want to be able to understand it and weld it. Would you show me around, Asterius?"

His eyes were dark and they glittered with the fullness of the joy her request gave him. He smiled, showing a flash of sharp, white canines. "I would be honored."

CHAPTER TWENTY-FOUR

W ALKING through her bedroom with him was an oddly intimate experience. Mikki saw his eyes go to her opulent bed. His long, powerful stride was suddenly thrown off, and, for the first time, she saw him move awkwardly. She had to force herself not to smile. If he wasn't thinking about getting her into bed, then why should the sight of said bed make him jittery? She thought it was an excellent sign. Then he opened the door and stepped aside so she could go through, and all bedroom thoughts fled her mind.

Her room was the last in the hall and her balcony wrapped all the way around the side of her bedroom, which also was the eastern end of the palace. To her left, the vast main hallway of the palace stretched on and on. The hall was wide, the ceiling incredibly high. Huge mullioned windows faced the south, showing a nighttime view of the torch-lit gardens. The north side of the hall held door after door, each ornately carved with mystic symbols and designs, and stretching as far as she could see. Torches blazed from wall sconces on either side of each door, as well as up and down the hall on both sides. Mikki's eyes were drawn to the long marble boxes that covered the area between the doors. The boxes were filled with flowers that were—amazingly enough—not roses.

The air in the hallway was filled with a sweet, delicate fragrance that reminded her of daylilies. Actually, the flowers did look a little like daylilies, only their leaves were too big and round, even though the huge, trumpetlike white blossoms were lilylike. But the blossoms were weird . . . they were . . . she walked closer. They were surrounded by a glittering haze, like mist that had been sprinkled with glitter. What the . . . ? Then something about those blossoms pricked her memory.

"They're moon flowers! We have them in Oklahoma. They only open up like this at night. During the day their blooms close tight and droop down so they look almost dead."

"Yes, we call them moon flowers here, too."

"But what is the foggy stuff that looks like it's coming out of the blossoms?"

"It's not coming out—it's being drawn in."

"It's being drawn in? What is it?"

"The essence of dreams. Every night the moon flowers capture the essence of dreams and draw them into the rooms beyond, where the women of the realm take that essence and fashion it anew to send back into the world to create the magick that is born of dreams."

"All that's happening behind those doors?"

"It is." He smiled at her look of innocent wonder.

The smile she flashed him in return was brilliant, and when she squeezed his arm he thought his heart would burst from his chest and he had to remind himself that it was the magick of the realm that had excited her thus, not his presence. But no matter. Her happiness pleased him, whatever its source, and he was determined to enjoy it, as well as the joy being in Mikado's presence brought him, for as long as her destiny allowed.

"Lead on, Mikado, and I will follow you into the rooms of dreams."

She nodded, drew in a deep breath and touched the knob of the first door. It swung inward. Mikki moved into the room and blinked, trying to make sense of what she was seeing.

The room was misty with the sweet scent of moon flowers. All the women were blowing glass bubbles—that much wasn't hard to understand. It was warmer there than in the hallway, though not as hot as the open ovens that stood in each corner of the room should have made it.

The women looked up from their tasks when she and the Guardian entered. They ignored Asterius but dropped quick curtsies to her and greeted her cheerfully.

"Don't let me interrupt. Keep doing . . . uh, whatever it is you're doing," Mikki said hastily.

"They are creating dream bubbles."

Asterius was standing very close to her, and his low voice rumbled into her ear, causing the skin on her neck to prickle.

"See how, as each bubble grows, so, too, does the dream within it?"

She nodded, watching raptly as the women blew into long, slender tubes, turning and fashioning, until the molten lumps at the ends of the tubes were formed into bubbles that looked like delicate, iridescent glass globes of all different colors. As the bubbles got bigger and bigger, Mikki could see that there was something inside them. She moved closer and realized that she was looking at fantastic scenes. In one bubble, a young girl leaped off a cliff, but instead of falling, the child floated through a violet-colored sky singing to birds that looked like flying penguins. In another bubble, two knights jousted while scantily dressed women cheered them on. In yet another, an old woman was looking into a handheld mirror, and within the mirror her face grew younger and younger, until she was a tight-skinned teenager.

"You're seeing the essence of dreams reworked."

"So those are actual dreams that people will have?" she whispered.

"Yes."

"How do they get from here to the people's minds?"

"Like that." He lifted his chin toward a woman whose bubble had reached the size of a grapefruit. She stopped blowing into the tube and lifted the bubble to eye level. In the scene taking place inside, Mikki could see a woman dancing through a knee-deep sea of blue grass as the sky rained flowers all around her. The palace worker tapped the bubble once with her fingernail, and it broke off neatly from the tube. But it didn't fall to the ground and break, as Mikki expected it to. Instead, it floated. The worker blew one last breath of air on it, and the bubble lifted, eventually disappearing into the ceiling.

"Would you like to create a dream, Empousa?"

Mikki jumped as the woman who had just sent the bubble through the ceiling offered her the newly emptied tube.

"Oh, thank you, but no. Tonight I'm just watching."

"As you wish, Empousa." The woman smiled at her and went back to work.

Mikki grabbed Asterius's hand and pulled him toward the door. "I want to see more!"

"As you wish, Empousa." He tried to sound formal and aloof for the benefit of the women, who were watching and listening, but the small hand that nestled so easily within his was a treasure beyond price, and he could not conceal the happiness that lit his face when she touched him so easily. He didn't care that they were watching; he didn't care that pain sluiced through his arm. All that mattered was that she did not take her hand from his until they reached the next door, which she touched open. He followed her in, smiling at her little gasp of pleasure.

This room was much cooler and smelled like moon flowers and spring rain. A clear stream bubbled through the center of the room, coming from nowhere and disappearing into nothingness. On one side of the stream, women lounged on puffy cushions the color of blushes, talking and laughing while their hands trailed into the water. Every so often one of the women would pull something that looked like a coin from the water, study it carefully, then, with a snap of her fingers, the coin would disappear in a puff of pink smoke.

On the far side of the stream, women sat comfortably cross-legged, dipping round hoops into the water. A young woman caught sight of her and called, "Greetings, Empousa!" and soon the rest of the Dream Weavers greeted her.

"Don't let me interrupt you; I just want to watch," Mikki assured them. Then she lowered her voice and moved closer to Asterius. "Okay, what are they doing?"

"The stream carries coins from all of the wishing wells in the mundane world. The women choose a coin, and if they like the wish, they turn it into a dream."

"What if they don't like it?"

"It stays in the stream and eventually becomes the sludge from which nightmares are formed."

"Can't they throw them away or something? I hate nightmares."

"There must be balance, Mikado. Light—dark, good—evil, life—death. Without balance, the circle of life would collapse."

"I still don't like nightmares," she grumbled. Then Mikki pointed to the women with the hoops. "What are they doing?"

"They're finding the right mixture of dreams, water, and magick to make scrying mirrors."

"Scrying mirrors?"

"Mirrors used for second sight—for discerning that which cannot be seen with the eye alone."

"Really? That's fascinating. You know, I think I'd like to get a closer look." Mikki marched over to one of the women fishing for coins.

"I would be honored if you would join me, Empousa." She smiled warmly at Mikki and scooted over to make room for her on the cushion.

Mikki sat and looked down into the water. It was clear, tumbling hurriedly over the white sand that formed the bottom of the magickal stream. Then a circle of silver rolled into view, and without letting herself think too much, she plunged her hand in after it. The water was pleasantly warm, a nice contrast to the cool room. Her fingers closed around the coin. Smiling triumphantly, she lifted it, dripping.

"Well done, Empousa." Asterius's deep voice rumbled from beside her. "Now look into it and see if the wish is a dream you will grant."

Mikki narrowed her eyes and stared at the coin. With a little shock, she realized she was holding a quarter! The mint date stamped on it was 1995. It was just a plain, ordinary quarter. No different than the ones she'd been seeing, and spending, her entire life. How could there be any magick within—

The skin of the coin rippled, and she almost dropped it. She looked closer. It was like putting her eyes to one of those old view masters, only the scene within the coin moved like a video. A man and a woman lay on a sheepskin rug in front of a crackling fireplace. They were naked and making love. Mikki could hear him telling her over and over how beautiful she was and how she tasted of honey and love. Then, as the woman orgasmed, snow began to fall in the room all around the couple, without touching them or getting them wet.

"Do you grant that the wish be made a dream?" Asterius asked.

Mikki looked from the erotic scene to the beast who stood beside her. She licked her lips, letting her gaze travel up the muscular expanse of his chest to the fullness of his very human lips. "Yes, I grant it," she said. Without having to be told what to do next, she snapped her fingers and the coin exploded in a puff of pink smoke, which drifted lazily up and then through the ceiling.

"Will you choose another, Empousa?" the woman sitting beside her asked.

"I'd like to, but I want to visit more of the other rooms tonight."

For the second time that day, Mikki held her hand out to Asterius. This time there was no hesitation before he took it and helped her to her feet. When she stood, he let go of her hand, but she didn't move away from him. Instead, she placed her hand in the crook of his arm, as if he was an old-time Southern gentleman escorting her from the room. "Let's go see some of the other rooms."

"As you wish, Empousa."

His words were still formal, but there was no mistaking the way his expression softened when he spoke to her and how they leaned their bodies toward one another, sharing intimate smiles and whispers. They walked from the room, neither paying any attention to the shocked stares of the Dream Weavers.

CHAPTER TWENTY-FIVE

MIKKI'S mind was a whirlwind, filled with the unbelievable beauty she'd witnessed in the dream-weaving rooms. Just when she thought she'd seen something so incredible it couldn't be topped, Asterius would lead her to another room and she would be amazed all over again. She wished her mother and grandmother could be here with her. Her mother, in particular, would love the room where women were painting tiny porcelain animals, which came alive as they floated up through the ceiling. Her grandmother would probably most like the dream weaving that had been devoted to magick, like the room where brightly colored scenes were painted on long rolls of parchment so fine it was see-through. When the scenes were finished, the filmy paper suddenly broke apart, and like dove's wings, fluttered up out of sight. Asterius had explained that the women had been creating the essence of Tarot cards. And then there was the room they'd entered where women had been using shining silver hooks to crochet diaphanous blankets ranging in color from buttercup to smoke. Moon veils, used for drawing down the moon, he had named them. And she realized that they were, indeed, all the colors of the different phases of the moon.

But her favorite room was the candle room. It had been filled, tier after tier, with thick, cream-colored pillar candles, on which women carved into the soft wax fantastic dream scenes. When a scene was finished, the candle was lit. As it burned, the dream scene was released and then carried to the waiting world on fragrant, snow-colored smoke.

"One more room," Asterius said sternly as they left the candle room. Before she could protest, he shook his head. "No, there are shadows beneath your eyes. You can continue your exploration tomorrow night."

"Is this more of your duty to care for me, or are you tired of me dragging you from room to room?"

"Neither," he said quietly as they approached the door to the next room. He cupped her face within his hands and let his thumbs trace the shadows under her eyes. "It is only that I do not like to see you looking weary, even though if I could choose, this evening would never end."

Mikki looked up at him, surprised and pleased at his words and the gentleness of his touch. She wanted to say she was sorry she had misunderstood, or thank him, or—hell!—tell she was having a wonderful time, too, but he was already opening the ornate door. Her eager attention shifted to the new room and the wonders it held.

Everything within the room looked normal. Women sat around in front of large frames of cloth, their needles flashing in and out as they created exquisite tapestries. As usual, the women greeted her, but this time they did not ignore Asterius.

"Guardian, did you bring more thread?" one of the older women said in a businesslike, no-nonsense tone of voice.

"I have none with me. This evening I have been escorting the new Empousa through the dream-weaver rooms," he said.

"Empousa, please do not think I mean any disrespect, but it is important that the Guardian collect more threads for us—tonight, if you would grant him leave to do so. While he was"—the woman paused uncomfortably for a moment before plunging on—"away from the realm, we had to make due with the threads the Elementals gathered. They sufficed but only just."

"The tapestries are becoming frayed," added a slightly younger woman with a thick mane of blond hair she had tied back in a braid. Several of the other women nodded in agreement.

Thoroughly confused—again—Mikki contained her frustrated sigh. "Of course I'll give the Guardian leave to, um, collect threads for you. We were just finishing here anyway."

"Oh! Thank you, Empousa!"

Mikki waved off their thanks and retreated from the room with Asterius close behind.

"All right, you're going to have to explain that," she said.

"Did you notice anything different about the scenes in that room?"

She frowned at him, not liking it that he answered her question with a question, but she thought about the scenes the women had been embroidering. There had been one with a mother holding a newborn child. Another had shown a man speaking in front of a huge crowd of people. Yet another had depicted a woman sitting at a writing desk chewing thoughtfully at a pencil. Mikki shrugged her shoulders. "I don't know. They all seemed totally normal."

"That is because in that room the dreams woven into the tapestries are those that actually come true."

"You mean they really happen! The things those women were creating in there actually happen in the real world?"

"Always," he said.

"That's why the thread has to be different." She spoke slowly, following her intuition carefully, as if it was a dimly marked trail. "They can't get it only from the stuff that the moon flowers suck in. Dreams that come true need something else . . . something more real."

He looked pleased. "Exactly! Dreams that come true must be woven with threads gleaned from reality."

"And you can do that?"

He nodded. "I can."

"Will you show me?"

He started to protest that it was too late and that she was overtired, but she touched his arm gently and said, "Please, Asterius."

"Very well. Come with me."

"Where are we going?"

"To the rose gate," he said, leading her back along the hallway.

"We're going into the forest?" Her hand tightened on his arm.

"We must. Reality cannot be gleaned from the realm of dreams and magick." Briefly, he covered her hand with his. "Do not be afraid. I would not let anything harm you."

She smiled up at him. "I'm not afraid. Not as long as I'm with you."

MIKKI thought the huge gate made of roses looked damn creepy at night. It didn't matter that there were torches nearby and lanterns hanging from the limbs of the ancient oak. It was still dark, and the rose wall seemed like something out of a book of fairytales by the sublimely twisted British author, Tanith Lee. Mikki liked Lee's weird fairy-tale retellings, a lot actually, but she absolutely did not want to walk into one. Ever.

"You could stay here. I'll go into the forest, gather the threads and then return as quickly as I am able," he said.

"No! I'm not staying here by myself. I'm coming with you."

With Mikki's hand wrapped tightly within the crook of his arm, he took the torch planted in the ground near the gate. After speaking the command that opened the gate, the two of them walked out of the Realm of the Rose.

Mikki shivered. "It's colder out here."

He barked another command, and a royal purple palla materialized around her shoulders.

"You're really handy to have around," Mikki said, trying to cover her nerves with a smile. Then she nodded toward the dark depth of the forest. "We're going in there?"

"Do not be afraid," he told her.

"Easy for you to say; you have the claws," she muttered.

His smile flashed white in the torchlight. "My claws are at your service, my lady."

"You say the sweetest things," she said with her best Southern accent, and Asterius's chest rumbled with a deep laugh.

They entered the tree line and were instantly swallowed in a blackness that completely blocked out the silvery light of the waxing moon. Asterius's torchlight cast eerie, moving shadows against the bark of the ancient trees. Mikki thought that if she hadn't been with Asterius she would have been scared shitless. As it was, she was just creeped out and looking forward to returning to the bright safety of the palace.

"This is far enough tonight. I need only collect a few strands to satisfy the women. Tomorrow I can return for more." He stopped and shoved the torch back into the ground. Asterius glanced down at where her hand gripped his arm. "I have to have both of my arms free," he said gently.

"Oh, sorry." She loosened her death grip and took a short step away from him, glad that one good thing the darkness did was to hide her blush.

"Do not be sorry," he said gruffly. "Your touch pleases me."

She blinked in surprise. Had she heard him correctly? The words were nice, but the way he said them made him sound pissed off. It was confusing. Just like his hands were gentle, but his face always seemed to reflect something that looked almost like pain whenever he touched her. "Really?" she blurted.

His sigh was like a storm wind. "Really." Then he enveloped her shoulders with his hands and moved her a couple steps to the side. "Stand here. This won't take long."

Silently, he stretched out his hands. The firelight glinted off the claws that suddenly extended from his fingers. He closed his eyes and lifted his head, moving in a circle until he was facing into the slight breeze. Though he was half turned away from her, Mikki could see his lips moving, as if he was reciting a soundless prayer. He raised one hand and thrust it forward; it looked like he was clawing the wind. Then his hand twisted and closed in one inhumanly quick motion. And from the tips of his claws, the air began to glow, as long, thin threads suddenly took form, which he pulled, hand over hand, to pile in a glowing pool of luminous filigrees around his hooves.

Amazed, Mikki watched him work. He moved in a small circle, always staying close to her within the torchlight. But he didn't just pull the threads from the breeze. Sometimes he reached into the leaves of the ancient tree above them and plucked heretofore unseen threads from the leaves. Then he'd shift his focus and sweep his hands through the forest plants that pushed up through the verdant loam. All the while the pile of exquisite threads grew. She couldn't look directly at the threads for too long. They made her dizzy with their shifting and glowing. In the pile she thought she glimpsed the shapes of people, but they were all disjoined. It was like trying to study a Picasso through the warped glass of a carnival mirror.

So instead of the threads, Mikki watched Asterius. He moved with the grace of a warrior coupled with the strength of a big cat. Despite the horns and cloven hooves, he seemed more lion than bull-like, with his mane of hair; his dark, bottomless eyes and his feral grace. And suddenly those eyes were focused on her. He was breathing heavily, and his arms were damp with sweat.

"Of all the wonders you've shown me tonight, watching you pull the threads of reality from the darkness is what I think is the most incredible."

"Would you like to try it?"

"Oh, yes," she breathed.

"Then this time, you must come to me."

With no hesitation, she walked to him.

"Do you trust me?" he asked.

"Yes."

"Then turn your back to me."

Mikki turned around. She felt him close the small distance that separated them. He bent so he could cup one of her hands in each of his. "Open your hands and press them against mine, so my claws become yours."

Mikki spread her fingers wide, fitting them against his much larger hands. Then she pressed her arms to his until she was molded against his skin. Their bodies met, and she felt the sharp intake of his breath and the shudder that moved through him—her own body answered with a heat that made the inside of her thighs tingle.

"Now, move with me."

And she did. Her hands combed through the night air along with his. She felt the tingle of the threads against her palms. When his hands closed on them, so, too, did hers, and suddenly the scenes within the threads were no longer dizzying. They focused in her sight and became clear. It was like she was watching a movie tape unreel as she pulled it from the darkness. She saw a woman whose back was turned to a man, as hers was to Asterius. The woman was naked, and the long, soft line of her back was only broken by her fall of copper-colored hair. *Like my hair . . . she has my hair . . .* Mikki thought dreamily. Then into the scene came two arms, thickly corded with muscles and covered with skin the color of burnished bronze. The arms cradled the woman, pulling her back so her body rested against his naked chest. The man tilted his head forward to nuzzle the woman's neck, and light glinted off his two ebony horns.

Asterius's growl fragmented the scene the thread was revealing. Mikki stumbled and almost fell as he lurched away from her. When she caught her balance and turned to him, he was standing beside the torch, with his head down, surrounded by piles of gossamer thread. She could see that he was breathing heavily, and as she watched, he wiped the back of his hand across his forehead. His hand was trembling.

"I need to take the threads back to the palace." His voice had retreated to emotionless formality.

"Have I made you angry?" Mikki asked.

"No."

"Then why are you being like this?"

He lifted his head and looked at her. Mikki thought she had never seen such haunted eyes.

"Did you see it, too? The scene in the thread?"

"Yes," she whispered.

Suddenly, with choppy, violent motions, he started gathering the piles of thread. "I do not understand what has happened. These are the threads of reality. They are to be woven into dreams that will come true."

Silently, she unwrapped the palla from around her shoulders and spread it on the ground near him so he could pile the threads on it.

"And?" she prompted when he didn't go on.

"And it is not supposed to show fantasies and falsehoods!"

The force of his voice caused the torchlight to flicker, but Mikki didn't flinch. Instead, she closed the two steps between them. She watched him fall suddenly very still. She reached up and let the tips of her fingers briefly caress the side of his face. He quivered under her hand, but he did not pull away from her.

"Do you dislike it when I touch you?" she asked him.

"No!"

"Do you want to touch me, too?"

"Yes," he snarled through his teeth.

"Then I don't understand why you say the scene we just saw is a fantasy and a falsehood."

"Because I am a beast and you are a mortal woman!"

"Stop it!" She glared at him. "You're the one making this impossible. I don't care about the beast! All of this"—she made two brusque gestures at his horns and hooves—"didn't stop me from wanting you way back in Tulsa when you started coming to me in my dreams—and I didn't even know the man within you then. Why would it stop me from wanting you now?"

"Mikado, you do not understand. There is more here at stake than what may or may not happen between the two of us. You are only—"

"Here for the roses! Damnit, Asterius! I know that. Do you think I'm incapable of doing my job and loving you, too? Jeesh! The people in this realm have said some ugly things about my old world, and some of it is even true, but I'm beginning to wonder about the priestesses who came before me. Were they not able to multitask?"

"Please. I beg you not to say things to me you do not mean."

Mikki thought he sounded as if his heart had been rubbed raw.

"What are you talking about? I'm being completely honest with you."

"A mortal woman cannot love a beast."

"Who told you that?"

He looked quickly away from her.

Mikki walked to his side and let her fingers brush his cheek again. He closed his eyes as if her touch pained him. "Was it the last Empousa, the one who caused Hecate to get angry at you?"

His eyes shot open. "Who spoke of her to you?"

"No one—no one would. But I'm not stupid. You made Hecate angry. The Empousa's gone. The roses are sick. I'm here, and it's you who brought me. Come on—it's just not that tough to figure out that something happened between the two of you."

"I am forbidden to speak of the past."

"I get that. You and everyone else around here are forbidden. But I'm not, so let me explain something to you. One—I am not her. I'm sure I'm quite a bit older, and, let's say for the sake of argument, quite a bit wiser. Two—I come from another world, which means I don't have the prejudices the women of this world have. For example, I don't have a problem getting my fingers dirty taking care of the roses. And I don't have a problem seeing the man within you. Now, I want you to answer one question honestly and clearly for me, and I don't want to hear any of this 'I am forbidden to speak of it' crap."

"Ask," he said.

"Is there a rule that says Hecate's Empousa cannot love her Guardian?"

His dark eyes met hers. "I know of no such rule, but there has never been any need for one."

Mikki held her breath and said, "There is now."

"Mikado, you say you see the man within me?" His voice was strained.

"Actually, what I'm saying is that I might be falling in love with the man within you. I think I have been since you came to my dreams." She wasn't touching him, but she was standing close enough that she could see that his body was trembling.

"That may be, and just hearing you say those words is a rare and wondrous gift, one I have never before been given. But you must understand that though I have the heart and soul of a man, I also have the passions of a beast. I force the beast to submit to me, but he is always present, and he is as ravenous as the man for love."

Mikki felt a rush of emotion that made her heartbeat increase. But she wasn't afraid. She was fascinated. She took his hand and slowly raised it to her lips.

"I could not love the man without accepting the beast."

"Does it not make you fear me?" his deep voice growled.

She rested her cheek against his hand. He cupped her face, and she kissed his palm. "Does the beast within you want to hurt me?"

"No! He wants to love you, but he doesn't know how."

"Then we'll have to teach him."

They finished gathering the threads in silence, but their hands met often and their eyes spoke of dreams yet to be fulfilled. They retraced their path through the forest, too preoccupied with one another to sense the presence that lurked in the shadows, its red eyes ravenously following their every movement.

CHAPTER TWENTY-SIX

ASTERIUS carried the threads wrapped in the silk palla, and they made their way quickly through the sleeping gardens. They walked closely together, with arms brushing. He welcomed the sizzle of pain that contact with her body caused him. It was a price he was gladly willing to pay for her closeness.

Asterius's mind was a blur of thoughts. *Her touch still pains me, so she does not love me yet, but could she be falling in love with me? Could it be possible? And if she isn't—if this is a sham or an odd impulse she deigned to follow, but will regret*... His chest tightened. He should leave tonight with the gift of words and hope she had given him. It was enough.

It was not enough! The beast within him roared.

But it must be enough. Even if by some miracle she could love me, it wouldn't change anything. Her destiny must remain the same.

Asterius's mind and heart were at war, and he remained silent, fighting internal battles and savoring the soft brush of her arm against his.

Mikki tried not to think at all. Every so often she would steal a sideway glance at his strong profile—the square jaw, wide forehead, pointed onyx horns . . . A chill shivered through her—part trepidation, part fascination. She wasn't going to think. She was going to follow her instincts.

Both of them were preoccupied enough that together they were surprised when the stairway to Mikki's balcony was suddenly in front of them.

"I will take the threads to the Dream Weavers," he said gruffly.

"That's a good idea. They're waiting for you." She made a motion as if she wanted to touch the pile of gleaming thread but seemed to think better of it and dropped her hand to her side. She looked from the threads into his eyes and said, "The dream that we were in—will the women see it and weave it into a tapestry, too?"

He looked thoroughly surprised by her question. "I do not know. I have no personal experience with dreams coming true."

Mikki tilted her head back so she could look up into his face more easily. "You don't have dreams?"

"I do, but they do not come true. Since I swore an oath to be in Hecate's service, I have been watching the dreams of others come true without being granted any of my own." He continued to look into her eyes. "You already know I am the son of a Titan and I have lived for countless centuries, with more centuries stretching endlessly before me. I also want you to know I will remember today for as long as my heart beats."

"You sound like today is over."

He smiled, flashing sharp, white teeth, but his eyes remained sad. "It was a pleasing day, but as with all things, it, too, must end."

Mikki didn't want it to end, not yet. She wanted . . . she wanted him to . . . Her mind fumbled through possibilities. What did she really want him to do? Standing so close to him she was, once again, struck by his size and the powerful melding of man and animal—the cloven hooves and furred legs—the muscular chest and powerful shoulders—the face that looked like it should belong to an ancient warrior god and not a creature who was part beast. In her dream she had been pursued by him and then had ended up in his arms. It had been erotic and exciting, but it had been a dream. Reality was much different. For one thing, he was definitely not pursuing her. For another, she had to remember what he'd said about the beast within him. She was no fairy-tale Beauty, and he was not going to turn into a foppish prince if she agreed to marry him. Hell, he hadn't even asked her. Who knew what his intentions were—half the time his expression was so masked that she couldn't even guess at what he was thinking.

But what were *her* intentions? She'd admitted to him that she might be falling in love with him. What did that mean? Just how hard and far was she willing to fall?

"If there is nothing else you require of me, then I bid you good night, Mikado."

When he finally spoke, she realized she'd been standing there staring stupidly, speechlessly at him. She blinked her eyes, feeling a little like she was coming out of a trance.

"There is one more thing you can do for me."

Mikki climbed quickly up three of the balcony steps. He started to follow her, but she turned so he had to stop abruptly. She was almost at eye level with him, and for a moment he just stood there, enjoying the exquisite sensation of being so physically close to a woman who did not shrink from him or treat him as if he was an errant hound. Then she put her hands on his shoulders.

"What may I do for you, Mikado?" Despite the instant pain that began to radiate through his skin at her touch, he tried to speak as softly as possible, mentally cursing his inhumanly powerful chest and the voice that boomed from it, afraid that he would frighten her again. Afraid that she would stop touching him . . . or that she would not.

"This," she whispered.

She leaned forward and touched her lips to his. He could not move. It was as if her kiss had turned him back into stone. She pulled away, but only by a hand's width, so she could meet his eyes.

"Your lips are warm," she said, still whispering.

"Yours—yours are unimaginably soft." He somehow got the words free from where they had lodged in his throat.

"May I kiss you again?"

He knew she could feel his body trembling under the uncommon and bittersweet pleasure caused by the weight of her small hands. Not trusting himself to maintain control of his voice, he nodded.

This time her lips lingered. With a supreme effort of will, he pushed aside the white-hot jolt of pain and drank her in. Her scent filled his senses. Mikado was sweet rose spice and warm mortal woman, and she was touching him—kissing him—almost in his arms. It was more intoxicating than any of the magick he had at his command.

"It's better if you kiss me back," she murmured against his lips.

As he had watched so often in other men's dreams, he opened his mouth slightly and tilted his head. When her tongue flicked briefly against his, Asterius's body responded automatically. With a growl that changed to a moan, he dropped the palla so the luminous threads spilled all around them on the stairs. His hands came up and circled the gentle curve of her waist. She leaned farther forward so her full breasts pressed against the leather of his cuirasse. He could feel the heavy heat of them, just as he could taste her. He wanted her with a lust that was as white hot as the agony that was coupled with his desire. His pulse pounded in his temples as his blood surged in streams of liquid fire through his body. There was nothing in the world except Mikado—her touch, her taste, her heat. He had to have her. Even if the pain destroyed him, he had to have her! He had to bury himself in her and pump an eternity of need into her seductive warmth. Her arms went around his shoulders, and the kiss deepened. He slid one hand up the smooth line of her back as the other dropped down to cup her irresistibly round ass and bring her closer, holding her tightly against his throbbing length.

Ah, Goddess! He'd never felt anything like the delicious pain of having her body pressed against his.

His pain-filled and lust-fogged mind didn't register her first cry. He only heard the second because she had begun to struggle to get away from him. Breathing hard, he forced himself to lift his mouth from hers. Then he smelled blood. Her blood. He stared at her lips. They looked swollen, bruised. One was cut and bleeding. Her eyes were wide and she, too, was panting for breath.

"No!" he growled. Releasing her, he staggered back a step.

She took a shaky step back, too, so her body pressed against the banister. When her back touched the marble, she winced.

"What have I done?" he rasped.

"Your claws . . ." she began, her voice sounding unnaturally shrill. "You must have scratched me."

He looked down at his hands. His claws were fully extended. His eyes shot to her. *Oh, Goddess! Please no! Please don't let me have harmed her!*

"Let me see your back," he said, but when he started to move toward her, she jerked back another step away from him. He stopped, as if she had driven a stake through him, impaling him into place.

"It's fine. I'm sure I'm fine."

Mikado's eyes were filled with fear—and something else. Something he was sure he recognized—loathing. He knew the look too well. He'd seen it the night the other Empousa had rejected him. Her eyes, too, had told him she feared and loathed the beast. Slowly, making no further move to touch her, he collected the spilled threads, gathering them into the palla. Then he straightened and walked down the staircase before allowing himself to look at her again. She was still standing with her back pressed to the banister, watching him with wide, stunned eyes.

"I did not mean to hurt you. I do not ask you to forgive me, because I know that is not possible, but I do ask you to try to believe that I did not want to hurt you. I would never want to hurt you." With a choked growl, he turned and fled into the night.

When he was gone, Mikki wiped a trembling hand across her mouth and winced. She felt the cut on her lip with her tongue. She hadn't even known his teeth had done that. Her knees were wobbly, and she climbed the winding staircase slowly, but she didn't go to her room. She kept walking along the length of the balcony and down the stairs that hugged the eastern side of it. Thankfully, she didn't have to call for Daphne. As she'd ordered earlier that evening, the servants had begun leaving thick towels and extra chitons and nightdresses, along with soaps and oils and jugs of wine in large baskets near the baths. They had, of course, protested that it was their duty to attend to the Empousa's needs at all hours. But Mikki had insisted. She'd known she would want the privacy to bathe without being attended to and watched—she just hadn't known she'd want it this soon.

She unwound herself from the chiton, filled a goblet from a jug of red wine and gingerly lowered herself into one of the steaming pools, sucking in a breath as the mineral water covered her back.

It had scared the shit out of her. She'd been kissing him and liking it. He'd tasted like man with something musky mixed in—something as alien as it was exciting. And he'd felt . . . she shivered. He'd felt like stone, only his body was warm and unbelievably powerful. And he'd wanted her. Desperately. She could feel his muscles bunch and quiver under her touch. She reveled in the hard length of his erection as it pressed insistently against her, and her own body responded with an answering heat and wetness that felt so damn good it made the back of her teeth ache. She'd rubbed against him, teasingly erotic, loving how easily she could feel his body through the thin silk of her chiton. The low, rumbling growl he'd breathed into her mouth had thrilled her. She was doing that to him! It was she who had held that incredibly powerful beast in her arms and made him tremble for her. She'd molded herself against him, fitting her softness to him. It had been like her dream, only better. She didn't have to wake up alone and limp from an unsatisfying solo orgasm. He was right there. She could have him—all of him.

Then the pain had mixed with the pleasure. She'd known he hadn't meant to extend his claws. He had simply been lost in her and passion had triggered an automatic response. She'd tried to tell him—tried to push him away. He hadn't seemed to hear her at first, and then . . .

She sighed and closed her eyes. Then he'd been horrified. He'd seen the fear in her eyes and he'd run, especially after she wouldn't let him get close to her. He'd misunderstood. Of course he would. How many women had looked at him with fear in their eyes? That's probably what that other damn Empousa had done. When he'd said that Hecate had no reason to make a rule stating that the Guardian and the Empousa could not desire one another, he'd been intimating that there had been nothing between the two of them, but she knew he was hiding something. They were all hiding something they didn't want her to know. The other Empousa had broken his heart. Maybe that's why Hecate had sent him away, so he could get over her. And maybe she'd fired the other priestess because she'd rejected him. Who knew why? Who knew the why of anything in this strange realm of dreams and magick and desire?

Mikki thought about the hopeless look on his face as he'd left her. She'd broken his heart, too. She hadn't meant to. It was just that she'd been so shocked—shocked and afraid—when his claws had scratched the length of her back and she'd felt the raw rush of lust that had been her response. She'd wanted to sink her teeth into his lip and demand that he fuck her right there, rough and fast, over and over. To feel his strength fill her and to know that his lust, his passion, his barely controlled violence was hers . . . Mikki shuddered with the pleasure of remembering how it had felt to imagine that she could claim him whenever she wished and that he would respond with that same flame until she was finally sated as none of the inadequate men in her life had ever been able to do. It had overwhelmed and intrigued and shocked her to get a glimpse of what would finally satisfy her—and know that "what" was not a man, but a beast.

The simple truth was that she hadn't been afraid of him; she'd been afraid of herself.

CHAPTER TWENTY-SEVEN

"I THINK we got a lot accomplished, especially for only working half a day." Mikki wiped her hands together and surveyed the neat beds of newly fertilized roses that framed Hecate's Temple. If she didn't look too hard or think about the weird sick feeling she carried around in her gut whenever she was near the unhealthy roses, the gardens appeared almost normal, especially in this area of the realm closest to Hecate's Temple. Here the roses were all in shades of lavender and purple, and even in their sad condition, their sweet fragrance filled the space. Water flowed from the huge multi-basined fountain to trickle steadily into the marble troughs that stretched from its base outward and all the way to the four corners of the gardens. Nera had explained that the fountain carried water to all of the rose beds. Mikki had never imagined such a beautiful irrigation system.

"The work proceeds well. Many of the women were smiling and laughing today," Gii said.

"That's just because rumor has it that I'm going to cast a spell to invite men into the realm." But Mikki smiled back at the Earth Elemental. The women had worked hard and done so with good attitudes, especially today. She was keenly aware of it, because she had been struggling all morning with a decidedly surly attitude, which she had gone to great pains to hide.

Damnit! Asterius had shown not one hoof or horn or hair all morning. True, she hadn't called him. There hadn't been any reason for her to. Most of the heavy work had been finished the day before. Today the women were focusing on deadheading and clearing out weak canes. Neither task required his brawn. But he could have shown up to say good morning or check in or something—anything!

Logically, she understood that he believed she had thoroughly rejected him after he'd hurt and frightened her. But the sad truth was that love and lust were not logical. She'd wanted to see him—expected to see him. And she didn't want to have to force him to come to her or even ask him to come to her. She wanted him to come because he couldn't stay away.

"Empousa, shall I dismiss the women, or would you rather they stayed while you cast the sacred circle and invoked the spells?" Gii said.

"Oh, sorry. Yes, dismiss the women. I don't want an audience yet." Mikki pulled her thoughts into line. "And tell the other handmaidens that I want to do the magick work first. We can eat afterward."

"Yes, Empousa." The Earth Elemental hurried away.

Mikki frowned and chewed her lip. Instead of obsessing about Asterius, she should have been deciding exactly what she was going to do for the garden spell. She sighed. The man-drawing spell was easier to figure out—or at least she hoped she'd figured it out. For the other, she still had only half-formed ideas and confused musings. Crap.

Much too soon the four Elementals were waving and calling to her from their places around the ever-burning flame within Hecate's Temple. Mikki hooked her hair back behind her ears and brushed at a smudge of dirt on her violet-colored chiton. She'd been leery that morning when Gii had brought her the piece of beautiful material, thinking it would be damn awkward to work until noon with one boob exposed, but Gii had laughed and said that exposing her breast was only the ritual dress for rites during the dark of the moon. Otherwise, it was enough that she simply wore the color of the Spirit Elemental for spell casting. Well, that had been a relief. Or at least it should have been a relief, but part of her mind whispered that she would love to see

Asterius's reaction to her wearing the more seductive garb—that is, if he had bothered to come to see her that morning.

Mikki climbed the steps and entered the goddess's temple. Its beauty soothed her nerves. She straightened her spine and walked with her chin up. She was High Priestess here, granted power by a great goddess. It was not appropriate that she moon over a guy (or a beast) when she should be focusing on the work of an Empousa.

Mikki took her place in the center of the circle. She closed her eyes and cleared her mind, breathing deeply and centering herself. Then she envisioned the threads of light she had seen the last time she'd cast the sacred circle and how they had formed a boundary of magick and power, linking the four elements together. When she felt ready, Mikki turned to the east and approached Aeras.

"Hello, Aeras."

"Empousa." The Wind Elemental fell into a deep, graceful curtsey.

Calling the elements to the circle was easier this time, and Mikki worked her way deosil through Air, Fire, Water, and Earth quickly and with much more confidence than she'd shown the first time. When she called upon Spirit, the protective threads that encompassed the circle's boundary were shining and clearly visible, even in the bright midday light. Then Mikki drew another deep breath and took a moment to listen carefully to her internal voice before she began the ritual.

"Hecate, Great Goddess of the Ebony Moon, I ask that you grant me the power and knowledge to call health and protection to the Realm of the Rose."

The spirit flame in front of her leaped in response, and she felt a sudden rush of energy within her body. Following her instinct, she turned first to Floga.

"Floga, you are Flame, and I command that your element protect the realm. Each night when the sun sets I want torches to blaze all along the rose wall, sending light into the darkness and causing that which would hide in the shadows to look elsewhere for camouflage."

Dancing flame licked the handmaiden's body as she ritualistically replied, "This you ask of me; therefore, so mote it be."

Next, Mikki approached the Water Elemental. "Nera, you are Water. Your part in today's spell will be health and not protection. Every fourth sunrise I want soft rainwater to wash the gardens in a brief, refreshing shower. It isn't enough that the realm is irrigated; the roses need the touch of your element on their leaves to keep them healthy."

Nera's pale blue chiton rippled around her body like waves lapping a shore. "This you ask of me; therefore, so mote it be."

Then Mikki stood between Gii and Aeras. She looked from one to the other as she addressed the personified elements. "Gii, you are Earth. Aeras, you are Wind. I command that you join to nurture the health of the roses. Gii, I want you to summon ladybugs from the forest." Mikki paused, picturing the kind little red-and-black-spotted insects in her mind. "And Aeras, I want you to call the wind to carry them into the realm so they can find a new home here"—she smiled at the pretty Wind Elemental—"just like I have."

Together, Gii and Aeras intoned, "This you ask of me; therefore, so mote it be."

Then she returned to the place of Spirit and said, "I thank you, Wind, Water, Fire, and Earth—powers of the elements—divine spirits of nature. With Hecate's blessing, I asked that you always be present in this realm of dreams and magick and beauty. So I ask of thee, and so mote it be."

As she finished the spell she had a sense of completion, as if she had just cleared a rose bed of particularly nasty weeds. *One spell down, one to go . . .*

This time she started with the Wind Elemental, just as she'd begun casting the sacred circle there. She'd already thought about what she would ask of the elements, already planned out the words and practiced them in her head that morning, so as she spoke her mind wandered . . .

"Aeras, I command that men be allowed within the realm again, but only by a woman's invitation. If she speaks the invitation aloud, carry the words on the wind to her lover and then let him come to her."

Asterius . . . that's the name I would call and the lover I would have the wind invite to me . . .

Mikki moved to the Fire Elemental. "Floga, your affinity is with flame. Use the heat of your element to ignite the passion of any man who is desired by a woman of the Realm of the Rose. Let their passion burn as bright and hot as fire."

I know he wants me. He proved that last night. I wish Asterius would burn for me so much that he couldn't stay away—couldn't let our differences separate us.

She stood before Nera. "Let your element ready our bodies for the sweet intrusion of accepting a lover. Hot and wet and ready—that's what I wish for each woman who desires a man in her bed, so each will experience the physical thrill of the consummation of love."

I want him in my bed. I want his body joined with mine, and I don't want to be afraid of my desire for him anymore.

Almost without knowing how she got there, she found herself in front of Gii. "Earth is rich and wild, fertile and lush. Let your element fill the senses of the lovers. Let them know the fullness of love that is as deep as an ancient forest and as ripe as the sweetest fruit."

Help me not to fear loving him so Asterius can finally know a love like this with me.

Back at the Spirit flame, Mikki's body felt flushed. Her nipples prickled against the soft fabric of her chiton, aroused and ready.

"Hecate, I ask that through your power and the powers of the elements that this realm be a place of passion and love, as well as peace and enchantment. So I ask of thee, and so mote it be."

Mikki closed her eyes against the rush of liquid desire that slid through her body, and she had to bite her lip to keep from moaning his name aloud.

Asterius . . .

SHE shouldn't have been surprised at the speed with which the hand-maidens made their excuses and drifted off to their separate rooms. By this time Mikki knew that the women of the realm lived in the west wing of the enormous palace, so far from her own room she could have gone ages without knowing they were there had Gii not told her. Mikki smiled to herself as she walked dreamily up her balcony stair. She could definitely imagine what was going to go on in the women's wing tonight. *I wish the same thing was going on in my room—only with more growling and biting.* A little bubble of laughter escaped from her mouth. She still felt hot and flushed—giddy. No. That wasn't right. She felt hot and flushed—horny. Mikki looked around her balcony. Empty. She'd hoped he would be there. He was male. He had to have felt the spell, and he had to have known she was the only one who could have cast it.

What if he thought she was opening the realm to men so she could call someone else to her? But how could he think that? She'd used his name during the ritual; she'd thought only of him.

The truth had to be that he was staying away because he thought he'd hurt her. Or maybe because he was afraid he would hurt her if he came to her.

Just the thought made Mikki shiver with erotic pleasure. All that power—a beast barely harnessed by the soul of a man. It was delicious beyond belief. And so damn poisonously seductive.

Okay, she could call him to her. He'd have to come. But is that what she wanted? Of course not. She wanted him to come to her of his own free will and . . .

. . . And that was it. He needed her to come to him. If she did, she'd be showing him she wasn't afraid of him and she cared enough—desired him enough—*loved him enough*—to come to him.

Gii had said his lair was below the baths. Mikki didn't stop to primp or to think; instead, she followed her gut and her heart. She hurried from the balcony and down the path that led to the hot springs. From the top landing, she descended the stairs that connected the large bottom pool to the separate baths on the landing above. She hadn't been down on this level before, but it didn't take long for her to find a second stairway, one that clearly was not as well used as the others. It declined sharply, turning to the north. The end of the stairs emptied into a grassy area that hugged the side of the cliff on which the palace and the springs sat. To her right the grounds opened up to the labyrinth of Mikado Rose beds that were, by far, the healthiest roses in the realm. She knew her private temple sat in the middle of the spiral arrangement of beds; she'd been through the whole area with Aeras and Asterius the day before. So she also knew that there was no lair stuck out there.

Mikki studied the wide patch of grass. It ran along the base of the cliff, just like a path. She smiled and followed where her instincts led. Turning the corner, the cliff wall abruptly opened into a smoothed out entrance to a cave.

"Or better yet, a lair," she whispered.

She held her breath, stepped inside and was instantly surprised. The entrance had only been a little larger than an average-size door, but inside magickally smokeless torches lent a warm, yellow light to the area, making it look very un-cave-like and welcoming. The cream-colored walls were high and smoothed like the baths of the hot spring. They were also covered with lush paintings. Awed by the talent of the artist, Mikki gazed at the walls. The scenes showed a rocky island surrounded by white sand beaches and water that was a brilliant turquoise. The only person in the landscape was the faint outline of a tall, golden-haired woman.

Crete—these have to be images he remembers from the island of his birth. And the woman? Is it his mother, or the Empousa who rejected him? Not sure if she really wanted to know, she turned away from the beautifully decorated walls. There was a large wooden table in the middle of the room. On it was a bowl filled with cold meat and cheese and a pitcher of wine. There were also several rolls of parchment and glass bottles filled with a thick, dark liquid. Intrigued, Mikki came closer and realized the liquid was ink. One of the parchments was unrolled and held into place with smooth stones. An almost-finished ink drawing was on it. She walked around the table to see what he had been sketching—and gasped. It was her in the ritual dress she had worn her first night in the realm. She was standing in Hecate's Temple, in front of the Spirit flame. He'd somehow captured the aura of power she felt within the sacred circle, as he depicted her hair flying around her and the look of rapture on her face. It was a beautiful sketch, obviously drawn with loving attention to detail as well as a master's talent.

A beast didn't do this. A man did this, and one who might be very much in love.

"You should not be here!" he snarled.

CHAPTER TWENTY-EIGHT

T HE power in his voice caused the torches to flicker madly, but Mikki didn't cringe or start in surprise. Slowly, she raised her eyes from the sketch. And then her stomach lurched. He was standing in a rounded doorway that led to another room deeper within the cave, and he was almost naked. The leather cuirasse was gone, as was the tunic. All he had on was something that looked like a short linen towel slung low and tied around his hips. She licked her lips and reminded herself that if she didn't speak he would assume fear had paralyzed her.

"You wouldn't come to me, so here I am."

She could see his angry facade falter, and when she smiled, he seemed at a total loss as to what to say. She tried to ignore his almost nakedness, and instead nodded at the walls of the cave. "The paintings are beautiful. Is that Crete?"

"Yes."

"You're very talented. Just looking at these makes me want to go on a long Mediterranean vacation." Before he could formulate a response, she pointed to the sketch of herself. "And this is flattering. I didn't even know you were there that night."

"It wasn't meant to flatter."

"I didn't mean that in a bad way. I meant you made me look pretty and powerful, and that's flattering."

"That is how I see you," he said.

"Really?"

"I will never lie to you."

"Some people would say evasion and omission are lies," she said bluntly.

"Mikado, if the goddess has commanded me to do or not do something—or to say or not say something—I must obey her. I have given her my oath."

"Okay, I understand that. I'm sorry. It's just extremely frustrating for me to be in a situation where I don't know all the facts."

"If I could answer all your questions, I swear to you that I would," he said.

"Well, that's something I guess." She sighed and looked back at the walls of the cave. "How about you show me around? This place is incredible."

He didn't move from the doorframe. "Is that why you came here, Mikado, to have me show you my lair?"

"No. I came because I wanted to see you."

"Why?"

"Because you didn't come to me today. I missed you, especially after I cast the spell that would allow men into the realm."

"I am not—" he began.

"Jeesh, enough! Didn't we go over this yesterday? I know you're not a man, but man or not, when I was casting the spell, you were who I thought of," she said.

He looked away from her, and she could see the tension in his jaw and the way his hands kept clenching into fists.

"I know." His voice sounded strained. "I felt the spell, and I felt you thinking of me. I wish you would not."

"Why?" It was her turn to ask.

"Because I cannot bear it!"

Mikki thought it sounded like he had to grind the words between his teeth to get them out.

"I wasn't afraid of you last night," she said abruptly.

"I saw the fear and loathing in your eyes, but I do not blame you. I wanted only to hold you in my arms and kiss you, and I couldn't do even that small, ordinary thing without becoming a beast."

"You didn't want to do any more than to just kiss me?" she asked, smiling seductively at him.

His eyes narrowed. "If I show you my lair, will you leave me in peace, Empousa?"

"Probably not."

"I thought you were not mean-spirited; I see that I was mistaken," he said woodenly.

"I'm not being mean-spirited! I'm just doing a really awful job of trying to explain myself. I'm nervous, and I don't know how to put what I'm feeling into words." She wanted to fidget or pace, but she forced herself to be still and look him in the eye. "You didn't hurt me last night, and I wasn't afraid of you. I wanted you, even more so when it got a little rough between us. I liked it, Asterius. Your power—the strength in your body that you barely hold in check—is more passion than I've ever known in my life. Until I met you, men were inconsequential to me. And now I think I know why. They always seemed weak, especially when I compared them to the women who had raised me. You see, Asterius, I need someone who is more than a man. Last night when I realized that, the truth of my passion did frighten me. My fear had been formed by the voices I'd heard all my life—the voices of a mundane world that would be shocked by what I feel for you."

Asterius didn't speak for a long time; he just stared at her as if trying to comprehend something she had said that was very important to him, but spoken in a language he barely understood. Finally, he said, "Would you still like to see the rest of my lair?"

"I would."

He stepped from the doorway. "This is my bedchamber." He gestured for her to precede him into the room.

She walked through the arched doorway and entered the room. She could feel him follow her. Her whole body was attuned to his presence, as if he was a cobra and she was attempting to charm him. Then the beauty of the room registered. It was smaller than the main room, and it, too, had torches that gave off no smoke. Only here there were fewer of them so the room was dimly lit. The floor was covered with thick animal pelts, in the middle of which sat a huge pallet covered with more pelts. *This is where he sleeps.* The thought sent a wave of wet heat through Mikki's body. She looked quickly from the bed to the walls and was amazed all over again. The walls were filled with scenes from a garden covered with tier after tier of magnificently blooming roses. Each level of the garden held a water element, and in the central tier sat a large statue of—

"It's Tulsa's Rose Gardens!" Mikki gasped. "How could you have had time to paint this since you've been back?" She approached the smooth wall and touched it cautiously. It was completely dry. "There's so much here; this should have taken you months, or even years to paint."

"It did," he said.

She looked over her shoulder at him, not sure she had heard him correctly. "How can that be?"

"I painted this from images I saw in my dreams."

Caressingly, she skimmed her hand over the wall. "It's perfect. You got all the details right."

"Does it make you long for your home?"

She could feel him getting closer to her, but she didn't turn around, afraid that if she moved, he'd shy away. "No. The Realm of the Rose is my home now. I don't want to be anywhere except here, with you."

"I ached to come to you today," he said.

"And I couldn't stop thinking about you." Mikki's hand was trembling, so she dropped it quickly to her side.

He was so close to her she could feel the heat of his body against her back. Then his hands were on her shoulders and his mouth was against her ear. "When you cast the spell opening the realm to men, I felt you calling to me . . . beckoning . . . asking . . ." He growled low in his throat, and Mikki could feel the vibration through the depths of her soul. "I thought it would drive me mad to stay away from you."

"Then don't stay away from me. I don't want you to stay away from me," she said breathlessly and she pressed back into him, feeling his erection push against the swell of her ass. His hot lips were on the side of her throat, and she could feel his sharp teeth barely graze her skin with his kisses. When his hands left her shoulders to cup her breasts, she arched to meet him. Her arms went up to pull his head down to her, and, just like in her long-ago dream, she felt his horns through the thick mane of his hair at the same time his teeth found the hollow between her neck and shoulder and teased her with a stinging bite. She moaned and pressed herself more firmly against him.

Suddenly he froze.

"No, don't stop," she pleaded.

"It—it's gone!"

With the words his breath came out in a rush, and she could feel his body begin to tremble violently. Worried, she turned in his arms. He was staring at her with an expression of mixed joy and shock.

"What's wrong? What's gone?"

He took her face between his hands. "You love me." His voice broke on the words, and tears dripped silently down his cheeks.

She smiled. "Yes. I love you, but what's gone?"

He closed his eyes, trying to contain the raw joy of his emotions. "The last of the spell, my Mikado, and the last barrier between us. No matter what the Fates may bring, I will love you until the end of time."

He bent and kissed her gently. Fisting her hand in his hair, she pulled his mouth more firmly against her. His growl moved through her already-aroused senses like a knowing caress. He lifted his head and opened his eyes. They were dark and fierce with desire. His bronze skin was already slick with sweat. She ran her hands down his body, from his shoulders over his chest, to the cords of his abdominal muscles, which quivered under her touch. When she'd begun touching him, he'd taken his hands from her face, and now they were braced against the wall on either side of her so she stood in a cage of his arms.

"Don't move. Just let me touch you," she said huskily.

"I do not know how long I can keep my hands from you." His chest rumbled, passion straining his voice.

"It won't be long." She touched the side of his face and then traced his lips with her thumb. "First I want to see you—all of you."

She saw the automatic doubt that shadowed his eyes, but he nodded slowly, acquiescing to her need. Her hands slipped down his body again, this time not stopping until her fingers hooked in the linen wrap tied low around his waist. She pulled at the fabric, and it came free easily. Mikki stared at his naked body.

"Your father's wife meant to curse you, but she had actually created a creature of incredible beauty," she whispered the words into life. "You're not an abomination; you're a miracle."

He was raw male power so perfectly blended with beast that it was difficult to tell where exactly the man ended and the beast began. His waist tapered to flanks and thighs covered with dark fur. From his waist down he was less thickly muscled than he had appeared to be when his body was clothed. Naked, his lean, powerful lines were visible. Mesmerized, Mikki stroked the place where the skin of the man gave way to the body of the beast. Asterius bowed his head and growled. She looked into his face. His eyes were tightly closed, and he was breathing heavily in an effort to control the creature within. Mikki felt a hot rush of desire as she watched the beast stir. Her eyes moved back down his body. He was fully erect and formed like a man. The skin that covered his shaft was the same bronze of his chest. Mikki took its heavy length in her hands, stroking with one, squeezing with the other. When she touched him, his eyes opened to find her watching him.

"You don't always have to keep the beast chained, Asterius," she whispered. Still stroking him, she leaned forward, circling his nipple with her tongue. "Let him loose, my love. I'm not afraid of him." She took the hard nub of his nipple between her teeth and bit sharply down.

His snarl was a wave of thunderous sound. He lifted her into his arms. His hooves thudded heavily against the pelt-covered floor as he strode to his pallet. He laid her there, but before he could cover her with his body, she stood, causing him, once again, to pull back. In his pained expression she read too easily what he was thinking.

"You've got to stop believing that I'm afraid of you. I'm not. I didn't stand up to get away from you. I just thought you would like this off . . ." Mikki began to unpin the silver rose brooch that held her chiton together over her right shoulder, but her hands were trembling and she could not unclasp it. Frustrated, she looked up at him and then her expression changed to a seductive smile. "Would you do something for me?"

"Anything," he rasped.

"Unsheathe your claws and get this thing off me."

With a movement catlike in its grace, he silently extended the daggers from his fingers. Quickly and easily, he sliced through the material at her shoulder. She shrugged and the chiton fell from her body. His dark eyes gazed at her. He lifted a hand to touch her breast and then jerked it back when the still extended claw met her soft flesh. Mikki caught his wrist.

"Your control is so great that you can create beautiful art with these claws. Use that same control to touch me with them. Let me feel your power against my skin." Unflinching, she pressed his hand against her breast.

Hesitantly, he let the sharp points graze the creamy smoothness of her skin as his hand moved from her breast to her stomach and slid slowly . . . slowly . . . over the wet, hot core of her. Mikki sucked in her breath and shivered.

"Don't stop," she moaned.

His eyes never left her face as his claws trailed down her thighs and then around to rake softly over the voluptuous swell of her ass.

"Turn around. I want to see your back," he said, his deep voice rough with desire.

Mikki turned. She felt his lips replace claws as he kissed the raised pink lines he had left on her back.

"I thought I had ripped through your skin." His breath was hot against her skin.

"Of course you didn't. They're just scratches."

His lips moved to the small of her back, and his tongue tasted her. "I didn't think I would ever touch you again."

She turned and wrapped her arms around his neck as he licked and teased her nipples.

"Don't ever stop touching me, Asterius."

She sank down to the pallet, pulling him with her. He knelt beside her. Sheathing his claws, he touched her face gently. "I could not stop now, Mikado, even if Hecate herself appeared and commanded it."

"Shh." She pressed a finger against his lips. "I don't want to think about anything else except you." Slowly, she lifted her hand until the same finger that had pressed against his lips traced the smooth line of one dark horn. "You are amazing. I don't ever think I'll get enough of touching you."

"Mikado, you are a rare and unexpected gift." His deep voice trembled with the depth of his emotions. "I have never known the love of a woman—never, in all the eons of my existence, has a woman touched me, accepted me, loved me . . ." He had to pause before he could continue. "I will love you for as long as there is breath in my body, and beyond, if the Fates and our goddess will it."

"Come to me, Asterius. Show me the power of your love," she beckoned.

He worshipped her with his mouth and hands. He drank in her body as if he would never get enough of it. He explored her and, with the superhuman senses of a beast, he read the flushes and changes in her body, learning what brought her the most pleasure. And then, when he thought he could never know anything sweeter than watching the passion he had built within her, she pressed him to the pallet and began her own exploration. When her tongue teased him and she whispered against his skin that the hard length of his body was magnificent and how much she desired him, Asterius thought he would die of such exquisite pleasure.

"I need to feel you inside me."

Mikki opened herself to him. He trembled with the effort of controlling himself as she wrapped her legs around him and arched against him. Blood rushed painfully through his body, and the roar of the beast filled his mind. The beast wanted to pound violently into her, to bury his aching hardness in her wet heat. He clenched his teeth, sliding carefully in and out of her, trying to focus on her soft sounds of pleasure through the tumult in his mind. And then he realized that she was meeting his gentle thrusts with a fierceness that blazed in her eyes. When he bent to kiss her, she bit his lip. He growled. She smiled.

"Let the beast loose. I want him," she said in a deep, sultry voice.

Her words ignited a flame of lust within him that he was afraid would consume them both. Unable to fight against the combined force of her desire and the power of the beast, Asterius grabbed her ass and lifted her up to meet him as he impaled himself within her, over and over again. Mikado didn't shrink from him. She answered his passion with a strength that was goddess-touched. The beast and the priestess blazed together, until finally the man within could no longer stop the raging force and he poured a lifetime of need into her as beast and man together roared her name.

CHAPTER TWENTY-NINE

H E couldn't stop looking at Mikado. She was asleep, her naked body pressed against him. She was using his arm to cushion her head. One of her long, smooth legs was thrown intimately over his inhuman one. Her hand lay limply on his chest. He drew a deep breath, letting her scent imprint upon his senses.

He'd never imagined this. Even when he'd wildly hoped that the other Empousa might care for him . . . love him . . . he'd only thought about the sweet softness of her hands touching him. It was only in his dreams that he'd allowed himself to imagine making love to a mortal woman. But his dreams never came true. Until now. Until Mikado. When he had touched her and realized that the pain of the goddess's spell had been lifted, and what that meant, she had spun reality into his dreams, and in doing so had healed the wound of loneliness that had been festering within him for an eternity.

What was he going to do? She had saved him. Could he do any less for her?

If he did not sacrifice her, the realm would die. It might not happen immediately. Hecate might find another Empousa, but irrevocable damage would already have been done. The betrayal of one Empousa had caused sickness in a realm that had never before known blight or pestilence or illness of any kind. Those things did not belong in Hecate's realm of dreams and magick. But betrayal and abandonment had caused the barrier to weaken. Asterius was certain that only Mikado's swift action had prevented further disaster.

So he must choose between destroying his dream or destroying the dreams of mankind.

It was really no choice at all. Only a beast could choose himself over mankind. He felt the agony of what he must do press against him like a flaming spear thrust into his entrails.

"I can feel you watching me," Mikki said. Sleepily, she opened her eyes and smiled up at him. "Don't you ever sleep?"

"I would rather gaze at you." He brushed back a thick strand of hair from her face.

"I should have guessed that you'd be a romantic when you put the rose in my wine."

"That is not romantic; it is civilized." He tempered the gruffness of his voice with a slight smile and caressed the graceful slope of her neck and shoulder, smiling again when she sighed happily and stretched like a contented feline.

"Don't burst my bubble. I prefer to think of it as romance."

"Then, for you, I will call it romance, too." Slowly, with a sweet hesitance and innocence that were at direct odds with the fierceness of his body, he bent and gently kissed her lips. "When you came to me today, you offered me more than your body and your love. You offered acceptance. And that is something I never imagined knowing the joy of."

She took his hand and threaded her fingers with his. "That's something you and I have in common. In my old world, I didn't feel like I belonged." She took a deep breath and made the decision. She wanted him to know. She needed him to know. "Hecate explained to me part of the reason I felt so out of place—because I was meant to be her Empousa in this world, that I carry the blood of a High Priestess in my veins. But there's another reason. It's why I never let anyone, especially any man, get too close to me. It has to do with my blood, too." She studied his dark eyes, silently pleading with him to understand. "The women of my family are tied to roses through their blood. If we feed roses water mixed with our blood, they grow. Always—incredibly. In the mundane world, what I could do was unheard of—outside of the women in my family, no one would understand. It made me feel like I was a freak. I had to hide my secret." Worried by how still and pale he had suddenly become, she felt herself shrinking inside. "I wish you'd say something. I've never told anyone else." When he still didn't speak, she started to move away from him, but with a low growl, he pulled her fiercely into the protection of his arms.

"You did not feel accepted there because it was your destiny to be Hecate's Empousa—to come here and to save the roses and their lonely Guardian. The blood that runs through your veins is this realm's life force, and it is your love that sustains us." He closed his eyes and buried his head in her hair, willing himself not to tremble . . . willing himself not to think . . .

Mikki relaxed and fitted herself more comfortably against him. "It still amazes me. If the exact sequence of events hadn't happened, I wouldn't be here." She leaned back in his arms so she could look into his face and wondered, briefly, about why he still looked so pale. "You know, it was my blood that woke you up."

"I did not know." His voice was gravely. "I just know you roused me and that I could smell your scent and knew you were Hecate's Emp-ousa."

"Actually, that's one of the weirder aspects of what happened. Just that day an exotic old woman had given me some perfume. On impulse I wore it. As strange as this sounds, it is the same scent I'm wearing now. Gii calls it the Empousa's anointing oil."

He frowned. "How can that be?"

Mikki shrugged and nestled back against him. "I have no idea, but she was really eccentric. And beautiful, even though she was old. She had the most incredible blue eyes. She was foreign, but I couldn't place her accent. She said she got the perfume . . ." Mikki had to stop and think about what the woman had said. "Somewhere in Greece, if I remember correctly. What I do remember for sure is her name, because, like me, she's named after a rose—Sevillana."

She felt the jolt of shock jerk through his body. She pulled back to find him staring at her with an unreadable expression on his unnaturally pale face.

"What is it? What's wrong?"

"It—it is . . . nothing. Nothing is wrong. I am only surprised that a woman in the mundane world would carry the anointing oil of Hecate's High Priestess. It is a mystery." He wrapped his arms around her. "Lie against me. Let me feel your body touching mine."

Mikado lay on his chest, and as he caressed the long, graceful line of her back, his mind whirled unbelievingly. Sevillana . . . the name had sent shockwaves through his body. It was she! He, too, would always remember the cold beauty of her calculating blue eyes as well as her name. The last Empousa was still alive in the mundane world. How could it be possible? Time moved differently there, he knew that. But at least two hundred of that world's years must have passed. Perhaps the absent Empousa had taken more with her through the crossroads than a vial of anointing oil. Perhaps she'd managed to steal some of the realm's magick.

Then the enormity of the truth sifted through his shock. Sevillana lived! In the spring when an Empousa must be sacrificed for the realm it would be Sevillana and not Mikado who must die. All he need do was to find a way to return the absent Empousa to the Realm of the Rose. It had to be possible. Sevillana had escaped—she could certainly return. He held Mikado more tightly. That was his answer. He would not sacrifice Mikado. He would exchange her for the errant High Priestess, returning Mikado safely to her home in the mundane world. He would still be without her, but Asterius could live with that. He would miss her for all of eternity, but he could bear that. What he could not bear was knowing that it was by his hand she would die. If she left, he would lose his love. If he sacrificed her, he would lose his soul.

He wouldn't sacrifice his love, nor would he lose his soul. He had his answer, and he had the powers of the son of a Titan. He would turn that vast store of magick to achieving his end. But not now. Not to-night. Tonight he would revel in the miracle of Mikado's love, and he would not think about the endless empty dawns to come.

MIKKI leaned against the smooth entrance to the cave and gazed out at the misty morning while she chewed a piece of bread. Asterius came up behind her, and she leaned comfortably into him.

"Rain," he said, sounding surprised. "It does not often rain here."

"I did it. It's what I commanded Water to do when I cast the health and protection spell yesterday. Every fourth morning it's going to rain for a little while. It's good for the roses, and it's good for the realm, too. Rainy mornings are restful—a perfect time to sleep in and rejuvenate the soul." She turned in his arms. "Unfortunately, I didn't think to tell the handmaidens yesterday that rainy mornings equate to taking the morning off. I imagine the four Elementals are wondering impatiently why I haven't called them to work. And because last night was the first time men could be invited into the realm in a long time, I would bet that at least a couple of them are tired and grumpy while they wait. I should go see to them. What are you going to do?"

"I will do the same thing I do every morning. I will follow the rose wall around the realm to be certain all is secure. Then I will collect more threads for the Dream Weavers." He caressed the side of her face. "Only this morning I go about my duties with your scent on my skin and the memory of your smile, touch, taste, in my heart." He smiled. "Some say rain is dark and dreary, but to me this morning is bright and filled with promise."

"An incurable romantic. Who knew?" Mikki tugged at his cuirasse. "Kiss me so we can be on our way." She wondered if he would ever lose that look of startled happiness that was reflected on his face when she surprised him with a touch, or, like now, with a kiss. She sincerely hoped not. "Can you take time to eat the midday meal with me?"

He kissed her again before he answered. "Of course. All you need do is to call me to you."

"And tonight?"

"Command me, Empousa, and I shall obey," he said, dark eyes shining.

"You say that now, but let's see what you think of obeying my every command in a year or so," she teased, raising an eyebrow at him cockily, and was surprised to see his look tighten and his eyes lose all their sparkling humor.

"I would never tire of you, or of your commands, Mikado, not if we had an eternity to share together."

His words pressed heavily on her heart. How had she forgotten that he was an immortal? She would age; he would not. She would die; he would not. No! She wouldn't think about that now, not at the beginning of their love. They deserved time to savor the sweet, heady feeling of new love—in that way they were no different from any other couple. She wouldn't ruin the honeymoon of their love with dire thoughts of a future with her, shrunken and tottering around the gardens, leaning on his perpetually virile arm. Would he let her? Would he still want her then? *Stop it! I'm doing exactly what I just promised I wouldn't.* Mikki made her lips smile.

"I wasn't being serious; I was just kidding you, Asterius. But since you mentioned the whole command thing, I'll be happy to command you to come to me tonight." She glanced over his shoulder at the cozy cave, as filled with his presence as it was with the exquisite art he created. "Actually, I think I'd rather come to you."

"I do not believe you received the tour you requested earlier."

"Well, that's one of the things you'll be doing tonight, but only one . . ."

THE light rain changed the appearance of the gardens, washing them with a watercolor brush, turning reality impressionistic. Mikki decided she liked it. It went with the theme of the place—dreamy.

She meant to go straight to the palace and call the Elementals—the poor girls were probably going to be thoroughly pissed at her, especially if any of them had kicked someone scrumptious out of her bed—but she wandered, letting herself get lost in the misty magick of the roses. They felt better this morning. Even as she made her way slowly in a southerly direction, the sickness that had been pulling at her stomach whenever she immersed herself in the gardens didn't come. She even saw several hearty Floribunda lavenders she recognized as Angel Face in full bloom, where yesterday they had just been weak buds. Mikki smiled. Inordinately proud, she dubbed herself *Goddess of the Rose.*

And she daydreamed about him. Her body felt deliciously sore in places she'd forgotten she had. It had been almost a year since the last time she'd had sex, but she'd never experienced anything like making love with Asterius. His body . . . the man/beast mixture had been intriguing . . . alluring, but what she'd found most seductive was the freedom she felt with him. She could let her own beast loose when they were together and trust him not to turn away from her. He matched her, passion for passion. And he knew her—he saw into her soul. Asterius, Minotaur, Guardian—he knew what it was to be an outlander. Well, they had finally found their home—together.

"The rain was a clever idea, Empousa."

Mikki thought she'd stroke out at the sound of Hecate's voice. "Good grief, you scared the bejeezus out of me!" Then she remembered to whom she was speaking, cleared her throat and turned around to face the goddess with a heart that pounded painfully in her chest. "I'm sorry, Hecate." Mikki curtseyed as she had seen the handmaidens do so often. The goddess was sitting on a marble bench just a few feet behind her. "You surprised me. I shouldn't have spoken to you like that."

Hecate waved her hand dismissively. "My Empousa is allowed liberties few others will ever know." She gestured beside her. "Come, sit with me."

Swallowing down her nerves, she approached the goddess. The enormous dogs were at their position by her side, and they ignored Mikki completely. Hecate was clothed in the colors of night—black, the deepest blue and gray. She had manifested as the striking middle-aged woman again, and the light misting of rain looked like jewels in her dark hair.

"The spell of protection and health you cast yesterday was well thought out. I agree with your instincts. The rain refreshes the roses and the realm. Also, the little insects you commanded Earth to provide were a lovely surprise, and Wind was delighted to carry them here"—the goddess paused and then surprised Mikki with a musical laugh—"although you cannot see their red-and-black bodies through this mist."

"Ladybugs feed on aphids, and roses hate aphids," Mikki said, a little overwhelmed by Hecate's effusive praise.

"The roses thrive again. I am pleased."

"Thank you, Hecate."

"It was also good that you instructed Flame to illuminate the rose wall, most especially at the gate. Now that men will be coming and going again, you must take special care with the gate."

Mikki rubbed a hand across her brow. "I didn't even think about that. Uh! I'm a fool. How did I expect them to get in and out of the realm?"

"It is not a bad thing that you have allowed men here again. You've made many of the women very happy. All night I heard the names of lovers whispered in invitation and carried to the ancient world where they were eagerly accepted." Hecate's expression became sultry. "Still this morning lovers are being called and enjoyed by my women, who have long been revered as some of the most beautiful and intelligent in the ancient world. Having males about means we will have new life in the realm. Girl children are a blessing, and I look forward to the births."

"But Dream Stealers are in the forest. We have to be careful if that gate is opening and closing at all hours."

"You are the Empousa, Mikado. You may place limits on when the men are allowed to come and go." Hecate gave her a kind look. "It is good that you understand the dangers that lurk on the other side of the rose barrier, but you need not worry yourself. The Guardian's strength will protect the realm. Couple his vigilance with your nurturing of the roses, and all will be well in the Realm of the Rose."

Mikki tried not to think or react at all. She kept her mind blank and nodded respectfully.

"Excellent. Now, what I came to tell you is that I have matters to attend to which will take me far from my realm. You are not to be concerned if I do not visit here for"—she moved a round, white shoulder—"some time. Within this realm my powers are always here if you have need of them. I sense that you are relying more confidently upon your instincts, and for that I applaud your wisdom. Let your intuition guide you. If your blood and heart and spirit tell you something, then you may always believe it. And remember, Empousa, I applaud what you have done for the roses, but it is not so much your actions that have begun their recovery. It is your presence, and the blood tie you have with them that assures they will thrive. Be wise, Empousa. The dreams of mankind depend upon you . . ." Hecate raised her hand and disappeared in a glittering of mist.

CHAPTER THIRTY

MIKKI couldn't say she wasn't relieved that Hecate would be gone for a while. Of course she'd have to tell the goddess about her relationship with Asterius. Telling her would be ever so much better than Hecate reading her mind or finding out on her own some other way. Mikki wanted to run and hide just thinking about it. So she'd tell her, but she sure as hell didn't want to do it soon. It wasn't that she was ashamed that she loved Asterius, and it wasn't that she was afraid of Hecate, though the goddess was definitely intimidating. It was just that Mikki wanted to keep Asterius to herself. Why couldn't they have privacy to discover the shared secrets of new love? Even had she fallen in love with a man back in Tulsa, Mikki would have wanted time for the two of them to get over the newness of love before she hauled him around and opened their lives up for everyone to poke and prod. She was private, and the more important something was to her, the more private she was about it. Asterius was very important to her.

When Hecate returned from wherever, she would have a conversation with her about Asterius. Then she'd deal with the goddess's response, whatever it may be. Until then she would cherish this honeymoon period they had been granted and thoroughly enjoy the fact that she had finally fallen in love.

Satisfied with her plan of attack, Mikki left the bench and checked the surrounding beds and fountains to make sure she was heading in the right direction. Hecate's comments about the men coming and going through the rose gate had worried her, and, no matter what the goddess said, she was going to keep that worry fresh. Right now her instincts were telling her to check the gate for herself—then announce a curfew, even though she loathed the thought of acting like a den mother at a naughty sorority. She'd like to talk with Asterius about it, but it only made sense to place some limits on when the gate could be open. And also, she needed to find out who exactly could open it. Asterius could, of course, and he'd said she could, too. The Dream Weavers had mentioned that the Elementals had collected the threads of reality while he had been bespelled, so they had to be able to open the gate. But who else? It would be a massive headache if every woman in the realm could wave her fingers and have the damn thing part like the Red Sea. Clearly, there was a lot of work for her to do.

Checking her mental watch, Mikki picked up her pace. She really did need to get a move on and call her handmaidens. She could, of course, call them right now and have them meet her out here in the gardens, but it seemed too Nurse Ratchet–like. She'd much rather get the gate checked, hurry back to her room, change out of her wet (and torn, then pieced back together this morning) chiton, have Daphne bring some lovely tea and eventually have a comfortable meeting with the girls over a late brunch. And anyway, it was still early. The handmaidens weren't stupid. They could certainly look at the weather and realize that there was little work in the gardens they could do in the rain. Maybe they would even climb back in bed. Mikki smiled to herself, hoping they weren't climbing back into lonely beds—tonight she certainly wouldn't be.

The rain had moved lazily from drizzle to mist to a moon-colored fog that drifted over the roses as if they were in the Lake District of England. The fog thickened the farther south she walked, and Mikki was preoccupied with thoughts of the evening to come, trying to decide if she could sneak Asterius up to the hot springs for a whole new meaning to "scrubbed clean," when multiflora roses reared in front of her nose and she almost smacked into the wall.

"Remember, next spell tell Wind to blow away the fog after the rain," she mumbled to herself while she scanned the gate for signs of wear and tear. "You look good," she pronounced, patting part of the foliage.

"Priestess! Can you help us?"

Mikki looked around, trying to see where the deep voice was coming from. It was unmistakably male, which seemed out of place in the gardens.

"Here, Priestess! We're out here!"

Mikki realized that the voice was coming from the other side of the rose wall. She bent a little so she could look through a less-dense part of the climbing branches, and her eyes widened in surprise. Four men stood just outside the gate, surrounded by thick gray fog. Three of them were dressed as she imagined ancient Greek men should dress. In toga-looking outfits, with one arm bare, and regal purple embroidered cloaks tossed over their broad backs. They were all tall, well built and youthfully handsome.

The fourth man was clearly their leader and the one who had spoken. He stood in front of the others and was dressed in much the same style she was used to seeing Asterius wear, with a cuirasse over a short, pleated tunic. But there is where his similarity to her lover ended. This man was beautiful, tall and golden. Even in the foggy morning he shined. His skin was tanned to that singular color only a few true blondes get naturally—a healthy, burnished brown that looked like the purest of honey. It covered a body that was perfection. He was athletically built, without being too heavily muscled and brutish. His hair was thick and wavy, cut short enough to be masculine, but left long enough to be endearingly boyish. His eyes were so blue that Mikki could feel them searching through the roses to find her.

She'd never seen a man that handsome in person. Usually such perfection was limited to Hollywood and the machinations of filmmakers and plastic surgeons.

"There you are, Priestess!" He smiled, and his incredible face lit with warmth. "We're here. We answered your call."

She smiled back (who wouldn't return a smile like that?). "My call?"

"Well, Priestess, I can only pray to the Great Goddess that I could be lucky enough to be called by a beauty such as you."

Ridiculously, Mikki felt her face flush. "I've heard that blue eyes are weaker than brown or green. I think you've just proven the rumor true."

He laughed, and the sound was as catching as it was seductive. "Ah, I see my prayers have been answered! The goddess has granted me a priestess who has wit as well as beauty." He took a few steps toward the rose gate. His friends followed.

Mikki watched him move with a natural confidence that was easy and attractive—and so unlike Asterius's inhumanly feral grace that the comparison was jarring. She didn't desire the golden man, but she did feel a sliver of envy for the woman who had called him, followed instantly by a rush of guilt. What the hell was wrong with her? She'd just left Asterius's bed after proclaiming her love for him! And here she was gawking all calf-eyed at a handsome stranger? Maybe the rain had seeped through her head and into her brain, waterlogging it.

"Priestess, will you open the gate for us, or shall my comrades and I woo you through the prickly wall?"

"No!" she said a little too loudly. And then, feeling like an idiot, she added, "I didn't call you, so you don't need to woo me at all."

His expression showed honest disappointment. "I must apologize, gracious lady. I assumed you were one of the Elementals—Flame perhaps, with your wealth of fire-kissed tresses and your extraordinary beauty. It was, after all, Flame who called me here. I would have been a fortunate man had you been she."

"Sorry, I'm not an Elemental." Mikki smiled. She wasn't being unfaithful to Asterius by being polite to him—she was doing her duty as Empousa. After all, *she* was the one who cast the spell to allow men within *her* realm. "I'm the Empousa."

The man's aquamarine eyes crinkled endearingly at the edges with

his joyous smile. "Empousa!" He bowed with a lovely chivalrous flour-
ish, which the other men copied, each calling gallant greetings to her.
"What a fortunate coincidence that you were passing at this moment.
There is word that a new Empousa reigns in the Realm of the Rose. We
are honored to meet you." His smile was boyish with good humor.
"Though the meeting was shouted through a barrier of roses."

"You say Floga invited you?"

"She did, Empousa."

"Did she invite your friends, too?" Mikki tried to keep the mischievous grin from her face, but she failed miserably. She could all too easily imagine the Flame Elemental needing four men to extinguish her
passion—even if one of them did look like Adonis.

For an instant Mikki felt a stab of jealousy as she thought about the
Elemental's freedom and the ease with which she could walk side by
side with any man she chose.

"She did not, Empousa," said one of the toga-wearers who had
thick, dark hair and a well-defined face, bringing her thoughts back to
their conversation. "The Earth Elemental is the priestess whose call I
answer."

"Water called me, Empousa," another man said.

"I am fortunate to be summoned by Air," said the fourth man, who
had long, auburn hair and remarkably green eyes.

Damn, but they were four deliciously handsome men! Her Elementals definitely had made good choices. Mikki made a mental note to ask
Gii just exactly how this whole man-inviting thing worked. It was a
little weird that they had been called by the girls this morning, but then
again, maybe it wasn't. She hadn't called them to work—it was
rainy—they'd decided to busy themselves in their own way. Clearly
they were as smart as Mikki had given them credit for being.

"I'm sure the Elementals will be here any second. I'll be happy to let
you guys in."

Their leader's eyes lit, and he bowed again to her. "To be invited
within the Realm of the Rose by its Empousa is truly an honor we do
not deserve."

"Oh, it's no problem. We can walk back to the palace together. I was just going to head in that direction." And being escorted by four to-die-for-handsome young men was definitely not a hardship. Neither was it wrong. She felt an unexpected surge of anger. Hell, no! It wasn't wrong. She was in love, not dead. And all she was doing was taking the men to her handmaidens. The only ulterior motive she had was maybe to engage in some harmless flirtation. And why not? She felt amazingly pretty and completely loved. But that didn't mean she wanted to be controlled and caged! Asterius could just think again if he expected to put his brand on her and treat her like a prize heifer! Is that what Asterius would expect from her? To allow him to own her every movement? She was suddenly afraid that he might. He was, after all, a beast. She couldn't expect him to know how to treat a woman.

Somewhere in the depths of Mikki's mind a warning tried to cry its way through the cacophony of unnaturally defensive thoughts that bubbled and brewed like a rancid stew. But they could not be heard over the hatred and envy, selfishness and fear that were shouting so loudly.

Feeling totally pissed off, she moved to the middle of the gate and frowned at it. No doorknob. No latch. No bar to slide back. Frustrated, and especially annoyed at the massive headache that pounded in her temples, she raised one hand and pressed her palm against the gate.

"This is your Empousa speaking. Open the hell up," she muttered angrily.

The living gate instantly swung open. The four men stepped out of the swirling fog, smiling at her as if she had just given them the key to paradise. Mikki smiled absently back at them, wishing they'd hurry and get inside. She didn't like the looks of the gray-cloaked forest, and she wanted to get the gate shut right away. The second the last man was through, she raised her hand again and whispered for the gate to close, breathing a sigh of relief when it obeyed her. Then she turned to the men.

"Okay, the palace is that way." Mikki gestured to the widest of the marble pathways.

"After you, Empousa," the golden man said.

Mikki began down the path but stopped abruptly when the dark-haired man stepped in front of her to block her way.

"Uh, it's that way," Mikki said, pointing over the man's shoulder and thinking that he may be handsome, but he definitely wasn't the brightest Crayola in the pack.

"Perhaps you would like to know our names before you lead us to the palace, Empousa."

The golden man's voice came from directly behind her. He was standing so close she could feel his breath on her hair. The other two men stepped in to close the tight circle so they had her neatly surrounded, and in that instant her mind cleared—the pain in her head stopped, as did the deafening emotions that had been seething in her mind.

Mikki was suddenly, horribly afraid. They were Dream Stealers, and she had opened the rose gate for them.

Instincts that had been silenced from the moment she had begun talking with the golden man screamed at her not to show fear. Mikki swallowed the bile that had risen in her throat, drew herself up regally and turned to face the golden man.

"What is this all about?" she snapped.

"We're simply saying that we would like to introduce ourselves to you, Empousa. You see, we already know you. We've enjoyed watching you. Now we'd like for you to know exactly who you have so graciously invited within your realm." His voice had changed from charming to sarcastic. His lip curled at her, and his handsome face twisted in disgust.

"I don't like your tone, and I don't like how close you're standing to me," Mikki said sternly, trying to imitate Hecate's intimidating tone. "I think it's time you left. I've decided my handmaidens wouldn't like you."

"Too late! You opened the barrier to us, and you will see that once invited, we are not so easily banished." He reached out and lifted a strand of her hair that had fallen over her shoulder. Mikki tried to jerk away from him, but hard hands grasped her shoulders and held her in place as the golden man bent and sniffed at her hair. Mikki struggled. Fisting his hand in her hair, he jerked her head to the side. Like a snake tasting the skin of its prey, his tongue flicked out to graze the side of her neck.

"Ah, the sweet taste of an Empousa. It has been centuries since I've sampled this particular delicacy."

"Stop it!" Mikki cried. "Let go of me!"

Surprisingly, the golden man let loose her hair. He smiled at her, but it was a baring of teeth, not an expression of humor. "We're going to enjoy our visit with you, Empousa. And we do appreciate the weather change you commanded—all better to cloak our little rendezvous, though it looks as if someone has already had the pleasure of your company this morning." With reptilian grace, he lashed out and ripped the brooch that held together the torn pieces of her chiton.

Mikki was frozen with fear. She clutched at her chiton, trying not to vomit as the men crowded closer around her, grasping her with hungry hands and watching her with ravenous eyes.

"Come now, Empousa. Don't be shy. You can't say you don't recognize me."

"Or me," the dark-haired man breathed into her back.

"Or me."

"And me."

"Look into my eyes, Empousa. I'm sure you've seen me before. Can you not guess my name?"

She stared into the golden man's blue eyes—and they changed. The pupils shifted and became slits. The color faded and washed from brilliant blue to the red of old blood. Mikki did know him. Who he was seared through her mind, and with his naming came a fury that burned away her fear.

"Get your fucking hands off of me!" She jerked violently. Surprised, the dark-haired man holding her from behind stumbled and lost his grip on her, and she was able to back several steps away from them.

The golden man laughed and followed her with smooth, serpentine grace. "Good . . . we like it when they struggle. It makes it more interesting. What do you see when you look within my eyes, Empousa?"

"I see an asswipe who needs to invest in color contacts." She kept backing away. He and the other men followed her.

"Ha! I will have to teach you better things to do with that sharp tongue of yours. But for now, tell me, Empousa, what name would you give me?"

"Hatred," she said without hesitation.

His smile was fierce. "Ah! You are a quick study. Perhaps I will take you with me when we leave here. Would you like that? I am a man who knows intimately the hidden desires of women."

"Man?" She laughed sarcastically. "You're not a man; you're a creature. A carrion eater that feeds on the carcasses of dreams. I don't care what kind of skin you wrap yourself up in! You're no man."

He lunged forward and grabbed her arms. "Not a man? I'll show you how much of a man I am!"

As the others closed on her, Mikki screamed the one name that filled her heart and soul, "Asterius!"

"Your lover, whoever he is, will not save you now, and if you truly care for him, I suggest that you remain very quiet. No mortal man could look upon us without losing a part of his soul." Hatred breathed stinking breath in her face as he grasped the front of her chiton and ripped it from her body. "Cover her mouth, and be certain she does not make a sound. In this fog there is no chance we will be discovered until it is too late for her, and too late for them."

They dragged Mikki off the marble path into a bed of Salet roses. She struggled, kicking for groins and insteps and using her fingernails to gouge any flesh they came in contact with, as every damned self-defense class in America taught, but the four of them easily overpowered her. They pushed her to the ground, and she saw that the newly worked dirt was covered with the pink petals of destroyed roses, as if blushing snow had fallen to the ground with her. One of them was choking her. She could not scream, so within her mind she shrieked over and over *Asterius! Come to me!*

"And now, I will show you that I am, indeed, a man," Hatred said, pushing aside the front of his short tunic and taking his engorged flesh in his hand. "Then Fear, Envy, and Selfishness will have their turns with you." His laugh was thoroughly mad. "It is an interesting irony that Selfishness chooses to take you last. Or perhaps it is not. Perhaps he will choose to keep you to himself while we visit the women in the rest of your pathetic realm, Empousa."

Mikki caught a blurred movement from the edge of her darkening vision and then Asterius burst out of the fog. His roar of rage was deafening. Hatred whirled to face him. As the Dream Stealer moved, his body rippled and reformed until he was, as Mikki had accused, not a man, but a creature, and one that should exist only in the realm of nightmares. His skin was scaled, and his snakelike eyes bulged from a head shaped like a cobra's flared hood. His body had remained humanoid, but he crouched on all fours, hissing black froth from his open mouth like an evil reptile. Asterius's hand whipped out as he charged past the creature, slicing a bloody trail across Hatred's chest.

Mikki heard angry hisses from the creatures who were holding her and then she was suddenly free as Fear, Envy, and Selfishness hurried to stand beside their leader. They were truly a horrifying group. Each had retained something of his man form, but with monstrous mutations. Fear was a rotting corpse, with long, filthy claws and misshapen features. Envy's all-too-human body was covered with a sickening plant whose spikes burst through his skin like deadly thorns. He crouched, hissing, reminding Mikki of a poisonous swamp creature. Selfishness's body had elongated, and he had grown several sets of snakelike tentacles. He gnashed gruesome teeth while his arms writhed independently of one another.

They all faced Asterius as the Guardian charged them. Fear went down first, disemboweled neatly by the great beast's claws. The Dream Stealer's body crumbled and then dissolved, turning into scarlet smoke that hovered in an oily cloud over the rose beds.

Mikki scrambled to her feet.

"Aeras! Come to me!" she cried.

Moments later the wide-eyed Wind Elemental rushed up to her Empousa.

"Oh, Goddess! Save us from—"

"Hecate's not here. We have to save ourselves. Aeras, I command your element present. Blow in a mighty wind from the north and rid us of the smoke of Fear. Now, Aeras!"

White-faced, Aeras flung her arms wide. When she lifted them, a blast of cold wind hurled past them, carrying the morning fog as well as the red smoke over the rose wall and into the forest.

A scream of agony wrenched Mikki's eyes from the dissipating cloud and back to the battle. Asterius's dark eyes flashed, and he roared his fury as he dealt blow after powerful blow against the evil creatures. Each movement he made was controlled by a grace that was as beautiful as it was deadly.

She thought Asterius was the most magnificent thing she had ever seen.

He lunged and struck, and Selfishness was writhing on the ground, sliced tentacles spurting dark blood in a scarlet arch across the roses. Envy clinging to his back, Asterius lowered his head. With one blindingly swift movement, he impaled the fallen Dream Stealer, and at the same moment he reached around, plunging his claws into the base of Envy's spine. Both creatures' bodies shivered and then they, too, disappeared into clouds of blood-colored smoke.

"Again, Aeras!" Mikki commanded.

Aeras called the north wind, which banished Envy and Selfishness far into the ancient forest.

"You interfering bitch!" Hatred shrieked at Aeras.

Like a viper, he struck at the Wind Elemental, but Mikki was quicker, shoving Aeras out of the way. The Dream Stealer collided with the Empousa instead of her handmaiden. Mikki felt a searing line of pain explode across her shoulder and arm as she went down beneath him.

Then Hatred screamed. His body bowed as Asterius clawed his back to scarlet ribbons. With a terrible snarl, the Dream Stealer wrenched Mikki from under him. He spun around, holding the Empousa before him like a shield.

Instantly, Asterius checked his attack.

Hatred hissed evil laughter. "Why do you hesitate, Guardian? I am shielded from your rage by only a weak, mortal woman. Are you not willing to sacrifice your Empousa, even to rid the realm of hatred? I supposed that's hardly surprising. I seem to recall you have a weakness for Hecate's High Priestesses." The creature rubbed his groin against Mikki. "Not that I blame you. Her fruit is ripe and sweet."

Asterius's growl lifted the hair on her arms and the back of her neck. His voice was that of a deadly predator. "I will make you suffer for an eternity for touching her."

"I think not, Guardian. Instead, you are going to open the gate for me, and I am going to pass through it unharmed." The creature began pulling Mikki before him as he backed toward the rose wall. "If you get too close, I will play Destiny and slice her throat right now." He pressed the point of one jagged claw against Mikki's neck.

"This is not finished between us," Asterius snarled, moving carefully with the Dream Stealer and his hostage to the gate. "If it takes an eternity, I will make you pay for touching her."

"Hatred is never finished, Guardian. You should know that by now." He halted, his back to the gate. "Now open it for me, and I will return your Empousa to you, though I would enjoy having her entertain me for a while." Hatred bared his teeth at the Guardian as he bent so he could flick his tongue out and taste the High Priestess's salty-sweet neck.

And that was it. Mikki had had enough. More than enough.

"Oh, hell no!" she yelled, driving her thumb into the bulging, insectlike eye that he had been foolish enough to get close to her.

The Dream Stealer's scream of pain was deafening, and he hurled her from him, but not before Mikki felt his talon pierce her skin and the rush of wet heat that followed the wound. She grasped her neck and fell to the ground, watching through a haze of pain as Asterius picked up the writhing creature and bent his evil body back farther and farther until the Dream Stealer's spine was broken with a sickening crack. Asterius lifted Hatred and threw him over the rose barrier.

Then he was on his knees by her side, crying her name, touching her face, stroking her hair.

She tried to smile at him. *It's okay. It's not your fault. I let them in.* Mikki thought she was saying the words aloud, but she couldn't seem to make them come out. Then her four handmaidens were suddenly there, too. They were crying—even Floga, who Mikki thought hadn't liked her at all. She wanted to comfort them, to tell them she wasn't afraid and to ask them to please treat Asterius nicer because she knew, without any doubt, that she was dying.

CHAPTER THIRTY-ONE

ASTERIUS refused to lose her like this—not to Hatred—not when Mikado had brought love, desire, kindness and acceptance, everything that was Hatred's opposite, into his life. He lifted her in his arms and faced the distraught Elementals.

"Let us take her to the fountain, Guardian. There we will wash her clean and then lay her in Hecate's Temple, where we will offer prayer to the goddess for her soul," Gii said through her tears.

"She is not dead," he said and snarled a warning as Gii tried to approach him.

"Not yet, but her wound is mortal; soon her spirit will be in Hades' Realm," Nera said brokenly.

"No! It is not her destiny to die today!"

"The Fates have deemed otherwise," Aeras said softly.

"Then I defy the Fates!"

"Guardian, what will you do?" Floga asked.

"I will claim my birthright." Carrying Mikado's limp, bleeding body, he began to brush past them, but Gii's soft hand on his arm made him pause. When he glared at her, she met his eyes unflinchingly and said, "How can we help you?"

He hesitated only a moment. "Come to the temple. Perhaps the power of the elements will help my plea reach Cronos's ears."

Without waiting to see if they followed, Asterius rushed to Hecate's Temple, his hooves striking thunderously against the white marble path. He tried not to think about how still Mikado was and how much of her blood soaked their bodies. The beast simply ran.

He took the temple steps three at a time and then drew himself sharply to a halt in front of Hecate's sacred flame. Asterius dropped to his knees and gently placed Mikado beside the flame. He heard the handmaidens hurry into the temple after him. They quickly took their places, surrounding him in their familiar circle.

"Does she still live?" Gii asked.

Asterius looked down at his love. Her eyes were closed and her face was colorless. Blood still pumped freely from the long, slender slash that dissected her neck while her chest rose and fell in shallow pants.

"She does," he said.

"Then do what you can, Guardian. We do not want to lose another Empousa before destiny requires it," Gii said.

He lifted his eyes to meet hers. "Then summon your elements and form the sacred circle."

"You love her, don't you?" Floga said suddenly.

His gaze swiveled to Flame. "I do."

"And are you going to save her just to steal her away from us?" the Fire Elemental asked.

"On Beltane the realm's Empousa will meet her destiny. I give you my oath on that," he said.

"Even though you love her?" Aeras asked.

"Not long ago you watched me battle Selfishness. It is not the first time I have faced that particular Dream Stealer. This time I was victorious. I will not sacrifice the dreams of mankind for my own needs ever again." He looked back at Mikado and gently touched her cheek.

"You are not a beast," Gii said softly.

"I am," he said without looking at the Earth Elemental, "but I am also a man, and Mikado's love has made the man the stronger of the two."

"Then the four elements will help you save your love." Gii nodded at Aeras. "Begin, Wind."

The Elemental threw her arms wide. "I call Wind to the sacred circle!" Instantly, the air began to stir.

Like an electric chain reaction, Floga flung wide her arms, embracing her element. "Come to me, Flame!"

"Water! I call you to attend me!" Nera cried.

"Earth! I call you to complete the circle and to magnify the powers of our Guardian who we shelter within," Gii said.

Asterius felt the power of the elements sizzle across his skin. He bowed his head and raised hands stained with his lover's blood. In a voice magnified by Wind, Fire, Water and Earth, as well as by the beast within him, he shouted to the faraway reaches of the heavens.

"Cronos! Great God of the World and of Time—Titan divider of the heavens and Earth—Father! I call you by your ancient names as well as by the one my blood has earned me. I have lived for ages, and never before have I asked anything of you. Not acknowledgment or power. Not love or acceptance. But today I call upon you by right of birth and ask that you grant me the power to save this mortal. Her life's thread has been cut before its time—her string is not yet unwoven to its end."

The sacred flame stirred, and within its flickering light a man's face appeared—ageless, but well lined, as if it had been chiseled from young rock by time and experience. It was a face he would have recognized anywhere, for it mirrored his own so completely.

"Father," Asterius said, bowing his head.

The Titan did not acknowledge Asterius. Instead, he jerked his chin at Mikado. "Is this the mortal you would save?"

"It is."

"She is Hecate's Empousa?" Cronos said.

"Yes."

"Then her salvation will be only temporary."

"She has not lived her allotted time. It is not yet Beltane," Asterius said.

"What did this to her?" the Titan asked.

"The leader of the Dream Stealers, Hatred. I would not have her die from that creature's touch."

Cronos shifted his attention to his son. "Hatred has killed her, and you want love to save her?"

Asterius's jaw tightened, but he nodded. "I do."

"Love . . ." Cronos chuckled. "I am surprised by your weakness, Guardian."

"I have learned that love is only weak when it is selfish," he said, a clear challenge in his voice.

Surprise flashed over the Titan's face. "You remind me of your mother."

"That is probably because she, too, understood the weakness of those who love selfishly."

Cronos frowned. "I am not accustomed to being insulted when my aid has been asked."

"I meant no insult. I only spoke the truth," Asterius said quickly.

"Regardless, I grow weary of this conversation."

"Cronos! Forgive me. I did not—"

"Silence!" The flame flickered madly, and the floor of the goddess's temple shook. "I have not finished. I grant your request. You may share a piece of the immortality that lives in your spirit with the priestess. A very small piece, mind you. It will steal her from Hades' realm only this once. But know that there is a price for the spark of immortality you share with her. Even after she dies, she will carry that piece of your spirit. You will only feel whole when she is beside you, and your spirit is whole. When she no longer walks this realm, your heart will be empty and your days filled with loneliness. Think carefully before you make this choice."

"I have already made my choice. The cost is something I knew I would pay if I allowed myself to love her. I accepted it then. I do not mind accepting it again for her life."

"Very well then, it is your birthright to ask a boon of me, but do not trouble me again. You chose Hecate, and it is the goddess you must beseech in the future." Without another word, the Titan disappeared from the flame.

Asterius looked down at Mikado. His father had granted him the ability to save her, but how? He had to give her a piece of his immortality—a piece of his spirit. And then he knew. Slowly, he bent forward and touched his lips to hers. As he kissed her, he willed her to live—to share what he offered her and to accept him all over again.

Mikado stirred and sighed softly against his mouth and then she opened her lips and their kiss deepened. When Asterius finally pulled away, her eyes were open and she was smiling up at him.

"She lives!" Gii cried.

And then the handmaidens were laughing and crying together as they closed the circle and rushed to their Empousa's side. Mikki sat up and blinked in confusion, not sure where she was or why Asterius knelt beside her and was holding her hand right in front of the Elementals. She looked around. They were in Hecate's Temple? That wasn't right. She wasn't supposed to be here, she was supposed to be checking the rose wall to make sure that—

And it all came rushing back to her.

"The Dream Stealers!" she gasped, trying to get to her feet but finding that she was so light-headed that any abrupt movement made the temple pitch and roll sickeningly around her.

"Shhh," Asterius reassured her. "All is well. The Dream Stealers have been banished from the realm."

"I'm so sorry." She looked frantically from Asterius to the handmaidens.

"Empousa, you need not apologize. Dream Stealers are masters of manipulation. We should have prepared you better," Gii said, crouching to take her other hand.

"Yes!" Nera nodded her head a little frantically, as if that could convince her Empousa. "How were you to know the cunning games they play?"

"But I let them in. They told me that—oh, God! The things they made me think and feel! It was horrible."

Aeras smiled through the tears that washed her cheeks and touched Mikki's hair reverently. "You were very brave, Empousa. You took the blow Hatred planned for me."

Mikki had forgotten all about that. She frantically looked down at herself. She was covered with blood. How could anyone lose so much blood and live? She remembered the pain in her shoulder, but when she looked, she saw nothing but bloody skin. And there had been something else . . . something much worse . . .

Her eyes widened, and she felt a wave of dizziness. He'd slit her throat. She had been dying. But now she was very much alive. Slowly, she lifted her eyes to meet her lover's.

"It's over now," Asterius said.

"I was dying," she whispered.

"No. I could not let that happen," he said.

"He saved you," Gii said with a little sobbing hiccup.

"He saved all of us," Aeras said, wiping her face.

"We will never forget it," Floga said.

"Never," said Nera.

Mikki smiled at the Elementals. "He did what any honorable man would do to protect his home and those he loves." Then she wrapped her arms around his neck and whispered into his ear, "Take me home."

CHAPTER THIRTY-TWO

ASTERIUS carried her through the garden. Mikki wouldn't normally like being carried around as if she was a child, but she wasn't sure she could walk on her own. Her insides felt weak and sick. And she needed to be in his arms. She needed to feel his heartbeat against her own to reassure herself that she really was alive.

"Hatred tricked me," she said faintly, her head resting against his shoulder.

His arms tightened around her. "That's what Dream Stealers do. They infect mortals until their poison actually twists thoughts so that dreams sicken, and eventually, die. Do not punish yourself for falling prey to that which has been destroying mortal dreams for uncounted ages."

"I thought awful things. I was filled with . . ." She shivered convulsively, not able to continue.

"You were poisoned by hatred, envy, fear, and selfishness. They weren't your thoughts, Mikado, they were sick shadows of your infected imagination. You must not punish yourself for their evil, for that is a type of a victory for them. If they can taint your life, even after they've been banished, then they haven't truly been defeated."

"I'll never let them fool me again. And I'll never go into that damned forest again, either." She raised her head and stared at him.

"How do you stand it? How can you go out there and collect the threads of reality and know they're out there, too, watching and waiting for a chance to attack?"

"It is my destiny to battle them. Many of them are old, familiar enemies."

"Aren't you afraid?"

"Only when I think about what would happen if I failed and allowed them to have their way with the realm."

"But you won't ever fail," she said.

"No. I cannot."

She thought he sounded incredibly tired, and she hoped desperately that he wouldn't have reason to battle the Dreams Stealers again until he was well rested and—"Oh, God! Put me down! You have to go back and make sure the rose wall is okay and that no part of those things stayed in the realm."

"The realm is safe. The north wind blew the last vestiges of their evil deep into the forest."

"But shouldn't you go back and make sure everything's really okay?"

"All is well, Mikado. When Dream Stealers have been faced and defeated, they are loathe to attack again soon. They know that once they have been recognized for what they are, their power to taint lives is drastically weakened. They must retreat to lick their wounds and plot a new attack for another day."

"I remember Hatred said he is never finished."

"He isn't. We must always guard against him."

Something she had read once surfaced in her mind, and she spoke the words softly aloud. "Good defeated is stronger than evil triumphant." She touched the side of his face. "You fight on the side of good."

"And I will not allow evil to triumph."

"I won't let them taint my life; they won't defeat me." She lay her head back on his shoulder and then said, "How did you save me from dying?"

"I beseeched a boon from Cronos," he said quietly.

Her head snapped up again. "Your father?"

He nodded.

"You talked to your father?"

"Briefly."

"How long has it been since the last time you talked to him?" she asked, wondering at the odd, wooden expression that had hardened his face.

"I have never before spoken to him."

She studied him, feeling angry as hell at the arrogant Titan who had so cavalierly created and then discarded a son, wishing that she could erase the centuries of pain and loneliness in his past. Not knowing what else to do, she kissed him gently on the cheek.

"Thank you for saving my life," she said.

His face softened into a smile. "I was just returning the favor, Empousa. Remember, you brought me back to life once, too."

"That's right." She nipped his jaw. "And I like you better this way."

"Because you find that you are weary of walking, and you enjoy being carried about by your beast?"

Mikki laughed. "Well, the myths do say that the Minotaur was half bull, but I don't think bulls make very good beasts of burden. Rumor has it they're not docile enough."

"In this case, the rumor," he said, giving her a quick, hard kiss that ended in a growl, "is true."

BY the time they reached Asterius's lair, Mikki was tired of being carried, even though when he finally put her down the cave rocked a little under her feet. Especially after she realized that her chiton was hanging in shreds from her body, which was sticky with drying blood.

She groaned through clenched teeth. "I'm going to puke my guts up if I don't get this stuff washed off me." She glanced up at Asterius. "You may have to carry me up the stairs to my baths."

He swung her into his arms again, but instead of leaving the cave, he strode to his bedroom.

"Okay, I realize that my head is truly screwed up right now, but I do believe you're going in the wrong direction. Not that I don't want you to take me to your bedroom, but *after* I've washed this mess off of me."

"We keep forgetting to finish your tour of my lair."

"We don't forget; we get interrupted," she said.

"Then allow me to show you the rest of my lair without interruption." He carried her through his bedroom and then to a rounded doorway that fit neatly within a corner Mikki hadn't noticed before. It opened to a torch-lit tunnel, at the end of which was another rounded doorway, which, Mikki noted with surprise, was framed in sunlight.

"You know, this place isn't really very lair-ish. I mean, it's actually comfortable and beautiful. I think you should call it," she paused, thinking, while he took them closer and closer to the light. Then he stepped from the tunnel and into a large round room, the ceiling over the center of which was open to show the clearing morning sky. And also to allow the rising steam from the contained hot spring bath to escape. "I think you should call it paradise!" she breathed.

He laughed and put her down. In seconds, she'd stripped off what was left of her chiton and, with a satisfied groan, walked down the smooth steps and sank into the deliciously hot water. From behind her, she heard him speaking quick, sharp commands in the magickal language he used to call things to him, and she turned her head in time to see two baskets burst into being. One was filled with soaps, clean towels and lengths of soft chiton material. The other—she sighed happily—was full of food.

Asterius lifted a crystal bottle from the first basket and then smiled at Mikki. She grinned back, wondering at why he suddenly looked so shy.

"What is it?" she asked.

"Your soap," he said, holding up the bottle.

"I didn't mean the bottle. I meant what's that expression on your face about?"

"I would like to ask you something."

"Okay." Then she laughed. "You look a little mischievous." Feeling much revived by the warm mineral water, she gave him a sexy smile. "Are you feeling like being a little bit naughty?"

"I—I would like to bathe you," he said in a rush. And then he thoroughly shocked Mikki by flushing a deep red against the bronze of his skin.

"I would love that."

He walked to the edge of the rock pool and put down the crystal bottle. Then he took off his leather cuirasse and the short tunic he wore underneath. She loved looking at his body, watching as more and more of it was exposed. He was so physically powerful, such an amazing blending of extremes—man and beast, just as his mind was a blending of extremes, too. He was fierceness and compassion—childlike innocence and ancient knowledge mixed together to form a being truly unlike any other who would ever exist in any world. She was so distracted by her happy contemplation that it wasn't until he entered the pool that she realized the blood that spattered his body had come from more than her wounds. His arms were covered with slashes and bite marks.

"They hurt you!" She pulled him down so she could begin soaking the wounds in the hot water. "I'm such an idiot! Do you have bandages? Ugh—some of these look like they need stitches. There has to be a doctor in the realm. Let's get these cleaned up and I'll call for her, and—"

Asterius caught her wrists. "I do not need the healer."

She frowned at him. "Look, I worked at a hospital. Just take my word for it. You need a doctor."

He smiled and kissed her gently. "Your care for me warms my spirit."

"Lovely. I'm glad it does. It would warm *my* spirit if we'd get the doctor in here."

"Mikado, I am an immortal. I do not require a healer. The wounds already heal themselves."

Still frowning, Mikki lifted his arm and stared at it. "You're right! They are healing."

"Are you satisfied?" he asked.

"I'm dumbfounded," she said. "But definitely relieved." She splashed water over his arms, touching the newly healed bite marks, watching as the flesh knit itself together. "Is there any wound you can't recover from?"

"If you said you no longer loved me, it would destroy me."

She met his eyes. "Then you will live forever."

Asterius took the crystal bottle from the edge of the pool. "Let me show you how much I cherish you, Mikado."

She stood so the pool's water covered her only to her waist and then took the bottle from him and poured a generous amount of the heavy liquid over her neck, arms and breasts before putting it back on the ledge. The heady fragrance of the Empousa's anointing scent mixed with the heat of Mikki's skin, subtly changing it and making it unique to her.

Slowly, Asterius slid his hands over her slick skin. He caressed her neck and shoulders before moving to her breasts and the seductive flesh of her stomach. His hands dipped below her waist, carrying the rose-spiced scent to her thighs. Mikki felt as if she had turned to liquid heat as his hands slicked over her skin. His fingers found their way briefly between her legs, where he used his thumbs to stroke her with quick, circular motions, but then those knowing fingers would glide away, to tease her stomach or breasts before returning again to her core. She felt as if his touch was calling awake sleeping parts of her body that the warmth of the water continued to caress even when his touch had moved on. He turned her, and this time took the bottle himself and poured the soap in a thick line down her spine. Weak-kneed, Mikki leaned forward against the edge of the pool while his hands caressed her back and then dipped down to knead and cup her ass.

"Remember the last time I came to your dreams?"

She felt his breath hot against the middle of her back as he stayed on his knees and worked his clever hands across her skin.

"I remember," she said huskily.

Both of his hands slid around her body. She leaned back against him as they caressed their way slowly up her thighs.

"We were in a pit of roses." His deep voice rumbled across her skin, sending little ripples of pleasure through her body. "I was on top of you. You opened your legs to me." His fingers found the center of her excitement. The tempo of his caresses increased. "I was engorged, and when I pressed myself against you, rubbing and stroking, I could feel your wetness and heat and how your body gathered itself and then exploded with release." With a choked cry, Mikki climaxed, hard and fast.

And then he turned her to him, and in one swift motion lifted her through the water and impaled her while her body still pulsed and throbbed. Mikki arched to meet him, using the edge of the pool as support. His hands gripped her hips, and with a throaty growl, he extended his claws. His sex plunged in and out of her, exquisite in the barely controlled strength of his thrusts. Mikki didn't close her eyes. She wanted to see him, to watch the terrible beauty of his face as he loved her. Her skin was tight and overly sensitive, and jolts of pleasure were sensual shocks every time his claws shallowly pierced her skin. The liquid sound of him moving in and out of her coupled with his growls and the husky way he moaned her name, and it became an erotic symphony, the crescendo of which broke through her body with pleasure so intense it verged on painful.

She collapsed against him, breathing hard and feeling limp and replete. She was smiling contentedly against his chest until she realized it wasn't just his breath that was causing his chest to shake. He was trembling violently. Mikki pulled back to see that his eyes were closed and tears were slowly tracking their way down his face.

"Asterius?" She put her hand against his cheek. "What's wrong?"

He opened his eyes and kissed her palm. "It is only that I have been alone for so long—I find that I am unprepared for the happiness you bring me." He reached up and felt the tears on his face as if he hadn't realized until then that he was crying. "Does this make me appear foolish and weak to you?"

"No, my love. It makes you appear human."

CHAPTER THIRTY-THREE

THEY didn't leave his lair. They ate and discussed more changes Mikki wanted to enact in the realm—like a specific limit to the time the rose gate would be opened to allow men into and out of the realm. And the fact that the weather was growing colder as winter approached, so it would be prudent if Mikki commanded Flame to warm the gardens, even if just briefly during the darkest part of the night. Black spot, she explained to Asterius, liked to creep out in cold weather, and it was hard to get rid of once it spread.

Mikki loved talking with him, and it didn't take long for her to realize why. Asterius listened to her. Truly and completely, he heard what she said. She tried to think of the last man she'd known who had actually listened to her, and she couldn't remember one. Not one man had ever shown her the quality of respect and sincere interest Asterius showed her. It was supremely ironic that a being who wasn't literally a man knew instinctively what so many "real" men didn't seem to be able to grasp: women want to be heard and respected. It was really that simple.

His power thrilled her. It was a seductive lure of which she didn't think she'd ever get enough. She loved the exhilaration she felt just to be able to touch him, to stroke that incredible body and know he was hers.

That night they made love on the fur pallet, tenderly discovering more of the secrets their bodies held. Mikki delighted in the fact that his skin was so sensitive and that a light caress could leave him engorged and ready for her. Satiated, they fell asleep in each other's arms, secure in their love and the knowledge that tomorrow would be another day they would spend together.

"EMPOUSA! You must come!"

Mikki thought she was dreaming. She knew she was in bed with Asterius—she could feel him tense and surge from their pallet—but she also clearly heard Gii's frantic voice. What was the handmaiden doing in Asterius's lair? Then her sleep-clouded mind cleared and understanding burst in.

"What is the danger?" Asterius boomed, pulling on his tunic and buckling his cuirasse.

"The roses . . ." Mikki's mouth had gone dry, and her stomach clenched. "Gii, what has happened to the roses?"

Gii hurried to her Empousa's side, quickly wrapping the chiton she'd carried with her around Mikki's naked body while she spoke in quick, short sentences.

"The Elementals and I went to the rose gate at dawn. We thought to be certain no trace of yesterday's violence was left to disturb you." Gii's voice shook, and her face was deathly pale. "They're dying, Empousa. All of them."

"The roses!" Mikki said.

Though it wasn't a question, Gii answered, "Yes."

"The wall—is the barrier still intact?" Asterius said.

"Yes, and there are no Dream Stealers in the realm. No one is in the realm who shouldn't be. We made certain all the men departed yesterday, and none have been invited to return."

"I must go," Asterius told Mikki.

"Yes—go, go quickly. I'll be right behind you," Mikki said.

He paused only long enough to touch the side of her face in a gentle caress before the sound of his hooves echoed from the cave walls as he thundered from his lair.

"Hurry," Mikki said. "I need to get out there, too."

Minutes later, the two women rushed into the gardens. Mikki felt the change the instant she left the cave. Her head ached, and nausea rose in her throat.

"Show me the quickest path to the gate," Mikki told Gii and then neither woman had breath to waste on talking. They ran.

Women were crowded around the rose beds that ringed the gate, milling like frightened sheep. And Mikki understood why. It was worse than she had imagined. She pushed her way past them, taking only a cursory look at the dying beds. She needed to get to the heart of the disease that had suddenly afflicted the roses, and she knew she would find its center at the gate. She broke through the last group of women and staggered to a halt. Asterius was already at the gate, his keen eyes studying the forest as he paced back and forth before it. The other three Elementals weren't watching him; they were staring at the roses in the beds adjacent to the gate. Their faces were strained and pale. When they saw Mikki, they rushed to meet her.

"Empousa, it is terrible," Aeras whispered.

"What has happened to them, Empousa?" Nera said, keeping her voice low.

"I don't know. I can't tell yet. Give me room and let me examine them." Mikki felt the press of the women's fear almost as much as she felt the roses' sickness. "Have the women move back."

All the Elementals except Gii hurried off to speak to the watching, waiting groups of women.

"Do not ask me to leave, too," Gii said quietly. "You look as if you might faint at any moment. I want to stay with you. If you fall, I'll be there to catch you."

"As will I," Asterius said, joining them.

"The Dream Stealers?" Mikki asked.

He shook his head. "There is no sign of them. Not within the realm, and not as far as I can see or sense in the forest." He looked around at the roses. "But it seems they need not be present to destroy."

Mikki drew a deep breath. "Okay, then let's see what I can do to fix it."

The Elemental and the Guardian shadowed her as she moved slowly from bed to bed, examining rose after rose, but soon she forgot they were anywhere near her. The roses consumed her. She'd never seen devastation so horrible. They looked like they had been afflicted with a mixture of Botrytis Blight and Brown Canker and then burned from the inside out. The leaves were shriveled and covered in a dirty-looking fungus, but it felt like no fungus she'd ever encountered. It was sticky, and it smelled like rotting flesh. The canes of the bushes were blackened, with swollen places that looked like an old arthritic woman's knuckles. The buds were shriveled and a deep, bruised purple color.

Mikki straightened from inspecting another dead bush and gazed out into the gardens. Like a poisonous wave, she could see that the sickness was spreading, and she felt a bone-deep chill of fear. This blight wasn't natural. It had been brought to the realm by the evil of the Dream Stealers. Intuition told her that the disease had been in the oily cloud of evil each creature had dissolved into. They hadn't really been dead. She didn't imagine that creatures like that could ever really be killed. Hatred, envy, fear, and selfishness were emotions that would always slither around the fringes of mankind, waiting for their chance to strike and destroy dreams.

It was true they had been banished from the realm, but not soon enough. And Mikki had no idea how to battle something that had infected her roses through creatures of nightmares.

"Empousa," Gii asked timidly. "What would you have us do to save them?"

Mikki looked from the Earth Elemental to her lover. Both were watching her with expressions that were concerned, but she could also see the hope in their eyes and the confidence they had in her.

"I—I have to think! Just stay here and leave me alone for a second." Abruptly, Mikki walked away from them. She left the dying beds and went down the wide marble path that led to the rose gate, thinking she'd sit under the ancient oak and try to come up with a plan—any plan.

A splash of color caught at the corner of her vision, and she stopped and stared. Pink blossoms, in full and healthy bloom, filled two plants that sat in the middle of an otherwise blighted and dying bed. She hurried to the bushes, breathing their sweet scent and caressing the vibrant green of their leaves as if they were prodigal children newly returned. Salet Roses—she recognized them easily. They were one of her favorite Old Garden varieties, with their double blooms and abundant midseason and fall repeat blossoming. But why had these two bushes been spared from the killing blight?

She looked around, searching for spots of brightness within the ocean of rot and disease. She found a splash of red in the bed closest to the rose gate. Quickly, she made her way there. Three bushes there, all at the edge of the bed, were in full bloom. Their color and the deep, true rose fragrance of the blooms identified them as Chrysler Imperials.

What did the two types of roses have in common? Chrysler Imperial was a Hybrid Tea Rose; Salet was of the Old Garden variety. One was red; the other pink. And they weren't even near each other. Mikki stared at the healthy pink where it sat, blooming contentedly, seemingly unfazed by the death around it. Mikki shivered. Hadn't the Salet bed been the one the Dreams Stealers had forced her down in the middle of? They'd meant to rape her there. Thankfully, Asterius had arrived in time and—

Mikki's breath caught. She knew why these roses lived, thrived even in the midst of others that had succumbed to death and disease; she knew what all five bushes had in common. Her blood had touched each of them.

Mikki walked unsteadily to a nearby bench, making it just in time for her to sit as her knees gave way.

She had been in the Salet bed when she had taken the blow on her shoulder. Absently, she touched her shoulder, remembering how freely it had bled. Then near the gate—that was where Hatred had sliced through the vein at her throat. She vaguely remembered lying there, half in the bed, half on the marble path, as blood pumped from her body.

Her blood had saved the roses, had protected them from the Dream Stealer's poison. She put her face in her hands and tried to understand the enormity of her discovery. Over and over the words *my blood saved them* played in her head.

"Mikado, the women await your command."

She looked up, blinking her vision clear. Asterius knelt beside the bench and wiped the tears from her cheeks.

"Trust yourself, my love. You will find a way to heal them."

She stared into his dark, expressive eyes and knew what he said was the truth. She knew how to heal the roses, and she did trust herself. Now all she needed to do was to find the courage to act.

"I'm going to Hecate's Temple to speak to the women. Have the Elementals gather them and meet me there."

"Yes, my Empousa," Asterius said. He bowed to her and then took her hand and kissed it gently.

MIKKI stood within the raised temple. The four Elementals had formed a semi-circle behind her. Asterius stood behind them, near the goddess's ever-burning flame. Mikki looked out at the large group of women. They were silent, their faces set with worry and fear, every particle of their attention focused on their Empousa. She lifted her chin and drew a deep breath, projecting her voice into the crowd.

"We have a lot of work to do. We need to move fast, and we need to be focused. The disease that is killing the roses must be stopped, and I give you my word that I know how to stop it." She paused as a sigh of relief rippled through the crowd. "They'll be no dividing into the four groups this time. All of us need to focus on the area closest to the rose gate and work our way out from there. First, I want buckets of the strongest wine we have brought out to the gardens." She saw the looks of surprise on the women's faces, and it almost made her smile. "What you are going to do is to cut the diseased roses down to the ground. Then take the canes and pile them outside the rose wall, where Floga will burn them. As you move from bush to bush, be sure to dip your shears in the buckets of wine. It will help stop the disease from spreading to parts of the plants that have not been infected. Your shears must be razor sharp, and you need to make each cut at an angle." Her eyes passed around the group, looking confidently into the women's eyes. "Are there any questions?"

No one spoke.

"Then let's get to work." The women hurried off in groups to gather cutting tools and wine, and Mikki turned to face her handmaidens. "I wasn't exaggerating. We have to work hard and fast. The disease is spreading at an unnatural rate." Her eyes found Asterius in the shadows. "Asterius, as much as I don't like the idea of opening that damned gate, my instincts tell me that burning the sick roses inside the realm would be a terrible mistake."

"Then we follow your instincts, Empousa," he said. "And I will be there to guard the open gate."

"I know you will. That's why I'm not afraid to open it." She smiled at her handmaidens and had to work hard to keep the tears from her eyes. "And I know each of you will do whatever it takes to help heal the roses. I'm proud of you, and I believe in you. The Realm of the Rose will thrive again, I promise."

"We believe you, Empousa," Gii said. She walked to Mikki and kissed her gently on the cheek before curtseying and hurrying out to the roses.

"We trust you, Empousa," Aeras said. She, too, kissed Mikki before dropping into the familiar, graceful curtsey and departing.

The Water Elemental walked forward to take her turn kissing the High Priestess, but Mikki's question made her pause.

"Nera, I seem to remember that someone told me that the fountain"—Mikki nodded her head in the direction of the massive water feature that bubbled and frothed beside Hecate's Temple—"is the main source of irrigation for the realm. Is that true?"

"Yes, Empousa."

"So water in those troughs actually reaches all the rose beds?"

"Of course, Empousa." Nera smiled and continued. "Before you commanded my element to visit every fourth morning, it rarely rained here."

Mikki made herself return Nera's warm smile. "Thank you. That's good to know."

"We support you, Empousa," Nera said. She kissed Mikki and then departed.

"We love you, Empousa," Floga said. The last to kiss Mikki, Floga hesitated before curtseying. A tear trailed slowly down her smooth cheek as the Elemental said, "Forgive me for doubting you, Empousa. As my element, I am sometimes too rash and my thoughts burn too brightly."

Mikki hugged her. "There's nothing to forgive," she whispered.

When they were alone, Mikki went to Asterius and stepped into his arms. For just a moment, she let herself absorb his strength and his love, knowing the peace that comes with finding that one person to whom you were meant to be bound. But she didn't allow him to hold her for long. She couldn't.

TIME surprised Mikki by passing slowly. Maybe it was because the work of cutting the rotting, diseased roses and dragging them outside the wall to their pyre was so damn hard and depressing. Or maybe it was because Mikki's mind couldn't stop thinking about what the future held. Either way, it seemed that several eternities had passed in that one, endless day. Mikki had fallen into a hypnotic rhythm of cut—dip—cut—dip, so she was surprised to look up and see that, finally, the sky had darkened enough for Floga to light the torches up and down the rose wall.

"Gii," she called to the Earth Elemental, who hurried to her side, smiling even though her eyes were bruised with shadows and her arms were pink with thorn scratches. "That's all we can do today. Have the women finish dragging what they've cut through the gate, and let's call it a day."

"Yes, Empousa," Gii said, looking relieved.

Mikki didn't blame her. Her own shoulders were aching and her hands were bruised and sore from the shears. Thankfully, they were razor sharp—a group of women had spent the day doing nothing but sharpening and re-sharpening blades. Mikki glanced down at the shears. Carefully, she dipped them in the bucket of wine and then cleaned them in the grass before hiding them at the base of the rose she'd just finished pruning.

"The women are finishing their tasks as you commanded, Empousa."

Gii's voice made Mikki jump guiltily, which she covered with a small laugh. Then she took the handmaiden's arm and said, "Walk with me a little?"

"Of course," Gii said.

They walked together silently, taking a meandering path back toward the rose gate. Mikki was satisfied by what she saw in the rose beds. The diseased bushes had been purged. It looked stark now, but she knew that in the spring they would grow back and be healthier and hardier than before. Roses were survivors—not the delicate fainting flowers too many people believed them to be. Mikki knew better. She knew about hidden strength and resilience. Too often people had misjudged her, discounting her as a pretty face and nothing more, or worse, considered her opinions inconsequential because she was "only" a woman. She thought about Asterius. He, too, had been misjudged, solely on his appearance. Little wonder they fit so well together.

"You were wrong about him," Mikki said softly.

Gii glanced at her, surprised by the High Priestess's words. "Him, Empousa?"

"The Guardian. He's not a beast, and he doesn't deserve to be treated like one."

Gii stayed carefully silent.

"I don't know what happened before. I don't know what he did, and now, I don't want to know. But let me tell you what I do know. He saved this realm yesterday when my mistake could have destroyed it. He would do the same today and tomorrow—or for every tomorrow until eternity. He's honorable, Gii. And he's kind. Did you know that he's an artist?"

"No," Gii said.

"He is."

"He loves you," Gii said hesitantly.

"I know. I love him, too." Mikki drew a deep breath. "And that's why I want you to promise me something. I want you to promise me that you'll treat him better. Don't ostracize him. He . . ." She paused, struggling against a wave of emotions. "He gets lonely, and I don't want him to spend eternity alone. If you change the way you react to him, so will all the handmaidens who come after the four of you. Would you do that for me?"

Gii stopped and gazed into the High Priestess's eyes. What she saw there made her breath catch. Then, slowly, she nodded. "Yes, Empousa. You have my oath."

"Thank you, Gii. Now, let's get out of here. It's been one damned long day," she said with forced cheerfulness.

They reached the rose wall in time to see Asterius closing the gate, much to Mikki's relief. For a little while the four Elementals, the Guardian, and the Empousa stood with the women of the realm and watched the diseased roses burn at the edge of the forest. Then the women began to move off in little groups, calling tired farewells to Mikki, until only the Elementals were left.

"You did well today," Mikki told them, meeting each of their eyes in turn. "I want you to know how proud I am of you."

The handmaidens smiled wearily at their Empousa.

"Tomorrow I want you to sleep past dawn—we'll all need the rest. Then eat breakfast and meet me at Hecate's Temple. We'll start again then, doing the same things we did today—pruning and burning the disease from the roses. But I believe they will be better tomorrow."

"Is that what your instinct tells you?" Gii said, grinning at her.

"That's most definitely what my instinct tells me." Mikki smiled through the tight, hot feeling in her chest. Then, impulsively, she hugged each of them before saying, "If you need me, you can find me in the Guardian's home." She enunciated "home" distinctly, deciding then and there that she would never call it a lair again. "Good night," Mikki called, turning to join Asterius where he waited in the shadows.

"Sleep well, Empousa." Gii hesitated only a moment and then added, "Good night, Guardian."

Mikki was facing him, so she saw the look of pleased surprise that crossed his powerful face.

"Fare you well, Earth," Asterius said somewhat stiffly.

Then each of the other three handmaidens called similar good nights, leaving the Guardian to gaze in wonder after them.

"In all the centuries I have been Guardian of this realm, that has never before happened."

"I told you I was going to change things." Mikki linked her arm through his. "Let's go home."

CHAPTER THIRTY-FOUR

MIKKI stretched out on the pallet beside Asterius. The softness of the thick pelts was soothing against her flushed, sweaty skin. Absently, she traced a finger along the ridges of his abdominal muscles, prominent even as he lay there completely relaxed with his eyes closed. They'd made love twice. Once in his bathing pool again. It had been rough and fast, and Mikki knew her skin still showed raised marks where his claws had shallowly pierced her ass during the climax of their passion. The second time had been long and slow and incredibly gentle. He'd brought her to climax with his tongue twice before he'd entered her and slowly, slowly, rocked them to repletion.

Mikki couldn't imagine leaving him. Couldn't imagine never feeling his touch again—never talking with him again, or never seeing the uninhibited joy and wonder in his eyes when she reached for him. She couldn't imagine it, and so she refused to think about it. She would do what she had to do when the time came. Until then, she wouldn't waste the hours she had with him mourning the future.

"I want to paint you."

Mikki jumped and made a little "squee" sound.

Eyes still closed, his chest vibrated with his low laughter. She smacked his belly. "I thought you were asleep."

"I cannot possibly sleep with you touching me like that," he said.

"Oh, sorry. I didn't realize . . ." She started to pull her hand back, and he caught her wrist.

"I do not mind." He let loose her wrist and smiled when she continued to trace a soft path over his stomach. "I still want to paint you."

"You already sketched me."

"Yes, but I want to paint you, too. Just as you are now. I want your image on the walls of my bedchamber."

He didn't say "so I can remember you when you're old and/or dead," but Mikki's mind shouted the words in her head, along with words that whispered that he might need the painting to remind him of her much sooner than either of them expected. She pushed down her morbid thoughts, but suddenly she wanted desperately for him to paint her—for him to capture even just a piece of what they had so he would remember . . .

"Would you do it tonight? Now?" she asked.

Asterius opened his eyes and studied her. "Yes," he said slowly. "I will paint your portrait tonight."

Mikki watched as he left their bed and began gathering bowls and brushes from niches that had been carved into the walls of the cave and lighting more torches until the bedroom was alive with warmth and light. He hadn't bothered to get dressed beyond the linen wrap he'd slung haphazardly around his hips. She was struck again by the raw power and untamed beauty of his body. He was beast, man, and god, all mixed together to form a miracle, and there was only one thing she wanted more than to spend her life by his side.

When he had readied the paints and had a brush in his hand, she sat up and smiled at him. "Okay, how do you want me to pose?"

He walked over to the sleeping pallet and gently pressed her back so she was lying on her side as she had been when he'd been beside her. He spread her hair out around her so it made a copper veil on the cream-colored pelt. He positioned her hands so one was draped over her head and the other lay, palm down, on the pallet next to her, as if she had just caressed him. Then he pulled the blanket that had been covering her from her waist down off her, leaving her naked. She raised an eyebrow at him.

His lips tilted up. "Are you cold?"

"If I am, will you warm me up?"

His laugh rumbled between them. "When I am finished. For right now, just lie still and close your eyes." He went back to the clay pots and brushes.

"Do I have to close my eyes? I'd rather watch you."

He looked over his shoulder at her. "It will forever be a surprise to me that you enjoy looking at me."

"I like to do more than look." She smiled seductively.

"Do not move," he chided, but his smile was clearly indulgent.

He began painting, working with bold, fast strokes, which he painted right over the top of the Tulsa Rose Garden scene, causing the garden to be cast in the background, as if he was superimposing one view of reality over another.

"Can I talk to you while you do that, or do you need to concentrate?" Mikki whispered, a little awed by the beautiful, glistening version of her that was taking form.

"You may talk. I may not answer, though. Sometimes I forget where I am when I paint."

"In my old world they call that The Zone. I read an article on it once. It happens to artists and authors and athletes. Something about brain endorphins. It's supposed to mean you're doing something right if you can find The Zone."

Asterius grunted.

"Do you always get in The Zone when you paint?" she asked.

"Yes. Usually." He squinted as he studied her and then turned back to the cave wall and drew the long, curving line of her waist, hip and leg.

She watched him paint and thought about his talent and the beauty he seemed to so easily create, even though he had, for centuries, been an outcast. *Please, Gii, keep your word.* Then she pulled her mind from the handmaiden's promise, afraid Asterius would study her face too closely and be able to read her melancholy thoughts.

She needed to think of him instead. As he was then—as he had been earlier—passionate, tender, loving and full of surprises like the exquisite paintings he could produce. Which reminded her . . .

"Asterius, who is the woman you drew on the wall of the front room?"

His hand stilled mid-stroke. Without looking at her he said, "It is Pasiphea, my mother."

"I thought so," she said. And she had. Asterius wasn't adding her picture to his wall as he would a trophy. He wouldn't do that—he wouldn't even think that way. "She's very beautiful."

"That is how I remember her."

Mikki wanted to ask him to please remember her as beautiful, too. To please forget her faults and the pain of their parting after she was gone. To just remember how much they loved. But she knew she couldn't. All she could do was to hope that when the time came he would forgive her for being mortal. Mikki closed her eyes, afraid if she kept looking at him she would blurt out what she was thinking—admit everything and beg him to help her find another way out of this mess.

SOMEHOW, Mikki slept. She only knew it because the next time she opened her eyes the room was much dimmer and Asterius was sleeping beside her. She lay there for a few moments, listening to him take deep, regular breaths. Then, tentatively, she eased up from their bed. Quietly, she wrapped herself in a length of chiton she'd discarded earlier. She didn't look at the wall until she had the material fastened at her shoulder. Then she stared, pressing her hand to her mouth to stop her gasp. He had made her look like a goddess! Her painted image was sleeping, with a slight upturn to her lips, as if she had been having a lovely dream. Her skin looked touchable, her body lush and inviting. And he hadn't painted her lying on his pallet. He'd painted her sleeping on a bed of rose petals—specifically, Mikado rose petals.

She turned back to the bed and looked at him, wishing she could wake him up and make love to him. But she couldn't take the chance. She had to check on the roses. *If my instincts are wrong,* she promised herself, *I'll come back and wake him up and make love to him all morning.* Without looking at him again, Mikki padded on bare, silent feet from the room.

The sun hadn't risen yet, but the eastern sky was starting to turn from night's black to a gray that would soon welcome dawn. The grass was cold and damp under her bare feet as she followed the path around the base of the cliff to the stairs that would lead her up past the hot springs baths, around to her balcony, and then down into the heart of the gardens. Mikki didn't allow her mind to wander. She hurried up the stairs, barely glancing at the steaming baths, not wanting to remember how wonderful it had been to soak there in the company of her handmaidens and how much she had been looking forward to doing so again. Her balcony was empty, as was her room, but she could see a welcoming fire burning in the hearth and a candelabrum tree still lit beside her bed. She bit her lip and turned away from the homey sight.

Mikki descended her stairs and stepped into the garden proper. She chose the path that would lead her most directly to the center of the realm and the temple and fountain that awaited her there. She was careful to keep her thoughts on the roses and away from the Elementals or Asterius. She didn't want them to misunderstand and think she was calling them. What she needed to do she could only do alone. And it was easy to keep her thoughts on the roses. They seemed to be consuming her.

Sick . . . God, she felt sick. The closer she got to the center of the realm, the worse she felt. Two or three times she stopped and inspected beds of roses that just hours before had been already responding to the care and feeding she and the women had given them. Now they were black with the Dream Stealer blight and smelled of death.

Her instincts had been right, but it was even worse than she'd imagined. The blight had spread at an impossible rate. No mortal sickness could have decimated a garden like this. But the blight wasn't mortal. It was the manifestation of evil, and intuition told her there was only one way to combat it.

Hecate's Temple was like a torch-lit dream, and the sound of the huge fountain's flowing water was the accompanying magickal soundtrack. But Mikki didn't pause there. She kept walking until the lights illuminating the rose wall blazed before her. It was easy to find the bushes her blood had touched. They were the only color in the midst of darkness, death, and disease.

I was right. I wish I hadn't been, but I was right.

Mikki retraced her path back to the temple, pausing only long enough to find the newly sharpened shears she'd hidden at the base of a rosebush. She climbed the steps to the temple and stood before the spirit flame.

"Hecate," she said softly, looking into the yellow-orange flame. "I know you're far from your realm, but I'm hoping you're still attached enough to it . . . to me . . . that you will somehow be able to hear me. I need to talk to you before I finish this. I want you to know how much I have loved being here. For the first time in my life, I know I'm where I belong. The four Elementals are good girls, especially Gii. If you could, please tell them that I appreciate everything they've done for me."

She drew a deep breath and wiped silent tears from her cheeks.

"I love Asterius. You probably don't like that, but you did tell me to follow my instincts, and everything inside of me led me to him. He's not a beast, you know. And he needs what we all need—acceptance and someone to love." Mikki had to stop and press her hand against her mouth to stifle a sob. When she had her emotions under control, she continued. "He's why I'm doing this—him and the girls and the Dream Weavers. I finally know the real reason I'm here, and it *is* for the roses. I can save them. I don't really have any choice. I've seen what waits in the forest, and I can't let those creatures destroy everything I love."

Mikki stared into the fire, wishing she was more articulate, wishing she had more time to learn the special words to prayers and rituals so she could do this right.

"When I pledged myself to you, I did so with two words, 'love' and 'trust.' And it's those two words that bring me full circle here. What I do next I do willingly because I want to preserve the love I've found within this realm, and I believe I'm doing the right thing, because through that love I've learned to trust myself—to believe in my own instincts, intuition and judgment. So if you can, Hecate, I ask that you be with me for what comes next. So mote it be," Mikki whispered.

Resolutely, she left the temple and approached the fountain whose water fed the realm. The graceful fountain was really very beautiful. It had been formed by a series of huge marble dishes that eventually ran from a pool-size basin to a series of troughs that spoked off into the gardens. Mikki dipped her hand in the water and was surprised at its soothing warmth. *An odd coincidence,* she thought as she took off her chiton and folded it neatly on the ground beside her. *No. There are few coincidences here. I'll just consider it a parting gift from the goddess.* Naked, with nothing except the shears in her hand, Mikki stepped into the fountain.

The water welcomed her and she sat, settling comfortably on the bottom of the basin, which was deep enough that she was covered almost to her shoulders with clear, warm liquid. *Get it over with. Do it quickly. It's only going to hurt for a second.*

Mikki lifted her left wrist. She opened the shears and pressed the blade against her skin. She shut her eyes and sliced—quickly—sucking in her breath at the sudden pain. Then, she changed hands. This time it was more awkward but no less effective. Mikki dropped the shears over the side of the fountain. She winced as she submerged her wrists, but she had been right. The pain wasn't bad, and it didn't last long. Mikki rested her head back against the lip of the basin. Gazing up at the sky, she thought how right it felt that the moon had set and the sun had not yet risen. Hecate . . . Goddess of the Ebony Moon . . . perhaps the absence of light in the sky was a sign that the goddess approved of her sacrifice. She had done the right thing. The roses would live. The dreams of mankind would be safe, as would her love. Mikki closed her eyes. She was so sleepy, and the water was so comfortable . . . soft . . . like a big feather bed . . . a warm raft on a summer lake . . . her mother's arms when she was a small, frightened girl who'd had a bad dream.

She sighed. There shouldn't be any bad dreams . . . there should only be love and beauty and roses.

She wasn't afraid. But she would miss Asterius. As her mind blackened softly, Mikki's final thought was of how much she loved him.

ASTERIUS woke up suddenly. Something was wrong. He shook off sleep as he always had—instantly—and sat up, already reaching for his clothes. Then, thinking he should wake Mikado, he turned and . . .

She wasn't there. At first that didn't trouble him. She could be in the bathing chamber. He pulled on his tunic and strode through the tunnel. She wasn't there, either. Foreboding had him lengthening his stride as he made his way back to the bedchamber and the room beyond. Still, she wasn't there. He buckled his cuirasse as he left his lair. The sun had risen, but it was still early morning. An unusually warm breeze was coming from the gardens, bringing with it—

Asterius stopped, testing the wind. Yes, he'd been right. The wind brought with it the rich and heady scent of blooming roses. He picked up his pace, and soon he burst into the gardens.

They were abloom. Clouds of color filled the beds, like the goddess had taken a divine brush to the realm and painted in life and health. But instead of feeling relief and happiness, worry broke over Asterius, and he ran, letting his instinct guide him.

Hecate's Temple was in sight when he heard the first cry of lamentation. The sound of it was an icy fist closing around his heart. Then another cry met the first, and another and another, until the gardens echoed with mourning.

His mind was screaming *No!* even though he knew what he would discover. Asterius thundered up to the temple. The four Elementals were standing beside the fountain, clinging to one another and weeping openly. Between them he caught sight of wet copper hair and the side of her colorless face. Slowly, as if he was moving through a bog of sinking sand and mud, Asterius approached the fountain. She was there, of course.

Mikado was dead.

Asterius, Guardian of the Realm of the Rose, fell to his knees and roared his grief over and over and over. One by one, the Elementals, led by Gii, moved to him and placed their hands on his shoulders, until the five of them, connected by their grief, mourned their Empousa.

Part Three

CHAPTER THIRTY-FIVE

G OD, her mouth was dry. And she felt like shit. Mikki tried to roll over, but she was too weak. All she did was twitch and make a muffled moan.

"Oh, fuck! Call 911—she's alive!"

Huh? Call 911? There weren't any phones in the Realm of the Rose. Nor did anyone besides her say "fuck." So what the fuck? She tried to move again, and this time she felt the strong hands that held her in place.

"Don't try to move, ma'am! It's going to be okay. I've called for help." Then he yelled, "Over here! Bring the EMTs over here!"

Mikki could hear the hurried tread of heavy feet, accompanied by a vaguely familiar voice.

"Oh, Christ! It's Mikki. Ah, shit, look at all that blood!"

Mikki's breath was coming in panting gulps. She placed the voice. It was Mel, the security guard at the Tulsa Rose Gardens. But it couldn't be Mel—she couldn't be at the rose gardens. She was . . .

Oh. She'd forgotten. She was dead.

"Mikki, hang on. The EMTs are here. You're going to make it."

She tried to say that she didn't want to make it. That her intention had been to save the roses, and the only way she could do that was to give them her blood. Unfortunately, it was a damn big realm, and a few drops in a bucket weren't going to do it.

But she couldn't speak. Her mind was working, but her body felt heavy and not her own. And she was wet, which made sense, because she was supposed to be in the fountain.

"Okay, on three roll her over."

They rolled her from her stomach to her back. Mikki blinked, trying to clear her blurred vision. It was morning. From what she could see of the sky over the EMTs' shoulders, the sun hadn't risen long ago. Then her gaze shifted to a blob to her right. She managed to let her head flop to the side to bring it more fully into her view. It was a massive stone pedestal, and it was even more familiar than her old friend the security guard. It was the base that had supported the great Guardian statue. Only now it was empty.

Mikki screamed soundlessly inside her head. Then everything went blissfully black.

"You look better today, Mikki. How are you feeling?"

"Is that a professional question? A test? Or are you showing genuine concern?" she said sarcastically.

Nelly flinched. "I don't deserve that, Mikki, and you know it."

Mikki chewed her lips and reached out to quickly squeeze her friend's hand. It was dead wrong for her to take out her shitty mood on her girlfriend. It wasn't Nelly's fault that nothing she could do or say would ever come close to making it "better" for her.

"Sorry. I'm just in a wicked bad mood today."

"Did something happen? Have the dreams returned?"

Mikki couldn't meet Nelly's eyes. She didn't want her friend to see the desperation she carried around with her every day.

"No. My dreams have been completely normal, which is to say I don't remember them. Everything else has been normal, too. I don't know what the hell's wrong. I guess it's just the weather that's gotten to me. I'm tired of the rain and the cold." She tried not to remember that once she'd commanded the rain to appear every fourth day, and that the first day rain had obeyed her it set up the circumstances that had brought her into Asterius's bed . . .

"Mikki?"

She turned her eyes and thoughts back to the present and lifted her cappuccino, trying half-heartedly to work up a thirst. "Just daydreaming. Sorry again. I'm not very good company today Nelly."

"You're my friend; you don't have to entertain or amuse me. You know that." The psychiatrist sighed. "Honey, what happened to you was traumatic. The men who attacked you and stole the statue from the rose gardens left you bleeding to death—and they have never been caught. It's normal to go through stages of anger and depression and resentment during your healing process, especially when you have no closure for the crime."

Closure for the crime . . . Mikki had the insane urge to laugh, which she quickly stifled. She didn't want to do anything that might make her appear nuts. She didn't want her story questioned too closely.

"I know. I just—" Mikki rubbed her hand across her forehead. For the zillionth time, she wished Nelly was right, that what she was feeling was just a part of a healing process. "I just wish I felt normal again."

"You will, Mikki." Nelly glanced at her watch. "Oh, hell! I'm going to be late."

Mikki managed to summon up a smile. "Is this a real kooky appointment, or just a kinda kook?"

Nelly laughed, standing and collecting her briefcase and purse. "Totally, absolute kook."

"Good job security."

"Exactly," Nelly said. "Hey, call me later if you need to talk."

"I will. Promise. See you tomorrow morning. Same time—same coffee place." She grinned at Nelly and then proceeded to feel guilty as hell at the relief she felt when her girlfriend walked out the door. It was so damn hard to talk to Nelly! She couldn't tell her the truth: "Hey, girlfriend. I wasn't mugged, cut up by criminals who ripped off the statue from the Tulsa Rose Gardens and left to die. I actually committed suicide, although I like to think of it as a sacrificial act—I'm not big on suicide, which should prove that I'm not really nuts. Anyway, I had to do it because the magickal Realm of the Rose in the crossroads between worlds was in danger and only my blood could save it. It was my duty as Empousa. So really, you shouldn't say I committed suicide because I was just fulfilling my destiny. And by the by, I'm desperately in love with a man-beast and the reason I'm so damn depressed is that I'm stuck here without him."

Uh, no. Nelly was her best friend, but even she would be sure to have her locked up in a lovely, yet totally exclusive, padded cell if she babbled the truth. She'd realized that as soon as she woke up in the hospital and *they*—social services and the police—had started to question her. The story that had evolved had come about more out of omission and accident than anything vaguely resembling the truth. But it still made her nervous to tell it, especially to her friend who just happened to be a savvy shrink who knew her too damn well.

Mikki checked her watch. It was only seven thirty. She didn't have to be at work until eight. She did have time for another cup of cappuccino before heading off to work. As she stood for a refill, she caught her reflection in the glass of the picture windows of Expresso Milano. Thin . . . she looked thin. And she could have done something with her wild hair besides pulling it back in a haphazard ponytail.

The problem was she just couldn't work up the energy to care.

Well, at least there were still plenty of her favorite, the giant orange sugar cookies that the coffee shop bought freshly made every morning from the popular Pani Del Goddess bakery just a few doors down the street. Mikki ordered two to go with her cappuccino and then changed her mind and ordered a third. She needed to put on weight, and the sugar rush added with the caffeine high might be enough to get her ready to face another meaningless, endless day at work. She grabbed a copy of the *Tulsa World* and made herself comfortable at one of the plush, silk-covered chairs while she waited for the multiply pierced coffee girl to bring her coffee and cookies on the café's elegant little silver trays. When she heard approaching heels on the tile floor, she didn't look up from her paper.

"Just go ahead and put it on the coffee table. Oh, and keep an eye on me. I have a feeling this is going to be a three-espresso morning."

"Is everything not well, Mikado?"

Mikki almost dropped the paper in surprise. "Sevillana! I'm sorry—I thought you were the coffee girl."

The old woman's amazing aquamarine eyes sparkled. "I have not been mistaken for a girl in a very long time."

Mikki smiled, and for a moment it felt genuine. "Would you join me?"

"Yes, I would like that." The old woman settled herself gracefully into an adjoining chair and rearranged her beautiful pale blue pashmina shawl around her shoulders.

"I didn't think you lived here." As on the first time they'd met, Mikki felt a little intimidated by the woman's presence. She was just so grand—in the old European fashion. There was an air of grace and culture about everything she said or did. And then, with a jolt, Mikki remembered, and in the remembering she wondered how she could have ever forgotten. "The perfume! Where did you get the perfume you gave me that night?"

Sevillana smiled, but the waitress's delivery of their coffee and sweets kept her from saying anything. Then, even when they were alone again, Sevillana took her time emptying the coarse sugar into her cappuccino and stirring carefully with the tiny silver spoon before she spoke.

"There is only one place you can find such perfume, and it is in a realm that is far from here."

Mikki felt a dizzying rush of an emotion she'd been missing for three months—hope. "You're talking about the Realm of the Rose."

The old woman nodded her head slightly.

"Oh, God," Mikki gasped.

"I believe, Mikado, that it would be more appropriate for you to exclaim 'Oh, Goddess.'"

"How? How do you know about it? How did you get there, and how do I get back? What are you doing here? Why did you—"

Sevillana's raised hand cut off Mikki's torrent of words.

"Everything has its order and its time. Drowning me in questions will not change that."

"I'm sorry." Mikki pressed her hand against her chest, afraid that her heart would pound out of her body. "I just—I need to know . . ." She ran a trembling hand over her face and began again. "I have to get back."

"I know, child," Sevillana said softly. "I know." Then the old woman's gaze went past Mikki, and when she spoke again her voice reminded Mikki of a sad little girl. "Did no one speak my name while you were there? Did they not remember me at all?"

"Your name? No. Why would they—" Mikki's eyes widened with realization. "It's you. You are the last Empousa."

"No, I *was* Empousa. I am no longer Hecate's High Priestess. I discarded that position when I was young and foolish. But I have paid for my betrayal. For two hundred years I have been separated from my realm and my goddess and have walked the mundane earth, restless and unsatisfied—a true outlander."

"Two hundred years!" Mikki could only stare at her. "But how?"

"I have never fully understood it myself. Obviously, I age, but I do so slowly. I used to believe it was Hecate's way of punishing me—extending my life long enough that I was well and truly sorry for my selfish actions. Then, in my travels decades ago I visited Tulsa and happened to attend the unveiling of its new rose gardens . . ." She paused, her expression pained. "I recognized the Guardian statue, and I knew it had been placed here for a reason, so I always circled back to Tulsa, waiting and watching . . . And then I met you, and I began to hope that perhaps Hecate had allowed me to live for so long for another reason." Sevillana's blue eyes returned to Mikki. "I hoped the Great Goddess had meant for me to give you the anointing oil so you could awaken the Guardian and return to the realm—and fulfill the destiny I left undone." Sadness filled the old woman's beautiful eyes. "Why did you make the same mistake I made? I did not mean for you to run away."

"But I didn't!" Mikki cried. Then she lowered her voice when several heads turned in their direction. "You know about the blood, don't you? Somehow you understand."

"Yes, your blood nurtures the roses. How could I not know it? We carry the same blood in our veins, Mikado." Sevillana touched her hand lightly in a caress that reminded Mikki so much of her mother that it made her breath catch. "At the hospital that day I told you my name was Sevillana Kalyca, and it is. But that is only part of my name. I rarely use my family name—it is too difficult for me to hear it and to know that I forsook it, even though the deed was committed long ago. My true name is Sevillana Kalyca Empousai. I was the first Empousa to flee from the Realm of the Rose. I had hoped when I met you and felt the strength of the blood within you that I was also the last."

"I didn't run away," Mikki said numbly, staring at the woman who was her ancestress. "I died."

"Time runs differently there, but still it could not yet have been Beltane in the realm."

"It was just starting to be winter." Confused, Mikki frowned. "But the weather didn't have anything to do with it. Dream Stealers got into the realm."

Sevillana's hand flew to her heart in a gesture that oddly mimicked Mikki's earlier one. "Oh, Goddess, no!"

"It was me. They fooled me. I let them in. Asterius killed them—or, I supposed they can't actually be killed, so that's not the right word, but he got rid of them, sent them back into the forest."

"Asterius?"

Mikki studied Sevillana, her mind beginning to catch up with her racing emotions. This woman was the one they'd all been forbidden to talk about. She was part of why Hecate had bespelled the realm and Asterius. Well, Mikki was no longer in the Realm of the Rose, and she damn sure wanted to know, once and for all, what had happened.

"Asterius is the name given to the Guardian by his mother."

Watching carefully, Mikki saw the flash of surprise and unease that passed through Sevillana's eyes. "I want to know what happened between the two of you. All of it."

Sevillana stared out the window as she spoke, and her voice took on a faraway sing-song cadence, as if she was retelling a story that had been passed down from generation to generation. "I was young and worse than foolish. I was selfish. I loved the power of Empousa, so much so that I was not willing to relinquish it. As the days drew closer and closer to Beltane, I convinced myself that it was only right that I escape the destiny planned for me. That I was different. But I knew I could not cross through the forest without protection. I convinced the Guardian to betray his duty and escort me through the forest to the entrance to the mundane world."

"You seduced him?" Mikki felt very cold.

"Only with words. I would not bed a beast, but I made him believe I would. It was not a difficult thing to do. He had little experience with women. It was odd, though, that he allowed me to escape even after I rejected him." Sevillana shook her head. "I have long wondered about that. He should have turned on me and, at the very least, forced me back to face Hecate's wrath. Instead, he said one small thing and then stepped aside and let me go free."

"He thought he loved you," Mikki said woodenly.

Sevillana finally met her eyes, and Mikki could see the surprise there. "That is the one thing he said—that he loved me. But it made no sense. How could a beast love a woman?"

"He is not a beast!" Mikki hissed under her breath, anger making her face pale. "And you're not good enough for his love if you couldn't see the man within him."

"You love him!"

"I do."

Sevillana stared at Mikki for a long time without speaking and then she bowed her head slightly to the younger woman. "Forgive me for speaking so cavalierly. I was a young girl then. I have come to understand since that I was wrong about many things, this, then, is simply one last lesson for me. You have my admiration, Mikado, as well as my respect. I have never known such courage as yours."

Mikki took several deep, calming breaths. There was absolutely no point in getting so pissed off at the old woman. What she'd done had happened two centuries ago. It was over. Finished. And she didn't want to alienate her. Sevillana Kalyca Empousai was her ticket back to Asterius.

"I forgive you. I think Asterius does, too. And what I did wasn't that courageous. I didn't have any choice. Asterius had gotten rid of the Dream Stealers, but it was too late. They'd already poisoned the roses—all of them except the ones I'd bled on. I tried to stop the blight another way, but nothing worked. I knew it wouldn't. The only way to save the roses was by my blood."

"And you do not think it courageous that you went to your lover and allowed him to sacrifice you? It was not even Beltane, yet you met your destiny early and saved the realm."

Mikki frowned. "Asterius didn't sacrifice me. He didn't even know what I'd planned. I knew he'd try to stop me, so I snuck out. And what's this you keep saying about Beltane? That's in the spring, right? What does that have to do with anything?"

"You truly do not know?"

"No!" she said, exasperated and thoroughly sick of mysteries.

"They must have been afraid to tell you. Afraid that you, too, would leave them. Mikado, the Empousa serves one true purpose. She is there for the roses."

"Yes, yes, yes! I know that."

"You also know that Hecate's Empousa is bound to the roses through her blood. What you do not know is that every Beltane night the Empousa is sacrificed by the Guardian, because her blood insures that the realm thrives for another year."

Mikki felt everything within her go very still. "They were going to kill me?"

"Not they. He was. It is the Guardian's duty to protect the roses."

It all made horrible sense. Asterius's behavior when they first met

328 P. C. Cast

and were attracted to each other . . . how he had said they could not be together . . . how he had struggled against loving her. It had been more than disbelief that she could ever see him as a man—more than the rejection of Sevillana. He'd known he would have to kill her.

The thought made her physically ill.

Sevillana's warm hand on her cold, numb one was a physical shock. "He had no choice."

"And Hecate, she meant all along for me to die," Mikki said.

"Life and death is different for the gods. Hecate is stern and powerful, but she is also a loving goddess. She would see your sacrifice as just another link in the great circle of life. The goddess would not forsake you, Mikado, even in death. Had you met your destiny at Beltane, Hecate would have made sure you spent eternity in the endless beauty of the Elysian Fields. The goddess cares for those who belong to her; she only turns away from those who betray her."

"It's a hard concept for my mind to grasp. Everyone I cared about, everyone I loved, they all knew I was going to die." She paused as the enormity of it hit her. "So even if you could help me figure out a way to get back, I'd just be returning to die again."

"Yes. Do you still wish to return?"

CHAPTER THIRTY-SIX

DID she still want to return? It was already the end of February. Wasn't Beltane the same day as May first? So she'd have a couple months and then Asterius would kill her.

The thought was impossible to believe. Yet even in the middle of her disbelief, intuition told her Sevillana was speaking the truth. It all fit, and she suddenly felt like the piece outside the jigsaw puzzle. She knew where she belonged, and it wasn't in Tulsa, Oklahoma.

"I want to go back, but I don't know if I'm brave enough."

"Listen to your instincts, Mikado. Trust what they tell you."

"They tell me that I don't belong here."

"Then perhaps you should return home," Sevillana said.

"Do you know how to get me there?"

"I can give you the anointing oil, but the rest you already hold within you. You sacrificed yourself for the Realm of the Rose, and you were selfless enough to love its Guardian. You were, my dear, the exact opposite of the realm's last Empousa. I believe Hecate will hear your call, and honor it."

"But how—" Mikki stopped herself. She knew what she must do. She had to listen to her intuition and follow her instincts. She glanced at Sevillana, who nodded approval at her introspection. *Calm down and think. I'm Hecate's Empousa. There has to be a way for me to return.*

330 P. C. Cast

Suddenly Mikki smiled. "That's it! I'm still Empousa. Hecate said I carry her power—that can't have completely gone away, not even here. I mean, look at you! You've lived two hundred years, and you walked away from the goddess."

"Her power should still be yours to wield," Sevillana said. "Even in the mundane world." The old woman reached into her leather clutch and pulled out a glass rose stem, exactly like the first one she'd given Mikki. "This is the anointing oil of Hecate's Empousa. It is the one step in the invocation ritual with which I can aid you."

"Thank you, Sevillana." Mikki took the stem, carefully folding it in a napkin before sliding it into her purse.

"I ask only one thing of you, Empousa," the old woman said. "I ask that you petition Hecate's forgiveness for me. I know I cannot return to the realm, but I am weary and I would like to be allowed to shed this life and embrace my eternity in the Elysian Fields. I cannot do so without Hecate's forgiveness."

"I'll ask her. But why not ask her yourself?"

"I wish I could, but I cannot return. I have tried, many times over the long, silent years. The goddess will not hear me. She has turned her face from me."

"But Hecate hasn't turned her face from me!" she said in a rush of understanding. "Why do you think I'm not a ghost in the Elysian Fields? I died. I should not have woken up back in Tulsa—unless there was a damn good reason Hecate wanted me to return here." Remembering, Mikki sat straight up. "She knew you were here. I told her your name when she asked me how I'd 'accidentally' gotten my hands on the anointing oil of an Empousa. I remember the look on her face now—she knew it even then."

"The Guardian Statue—the goddess did put it here so I would find it—and find you," Sevillana said through a voice thickened with tears.

"Hecate meant for me to come back so I'd see you." This time it was Mikki who took the old woman's trembling hand in hers. "Hecate's forgiven you, Sevillana."

"Oh, my dear, if only that was true . . ."

"Let's find out. Tonight is the night of the new moon. Come to the rose gardens. Stand inside the sacred circle with me. Let's try to go home, Sevillana."

MIKKI was glad for the rainy night. It was cold and miserable, but it was also so dark that even the illuminating lampposts in Woodward Park cast only the smallest halo of weak, iridescent light in limited bubbles around the park. It was easy for someone who knew the park well to avoid the lights. And Mikki knew the park well.

She clutched her briefcase in one hand and held tightly to Sevillana with her other, helping maneuver the old woman through the darkness. They didn't speak; they didn't need to. Mikki kept up a running commentary in her head that prayed over and over that no one would be in the park or the gardens. By the time they'd reached the boundary between the park and the gardens, Mikki had relaxed a little. Clearly no one was crazy enough to venture out into the park on a night like this, especially a couple hours past midnight. Still, Mikki didn't say anything until they passed beneath the rock archway and stepped lightly onto the third tier of the gardens.

The illumination from the fountain lazily lit the area surrounding it in a watery light that, coupled with the drizzly mist that hung in the cold air, washed the tier with dreamlike color.

"It's appropriate," Mikki said softly.

"Yes. The lighting evokes dream images," Sevillana said in perfect understanding. "It is a good omen, Empousa."

"Let's hope so," she muttered. Then she looked at the empty pedestal. She hadn't been back since that horrible morning they'd found her. She couldn't bear it. Mikki hadn't quit as a volunteer; she'd asked for a leave of absence, which was granted immediately. Everyone said they understood how hard it must be for her to come back into the gardens where she'd been attacked and left for dead. But of course, they didn't really understand. How could they? They'd never know the truth.

"Mikado?" Sevillana touched her arm gently.

Mikki turned her back to the empty pedestal. "You're right. We need to hurry. This will definitely be impossible to explain if we get caught."

"Then we must not get caught," the old woman said firmly.

"Agreed. Let's get busy."

Mikki chose a place near the fountain. She opened her briefcase, and Sevillana helped her place a candle in each of the four Elemental positions of the circle: yellow in the east for Wind; red in the south for Flame; blue in the west for Water; green in the north for Earth and, finally, purple in the center of the circle for Spirit. Then she took the long, narrow fireplace matchbox from the briefcase as well as the little razor-sharp knife that usually stayed hidden in her apartment, and placed them beside the spirit candle.

Stepping outside the ring of candles, Mikki took one last thing from the briefcase before she placed it in the shadows beside the empty pillar. She pulled free the cork that closed the end of the delicate glass stem and then applied the perfumed oil liberally to the pulse points at her neck, wrists and breasts. Then she handed it to Sevillana. With only a small hesitation, the old woman took the bottle and applied the perfume to her own body. The scent of roses and spice was heavy in the damp air, and Mikki's stomach clenched with remembrance.

This had to work; she had to return.

"Are you ready?" Mikki asked.

The old woman nodded and tugged two long hair pins from her elegant French knot, setting her waist-length fall of silver hair free. Then with a flourish that showed grace and beauty that belied her years, Sevillana whirled off her long raincoat, under which she was wearing a beautiful silk chiton the color of lilacs.

Mikki discarded her own coat and ignored the cold as she, too, was now dressed in a violet-colored chiton. The only difference between her chiton and Sevillana's was that Mikki's was a shade darker, and, as was proper for a new moon ritual, it left one of her breasts bare.

"One thing you can say about chitons is that they are definitely easy to make," Mikki said.

"I have missed them dreadfully." Looking down at herself, Sevillana smiled. Then she glanced at Mikki and dipped into a fluid curtsey. "Shall we continue, Empousa?"

"Absolutely."

Together the two women walked to the center of the circle. With the purple candle between them, they faced north. Then Mikki picked up the box of matches, thinking how much she missed the company of the Elementals, especially tonight. Shaking off doubts, Mikki approached the yellow candle and lit the match.

"Blowing winds, strong and everywhere, even in the realm of the mundane, I summon you, Wind, as the first element in the sacred circle." Mikki touched the match to the candle and held it there until it lit. Without letting herself worry about whether or not the element actually heard her and would answer her call, Mikki moved quickly to the red candle. "Blazing force of cleansing fire, dancing flame of light, even in the realm of the mundane your power is rich and true. I summon you, Flame, to the sacred circle." When the match touched the red candle's wick, the flame burst into being and Mikki felt a surge of hope. Without hesitation, she moved to the blue candle. "Sparkling, glimmering tide of life, you bathe us, cool us, quench us, even in this realm of the mundane you cover more than half our world and give us life. I summon you, Water, to the sacred circle." Through the lit wick, Mikki thought she saw the blue candle waver and shimmer like waves. Then she was facing the green candle. "Lush and fertile, familiar and wild, even in this realm of the mundane you hold us and care for us. I summon you, Earth, to the sacred circle." Mikki moved back to her place beside the purple candle. "I summon you, Spirit, to the sacred circle with the two words that bound me to my goddess—'love' and 'trust.'" She lit the purple candle and then dropped the match. Staring around her, she was disappointed that she saw no luminous threads weaving together to bind the elements to the circle.

"Do not despair that you cannot see them in this realm," Sevillana said as if she could read Mikki's thoughts. "See them within your mind. Believe they are there. The power of an Empousa's belief is a magick all its own."

Mikki nodded, and within her mind she imagined the gossamer threads outlining the circle.

"Now, let's finish it," Mikki said resolutely. She bent and picked up the knife. She looked at Sevillana, and the old woman gave Mikki her hand, palm up. With a quick, practiced movement, Mikki pressed the sharp blade against Sevillana's thin skin and drew a long line across her palm. As her blood welled, Mikki handed the knife to Sevillana. The ex-Empousa took Mikki's hand firmly, and with one quick stroke, cut a similar line in her palm. Then she dropped the knife and the two women clasped their hands together, palm to palm, mingling the blood of generations of Hecate's High Priestesses.

Mikki closed her eyes and cleared her mind. When she spoke, she gave no mind to lowering her voice. If it worked—if the goddess was really invoked—the circle would hold and no mortal would be allowed to intrude. And if it did not . . . if it did not, then Mikki didn't care what happened to her.

"Hecate, Great Goddess of the Ebony Moon, Crossroads of Mankind and Beasts. I am Mikado Empousai, High Priestess and Empousa of the Realm of the Rose. In a land far from you I have anointed myself, cast your sacred circle and by the right of my blood I call upon your name. We have a pledge between us, an oath sealed with love and trust. And by the power of that oath I invoke your presence and ask that I be heard."

Suddenly, wind whipped around them, causing the candles to shiver madly. The mist swirled, and as Mikki watched, it became filled with glitter until from the center of the vortex of wind and sound and light, Hecate appeared. The goddess was dressed in full regalia—robes of night, the headdress of stars and the golden torch. At her feet the massive hounds snarled and snapped at the misty garden.

Mikki started to cry the goddess's name, but Sevillana's tearful voice interrupted her. The old woman pulled her hand from Mikki's and fell to her knees.

"Great Goddess! Forgive me!" Sevillana sobbed, tears falling freely down her well-lined face. "What I did was wrong. I have spent lifetimes trying to atone for my unforgivable error. The foolish, selfish girl who betrayed you no longer exists."

Hecate's face was unreadable, but her voice was soft. "What is it you have learned, Sevillana?"

"I have learned that there are things more terrible to lose than my life."

"And what are those things?"

"My honor . . . my name . . . and the love of my goddess."

"You never lost the love of your goddess, daughter."

Sevillana pressed her hand to her mouth, trying to stifle her sobs. Mikki put her hand on the old woman's shoulder, lending her strength through touch.

"Will you forgive me then, Hecate?" Sevillana was finally able to say.

"Child, I forgave you long ago. It is you who have not been able to forgive yourself," said the goddess.

Sevillana bowed her head. "May I rest now, Goddess?"

"Yes, Sevillana. All you ever needed to do was to ask. I would never turn my face from my Empousa—even an errant one. Behold!" Then Hecate swept out her hand and a section of the mist opened, like a door made of night. Suddenly a lovely scene came into view. It was a beautiful meadow, filled with clover and ringed by tall pines whose needles looked like giant feather dusters. As they watched, a lithe figure skipped and danced into the meadow, followed by a group of young, beautiful women. Their flowing chitons were draped alluringly around their bodies, which looked strong and young, even though each of them had an odd, semi-substantial look.

And then Mikki felt a jolt of shock as she recognized one of the women.

"Mama!" she cried.

Before Mikki could rush forward, Hecate said softly, "It is not your time, Mikado. Your destiny is not complete yet."

Through streaming tears, she stared at the goddess. "But it is my mother, isn't it?"

"It is, indeed. And look closely. You will see your grandmother, as well."

Mikki watched breathlessly. Yes—she did recognize the stunning young woman who danced holding her mother's hand. She had looked into that beautiful face countless times, only when she'd known her it had been lined by life and wisdom.

"Where are they?"

"The Elysian Fields," Sevillana said, her voice filled with awe. "There they will be eternally young and happy and free."

"Take your place beside them, Sevillana. Your banishment is over."

Slowly, the old woman stood. She turned to Mikki and hugged her tightly. "Have a blessed life, my dear," she whispered.

"Tell my mother and grandmother that I love them," Mikki whispered back to her.

"I shall. They will be as proud of you as I am, daughter."

Sevillana walked through the boundary of the sacred circle to the goddess. She stopped before Hecate, and, sobbing again, she curtseyed deeply. The goddess reached out and embraced her, kissing each of the old woman's cheeks.

"Enter Elysian with my blessing, Sevillana."

The old woman walked through the door the goddess had opened to paradise, and as she did her body changed. Old age fell from her like a discarded cloak, until with a shout of joy the beautiful young Sevillana took her place with the group of dancing maidens. Then the door faded and was once again nothing more than rain-heavy mist and darkness.

"I am pleased to see you again, my Empousa," Hecate said.

Mikki wiped the tears from her face and smiled at the goddess. "I'm unbelievably glad to see you, too. If I had known I could do this— invoke you here—I would have cast the circle and called you months ago."

"Ah, but then you would have been missing one piece in the invocation—the anointing oil of an Empousa. You needed Sevillana for that."

"You're right—you're right. I don't know . . . I've learned so much today that my mind can't seem to hold it all. I'm so glad you forgave Sevillana." Then Mikki blinked in surprise, as more of the pieces of the puzzle fit together. "The first night I was in the realm—you said you'd made a mistake and you wanted to fix it. That mistake was about Sevillana and Asterius, wasn't it?"

"It was." Hecate sighed, a sound that Mikki found amazingly mortal and fallible. "I should not have punished them as I did. Sevillana was young and selfish—I knew that when I chose her as my Empousa. I mistakenly hoped the power in her blood would mature her. It did not."

"And what about Asterius?" Mikki asked, feeling like she should hold her breath.

"That was my biggest mistake. I gifted him with the heart and soul of a man and then refused to truly acknowledge that he was, indeed, more than a beast. In that respect I was even more selfish than his mother, who could not see more than her own mistakes whenever she gazed upon him. I was wrong to disallow him a mate—to believe he was a creature who needed no more than duty to exist. It was my fault his need drove him to choose unwisely when Sevillana tempted him. It was anger at myself that caused me to banish her and bespell him. Unfortunately, I understood that too late. Then all I could do was to wait for the right mortal to be born. One who could see the truth and have the courage to act upon it."

"Then you'll let me love him, if only until Beltane?"

"No, Mikado."

Mikki's body went cold and still. "Please, Hecate. I love him. Let me make him happy, even if it's only for a little while."

"The roses thrive, Mikado."

Confused at the sudden change in subject, Mikki said, "Good. I did what I felt had to be done."

"You sacrificed yourself willingly, calling upon the oath of love and trust with which you were bound into my service."

"Yes, Hecate."

"That has never before happened in the Realm of the Rose. Oh, yes, for generations Empousas have given their blood to nurture the realm, but they did so because they had to, because it was the thread of life Fate and Destiny had together woven for them. But you, Mikado Empousai, a mortal woman from a land almost completely bereft of magick, willingly sacrificed yourself to save something as nebulous as the dreams of mankind. And you also saw the man within the beast and let yourself love him, breaking his spell of loneliness and isolation."

"I—I just did what my instincts told me to do. I loved the realm. It was my home, and protecting it, and everyone in it, was worth dying for," Mikki said quickly, feeling completely overwhelmed by the goddess's praise. "Asterius wasn't hard to love." She smiled and moved her shoulders nervously. "Isn't there always something of a beast within every strong man? It's part of what makes them so deliciously different from us." She took a deep breath. "Can't you please let me return to him? I give you my word that I will willingly go back to the fountain on Beltane night."

"What you have done has changed the fabric of the realm, Empousa. Your sacrifice was pure—unsullied by the bonds of duty or force or fear. There need never be another Beltane sacrifice; your blood has insured that."

When Mikki began to speak, Hecate raised her hand to silence her. "But simply returning is not that easy. You have also been changed by your sacrifice. As long as you stay in the mundane world, you will live a normal lifespan. But should you return to the Realm of the Rose, your blood ties you to it irrevocably. Which means you would be an immortal, reigning in the realm eternally as more than my Empousa—you would become Goddess of the Rose."

Mikki heard Hecate's words, but they were almost drowned out by the dizziness and disbelief that hummed through her mind. Did Hecate just say that she would never die? That she could become a goddess?

"But you should know that a goddess's path is not an easy one to tread, Mikado. Eternity is a daunting companion—sometimes he is glorious—sometimes he is melancholy and petulant as a spoiled child.

Think carefully, Empousa. I give you a choice, but that choice is irrevocable. You may stay here, in the mundane world, and live out your mortal life's thread—at the end of which I will not desert you and will welcome you to the Elysian Fields as I did your mother and her mother before her."

"But Asterius—" she began.

"Because I regret the mistakes I made, I will grant him a boon. If you so choose, I will gift him with a mortal man's body." The goddess smiled and her eyes glittered mischievously. "I will gift him with a mortal man's body, but for you, my favorite Empousa, I give you my oath that his new form will be more pleasing to look upon than Adonis. But it is impossible, even for my powers, to change his form in the Realm of the Rose. I will have to bring him here, to live out his mortal life by your side. You will have children and grow old together and find solace in each other's arms when your lives are finished."

"Or I can return?" Mikki prompted, when it didn't seem like Hecate was going to continue.

"Yes. You may return as Goddess of the Rose—I will relinquish the realm of dreams to you eternally. But remember, in that realm I cannot change Asterius's form. He will remain eternally a beast, but with the heart and soul of a man. Make your choice, Mikado."

Mikki started to consider and then realized that she actually had no choice. She knew exactly what she had to do.

"I choose the Realm of the Rose and my beast. I don't want to live anywhere else, and I would not ask Asterius to change. I love what he is, not what others would have him pretend to be."

Hecate's smile was radiant. "Then let us return you to your realm."

Chapter Thirty-seven

THE forest had certainly not changed. It was still dark and creepy—especially now that Mikki knew what lurked out there. Of course now she was a goddess, so the Dream Stealers would have a whole new ball game to play if they tried to trap her again. And they would—Hecate had already warned her about that. Just because she was an immortal now, it didn't mean she wasn't still fallible and able to be manipulated by darker emotions. Hecate herself had been proof of that. Mikki shivered and wrapped her purple palla around her shoulders more tightly. She'd be careful.

Weird that she didn't feel any different. Or at least not that much different. She'd felt the roses when she'd returned. Really *felt* them. Embarrassingly enough, they had rejoiced when she entered the realm. Although now that she knew they had real emotions and bright little spirits, she felt decidedly less ridiculous about all those years she'd talked to her bushes. Still, it was a wonderful yet odd sensation that she'd have to get used to.

The handmaidens would be really glad to see her, and Mikki was looking forward to surprising them in the morning. But not tonight. Tonight there was only one person she wanted to see—only one place she wanted to be—and that was in Asterius's arms.

Mikki could feel that he was out here somewhere, gathering the threads of reality to take to the Dream Weavers. She could have waited for him in his home. She could have called him to her bedroom in the palace. She hadn't wanted to do either. She would come to him because she loved the innocent joy he so obviously felt every time she chose him. And she wanted him to know she would keep choosing him for all of eternity.

A flicker of light drew her to the right. She followed it, and the flicker became a torch. Holding her breath, she made her way slowly and silently toward it. He was standing with his back to her, combing the limbs of the ancient tree above him. Glittering threads appeared within his hands, and he pulled and spun them into a luminous mound of magick on the forest floor.

She moved closer and then stopped when he made a low moan. He turned to the side with a sudden flinching movement, as if the thread he was weaving had caused him pain. But he didn't drop it. Instead he stared at it with an agonized expression filled with despair and longing.

Mikki looked within the thread and saw herself. She was heavy with child, which was truly a shock, but her shock shifted to joy as she watched Asterius enter the frame and pull her into his arms. He kissed her and then dropped to his knees, placing his lips gently against her swollen belly. In the dream vision, Mikki saw herself smile contentedly and reach out and stroke her finger down one of his ebony horns, just as she had done long ago.

With an anguished cry, Asterius hurled the thread away from him. "Why do you torment me?" he roared.

Mikki stepped from the shadows. "It torments you to think of me being pregnant? I think I'm the one who should be tormented. I mean, the whole horns and hooves issue in utero is a little daunting."

Asterius didn't move. He only stared at Mikki with eyes filled with hatred. "Begone apparition! I will not fall prey to your evil lies." Growling menacingly, he started moving stealthily toward her, holding his deadly claws before him like blades.

"Asterius! It's me! I just wanted to surprise you."

His look darkened. "I said begone, nightmare creature!" He closed on her.

Mikki squealed and stepped back, blurting the first thing that came in her mind. "The first night we met you put a rose in my wineglass!"

As if he'd run against a wall, Asterius halted.

"Mikado?" he said tentatively.

"That's what I've been trying to tell you." She sighed when he still didn't seem to thaw. "You know, as often as you've rejected me, it's a wonder we've ever gotten together at all."

"Mikado!" He lunged forward, pulling her into his arms.

His powerful body was trembling so hard he didn't seem to be able to do more than just hold her and repeat her name over and over again. She held him in return, touching him and murmuring wordless endearments, until his shaking stopped and he was able to loosen his grip on her.

She looked up into his beautiful, terrible face, which was wet with tears.

"How did this happen? How can you be here?" he asked.

"Hecate gave me a choice."

"But the realm—your blood—it is safe, eternally. The goddess said that after your sacrifice, no other Empousa's blood would be needed to make the realm thrive, not for an eternity."

"I know. I chose the eternity, and I chose to spend it with you."

At first his eyes were blank and then understanding flashed joyously across his face. "We will never be parted?"

"Never," she said.

"Then the threads—they were not tormenting me. They were showing . . ." He broke off, unable to speak through the swell of emotions.

"They were showing you our happily ever after. And, yes, my love. That particular dream has finally come true."

Slowly, he bent and kissed her, cupping her face between his massive hands. Mikki wrapped her arms around him and held on to their future—their eternity.

In the shadows, Hecate smiled and patted one of her great beasts on his dark head.

TURN THE PAGE TO READ AN EXCERPT
FROM THE NEXT BOOK IN
P. C. CAST'S GODDESS SUMMONING SERIES

Goddess of Love

NOW AVAILABLE FROM BERKLEY SENSATION!

P EA felt a wash of relief, which was quickly followed by embarrassment when she heard the fire siren getting closer. Crap crap crap!
What a way to start Saturday morning.

"They're almost here, Chlo-chlo-ba-bo!" she yelled up at the tree.

The pitiful whine that replied from the middle of the winter-bare
branches squeezed at her heart, but Pea shook her head sternly at the
dog, refusing to give in to Chloe's manipulation.

"Okay, look! How many times do I have to tell you? You. Are. Not.
A. Cat."

A black nose appeared from a top branch of the tree. Behind it Pea
could see the glint of bright, intelligent eyes staring down at her.

"Hrumph!" Chloe barked the strange, deep growl sound she made
when she was highly annoyed.

"Whatever! You can love cats. You cannot be one."

Chloe had just *hrumph*ed indignantly at her again when the fire
engine glided to a smooth stop at the curb. Pea sighed and gave Chloe
one more glare. Then she started to walk toward the men who were
climbing out of the traditional shiny red fire truck. Instantly Chloe
erupted in a pathetic chorus of whines and yaps. Forgetting all about
embarrassment and doggie manipulations, Pea rushed back to the tree.

"Chlo-chlo! It's okay, baby girl. I'm right here."

"Bring the ladder over here, Steve." A deep male voice called from close behind her. "This is the tree."

"Hurry!" Pea yelled without taking her eyes from the frightened dog. "She's really scared, and if she falls she's definitely going to break something."

"Ma'am, cats rarely hurt themselves when they jump from trees. The whole land-on-their-feet myth actually has quite a bit of truth to it," the voice over her shoulder said.

Chloe whined again.

"Hey, that's not a cat."

Pea turned to the fireman, an annoyed frown on her face. "I clearly told the dispatcher that my *dog*—" she began, putting her fists on her waist and letting the worry she felt for Chloe shift over to irritation, but one look at the man had her anger fizzling and her tongue stammering. She felt her cheeks flame with heat. Quadruple crap! It was *him*. Griffin DeAngelo. The most gorgeous man she had ever seen. Ever. Even on TV. He was also the guy she'd been crushing on for the entire past year—ever since she'd walked Chloe by his house (which was just down the street from hers) and seen him mowing his yard. Without a shirt on. And here he was. Standing in her front yard like he'd walked right out of one of her very graphic dreams.

Naturally he wasn't looking at her standing there in her baggy sweat-pants and sweatshirted glory, and he hadn't noticed her sudden pathetic inability to speak. He was peering up at Chloe with a quizzical smile tilting his delicious-looking lips.

"How in the hell did he get up in that tree?"

"She's not a he, she's a she. And she climbed," Pea said.

"Oh, pardon my language, ma'am; I forgot you were there. I'm Griffin DeAngelo, captain of the Midtown Station." He tapped his helmet in an archaic and adorable gesture of a gentleman greeting a lady.

"I know!"

"You know?" He raised an eyebrow as if to punctuate his question.

"Yeah, you live down there." Pea pointed down the block directly at his house. Like a stalker. "Remember, we met at the fourth of July block party last fourth of July, and also at the summer weenie roast and again at the pre-Christmas light hanging neighborhood meeting," she babbled, sounding exactly like a stalker.

His beautiful forehead wrinkled in confusion. "I'm sorry, ma'am. I don't remember."

Of course he didn't. No one remembered meeting her. "No problem, I'm um . . ." She paused as she stared up into eyes that were so big and blue and beautifully dark lashed that she suddenly and moronically forgot her name.

"Ma'am?"

"Dorreth Chamberlain!" she blurted, holding out her hand like a dork. "And the dog caught in the tree is Chloe."

He took her hand gently, like he was afraid she might explode at his touch. And why wouldn't he think that? She'd just told him that they'd met three times, none of which he remembered, and she was still standing there gawking at him like a kindergarten kid in a bubble gum factory. And her hair! Pea forced herself not to groan and pat manically at the frizzy mess she'd tied back in her favorite scrunchie.

"Check it out. It's a dog," said a young fireman who had joined them with two other men carrying an extension ladder.

"How the hell did it get up there?" said another fireman, with a laugh.

Griffin cleared his throat and gestured at Pea.

"Sorry, ma'am," was mumbled in her general direction.

Pea laughed gaily, gesturing up at the tree, trying hard to sound perky and interesting. "She climbed!" As usual, none of the men so much as glanced at her.

"Climbed? She must be twenty feet up in that old oak," one of the unnamed guys said.

"She's a good climber. She's just not a good climber downer," Pea said, and then wanted to dissolve into the sidewalk in embarrassment. *Climber downer?* God, she really was such a dork.

"Well, let's get her down," Griffin said. The men went to work extending the ladder, and Chloe started growling.

"What kind of dog is she, ma'am?" Griffin asked her.

"She's a Scottie, but she thinks she's a cat. See, I have a cat named Max, and Chloe is totally in love with him, hence the fact she is clueless that she's a Scottie *dog*. Chloe is in denial. She believes she's a Scottie *cat*. I'm not sure whether to get her another dog, get her some Prozac or take her for a visit to the pet psychic."

Griffin laughed, a deep, infectious sound that made Pea's skin tingle with pleasure. "Or maybe you should just invest in a safety net."

Pea giggled and tried to have one of "those moments" with totally, insanely gorgeous Griffin the Fireman—one of those eye-meeting moments where a man and a woman share a long, sexy, lingering, laughter-filled look.

Naturally the moment did not happen.

First, her coquettish giggle turned into—horror of all horrors—a snort. Second, blonde and beautiful appeared on the scene.

"Pea! Don't tell me Chloe got caught in a tree again!"

Griffin immediately shifted his attention to her neighbor, who was hurrying up to them, her six-year-old daughter in tow. "Hi, Griffin," she said.

"Good to see you again, Stacy," he said, and tilted his hat to her, too.

Pea sighed. Of course he remembered Stacy—tall, sleek, always together-looking Stacy—even though Pea knew for sure that Stacy had only made *one* of the neighborhood meetings in the past year. With Stacy there was no way in hell gorgeous Griffin would give her another thought. If he'd ever given her a first thought. Even with a kid at her heels, Stacy was ridiculously attractive.

But, surprisingly, the fireman's eyes slid back to her. "Pea?" he asked with a raised brow.

"Yeah," she said, shrugging and launching into the short version of her all too familiar explanation for what everyone called her. "Sadly, Pea is an unfortunate childhood nickname that stuck."

"Oh, come on! There's nothing wrong with your nickname. Pea's adorable," Stacy said, grinning at her.

"Yea for Pea!" Stacy's daughter Emili chimed in. "I like your name.

It's cute. But it's not as cute as him." Emili pointed up at Griffin. "Are you married? Pea's not married. Maybe you could marry Pea. She doesn't even have a boyfriend and my mommy says that's a shame because she really is cuter than people think she is 'cause—"

Pea sucked in air and felt her face blaze with heat while Stacy clamped her hand over Emili's mouth and tried unsuccessfully not to laugh.

Thank the sweet weeping baby Jesus that Chloe chose that moment to snarl a warning at the young fireman who was positioning the ladder against the tree.

"Chlo! It's okay." Pea hurried over to the trunk of the tree and looked up at the black snout and bright eyes. Chloe whined. "Sorry, she doesn't like men," she said to the fireman. "I really don't think she'll bite you. But she will complain. Probably a lot."

"I'll get her," Griffin said.

"She's all yours, Captain."

Griffin started up the ladder and Chloe's low, rumbling growl intensified.

"Chloe! Manners!" Pea called up to the perturbed Scottie. *Please, God, please don't let her bite him*, she mentally telegraphed over and over. . . . Until Griffin did something that made Pea's thoughts, as well as Chloe's growls, come to an abrupt halt. He was calling Chloe, but he wasn't calling her like someone would call a dog. He was, unbelievably, kitty-kittying her.

"Come here Chloe, kitty-kitty. It's okay little girl. Come here, kitty-kitty-kitty. . . ."

Dumbfounded, Pea watched her dog's ears lift and her head tilt toward the approaching man.

"Good girl," Griffin murmured. "Good kitty-kitty, kitty-kitty." He held his hand out slowly and let Chloe get a good sniff of him. "See, you smell her, don't you? That's right, kitty-kitty-kitty, come on down."

Pea could only stand and stare as Griffin reached into the tree crevice and pulled Chloe, who was still sniffing him curiously, into his arms and began the descent down the ladder.

"Amazing," Stacy said with a deep breath. "How did he do that? Chloe hates men."

"He's too pretty to hate, Mommy," Emili said.

"Honey, let's keep that for our inside thoughts, shall we?" Stacy said. Then she glanced at Pea and whispered, "Even though it's totally true."

Pea pretended not to hear either of them, which was easy. Her entire being was focused on her dream man striding toward her with her dog—who was actually wagging her tail—held firmly in his arms.

"Here ya go, ma'am." He handed Chloe to Pea.

"Th-thank you," Pea stuttered. "How?"

"How?" he repeated.

"The kitty-kittying. How did you know to do that?"

"Just makes sense. You said she thinks she's a cat, and you have a cat, right?"

Pea nodded.

"That's how you call your cat. Right?"

Pea nodded again.

"I figured she'd recognize the call."

Griffin scratched Chloe on the top of her head, and Pea watched in astonishment as her dog—her man-hating dog—closed her eyes and sighed happily.

"That's just part of it, though," Griffin said. "I was counting on Chloe smelling Cali."

Pea suddenly understood. "Your cat?"

"My cat." Griffin gave Chloe one last scratch, then turned back to his men. "Okay, let's get this loaded up. Have a good day, ma'am." He nodded politely to her and then to Stacy. He winked at Emili, and then he was gone.

"Em, honey, go on inside and wait for Mommy. I'll be there in just a second," Stacy told her daughter.

"Are you and Pea going to talk about how pretty that fireman was?"

"Of course not, honey. Now go on."

"'Kay! Bye, Pea." Emili skipped off to her house, singing a song about lemon drops and unicorns.

"Okay, I'd forgotten how drop dead Mr. Tall Dark and Fireman is. I can definitely understand why you've had a thing for him for ages," Stacy said.

Pea put Chloe down and the dog trotted over to the tree and began sniffing all around the trunk. "Do not even think about climbing up there again," Pea told her sternly. Chloe glanced back at her and snorted. "I swear that dog understands every word I say," Pea muttered.

"Hello! Sexy, incredible man. We were talking about him and not your insane Scottie."

"She's not insane," Pea said automatically. "And yeah, he's gorgeous and I might have a little crush on him."

Stacy rolled her eyes, which Pea chose to ignore. "But now he's gone. I don't see the point in going on and on about him."

"Like you haven't gone on and on about him before?"

Pea silently chastised herself for the one or two—okay, ten or twelve—times she'd mentioned to Stacy how hot she thought their neighbor was. "Whatever," she said, trying to sound nonchalant and dismissive. "He's still gone, and there's still no point in talking about how gorgeous he is."

"The point is, Ms. Totally Single, that he seemed interested in you."

"Get real, Stacy. He wasn't interested; he was polite. There's a world of difference."

"Bullshit."

"Stacy, he didn't even remember me, and today makes the fourth time we've met. Men like him are not interested in women like me."

"So he has a crappy memory. Lots of guys do. And women like you? What does that mean?"

Pea sighed, and didn't feel up to mentioning that Griffin's memory hadn't failed when she'd walked up. "Women like me—short, plain, forgettable. He belongs with a model or a goddess. He doesn't belong with me."

"You know, that's your problem! You defeat yourself before you even start. I've told you before that all you need is a little self-confidence. You're perfectly fine looking."

Perfectly fine looking. Didn't that just sum it all up? There was sexy Stacy giving her what she really considered praise and encouragement, but the best she could come up with was perfectly fine looking. She studied Stacy—tall and blond with her great curves, fabulous boobs and those cheekbones that made her face look like someone should carve it out of marble. How could she possibly understand what it was to be so average that you went through life being invisible? She'd never walked into a room and not turned heads. Pea would bet the great raise she'd just got that gorgeous Griffin had already forgotten her. Men always did, but she would also bet that the firemen were discussing her hot blond neighbor all the way back to the station. And then someone might say something like: "Oh, yeah, that *other* girl was there, too." Pea was the other girl. The forgettable girl.

"So will you do it?"

"Huh?" Pea said, realizing Stacy had been talking and she'd not heard anything she'd been saying.

Stacy sighed in exasperation. "I said, it's not even noon yet. You have plenty of time to go into that fabulous kitchen of yours and bake a big plate of your to-die-for brownies and deliver them to gorgeous Griffin at the station as a thank you."

"Let me think about that." Pea paused for half a blink. "No."

"And why not?" Stacy didn't give her time to continue. "Because you have so many men beating down your door to go out with you tonight? Because you're in an incredible relationship with your dream man? Hmm? Which one is it?"

"You know I'm not dating anyone, and thanks for reminding me," Pea said through her teeth, and then thought *for the zillionth time.*

"Okay, so is it because you don't find Griffin attractive?"

"As you very well know that's definitely not the case."

"Then is it because you're hateful and rude and you don't believe in thanking the man who just saved your weird Scottie cat's life?"

"Chloe isn't weird and she wasn't about to die," Pea said.

"She definitely could have broken something if she'd fallen out of that tree."

"Stacy, it's stupid and pathetic to bake brownies as an excuse to see a man who has no interest in me."

"He smiled at you and asked about your nickname," Stacy countered.

"He was being polite."

"Maybe. Maybe not. If you don't bake the brownies, you'll never know."

Pea opened her mouth to say no. Again. But Stacy interrupted. Again.

"Take a chance, Pea. Just one small chance. The worst that can happen is that a bunch of overworked firemen will get a treat. On the other hand, maybe your brownies will work magic and you might actually live out one of those fantasies you usually only dream about. . . ." Stacy waggled her brows at Pea.

"Fine!" Pea surprised herself by saying. "I don't have dance class till this afternoon. I'll bake the damn brownies and drop them off on my way to class."

"Finally I'm victorious with the Pea-and-men issue! Okay, look, be sure you write a little thank you note, too. On the stationery that has your new work title and letterhead."

"Huh?"

Stacy rolled her perfect eyes. "It serves two purposes. He'll know how amazingly successful you are, and he'll also know how to get in touch with you."

"Great. Yeah. Okay. Whatever." Pea called Chloe and started to retreat up the steps to her homey porch.

"You'll write the note?" Stacy called.

"I'll write the note."